MW01632290

Dead and Gone

by Robert L. Gold

Printed in the United States of America.
Published by Marcinson Press, Jacksonville, Florida

For bulk purchases or to carry this book in your library, school, or bookstore, please contact the publisher at marcinsonpress.com.

ISBN 978-1-946932-04-4

Published by
Marcinson Press
10950-60 San Jose Blvd., Suite 136
Jacksonville, FL 32223 USA
http://www.marcinsonpress.com

Dead and Gone

Robert L. Gold

In memory of my father and mother,

whom I credit for the best in me;

the worst is of my own making.

ACKNOWLEDGEMENTS

First of all, I want to thank Trish Diggins and Kat LaMons for the four beautiful books Marcinson Press has produced for me. I am absolutely delighted with their design and appearance. And it is no wonder that the books have received so many compliments since they were published. *Dead to Rights, Cut of the Cross, Dead and Gone* and *St. Augustine: A Brief History of America's Oldest City* simply look spectacular.

The meticulously drawn maps in *Dead and Gone* are the work of Terri I. Bailey. Ms. Bailey has adapted two colonial maps of the city of New Orleans and the Lower Mississippi Valley to enhance the murder mystery. The maps reveal and locate the significant sites mentioned in the story and provide a picturesque view of colonial Louisiana in the late eighteenth century.

Kent Stark, my friend and former neighbor, also gave me invaluable help. An architect and experienced sailor, he designed the cabin door on *La Bonne Chance* where the first murders take place. The door was critical to the story and, although I visualized it, I could not describe its precise appearance, position or how it opened and closed. Only a day or so after I phoned Kent for his advice, he sent me a detailed drawing showing, not only the cabin door's placement in the sloop, but how it operated as well.

I am also appreciative of the assistance given to me by my friend Bridget Boix, Sister Kathy, Archivist of the Roman Catholic Diocese of St. Augustine, James Cusick, Curator of the P. K. Library of Florida History, and Charles Tingley, Senior Research Librarian of the St. Augustine Historical Society Research Library. I called them for information any number of times and they always spent time helping me.

Professor Michael M. Smith, my old friend and history colleague, was likewise willing to help me whenever I phoned him in Oklahoma. Mike scrutinized the first two novels in the mystery series and made sure my use of Spanish was grammatically correct and appropriately employed. Fluent in Spanish, he was particularly helpful correcting my all too frequent misuse of accents.

For *Dead and Gone*, the final novel in the mystery series, I am extremely grateful that Susan Collatz proofread the manuscript. She examined the book with an eagle eye and I thank her for the careful and conscientious effort.

Finally, in the process of writing *Dead and Gone*, I continued to be dependent on my wife's computer expertise. Her availability, constant concern and commitment have been essential to everything I have written.

Despite all the assistance I have received, there still may be errors yet to be found in the three books. If and when errors are revealed, I alone am responsible for them.

LOWER MISSISSIPPI VALLEY

1799-1800

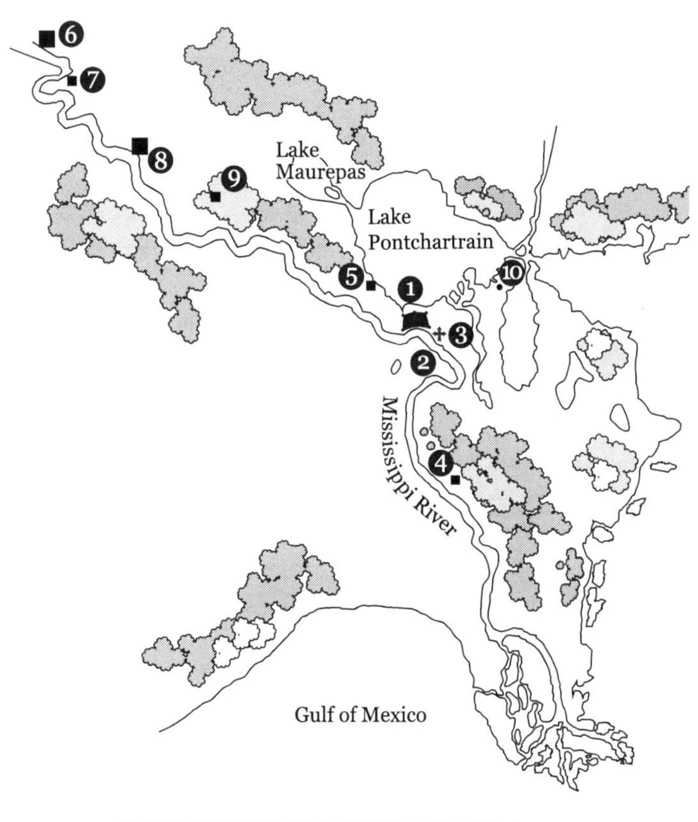

1. New Orleans
2. Hidden Lake
3. Santa María (St. Mary's) Church
4. Mosquito Creek
5. Menard's Hog Farm
6. Natchez
7. Mitchell's Farm
8. Baton Rouge
9. Galvez
10. Swamp Cabin

Terri L. Bailey 2018

NEUVA ORLEANS 1799-1800

1. Catedral de San Luis
2. Cabildo
3. Madame Boudreaux Home
4. Madame Lefevre Home (Olivier's Rooms)
5. Jean Bertin's Office
6. Dumont Family Home
7. Governor's House
8. Laroux's Home
9. Attack on Laroux
10. Ursuline Convent
11. Attack on Olivier
12. San Carlos Gate

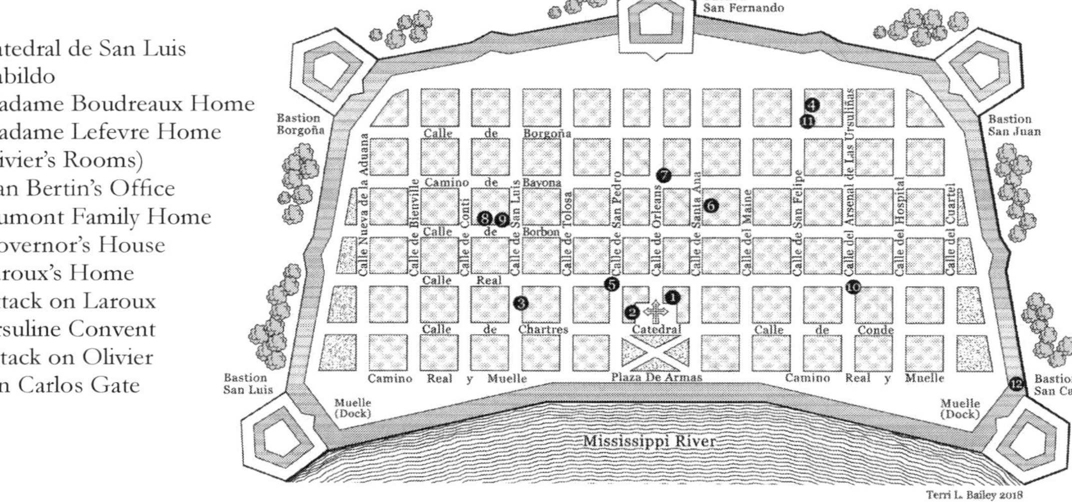

CHAPTER ONE

NEW ORLEANS: AUGUST 15 - 30, 1799

Even in the night air, the man was soaked in sweat by the time he paddled the pirogue to the stern of *La Bonne Chance* (*Good Fortune*). It had been easy paddling in the barely moving water, but the mid-August humidity left him tired and winded. He needed no more than twenty strokes to reach the anchored sloop from the shore and he withdrew his paddle from the water a few feet from the stern. The wind on the lake carried the light pirogue the rest of the way.

At the stern, he stood carefully to avoid tipping the tiny boat over. He put one hand on the sloop's hull and eased the pirogue carefully against its side. The two boats touched without a sound. Hoping to board the ship noiselessly, he had padded the sides of the pirogue with a thick layer of cloth. The man maintained his balance by pressing one hand against the hull. With his other hand, he tossed a bowline up and over a cleat on the deck. He pulled the line taut and tied it to the bow of his pirogue. He paused a few seconds to remove his shoes and, with both hands tightly gripping the line, he hoisted himself up to the deck and crawled over the gunwale.

The man stood cautiously and listened for several minutes. It was a quiet moonless night. He heard nothing except the marsh crickets, the occasional croak of a frog and the water lapping softly alongside the sloop. There was no sound from inside the cabin.

He walked stealthily on tiptoes to the cabin door which was wide open to let in whatever wayward breeze might blow over the water. The door led to a four-step stairway that went down below the deck into the cabin. In the darkness, it suddenly loomed up in front of him sooner than expected and he stubbed the toes of his right foot on the base of the doorway. Barely stifling his scream of pain, he gritted his teeth and kneeled on the deck to massage his toes. He remained on one knee until the pain subsided and then rose slowly to stand on his sore foot. He sighed in relief, realizing a scream would have ruined everything.

A few feet back from the doorway now, the man got down on his hands and knees again and crawled forward to lean his head into the stairway. Listening for any sound of movement, he smiled when he heard snoring from inside the cabin. He listened for a few seconds more and then stood to close the door.

The back of the sloop's cabin was built at a forty-five degree angle above a twenty-inch high base and its sliding door was set into the angular portion of the cabin's back wall. Almost hidden in the left side of the wall when open, the door was closed by sliding it sideways across the opening to the right side. Ending there, the door slid into a deep grove that held it tightly in place. A ring in the door's outer edge was used to open and close it. The door itself, built with four one-inch thick and seven-inch wide boards, was forty inches high and twenty-eight inches wide. It was held together by four similar horizontal boards which were nailed across the top, bottom and center of the vertical boards.

He put his right forefinger in the ring and began to pull the door to the right. It squeaked loudly and he instantly stopped. He stood still and again leaned his head down into the stairway. Hearing the continuing and unchanged snoring, he resumed pulling the sliding door a faction of an inch at a time. His forearms ached from the effort. He only stopped when the door squeaked and he would immediately drop to the deck to listen for any sounds other than snoring from the cabin below. It took time, but no one was awakened and he finally slid the door into the right side groove. It fit snugly with only a faint click.

The man paused again to listen and, hearing no sound from inside, he removed the iron crossbar from the chocks beside the door. The crossbar had been installed on *La Bonne Chance* a month earlier to prevent thieves from entering the cabin. Careful not to let the bar hit anything and make noise, he eased it slowly through the iron rings that secured the door to the side posts. There were four rings in all, one on the left side post, two on the door itself and the fourth ring on the right side post. The bar had a rounded knob on one end to keep it from slipping through the rings and a hole in the other end for a padlock, which at night hung on a hook in the cabin. He took a nail and a rawhide thong from his pocket and laid them on the cabin roof. He then put the nail in the hole and, while holding it in place with one hand, he bound the thong around both ends of the nail with his other hand. The crossbar was now secured as if it was padlocked. The man stepped back from the door and exhaled his breath. The hardest part was over.

Even if they awoke, they were locked inside the cabin and could not escape. They could not get out the locked door or the portholes. The portholes, built into the walls above the bunks, were no more than six inches in diameter and would not allow anything thicker than a man's arm to reach through them. They were incarcerated as if in a prison cell. He smiled, thinking the tiny cabin might be better termed a coffin and the sloop a sepulcher. They, of course, would not think of such terms; they would be too horrified, knowing there was no escape from the cabin and they would die. He saw them in his mind's eye, their frantic gestures, the futile screams for help – all in vain. No matter what les plus choyés (pampered ones) tried to do, they were doomed.

The man tiptoed silently back to the stern and climbed down to the pirogue. He took off all his clothes except his drawers and, with his knife in hand, dropped quietly into the water. He swam below the anchored ship to open the three plugged holes he had previously drilled into the bottom of the hull next to the keel. One had been bored into the bow, another amidships below the cabin floor and the third in the stern. The man had drilled the holes in the underside planks while the ship had been docked for repairs. He situated them in the seam between two planks that ran the entire length of the sloop. The openings were an inch in diameter and drilled deep enough to pierce both the inner and outer planking.

At the time, he had pushed a foot-long stick into the holes to make sure the hull had been breached. He then had plugged the holes with tapered wooden dowels to prevent leaks when the sloop was returned to the water. When he finished, no one could find the plugs unless guided to them. At sea, they would be well under water and completely out of sight. Knowing he would return to *La Bonne Chance* at night, he marked their location on the edge of the deck in a way no one else would notice. Only he would be able to feel the tiny carved crosses in the wood.

It had taken him almost an entire night to finish the task at that time, but he knew then his effort had been well spent. The wooden dowels could now be removed as easily as a cork from a bottle of wine. He had only to pry them out with a sharp pointed knife. As expected, it took him eight dives below the sloop to find and open the holes. On his last dive, he swam along the keel to all the openings to make certain water was flowing into the hull. He inserted his forefinger in each of the holes and felt the water flowing steadily into the sloop. A few minutes later, he sat in the pirogue drying himself with a towel he had brought from home. It was now only a matter of time to wait for the ship to sink.

Once dressed, the man untied the bowline from the sloop and paddled to a spot near the shore. He was near enough to see the ship's outline in the dark and hopefully far enough away from the clouds of mosquitoes that converged in the swamp land around the lake. But, no sooner had he laid the paddle at his feet than he heard them buzzing behind his head. The man hurriedly paddled into deeper water, slapping futilely at the mosquitoes following him. They relentlessly pursued him no matter how many he swatted or where he paddled in the lake. He finally gave up all attempts to elude them and put the wet towel over his head while waiting for the ship to sink.

For a while, the sloop looked unchanged as it floated serenely on the lake's surface. But, when the man paddled the canoe closer, he could see the waterline had risen almost a foot on the side he approached. He felt relieved and, on his next examination, the line was six inches higher. An hour later, the rising water looked to be only a foot from the deck. He knew the cabin floor must be flooded, but those inside apparently slept unaware of the rising water around them.

"How can they possibly sleep with the water flooding the cabin?" he wondered aloud.

He had a moment of fright, thinking they somehow had opened the door and escaped. It occurred to him that they could have found an unknown implement in the cabin allowing them to break through the door. But, then, he calmed himself, realizing there were no sights or sounds of the door breaking or anyone moving on the deck. They were trapped inside the cabin and could not break through the barred door no matter what they did. Still, the man wondered why he had heard no shout or sound from *La Bonne Chance*. Seconds later, he heard shouts from the cabin. It was almost as if they had heard his question and answered him.

The shouts were followed by sounds of them pounding on the locked door. He guessed they must be using their fists and feet since the small stairway entrance into the cabin would not allow them to throw their bodies or shoulders against the door. Only one man at a time had room enough to pound on the door and, as the water rose to their knees, they could only use their fists. Their muskets or pistols were of no use since they were stored beneath the bunks and would be much too waterlogged to shoot. The butts of the heavy weapons might have been used to batter the closed door, but that possibility had not occurred to them. Instead, they apparently took turns pounding their fists on the door. It was the only way they knew to escape the flooding cabin.

The hammering sounded much louder a few minutes later and he assumed the men inside the cabin had finally begun to strike the door with the butt of a musket. He doubted they could break through the inch thick oak door with its similarly thick cross-board supports, but still the possibility worried him. It would have relieved him to know the imprisoned men were having little success battering the door with the musket. They found the heavy weapon too big and too awkward to wield in the close quarters of the entrance. It was also too tiring to stand on one of the steps and try to strike the door from below. Although they dented the door with the musket, the men, even taking turns, could not break through the oak planks. The iron crossbar outside held it firmly in place.

One of the men continued to batter the door, while the other tried to close the portholes. They had been left open in the hope of a breeze blowing into the cabin sometime in the night and now could not be closed. The porthole hinges had been bent the afternoon before by the man in the pirogue. With the portholes partially open, water was streaming over the deck and cascading down into the cabin. As water was also steadily rising through the floor boards, the small space was being inundated from above and below and nothing could be done to stem the flow.

The man in the pirogue and watched as water first splashed and then streamed over what little of the sloop's deck still remained to be seen. He could see somewhat better now that the sky had lightened as morning approached. On his knees in the pirogue, he stood to look at *La Bonne Chance* for the last time.

"They're now doomed," he said quietly.

As the ship started to sink, there was little time left for those trapped inside the tiny cabin. Flooded below deck, the weighted vessel settled into the water. Only its mast and the top of the cabin were now visible, the deck had disappeared in the darkness. As the man watched, the sloop suddenly pitched forward and vanished from view. It sank with a soft whisper, leaving a series of silent ripples that rolled away over the lake. *La Bonne Chance* was gone.

The man thought he heard an anguished cry that ended abruptly as the sloop went down. It made him shiver and he wrapped his arms around his chest. The shiver lasted only a second and he turned his mind to what yet had to be done. Unless there were unexpected complications, he had at least another half hour of work. Reminding himself of the importance of his tasks, he waited a moment more and then paddled over to where the sloop had been and began searching for its mast. Using his paddle, he eventually found it a foot below the surface of the water. The mast appeared at an angle from the bottom and he knew the sunken ship lay on its side.

He tied the pirogue to the mast and once again took off all his clothes. He dove into the water and swam down to the deck of the sloop. It now lay tilted to the starboard side.

The man looked into one of the portholes before swimming up to the surface for air. Everything had gone as exactly as planned he thought as his hand reached above the water and touched the side of the pirogue. His head above water, he took several deep breaths, swept the hair out of his eyes and rested his head against the side of the pirogue.

The man made two more dives down to the ship. On the first, he used his knife to cut away the thong holding the nail in the crossbar. He discarded the nail and thong and resurfaced beside the pirogue. On his last dive, he removed the crossbar from the cabin door and dropped it to the bottom. Seconds later, he climbed into the pirogue, quickly dried himself and dressed. As he paddled away, the sun's first rays lit up the sky above the trees. Later at home, the man took a bath, ate breakfast and scanned the *Moniteur de la Louisiane (The Louisiana Monitor*). He then strolled into town, humming the popular ballad, *La Dama Jacinthe* (*The Hyacinth Lady*).

The two elderly women stood outside the cathedral talking after Mass. It was already hot at seven o'clock in the morning and a sultry mist hovered in the air above them. Everything was wet to the touch even the pews inside the cathedral. The women had begun to perspire as soon as they sat in the usually cool church and, by the middle of the Mass, they were soaked to the skin. They patted their faces and necks with handkerchiefs, but still drops of perspiration ran dripped down into their dresses and underclothing. It seemed as if every piece of clothing they wore was wet and stuck to their bodies. They instantly fanned themselves once outside the church.

"What an awful morning; I can hardly get a breath of air. It was intolerable inside." The white-haired woman spoke French. "I thought I might faint before Father Antonio finished his sermon." She sighed and dabbed her fleshy cheeks with a handkerchief.

"It was stifling in there." Her companion was a slender woman with dark skin. She had gray hair streaked with black and striking black eyes. "Will you join me for breakfast, Aveline? We should get a breeze off the river on my porch; it's blown every morning this month."

"Yes, thank you, María Adela. I'll be grateful for any breeze. It's so beastly hot today. What an August and it's only half over. When I get home, I'll stay inside the rest of the day."

"I'll do the same. There's nothing I have to do outside."

The two women walked to their coaches, which stood on the unpaved street in front of St. Louis Cathedral. They lifted their long dresses and cautiously stepped over the puddles and mud left from the previous night's rainstorm. The white-haired woman turned her ankle and stepped into a puddle. She uttered an anguished cry as dirty water splashed over the hem of her dress and soaked her stockings.

Her driver immediately rushed over to guide her to the coach. He had been talking to the other woman's driver, his back to the cathedral, and did not see her until she cried out. Worried of a reprimand, he laid a long piece of canvas on the muddy street in front of her. The length of canvas was not long enough to reach the coach and he laid it out a second time. He walked along beside her so she could grasp his arm if needed. The other driver also used a piece of canvas for his mistress, but she arrived at her coach without incident.

"Lucien, I'm going Madame Boudreaux's home this morning." The white-haired woman held the driver's thick forearm as he helped her into the coach. She gave him a severe look as he shut the door, but said nothing about her mud-splattered dress.

"Immédiatement, Madame Dumont." Luicen quickly climbed up to his seat and, looking back to make certain the other driver was ready to leave, he clicked his tongue to urge his horses forward. The coaches moved simultaneously and, in seconds, they had reached the next block. There was little traffic that early in the morning and the horses increased their gait to a trot.

The coaches left the cathedral and proceeded along Chartres Street toward San Luis Street where Madame Boudreaux lived in her newly constructed house. Chartres Street was the most important thoroughfare in New Orleans. The cathedral, Cabildo (city hall) and Presbytére (court house) had been built on the busy street and the Spanish Army's headquarters was situated on a nearby cross street. With five city blocks on either side of the large building, La Catedral de San Luis (St Louis Cathedral) stood on Chartres Street in the middle of New Orleans, across from the Plaza de Armas. Chartres Street extended the entire length of the city, though half the length of it had been named Conde Street by the Spaniards. That portion of the road ran from the cathedral to the northeastern city wall.

The former French capital of Louisiana had been laid out along the Mississippi River in a rectangular form, eleven blocks long and six blocks wide. Running northeast to south-west, the principal streets were named Chartres, Real (Royal), Borbón (Bourbon), Bayona and Borgoña (Burgundy). The streets extended from one end of the community to the other. Nueva Orleans, as the arriving Spaniards re-named the city when they took possession of it in 1764, was walled and fortified for much of the late eighteenth century. It had stone walls on three sides, the river on the fourth and five forts to defend the city from attacks by land or sea.

In a century of intermittent warfare, both French and Spanish governors built the defenses to make the city as secure as possible. They worried that an enemy army would try to seize New Orleans to control trade on the Mississippi River and take Louisiana. It was a reasonable worry since

England, France and Spain had been fighting over North America for much of the century. The wars raged along the eastern coast from Canada all the way south to Florida. There also had been a number of Indian wars. Fortunately for New Orleans, the hostilities did not extend to the Lower Mississippi Valley or ever menace the capital. Colonial Louisiana escaped the ravages of both the French and Indian and the American Revolutionary Wars and the city never confronted an attacking army. The transfer of Louisiana from French to Spanish rule by treaty in 1763 was the only event that affected the colony and its capital.

The first Spanish governor faced an insurrection of French creoles and the next governor from Spain, in reaction to the rebellion, ruled the colony with severity. French resentment of the foreigners remained for years, but, after a decade, the creoles accepted their new administrators. The mood of the community improved after 1769 with the arrival of Luis de Unzaga y Amézaga, the newly assigned Spanish governor. The governor treated the creoles fairly and, within a few years, despite their unending distrust of each other, the Spaniards and the French colonists lived peacefully together.

Fire caused much more damage than either international politics or war. Two great fires devastated New Orleans in the last years of the eighteenth century. The first in 1788, on March 21, *Good Friday*, destroyed 856 buildings, and the second, on December 8, 1794, consumed 212 structures in the city. Most of central New Orleans, including all the major buildings, was razed in the first fire and the city had been almost rebuilt when the second struck and burned down all the buildings in the southwestern part of the city.

Five years later, New Orleans still showed signs of the last fire even though much of the community had been reconstructed. Three new suburbs also had been built in the last years of the century. Santa María and San Carlos appeared outside the walls in the upper and lower ends of the city and

Bayou San Juan stood behind the rear stockade. Santa María became the preferred residential site of many merchant and planters, but the older families still lived in town.

Despite seemingly constant construction everywhere, blackened foundations and empty lots with broken boards and stone rubble were still common sights in New Orleans. But as the population of the city increased, the burnt out areas began to disappear. Bargain prices for lots still full of fire debris convinced local and newly arrived residents alike to buy them up and build houses. The existence of usable foundations on many of the littered lots made them even more appealing to buyers hoping to erect homes as quickly as possible.

Madame Boudreaux was one of the local residents who took advantage of the low prices and purchased a lot in a block that had lost all its houses. The wealthy widow of a rum merchant, Madame Boudreaux shrewdly bought the lot a few months after the second fire. A year later, in the spring of 1795, she contracted an Acadian carpenter to build a two story house with an upper porch that provided an unobstructed view of the river. The house stood on San Luis Street and crossed Chartres Street only three blocks from the cathedral. Madame Boudreaux chose the site because of its distance from the noisy center of the city and its nearness to the Mississippi River.

Though Madame Boudreaux had always enjoyed looking at the river on her walks to the cathedral, she did not realize how important it would become to her when the house was erected. The building was still under construction the first time she went out to the porch overlooking the river. Instantly entranced by the view, she remained almost unmoving for a half hour looking at the river and the forested land that bordered it. From that time on, not a day went by without her taking at least one look at the river even in inclement weather.

Madame Boudreaux usually went onto the porch at dawn

and dusk to see the spectrum of colors the sun produced as it rose and fell each day. At first light, the landscape looked orange and yellow and, at sunset, the river often was colored pink and purple like the clouds that passed overhead. During the day, she enjoyed seeing the seemingly endless variety of ships gliding up and down the river. The porch and its proximity to the river also provided refreshing breezes in the summer, when the 12,000 residents of the city sweltered in the humidity. Some movement of air seemed always present on the porch and she often spent time there during the heat of the day. At dawn and shortly after dusk, a gentle wind usually arrived as if scheduled, wafting into the porch and through the bedroom windows. Even in August, she could count on a cooling breeze blowing into her bedroom sometime during the night and often in the mornings after first light.

The coaches rode quickly along Chartres Street and turned on San Luis to reach the house of Madame Boudreaux. There was little traffic that early in the day and they arrived only a few minutes after leaving the cathedral. Shortly afterwards, the two women were sitting on the porch sipping tea. No sooner had they seated themselves in cushioned chairs when a cool breeze began to blow up from the river. Though slight, the breeze was strong enough to move the edge of the awning that extended over the porch.

"Ah, that feels good." The white-haired woman put her fan in her lap and closed her eyes momentarily. "I must say I envy you this porch, María Adela."

María Adela smiled. "I was fortunate to hire that wise old carpenter, Monsieur Clermont. He told me to spend a little more money and put an upper porch on the house. I still remember his words. He said, 'Madame, spend a few more pesetas for a porch. The river will reward you in more ways than you now can foresee.'"

"He was quite correct. I should have followed your example and bought one of those lots while they were cheap. Oh well, I am right next door to Jean-Bertin and my grandchildren; that more than makes up for the summer heat. Thank God, there's only a month of it left. I find the summers harder to bear each year now, especially with that disgusting odor coming up from the levee. It's about time the Spaniards cleaned up that stench. But knowing them, I suppose that's too much to ask." Aveline made a face, twitching her nose. "What about you, María Adela? Do the summers wear on you as well?"

"They're harder every year for me, too. It's our age, I'm sure. Tell me, Aveline, what do you think about what has befallen Father Olivier?"

"I don't know what to think. I wasn't in the cathedral at the time, but I heard about it that afternoon. Knowing Father Olivier, I'm not surprised."

"Nor am I. He's a Dominican after all and probably had to bite his tongue any number of times listening to the sacristan. I suppose it was only a matter of time before he lost patience with him. Even I sometimes question what Simón Mendoza says and I have little knowledge of Church history. I can't imagine what Father Olivier thinks and he's a scholar of history."

Aveline nodded. "The imbécile thinks he knows much more about Church doctrine than anyone else. The man's not a priest, though he prances about as if he is – an all knowing one at that! It was foolish of him to argue with Father Olivier. Mon Dieu! About the writings of Saint Thomas of all things. I heard he questioned the saint's use of reason to prove God's existence."

"It was *very* foolish. Father Olivier is the most erudite man I have ever known … That is with the exception of a Portuguese physician I knew many years ago when I was young."

"I have the same opinion of him, but unfortunately that won't help him with the bishop. I understand Father Olivier will have to appear before Bishop Meléndez over the matter."

María Adela frowned. "Why will he have to appear before the bishop? The sacristan's complaint is a parish problem. I would think Father Antonio would be the one to hear it, not the bishop. Unless, of course, *something else* involving Father Olivier is the reason for his meeting with the bishop." Both women had heard the rumors of the priest's excessive drinking.

"That's what I think. I don't know why the bishop is involved. I certainly don't envy Father Olivier. The bishop's a humorless man. I don't know if I have ever seen him smile. He always seems to have a sour look on his face. I wonder if he suffers from dyspepsia."

"I wouldn't doubt it, he does look sickly. Of course, the bishop is probably weary from his trip to Florida. I understand he sailed to Pensacola and then went by coach to St. Augustine. Even though the bishop returned by ship, he must be exhausted from the journey. Would you like more tea, Aveline, or some more bread and preserves?"

"No, thank you. I'm sure the journey was tiring, but I think he looked as sour before he went to Florida. I certainly look forward to the return of Bishop Peñalver y Cárdenas from Cuba. He's been gone three months now. I wonder why he has remained there so long."

"No one seems to know, not even Father Antonio." María Adela shook her head. "I too look forward to our bishop's return. I find the visiting bishop aloof and hard to approach."

"That's my impression of him as well. On the two occasions I spoke to him, he seemed preoccupied and in a hurry to end our discussions and I was talking to him about our willingness to contribute to the Church's construction funds."

María Adela made a face. "That's peculiar especially since he has so often spoken of the parish's need to support the construction of a new Vicaría (priests' residence)."

"Isn't it?" Aveline frowned and fanned herself.

"It may be the bishop wants Father Antonio to be responsible for all contributions to the parish. Bishop Meléndez appears to be a pious man, apparently without worldly interests. That also might be why he spent little time talking to you about money."

"Perhaps. If so, the bishop would be *one* of a kind in my experience." Aveline smiled knowingly. "But you may well be right about him. He's pious and spends little time outside the cathedral. As you know, Bishop Meléndez is often in prayer at the main altar. It's said he prays there at least four times a day." Aveline smiled mischievously. "Of course, I can't imagine what could possibly concern a Church bishop to make him pray so many times a day. You don't think he's praying for the sins of his youth to be forgiven, do you?"

María Adela laughed. "No, I believe his only concerns are the Church and its teachings. That's why I say he has few, if any, worldly interests. I certainly wouldn't expect the bishop to be interested in history or philosophy like Father Olivier."

"No, such worldly subjects wouldn't interest him. I doubt he thinks about anything other than what the Church has ordained. When he speaks it's invariably about our need to love God, live a spiritual life and follow the teachings of the Church. He's a man of faith, not mind."

María Adela sighed and shook her head in agreement.

"The bishop will not be impressed with Father Olivier's mind or knowledge. His concern will be the manner in which he serves the Church and carries out his duties in the cathedral.

"If so, Father Olivier can't be faulted. From what I've seen, he does everything in the same manner as all the other priests in the cathedral. If I didn't see their faces, I wouldn't know one from the other. Of course, in the confessional, Father Olivier's voice and Paris accent are much too distinct to be confused with the voices of the others."

"Who wouldn't recognize his voice?" Aveline smiled.

"His voice sometimes makes me shiver especially when he's making one of his inspiring sermons."

"His sermons *are* truly inspiring. And none of the others, including Father Antonio, can give such sermons. I always attend Mass when it's his turn. " María Adela refilled her guest's cup of tea and handed it to her.

"Thank you. No, they certainly cannot." Aveline shook her head. "As much as I admire Father Antonio, he's not nearly as knowledgeable as Father Olivier."

"Nor does he have Father Olivier's gift of speaking in God knows how many languages. Of course, no one else in New Orleans has that ability either."

"I agree, María Adela, but I doubt his learning will mean much to the bishop. Not only is he humorless and narrow-minded, he is, I fear, disposed against us French. Although the colony has certainly prospered since the Spaniards arrived, the French are treated with less respect than their people. The Spaniards see themselves as superior to us and hold the important government positions. It's true in the Church as well. Not one of the bishops of Louisiana has been French since Spain acquired the colony. That's more than thirty years ago!" Aveline's cheeks reddened. "We are treated no better than the common people no matter our background or family lineage. It infuriates me!"

"It's true. I was surprised to find most of the priests here were Spanish, not French when I came to New Orleans with my husband in 1778." María Adela had been born in a small village outside of Spanish St. Augustine and spent her youth in the old presidio by the sea.

"Not only does the bishop have that haughty Spanish attitude toward the French, I have heard he looks with suspicion at the Dominican Order. Of course, that's quite common among many of the secular clergy as well. So, as a *French Dominican*, Father Olivier faces a superior who probably holds him in low regard even before he is to be judged for the complaint made by the sacristan." Aveline clucked her tongue.

María Adela nodded. "It's true. Father Olivier's birth in France and Dominican learning will probably weigh against him, especially after what the Jacobins and Bonaparte have done to the Church in France. I do hope we don't lose him over this incident. I've so much enjoyed our afternoon women's meetings with him."

"So have I." Aveline sighed. "It's the only time of the week when my mind awakens from sleep. I seem to spend most of time with my grandchildren and gossiping about the other French families in New Orleans."

"It's the same for me, though, of course, I don't have grandchildren. How are they by the way? I saw Paulette and the girls at the market Monday morning. They're growing like weeds."

Aveline smiled. "They are. Colette has me measuring her height every time she comes to see me. I use the edge of the bedroom door and there are quill lines on it from the time she was five years old. Colette's so clever – at times, too clever for her own good. I have to watch her when I measure her or she will raise her feet to get a higher line on the door." She chuckled.

María Adela laughed with her. "Children can't wait to grow up. Colette's eleven now, isn't she? I suppose she can't wait until her next birthday in February."

"Yes, though she announced last week that she was not eleven. 'I'm eleven and a *half,*' she corrected her mother. My God, María Adela, it seems like only yesterday when I saw her round little face and tiny wrinkled hands."

"I recall seeing her in church in Paulette's arms. She was truly a beautiful baby."

"She was indeed. But so was Jacqueline, who now sees herself as ugly. At thirteen, she has a poor complexion and that ungainly look that girls get at her age. So, she's quite miserable these days and takes it out on everyone – especially her little sister. Jacqueline can be quite cruel to Colette and delights in making her cry. It's her age I'm sure and she should grow out of it."

"That's what I would think. I see that Jacqueline is beginning to show a bosom beneath her dresses. I assume, she will be having her monthlies soon."

"Paulette has prepared her for it. She's a good mother as well as a good wife. I couldn't ask for a better daughter-in-law." Feeling warm from the hot tea, Aveline picked up her fan.

"How about the boys? I haven't seen them for ages."

"Alain hasn't written for a fortnight. I'm sure it isn't because of his studies. It's life in Paris, I imagine. As my mother would say, "A boy in Paris is a boy in a sweet shop."

"What about the chaos in Paris with the execution of the king and the Reign of Terror?"

"In his last letter, Alain said his law studies continue though with occasional disruptions."

María Adela smiled. "And the other two boys?"

"Jacques and Matthieu are off somewhere. God knows where they are and what they're doing. Against my wishes, Jean Bertin let them take the sloop out by themselves. "

Father Olivier Blanchard sat in the bishop's small office at the back of the cathedral. He arrived at eight o'clock exactly as he had been told a day earlier by the bishop's assistant. The timid young man, a Capuchin novice, had silently ushered him into the office and pointed to the hard chair where he was to sit and wait. Father Olivier did not look at his pocket watch, but he guessed at least ten minutes had passed since his arrival.

He stretched his long legs out and crossed his arms over his chest. A lean man well over six feet tall, Olivier stood out everywhere he went. In New Orleans, he was called El Águila (the Eagle) by the townspeople. His nickname came from a quill and ink drawing made of him by a street artist outside the cathedral. The artist had accentuated Olivier's thick black eyebrows and beaked nose and drawn him looking grim as he strode forward with his long arms swinging at his sides. With his black skullcap made to look like feathers, the Dominican priest appeared to be a hawk taking flight from the ground.

Olivier squinted trying to examine the dark office. Lighted by a dying candle burnt down to a tiny nub in the holder, the windowless room seemed more a monk's cell than a bishop's office. Olivier could barely make out the table the bishop used as a desk and the chair behind it. Leaning forward, he could see the outline of a bookcase near the door, but none of the books on the shelves. He did notice a black Bible on the desk top as he walked into the room. There was nothing else there except the candle.

Father Olivier turned his eyes to the doorway when he heard footsteps on the stone floor outside the office. The footsteps stopped at the door and the man in the hallway sneezed twice and blew his nose. A moment later, Bishop Meléndez walked into the room and greeted him.

"Father Olivier." The bishop nodded formally.

"Most Reverend Bishop," Olivier stood and bowed his head respectfully. He watched as the bishop replaced the dying candle with a new one that lighted the center of the room. Most of the office still remained in semi-darkness, but Olivier now could see the table clearly and the few volumes on the shelves. Except for the Spanish editions of St. Augustine's *Confessions* and *The City of God*, the titles on the narrow spines were too small and unclear to read. Olivier resumed his seat when the bishop gestured to the chair.

"I trust you know why I have summoned you here, Father Olivier." The bishop, a slender man with a long sad face, sat with his thin fingers laced together on the desk. He spoke softly in Spanish, his lips compressed in a tight line.

"Sí, Mi Obispo." Olivier replied in flawless Spanish. It was one of the six languages the Dominican spoke fluently.

Olivier decided to say as little as possible and let the bishop state the sacristan's complaint against him. He intended to be respectful, but not submissive to the man sitting behind the desk. Olivier, who arrived in New Orleans six months before the bishop, had not liked Meléndez from his first meeting with him. Two weeks after his arrival in Louisiana, the visiting bishop had met with all the cathedral priests and told them his expectations for the local parish.

Meléndez told them their mission was to make certain their parishioners understood and followed Church doctrine. The parish, he said, should function as one would in Spain. Meléndez did not criticize the French priests who preceded the Spaniards in Louisiana, but Olivier knew he implied the French clergy had been incompetent. As he now sat waiting for the Spanish bishop to speak, Olivier remembered how angry he had been listening to his tone of superiority.

He saw the bishop as an ignorant man content with a medieval understanding of God and almost no knowledge of the world outside the Church. From Olivier's few brief conversations with Meléndez, he realized the man knew or cared little about the Enlightenment and the many changes it brought about in Europe and America. The man was in Olivier's mind a fanatic whose religious convictions kept him isolated from secular life in New Orleans. Meléndez, he thought, should have been assigned to a remote Church district with few priests and parishioners instead of to a populous diocese where he supervised a cathedral and dominated the parish priests.

"Ah, Father Olivier, I'm sure you are aware of the sacristan's complaint against you. It concerns an incident that occurred a week ago on the twenty-first of this month."

"I am aware of the sacristan's complaint, Bishop Meléndez,

but I don't know its content. He wrote it to Father Antonio, not to me."

"I see. Well, then, I'll read it to you." The bishop reached into the top desk drawer and withdrew a piece of white paper. He took a pair of spectacles from his pocket and put them on. Before beginning to read, he looked over his glasses at Olivier and narrowed his eyes. Meléndez suspected the Dominican knew every word of the complaint and was simply trying his patience.

"I'll skip the salutations and other unrelated matters and read only the paragraph relating to you. 'I regret to inform you of an unpleasant incident involving Father Olivier. He insulted me publicly in front of Father Tomás and three of the parishioners. He told me I was ignorant and should only speak about subjects I knew something about. He said foolish *babbling men* like me were the source of much of the ignorance of the Catholic laity. I believe Father Olivier was in his cups at the time and he shouted loudly in the cathedral. As he left us, he stumbled against the altar and knocked over a burning candle. Father Tomás and I had to hurry over to put out the resulting fire. I'm certain we prevented a conflagration in the cathedral.'"

Meléndez removed his spectacles and looked across his desk at Father Olivier. "Before you respond, let me advise you that Sacristan Mendoza repeated those accusations yesterday in person. Father Tomás also spoke to me and substantially confirmed what the sacristan stated in this letter to the parish priest."

Father Olivier looked at the bishop, but said nothing.

Annoyed, Meléndez raised his voice. "Well, Father Olivier, what do you have to say to these accusations? Is your silence to be regarded as agreement to the complaint?"

"No, Bishop, I do not agree to the complaint. The sacristan's account is inaccurate and incomplete. Among other inaccuracies, the candle fell on the marble floor and never could have produced a conflagration. And, though Father Tomás and the sacristan rushed over to the candle, I was the one who put out the flame." Olivier showed the bishop a burnt spot of the palm of his right hand. "I would appreciate hearing Father Tomás' account of the incident. I believe you said he '*substantially* confirmed what the sacristan stated.' "

The bishop glared at the priest. "Father Tomás' account is *not* the subject of this meeting. It is the sacristan's complaint that concerns me, Father Olivier. He said you insulted him in front of Father Tomás and three parishioners. What did you say to the sacristan?"

"I told the sacristan he should read at least one of the works of St. Thomas before talking about his thinking. I offered to loan him my copy of *Summa Theologica*. It's in Spanish, I told him, if he decided to read it."

The bishop nodded knowingly. "So, it's true – you did insult him publicly."

"It might be said my remarks to him, rather than insults, were words of encouragement for him to learn more about the theology of St. Thomas Aquinas. The philosophic contributions of St. Thomas are much too important in the Church's history to be misunderstood."

"Don't bandy words with me, Father Olivier." The bishop's raised his voice. "You know very well that you insulted the sacristan. You insulted him amidst our parishioners in the house of God. How dare you? The Church is solely for the worship of God. It is not for the idle and endless debates you Dominicans seem to enjoy. Do you hear me, Father Olivier?"

"Si, Más Reverendo Obispo."

"The Church is where man can reach out to God, where he can redeem himself from sin. It is the only place left in this sinful world where he can come close to God and feel his love and presence." There was spittle in the corners of the bishop's mouth when he finished speaking.

Olivier said nothing. He saw the bishop as one of the

dour-looking priests often present in an El Greco painting. Bishop Meléndez, he thought, belonged in the same century as El Greco and not two centuries later when the Church faced the challenges of a more materialistic world. As he waited for the bishop to control his anger, Olivier pictured him in the sixteenth century as a grim interrogator in the inquisition. He saw him glaring at a torture victim on the rack.

"Now, we must consider the sacristan's last statements in his complaint." The bishop had calmed himself and now spoke softly once again. "Sacristan Mendoza has accused you of drunkenness in the cathedral, a charge that was reluctantly confirmed by Father Tomás. He said you shouted at him and, in a drunken state, stumbled against the altar, knocking over a *burning candle*. What do you say to those accusations, Father Olivier?"

"I was *not* in a drunken state when I fell against the altar. It was simply a misstep."

"Is that so? Do you deny your drunkenness? Speak up, Father Olivier!"

Olivier sighed. "I may have taken a touch too much that afternoon."

"A 'touch too much,' you say. In the saint's cathedral! That's blasphemous!" Meléndez, his face flushed, raised his voice loudly. "This is not Paris, you know, where the French brutes have reviled the Church and rejected God himself."

"I did not drink in the cathedral." Olivier spoke softly. "I drank outside while eating my lunch behind the cathedral."

"I see." Though still incensed, the bishop only sighed and shook his head sadly. "Well, Father Olivier, this is the fourth such incident as you must be aware."

Olivier sighed again. "I thought it was the third …"

"No, it is the *fourth* such incident! That is why Father Antonio has brought the matter to my attention. He should have come to me after the third – that's the rule, but the parish priest is far too lenient. Well, never mind that. The fact is that you have been guilty of four incidents of drunkenness as well as insulting the sacristan in the cathedral – in front of parishioners! Do you question those facts?"

"No, Most Reverend Bishop." Olivier knew there was no point arguing with the bishop. Meléndez had already made up his mind.

"Well, then there is nothing more to be said. I will consider your case and notify Father Antonio of my ruling. In the meantime, I suggest you pray to God for guidance and penitence. It is certain that you are guilty of the sins of pride and drunkenness. There may well be others, but only you know of their existence and what you should do about them."

Reynaud Fournier had pulled his net full of fish against the side of his pirogue when he saw a hole in the hemp webbing. About to heave the heavy net into the pirogue, he stopped and stared at it. There were several broken stands which he had not noticed on his previous cast. He wondered if one of the crabs in the net had torn it. But then he recalled tugging at the line to free it from something. He looked out to where he had made his last cast, but saw nothing floating or sticking out of the water that could have torn the net. Thinking something below the surface must might have caused the tear, Fournier decided to search there after emptying the net. He frowned, annoyed he would have to repair the net again. It was the sixth time that week and he wondered what sin he had committed to bring him such bad luck.

Fournier hauled the net out of the water and sorted through the mass of wriggling fish and crabs. Most were too small or inedible and, one by one, he threw them back into the water. The keepers, three good-sized bass, two catfish, an unusually big flounder and three hand-sized crabs, he dropped into his fish-holds. The smaller hold for the crabs was almost full; Fournier guessed he had at least a couple of dozen good-sized crabs. He lifted the top of the large hold and looked at the swimming fish. The hold appeared to be about two thirds full and he assumed another two casts of the net would fill it completely.

It had been a good day and he expected it would be even better when the last netting was emptied. The shaded pool in the east end of the lake had never failed him. Surrounded by cedars, water oaks and marsh grass, a variety of edible fish seemed to congregate there and he invariably came away with at least a twenty-five-peseta catch. It was one of his secret fishing spots and he hoped no one else would ever find it.

Taking a wrinkled handkerchief from his pocket, Fournier wiped the sweat from his face and looked at the place where he thought the net had been torn. He paddled slowly to the spot, looking down into the water. Fournier knew he had plenty of time to reach the docks and sell his catch before the fishmongers opened their stalls. He usually sold most, if not all of his catch to Jean Gaudet who would wait for him, knowing he brought in fresh fish caught that morning. He had never been one of those lazy and deceitful fishermen who kept their catch alive a day or so before selling it in town.

Fournier reached the spot where he thought the net had been torn, but saw nothing below the surface. The lake at six-thirty was still in early morning shadow and it was hard to see more than a couple of feet beneath the rippling water. He bent over the gunwale to look down into the deep water and leaned as far over as possible, careful not to tip the heavily laden boat over. The fisherman did not intend to lose his catch simply to find what had torn his net. About to give up his search after seeing nothing below, Fournier turned his eyes upward and toward the starboard side where the pirogue was slowly drifting. And, there less than six feet away, he saw the top of a ship's mast just below the surface of the water. He reached the mast with one paddle stroke and tied the pirogue to it.

Fournier climbed over the crab and fish holds and went to the bow where a shaft of sun shown on the mast. Again, he bent over the gunwale and peered down into the deep water. His movement from the stern to the bow had rippled the water and he had to wait impatiently while the surface calmed. This time when Fournier leaned over the side and looked down, he saw the dark shape of a sunken ship and knew his fishing was over for the day.

María Adela Boudreaux left the funeral with Father Olivier. They walked side by side along the path from the grave site to the street. They walked in silence. María Adela had waited for Olivier, who had been among the last mourners to leave the cemetery. He had remained with the grieving family and Father Antonio, while the diggers filled the graves. They left only when the last shovelful of dirt was patted into place on top of the second grave. Father Antonio walked away with the family and Olivier joined María Adela on the path behind them.

At the street, the elderly woman offered the priest a ride in her coach. His mud splattered cassock and shoes showed her that he had walked all the way from the city, a distance of almost three miles. María Adela wondered why he had not come to the funeral with the parish priest, whom she saw climbing into his carriage over Olivier's shoulder.

"Do join me, Father Olivier." She gestured to her carriage. "I am going directly back to town and I'll take you to the cathedral."

"Thank you, I would appreciate a ride into town, though I'll not be going to the cathedral. I walked here, thinking the walk would do me good. In the last few months, my stomach seems to have grown substantially. Gluttony apparently is another of my sins." He smiled ruefully.

María Adela returned the smile. "It's a problem all too many of us face in New Orleans." She turned toward her carriage and the priest walked behind her.

Her driver held María Adela's elbow as she climbed up into the carriage. Father Olivier, refusing assistance, followed her. They sat on opposite sides of the open coach so Olivier could stretch his long legs out sideways. María Adela removed her wide-brimmed bonnet and began to fan herself. It was already hot though dark clouds covered the sun.

"I thought it might rain at any time." María Adela sighed. "I'm so glad the family was at least spared the rain. They have suffered so much."

"What a terrible tragedy!" Olivier nodded. "Their two youngest boys … lost."

"Yes, Jacques was sixteen and Matthieu seventeen. Jean Bertin was grooming the boys to run the business in the future, of course, with the help of their cousin Charles Laroux. God only knows what Jean Bertin would do without his nephew, now. Alain has said he will not be involved in either the saw mill or the sugar refinery – despite his father wishes."

"Alain is the boy studying law in Paris – the oldest boy?"

"Yes. Jean Bertin was willing to send him abroad to study because he had the very able assistance of Charles Laroux. Are you acquainted with him?" María Adela saw Olivier shake his head. "He's the blond man who stood behind Jean Bertin. Charles is his nephew, the son of Estelle Laroux, Jean Bertin's older sister. Estelle is a bedridden widow and Charles is her only child. Her husband, Louis, died in 1782 and Jean Bertin hired the thirteen-year old boy to run errands for him. Charles has been with him ever since and now is indispensable to him. He's quite clever and knows the business as well as Jean Bertin. Charles has been a Godsend to him since Alain is not interested in his father's enterprises and Jacques and Matthieu are … " María Adela paused as tears filled her eyes … "*were* too young to assist him."

Olivier nodded. "I see. I've never met Charles Laroux. In fact, I don't remember ever seeing him at the cathedral."

"I'm not surprised. He rarely comes to the cathedral." María Adela sighed, pressing a handkerchief to her swollen eyes. "It hurts to mention the boys' names. I've known them since they were babies. Oh, Father, it breaks my heart!" María Adela's eyes filled with tears and her chin trembled. She again gently touched a handkerchief to her eyes.

"I didn't know them well. Father Antonio was their confessor. I know the girls better. I confirmed Jacqueline this past spring and I have enjoyed several animated conversations with little Colette. She is very curious and questions everything."

"That's Colette. "*Why* is her favorite word and she can *why* you to death." María Adela had dried her eyes and now smiled broadly. "Though Aveline would never admit it to anyone, Colette is her enfant gâté (spoiled child). The proud grandmother talks about her constantly."

"Colette is a delightful child. Though, I must say, she has asked me some *embarrassing* questions. The last time I saw her, she wanted to know why priests wear *dresses*. When I told her a cassock was a robe, not a dress, Colette said, 'Call it what you want, Father, it's a dress and you know it.'"

María Adela laughed. "Colette's a precocious child and you never know what she will say next." She looked at Olivier and her smile faded. "I'm glad you came today, Father. The family needs as much comfort as possible. The loss of children is a family's worst nightmare."

Olivier nodded. "It is and I'm glad Monsieur Dumont asked the pastor if I might attend the funeral. It surprised me since I don't know him or his family very well, but I was pleased to be asked. Of course, I know Aveline and I hope my presence was helpful to her in some small way. Father Antonio certainly did not need me there and he gave each of the boys a touching eulogy. He speaks from his heart and everyone knows it."

"Yes, he does. As you probably know, Father Antonio has known both boys from birth. He baptized them in the old cathedral. Of course, well before the Great Fire."

Olivier nodded. He saw that the coach was approaching the walls of the city.

"Father, what have you heard about the accident that sank the *La Bonne Chance*? I know Jean Bertin would not have let the boys take the sloop out unless it was seaworthy."

"I've heard almost nothing – except that it was a peculiar accident. It's certainly hard to understand the sinking of a sound ship in calm waters. *La Bonne Chance* was only three years old and well maintained by Monsieur Dumont. The city magistrate has asked the captain of the guardiacostas (coast guard), Capitan Ricardo Ordoñez y Rosas, to investigate the incident."

"Is the captain reliable?" María Adela made a face showing her doubt.

"He is *very* reliable. Despite the poor opinion of the Spaniards in New Orleans, there are many conscientious and intelligent men in the king's service and the captain is one of them."

"It's not only the Spaniards who concern me; it's the incompetent colonial officials I've seen over a lifetime. I have lived under the English as well as the Spanish and, with all too few exceptions, I have seen men of little mind and consequence in charge of the colonies."

"That may well be, but I'm certain Ordoñez y Rosas will do a thorough investigation of the sinking." Olivier could see a long line of carriages and carts waiting to move through the gates. As he looked at the line, he saw the Dumonts' covered coach, draped in black, entering the city. One of the sentries had waved it forward in front of fifteen other horse-drawn carriages.

"I'll be leaving you inside the gates on San Felipe in the middle of the block. I now have rooms in the home of Madame Lefevre. I assume you know her."

"I do, but why are you living with her" María Adela knew the answer to her question as soon as she asked it. "So, the bishop has pushed you out of the parish."

"Not exactly. I've been assigned to serve the poorer people of the parish outside the city at Santa María. Father Etienne's ill health has forced him to retire as pastor and I have replaced him for an indefinite period of time."

María Adela frowned. "Is this assignment the bishop's punishment for the incident with the sacristan? From what I've heard, he deserved what … "

"I don't consider it a punishment, María Adela. Not at all! Keep in mind, I serve God and the children of God, whether they be rich or poor. Hopefully, I will be helpful to those less fortunate people who live outside the city walls. It may be God's will that I now devote myself to those parishioners rather than the wealthy of the cathedral. It should be good for me as well."

Olivier did not tell María Adela what the bishop had conveyed to him through the parish priest. Embarrassed, Father Antonio had awkwardly related the bishop's words a week earlier. He spoke to Olivier after the Dominican heard confession on a Friday morning. Father Antonio, a gaunt, gray-haired man, stammered as he told him of his new assignment.

"Olivier, you know this is awkward for me." He sighed loudly. "I would have wished the b-bishop spoke to you himself."

"I understand, Father. I know you are only doing what the bishop instructed you to do. Now, please tell me what the bishop has decided and what he told you to tell me."

Father Antonio exhaled his breath loudly. "Yes, well, Olivier … the bishop wants you assigned as pastor at Santa María. Father Etienne is no longer able to cope with the multitude of problems the church has faced, especially after July's storm. He has asked to be relieved; as I'm sure you know, he is well over sixty and in poor health. Santa María, in the bishop's words, 'is in desperate need of renovation as well as the restoration of its spiritual meaning in the parish.'"

"I see, the bishop expects me to restore Santa María. Now, please tell me what he said."

"I should remember his words, he repeated them *twice*." Antonio sighed. "The b-bishop said, 'Tell Father Olivier that I expect him to use this new assignment to s-strengthen his moral character and d-dedicate himself to the humility and sobriety that his p-priestly office demands.'"

CHAPTER TWO

New Orleans: September 2 – October 25, 1799

"At this time, Señor, ah, pardon, Monsieur Dumont, we do not know why the *La Bonne Chance* sank." The Mississippi River flowing behind him, Captain Ordoñez stood at the edge of the quay, supporting himself on an oak cane. The coast guard captain was an elderly man with gray hair and the lined, weather-beaten face of a man who had spent much of his life at sea. He held his mouth in a tight line and it was apparent his left leg caused him severe pain. His hand trembled from the strain of pressing down on the cane's handle to keep his weight off the leg.

Jean Bertin Dumont frowned.

"I am sorry to say, Monsieur Dumont, we could not find anything under water to show us why the sloop went down. The divers were there for four hours this morning and looked all over the sunken vessel; they swam around the ship countless numbers of times and could find nothing broken of any kind. The hull looked to be as sound as the day the ship put to sea. There was no sign of a puncture, split plank, leaking seam – nada!"

Jean Bertin exhaled his breath in exasperation. He was a short, stout man with a round face and striking blue eyes. He leaned wearily against the dock's railing, his arms crossed over his chest. Dumont had dark circles around his eyes and looked as if he had not slept for days.

"The sloop looks seaworthy and I expect it could be salvaged." Captain Ordoñez nodded. "It's down a little more than three fathoms and near the shore. Since the lake is also quite close to town, the salvage ships would have no trouble reaching it from the river. The outlet channel from the lake to the Mississippi is deep and wide enough for even the biggest salvage ships. In calm weather, it would be an uncomplicated operation."

"I see." Dumont exhaled again. "The lake is west of the river, isn't it?"

"Yes, Monsieur Dumont, it flows out where that sunken warship lies on the bottom."

"What you say makes sense. We probably should salvage the sloop." Dumont wiped the sweat from his face with a damp handkerchief.

"Bueno (Good)."

"Captain, please tell me what you think happened to *La Bonne Chance*? I know you hesitate to say anything official about the sinking at this time, but I would appreciate hearing your opinion of the cause."

Ordoñez limped to the railing, faced Dumont and shook his head. "To be quite candid, Monsieur, I don't know. I've examined sunken ships for twenty years and *La Bonne Chance* is the first sinking I cannot explain. I usually know as soon as the divers come up from their first dive. I'm sure the cause will be found in time, but, for now, I can't offer an explanation."

"I see. What about a sudden swell – a flood wave sweeping in from the river? I know such waves are common. I've seen a couple myself over the years."

"They are indeed, Monsieur Dumont, but I haven't heard of a tidal wave anywhere in the bayous this summer. I asked several of the fishermen, but no one has reported any unusual tidal movement in the last couple of months. Fournier, the Acadian who found the sloop said the tidal waters have been exceptionally calm so far this year."

"I realize it would help if the sloop was brought up and the water drained out of it. You could them examine it from bow to stern." Dumont made a face. "The only reason I hesitate to salvage it is because of my wife and mother. I fear they might faint or worse simply seeing the ship where our two boys drowned." Dumont's eyes filled with tears and he turned away to wipe them with the back of his hand.

"I understand, Monsieur Dumont. "We certainly can wait awhile until you decide when would be a better time. However, I must remind you that this is the season of the worst storms and if one strikes the lake the sloop may well be destroyed or lost. As you will recall, the storm of 1790 changed many of the bayous and channels as well as the course of the river itself."

Dumont nodded. "August and September are the worst months of the year."

"Yes, Monsieur, September usually brings the most destructive storms of all."

"Well, then, we can't afford to wait, can we? I want to know what happened to *La Bonne Chance*. I'll not rest until I know why my boys died. How long will it take to raise the sloop out of the water? I hope it can be done this month."

"I would think so. I know of no other salvage operation now in progress. From what I've have seen of such efforts, I think it could be done in two to three days. The sloop lies in shallow water and shouldn't be too hard to raise unless there's a serious puncture in the hull that no one has seen."

Dumont sighed again. "Then, let's do it as soon as possible. Can I leave you in charge of the salvage operation, Captain? I'll see to it that you are well compensated."

"Yes, Monsieur, you can leave it to me. I know the reliable salvage companies in town and I'll choose the one best suited to bring up the sloop. I'll also make certain the charges are reasonable. I'll inform you of my findings as the salvage proceeds."

"Thank you, Captain. I would appreciate the ship's salvage remain as secret as possible. Please see to it that the salvage men are given extra pesetas for their silence. I don't want my family to know about it until I tell them. Contact me at my office."

"Yes, Monsieur Dumont. "I'll try to keep it secret, but the gossip in this city will make it difficult. You know how fast rumors spread in New Orleans."

Later that day, Jean Bertin told his nephew the *La Bonne Chance* would be salvaged. He spoke to Charles Laroux when he returned to his office following a weekly meeting with the saw mill's superintendent. Jean Bertin reclined on the soft couch across from his desk as he related his conversation with the captain of the coast guard.

His nephew, a short muscular man with blond hair and blue eyes, nodded when he heard the sloop would be brought up and towed to New Orleans.

"*La Bonne Chance* should be salvaged and thoroughly examined. That's the only way we will know why it went down. I intended to suggest the salvage, but hesitated to say anything since the funerals were so recent. I also worried Aunt Paulette would suffer terribly if she saw the ship at the dock. I fear Grandmother Aveline would also suffer."

"That was my fear as well. But the Coast Guard captain

convinced me to bring the sloop up now. He warned me if we waited a storm might destroy the ship before an investigation can be conducted. As you well know, we are in the midst of hurricane season and a storm can strike New Orleans at any time."

"That's true. How will they salvage it?"

Laroux moved a chair near the couch to sit facing his uncle. As he turned to Jean Bertin, the left side of his face stood out revealing a purple birth mark on his cheek. The mark began at the far corner of his eye and covered most of his cheek. To avoid stares, Laroux tried to speak to people with the right side of his face tilted toward them. Outside in the streets, whether riding or walking, he wore a wide-brimmed hat slanted to the left to hide his disfigurement. The hat had been specially made by a hat-maker in Paris and he wore it in all weather. Laroux even averted his left cheek from his uncle who had known him since his birth.

"As I understand it, Charles, they will bring it up between two other ships using winches. The sloop lies in only eighteen feet of water and divers will be able to dig out enough sand to tie lines around its hull and haul it up. Once above the water, the flooded interior will be emptied – they now have pumps these days that do it and then they will tow it here to the city dock. If the sloop still leaks, they will take it ashore there and beach it for a thorough examination."

"I've never seen a sunken ship brought up, though I've heard about it."

"I haven't either. Apparently, the size of the sloop and the shallow depth of the lake make it possible. Under other conditions, such as bad weather, it would be questionable."

"We are indeed fortunate that it's possible." Laroux frowned. "Though I for one, dread seeing the interior of the cabin where the divers found Jacques and Matthieu."

"I dread it too, Charles, but the sloop must be brought up to find out why it sank. I don't think I'll be able to sleep at night until we know."

"I understand, Uncle Jean. I can't believe there was something structurally wrong with *La Bonne Chance.* It was refitted only a month ago when we made the renovations. If there had been something amiss, surely the carpenters would have told us."

At that moment, Tristan Surette entered the office carrying a heavy silver tray held high on one hand; the tray contained coffee, milk, beignets as well as cups, saucers, additional plates, spoons and white napkins. Surette, a dark bearded Acadian in his late thirties, served Jean Bertin doing a variety of tasks for him at both his home and office. He had been hired by Jean Bertin's father as an orphaned child and had worked twenty-five years for the Dumont family

Jean Bertin scowled, looking at the tray Surette had placed on the small table in front of the couch. "You forgot the sugar bowl again, Tristan. This is the second time this week and it happened at least once last week as well."

"I'll get it immediately. Is there anything else?" The neutral expression on Tristan's face remained unchanged, but his black eyes narrowed as he stared at Jean Bertin.

"No, nothing." Jean Bertin did not look at him as he reached for a beignet. He heard the office door close and sighed as he spoke to his nephew. "Not only is he forgetful these days, he's clumsy. As you well know, a fortnight ago he spilled a bowl of hot soup on me and damned near scalded my stomach, never mind ruining my breeches. I would have let him go a long time ago, but my mother wouldn't hear of it."

"I don't know why he's forgetful, but I can understand his clumsiness. The man's so big and strong I imagine objects such as soup bowls, which seem quite heavy to us, are like feathers to him and therefore easily dropped. I would think his occasional clumsiness is not meaningful, considering his great strength which is available to the family whenever needed."

Laroux saw his uncle nod as he thought about what had

been said. He actually wondered if Tristan Surette's mistakes, whether careless or clumsy, were deliberate. The taciturn Acadian did everything he was told without a word of complaint, but something in the large man's eyes told Laroux he hated Jean Bertin. Of course, many men in town hated him, some envious of his wealth, some because of their disappointing business dealings with him, but most because of the contemptuous manner in which he treated them. Laroux had heard any number of criticisms of Jean Bertin from commercial associates and clients alike who asked to meet with him rather than his uncle, the owner of Dumont enterprises.

Surette returned a moment later and put a small sugar bowl on the platter. He left without a word. Laroux said, "Merci," but the Acadian did not acknowledge it.

"Where were we?" Jean Bertin, holding another beignet in his fingers, did not look up at the man during his arrival or departure. Finishing the sugar-covered pastry in two bites, he then dropped two teaspoons of sugar in an empty cup, added milk to a half the height of the cup and filled the rest of it with coffee. Stirring the mixture, he looked at his nephew awaiting his reply.

"We were discussing the structural soundness of *La Bonne Chance* and I recommended we ask the carpenters who completed its recent renovation about it." Laroux filled another cup with the same mixture as his uncle, stirred it similarly and drank half of it immediately.

"Ah, yes, we should ask them about it. We used those two Acadian brothers, didn't we? The Laroche brothers?"

"Yes, Uncle. They've worked for us many times before. They built the additions to the mill and repaired the roof on your house among other carpentry projects. We always have been well satisfied with their work. I'll talk to them as soon as possible – perhaps tomorrow."

"Good. What renovations did they make on *La Bonne*

Chance? I recall the new decking and cabin door, but not the other renovations. The sloop was out of water for more than a month. The boys kept nagging me to complete the carpentry so they could take it out before the summer storms. Matthieu was so persistent. Remember how he came to the office every day inquiring when everything would be done? Mon Dieu, how I wish I had taken it out myself first." Jean Bertin's eyes watered and he dabbed them with his handkerchief.

Laroux was silent, while his uncle wiped his eyes and blew his nose. He looked down and wiped his own eyes with a handkerchief. When the young man finally looked up, he saw his uncle wave his hand for him to continue.

"I'll get the invoice, Uncle Jean. I don't remember all the renovations either. I know we wanted to make sure no one could break into the cabin again."

Laroux stood up and went to the closet, where the files were stored. A moment later, he returned to his seat with a thick folder in hand. *Billings, August, 1799* was written on the cover. The folder held a sheaf of papers and Laroux looked through them one by one until he found the invoice for the renovations of *La Bonne Chance*. It was dated, 12 August 1799.

"Here it is." He held up a piece of paper. "Do you want me to read it to you or …"

"You read it, Charles. I don't want to use my spectacles." Jean Bertin had finished half his coffee while his nephew found and returned with the folder.

"They began the work on July eleventh and finished on August twelfth. Marcel Laroche, the younger brother, signed the invoice. Apparently, he can write."

"I doubt it, Charles. Very few craftsmen can read or write and, of course, fewer Acadians. Laroche probably paid someone to make out the invoice, perhaps one of those writers who loiter about the Plaza de Armas. They would even sign it for him."

"True. Anyway, he listed everything they did on the sloop

in order of its completion. They began by scraping the barnacles off the hull. That took them a week. They then caulked and filled in cracks, split planks and holes both inside and outside the hull. All weak-looking and water-logged wood was replaced as well as that broken railing on the starboard side of the sloop. They also replaced some of the decking."

"Didn't they paint the ship?" Jean Bertin finished the last of his coffee and fixed another.

"The entire sloop was painted after the carpentry was completed and the pitch applied to it. The hull was given three thick coats of pitch alone. I remember telling them to make certain the pitch was applied thickly, each coat, at least, a half-inch thick. As you well know, with all the oyster beds in the bayous, the ship bottoms always get cracked and scraped around here."

"That may well have been what happened to *La Bonne Chance*." Jean Bertin sighed. "A cracked plank or seam in the hull might have been scraped open and flooded the sloop while the boys slept. Mon Dieu, there are so many possibilities!"

"There are. We'll know more when the sloop is examined. It's possible that something unknown in the lake sank *La Bonne Chance*. Perhaps, a swell from the river."

Jean Bertin nodded. "That's also a possibility, though the captain didn't think so. You know, it might be a good idea to have Tristan ask the Acadian fishermen about any unexpected swells from the river. Though Ordoñez is certainly an experienced seaman, he's a Spaniard and, as you know, I'm never confident of their competence or what they say."

"I see, so you want Tristan to verify if the captain has told you the truth."

"Yes, I'll send him to the lowlands in the morning. Meanwhile, I want the sloop brought up as soon as possible." Jean Bertin drank half of his second cup of coffee.

"Do you want me to speak to the captain and urge him

to get started? As I recall, he said there were no salvage operations in progress at this time." Laroux was relieved that Jean Bertin would be the one to send Surette to speak to the fishermen. He always avoided ordering the big Acadian to do anything that his uncle required.

"Yes, offer him an incentive. Spaniards are greedy. Let's get the salvage started the first of next week at the latest. I probably should go out to the lake and watch them bring it up."

"Would you like me to take charge of the salvage, while you supervise the installation of the new machinery at the mill?" Laroux knew his uncle wanted him to go to the lake rather than himself. Jean Bertin hated the humid, insect-infested bayous and lowlands and had not been near them in years. "If agreeable to you, Uncle Jean, I'll supervise the entire salvage operation and advise you of its progress." He paused to take two swallows of his coffee.

"That's a good plan, Charles. Was there anything else on the invoice?"

"Yes, the installation of the new cabin door with its iron crossbar was included next. The carpenters were told to strengthen the cabin door and install an iron bar …"

"I remember it well! We ordered a heavy new door after the other cabin door had been broken open and our sea charts stolen. We also had them install a crossbar on the forward hatch of the ship." Jean Bertin glared at his nephew. He did not like being reminded that he frequently forgot the details of his business discussions with his nephew.

"The last item on the invoice is the sloop's painting. We provided all the materials for the renovation – the oak planks, paint, pitch and all the iron work including the crossbars. Their bill therefore only lists the charges for their carpentry and other work on the sloop."

"What about the installation of the crossbars over the cabin door and hatch?"

"There's no mention of charges for either installation."
"That's too bad. It's their loss, isn't it?"

Two days later, Laroux spoke to the carpenters at the dock. He met the Laroche brothers in the late afternoon as they were finishing their day's work on a tied-up schooner. The approach of dark storm clouds from the gulf made them pack up their tools for the night. Thunderstorms usually struck New Orleans every afternoon in September and the heavy clouds moving in from the southwest across the Gulf of Mexico signaled the coming of another storm.

"I think we have a few minutes to talk before the rain falls." Laroux and the two brothers stood on the schooner's deck near the main mast. "I'm sure you have heard, we lost my cousins, Jacques and Matthieu …" Laroux sighed … and *La Bonne Chance* a few weeks ago."

"Oui, Monsieur Laroux, we hear a tha sinkin.' Teribel loss. So sad." Marcel Laroche, the younger of the two brothers, looked down and shook his head from side to side. Marcel was a short, sun-burned man with muscled arms and big rough hands. He looked at his older brother who also had been shaking his head. "We speek ta da boys evry day when we work on *La Bonne Chance.*" He motioned to his brother, a bigger broader man, but with the same raven-black hair as Marcel. "Pascal fish wit Jacques."

"I know. Jacques showed me that big bass he caught the last time he fished with Pascal." Laroux paused, thinking how he should inquire about the sloop's condition. "I need to ask you about the condition of *La Bonne Chance* when you finished the renovation last month. Was it sea worthy?"

"Oui, Monsieur! We sail the sloop ta le Golfe du Mexique before we give keys ta you. The ship sail en douceur (smoothly)." Marcel shook his head up and down emphatically.

"*La Bonne Chance* – un beau navire (a fine ship)."

Laroux nodded. He recalled Marcel telling him about their testing the ship's handling on the trip to the gulf. At the time, Marcel gave him the keys to the crossbar locks. He handed them over as the two brothers guided him around the sloop showing him what they had done.

The first drops of rain pattered on the deck as Laroux thanked the carpenters and walked down the gangplank to the dock. Mounting his horse, he saw a brilliant flash of lightning over the river. An explosion of thunder followed as he urged his stallion to a trot toward his office. With luck, he would be inside before the rain fell.

Charles Laroux stood at the railing of *Le Cavalier* and watched as the deck of the sunken sloop appeared below the water. It was a foot or so from the surface and slowly emerging from the bottom of the lake. The salvage ship's captain, Corbin Blanc, paced back and forth between the two winches on *Le Cavalier*, making certain the ship rose at the same level at both its bow and stern. At each winch, he leaned over the railing and dropped a weighted sounding-line down on the ship's deck to measure the length of the hauling ropes.

Laroux exhaled his breath in relief when he saw the wooden deck so close to the surface. The top of the cabin had been visible for a while and now the metal edges of the portholes came into view. He shared a smile with the Captain Ordoñez, who stood beside him looking over the side. It appeared the sloop soon would be above water.

Le Cavalier and a second large vessel, *Le Bon Voyage*, were on either side of the sloop as four winches, two on each ship, hauled it up. The salvage ships had heavy rope mats hanging on their sides to prevent the rising sloop from scraping their hulls. Both ships had been anchored at the bow, stern and amidships. Amidships, two anchors were dropped, one on the port side and the other starboard, to limit the ships' movement during the salvage.

Laroux had arrived at dawn with the coastguard captain. They sailed into the lake on a small cutter that glided quickly through the inlet on a strong current. Entering the bayou, Laroux was glad to see the salvage ships already anchored and the crews setting up their winches. The captain anchored the cutter a short distance away from the site and Laroux paddled the dinghy to *Le Cavalier*. Tying the dinghy to the side of the salvage ship, they climbed aboard.

On the deck of *Le Cavalier*, they stood at the starboard side railing well away from the winches and crew. Captain Blanc gestured them to stay out of the way. The crew experienced from many salvage operations in the waters around New Orleans, went about their work without any interest in the observers.

Two Indian divers stood on the other side of the deck at the port railing. Out of the corner of his eye, Laroux saw them remove all their clothing except for loincloths. They then tied their hair behind their heads and rubbed an oily substance on their bodies. He later learned it was the milk of a weed that supposedly kept bull sharks away. Laroux noted that the Indians had broad chests and muscular arms. Their upper bodies appeared out of proportion for their slender legs.

Moments later, they crossed the deck to the starboard side, climbed over the rope railing where Laroux and the Spanish captain stood watching and dropped into the water. They swam to where the lines hung from the winches, one diver to each line, took deep breathes and dove downward disappearing into the water. With the dawn light still low in the sky, it was too dark to see below the surface.

Laroux timed the divers on his pocket watch and saw them resurface four minutes later. They repeated the same procedure along the side of the other salvage ship. They swam back and forth between *Le Cavalier* and *Le Bon Voyage* diving in turn beneath the ships. Neither of the divers said anything or signaled each other when they came up for air. Yet, they dove down into the water and surfaced in unison.

Laroux noticed that their time below water increased the more dives they made into the lake. They remained down five minutes during most of their dives. The divers stayed below the water even longer on their final dive. They were down for almost six minutes. Laroux held up his watch so the Spanish Captain could see it and they both shook their heads in astonishment.

The divers needed only ten dives to dig two channels under the sloop's hull; one channel was dug beneath the ship's stern, the other was dug beneath the hull a foot and a half from where the ship's main beam curved to become the bow. Only three more dives were needed to push the hauling lines through the channels and to tie the lines securely around the sloop. After their final dive, the Indians stayed in the water only long enough to hand up the ends of the hauling lines to the winch crews.

They were on deck toweling off when the rising sun appeared above the trees around the lake. A glass of rum was given to the divers as they dressed and another when they were paid for their work. Seeing the sunken ship beginning to rise, the Indians paddled away in their pirogue.

The sun shined for no more than a half hour. Dark clouds appeared out of the east and partially covered it. A light wind accompanied the clouds, followed by a sprinkling rain. The rain stopped an hour later, but the wind was stronger and the lake, which had been calm earlier, now began to roll with white caps appearing here and there.

Captain Blanc looked up from the rising sloop and studied the clouds in the sky. He spit on his finger and held it up to the wind. He then looked out at the surface of the water and made a face. A moment later, he turned and walked over to Laroux.

"I don't like tha look a tha day now – not atoll." The captain stared at Laroux. A big-bellied man with a black mustache that almost covered his lips, he spoke French with a distinct Acadian accent. "I won't stay ifn tha weatha gets any wors."

"The weather hasn't changed much in the last hour. I'm certain we have enough time to bring up the sloop." Laroux spoke as if he were in command of the salvage.

"I'll be tha one ta decide tha. I'll na be riskin' my ships or my men."

"I understand, but it doesn't look bad, now." As Laroux spoke, a shaft of sunlight came through the clouds and lighted the stern of the ship. "Look Captain. See, it may even clear soon."

"I dowt it. I don't like tha look a tha sky. I didn't like tha look this mornin' an I shurly don't like it now. It looks like a storm's comin' an my achin' bones says it is, too."

"Will you wait a little longer – an hour or so?" Laroux hoped the weather would hold at least until the sloop could be raised and pumped out. If the ship could not be floated to the city dock, perhaps it could be beached with its bow out of the water.

The captain nodded. "I'll wait abit, but I'm warnin' ya now, Monsieur Laroux, ifn it gets any worss I'll cut tha lines." He walked away without another word.

Laroux looked at the coastguard captain. "What do you think, Captain Ordoñez?"

"It doesn't look good, Monsieur Laroux. The captain is right, a storm is coming. A big one I think. I can feel it in my bad leg and the increasing wind is a warning sign. I've seen all too many of them in my twenty years at sea."

"But the rain has stopped."

"It's the dark clouds and wind that matter – not the rain."

"How much more time will it take to raise the sloop

high enough to pump out the water?" Laroux glanced down and saw the ship's deck a few inches above the water.

Captain Ordoñez leaned over the railing and scrutinized the slowly rising sloop. He sighed and looked at Laroux'. "I must be candid, Monsieur, it will take another hour, at least, to raise the sloop high enough for pumping and, then, at least three to four hours to pump out enough water for the vessel to float."

"What about beaching the sloop with its bow out of the water? Surely, we have enough time to drag it to shore. All we need is another couple of hours …"

The Spaniard raised his hand to stop Laroux. "Unfortunately, Monsieur, we don't have another couple of hours. Look at the sky."

Laroux looked up and saw ominous-looking black clouds covering the sky. He grimaced, knowing the salvage operation was done for the day"

Moments later, rain fell again, this time, much harder. A powerful wind blew the drops of rain like musket shot on the decks of the salvage ships. The sky darkened and it looked like dusk had come early and night was near.

Captain Blanc turned to Laroux and shook his head. He shouted to the crewmen cranking the winches and waved his hands signaling the men on the other salvage ship. They stopped the winches and watched as Blanc hurried to Laroux. He again shook his head.

"We're sailin,' now. I'm takin' my ships ta dock. I'll not be takin' any chance a losin' 'em. This storm's gonna be a bad one. Ya better get ta tha cutter afor it hits." He bent his wrists and threw his fingers forward as if sweeping them away.

"What about *La Bonne Chance*?" Laroux pointed to the partially surfaced sloop.

"I'll cut tha lines. With a bita luck, it'll still be here afta tha storm an we can bring 'er up again in aweek or so. I don't 'xpect ta be paid. Tha 'greement with Monsieur Dumont was fer tha salvage an we didn't do it."

"But can we at least beach the sloop?"

"There's no time. I'm cuttin' tha lines, Monsieur Laroux." Captain Blanc turned to his crew and ran a forefinger across his throat.

The taut lines were immediately cut and the sloop once again settled quietly down into the lake. Laroux made a face as he watched the deck and then the cabin disappear from view. He knew Jean Bertin would be angry and complain about Acadian incompetence.

As Captain Blanc had predicted, the storm was a bad one. In fact, it was a hurricane with exceptionally high winds. The hurricane lasted only two days, but it devastated New Orleans and the surrounding areas. Heavy winds broke up wooden buildings and flood waters inundated city streets as well as the outside farms and pasture lands. The wind driven water drowned herds of cattle and hogs and ruined the crops still in the fields. Already harvested cotton, rice, sugar and tobacco were water-soaked or seized by the incessant wind and blown over southern Louisiana. Inside New Orleans, eleven people, six of them children, died in demolished houses and, outside, thirty-nine people drowned in the lowlands. Long-time residents of Louisiana said the hurricane was the worst storm in thirty years.

In New Orleans, most of the dock disappeared in the flood along with a number of houses near the river. On the second day, high winds drove water over the quay, flooded the streets of the city and flushed dock timbers and house debris into the river. If the hurricane had not finally abated that evening, the combination of wind and rain would have destroyed the entire city.

The flood left only three inches of water on Chartres

Street, but as much as a foot of mud on the quay and the lower sections of the streets that ran down to the river. Most buildings in the city lost a portion of their planks and some structures were stripped of their roofs. The majority of cheaply built houses had been broken apart with windows and doors smashed and roof beams exposed. One house had been blown off its foundation and propelled down San Felipe Street into the Mississippi River. Another shattered house had been blown into San Pedro Street, where it leaned precariously at an angle against the Munitions Supply Building.

It took a month for civic order to be restored and another three weeks for the removal of the stinking debris left from the storm. Dead animals, fortunately, were carried away within the first week. House reconstruction and repair required two years of work, but additional carpentry on damaged buildings actually continued into a third year. Local carpenters and masons worked every day from dawn to dusk and even on Sunday, after morning Mass.

The bishop, at first, forbad all Sunday labor, saying it was sinful. He refused to permit reconstruction efforts on Sundays even when confronted one morning by an angry congregation in the cathedral. His assertion that the Edict of Constantine, the first Christian emperor of Rome, forbade it had no effect on the residents, who insisted the craftsmen be allowed to work. After a week of widespread protests, the bishop finally yielded to their demands and permitted the parish six months of Sunday labor. In the end, Sabbath work continued in New Orleans well after the deadline had come and gone. The bishop made no mention of it despite his fury at the *brazen disobedience* of the colonists. After his confrontation with the parish congregation, he hesitated to oppose the construction, fearing additional public protests and the possibility of petitions sent to the Archbishop of Havana.

The lowlands had been hit harder by the summer storm. Trees of all kinds were uprooted and many of the largest trees lay sprawled like dead bodies over the crop fields as well as in the roads and waterways used to reach New Orleans. Leaves and tree debris seemed to be dispersed everywhere in sight. The land looked as if the greenery had been dropped from the sky to cover the earth. The flooding increased the size of bayous and tidal pools around the city and most high and dry places in the woods now were under water or had reverted to marshes with sinking sand.

Dead animals, both domestic and wild, littered the countryside. Cattle and hogs made up most of the carrion, but numerous armadillos, rabbits and raccoons were also seen lying bloated on the ground. A number of larger animals died in the storm as well, but their corpses appeared less conspicuously in view. Seen or unseen, dead animals did not remain long on land or in the marshes. Alligators, vultures and insects quickly disposed of them.

River and bayou boats had not fared any better in the storm. With the exception of heavy and well anchored vessels, more than a hundred boats and ships of all size were cast all over the area. Some were sunk, others lay over-tuned or on their sides in shallow water and a number of vessels ended up on farmland adjoining the river. A schooner and two sloops had been wrecked against the docks and four pirogues were found above the quay at the bottom of Tolosa Street. Another sloop lay on its side in the Plaza de Armas as if a giant had picked it up out of the river and carefully placed it there in front of the cathedral. Weeks later, when New Orleans had begun to resume its normal everyday life, house and ship wreckage still littered the riverside streets as well as the surrounding lowlands and waterways.

Five weeks later, Laroux and Ordoñez returned to the lake where *La Bonne Chance* had been found. They boarded the cutter before first light and were well on the way south as the sun appeared on the eastern horizon. Sailing on the fast-moving current, they reached the channel to the lake a little after seven o'clock. The day ahead looked to be sunny and pleasant with a cool breeze blowing off the gulf.

At first, they could not find their way to the site. The waterway they followed earlier was now obstructed by broken branches, vine entangled tree limbs and, in two places, the trunks of uprooted oak trees. They managed to bypass one of the large trunks, but spent an hour trimming the top of the other that obstructed their passage.

Additional time was spent cutting away branches that leaned over the bayous and raked the sides and deck of the ship. Their work was not only tiring, but perilous in the snake infested lowlands. Venomous snakes often lurked in the low lying trees especially on the thick limbs that leaned over the water. Before touching them, they looked over every branch to make sure none of the snakes were hidden among the leaves. All too many fishermen had died after being struck by one of the brown water snakes that thrived in the bayous. Well aware of their presence, the captain guided the cutter cautiously through the cluttered channel, while Laroux stood amidships scrutinizing every branch and limb he saw leaning over or in the way of the ship.

They saw three water snakes, but none of them posed any danger. Two dropped into the water from overhead branches and the third, lying curled up at the foot of a tree, slithered away into the swamp. Laroux saw the third one, more than four feet in length, as he trimmed the top of a downed tree that blocked their passage. The snake showed him its distinctive white mouth and fangs and then disappeared into the brush.

As Laroux and Captain Ordoñez hacked their way through the channel, they realized it had changed direction and now veered much farther to the east than before. The hurricane had not only altered the Mississippi River's previous course to the Gulf of Mexico, it also rearranged its tributaries as well as countless number of creeks and streams that flowed from the river into the lowlands and swamps.

It was almost noon when they reached a thicket of cedar trees and could not proceed any further. The previous channel to the lake had been emptied and the water now flowed through the cedar thicket, where not even the small cutter could enter. After all their effort, they were obstructed without a way into the lake.

Captain Ordoñez stared at the cedars. "There are only two choices left to us, Monsieur Laroux. We can row a dingy into the lake or we can look for another passageway. I suggest the latter choice. The lake is spring-fed and I'm sure there are other channels flowing from it."

"How long will take us to find another channel to the lake? Do we have enough time today?" Exhausted from all his exertion, Laroux exhaled his breath loudly.

"I think there's another channel a little farther north. I recall passing it a few days after the storm. If it still exists and is in a similar state as this one, we should be able to reach the lake by the mid-afternoon. That will leave us, at least, five hours before dark. I think that's our best way into the lake – rather than take the dinghy from here."

"Laroux nodded. "I agree with you. With all the alligators and snakes I've seen today, I don't think it wise to take the dinghy through the trees."

"Exactly. If we don't have any luck by two o'clock, we can try another day."

"That seems sensible. Let's get out of the swamp and have some lunch. I brought bread and cheese and a bottle of wine."

Their return trip through the channel was easier than expected once they turned the cutter about and cut away a vine that had entangled the rudder. They anchored the cutter at one of the bends in the river and ate their lunch quickly. The captain studied a detailed chart he kept of the river south of New Orleans and then looked through the cutter's log book for the location of the sunken sloop.

There were two hundred some citations since the storm and it took a few minutes to find the date and his written notation. The cutter had been used for a variety of search and salvage operations in the weeks following the hurricane. The captain smiled when he finally found it.

"Here it is." He held his forefinger on the notation and read what he had written earlier. "September 10, 10:15 a.m. Location of *La Bonne Chance*: Some four miles west of the three boulders at the bend of the river, beyond the ten mile marker south of New Orleans. See dark square on chart."

"Will that mark help us find another channel?" Laroux drank the last of the wine.

"Let's hope so. It appears there were other channels; my chart, which is a year or so old, shows five channels flowing from the lake to the Mississippi River. Hopefully, one of them will still be open and will have a deep enough draft for the cutter. If not, we'll have to look for others another day. Is that agreeable to you?" He saw Laroux nod his head.

They followed two channels without success and turned back in a third that soon became too shallow. The fourth passageway was blocked by a downed tree where a dead deer had been caught in its branches. Three alligators were hissing at each other as they devoured the deer. A few minutes later, they found the last channel shown on the chart. To their relief, it appeared to be open, navigable and almost free of tree debris. But when they sailed into the lake, neither of them thought it was the site of the sunken sloop.

The lake looked nothing like the one where their salvage of *La Bonne Chance* had been attempted. Even when the compass confirmed the site, they remained dubious. They looked at each other shaking their heads. The lake seemed twice as large as it had been and now was open and full of sunlight, instead of shaded by a surrounding forest of trees. Few of the tall leafy trees that bordered the bayou still stood. Many lay flattened along the shore and in the swamp beyond the lake. Others were uprooted, their limbs and branches stretched out over the water. As many as fifty of the trees floated in the lake, some of them lying side by side held together by branches that seemed to be embracing.

The two men stood at the bow and looked for landmarks to show them they had arrived at the right spot. According to their compass, the passageway had taken them only a short distance north of where the former channel entered the lake. The captain estimated they had arrived about a quarter mile from that entrance.

"There's a current flowing southward. Let's take it and see if we can find the marker left by Captain Blanc." The captain saw Laroux nod and he moved the tiller to catch the current.

A few minutes later, he anchored the cutter within sight of the previous outlet of the lake. They looked in all directions, but saw nothing that resembled the site where the top of the sloop's mast had been before the storm. Seeing only floating trees and branches, they studied the shore and surrounding woods in search of something recognizable.

"The sloop should be located somewhere near here." Laroux pointed to a huge live oak still standing at the east side of the lake. "See that hole in the trunk just below the second main limb. I remember seeing a couple of squirrels there."

The captain nodded. "I also see a landmark – that dead pine lying there behind the oak. I recall seeing it when you paddled the dinghy to the *Cavalier*. It's noticeable because of the crack down its length, probably made by lightning. So, this is the lake after the storm. Dios mío! (My God!) Without the compass reading, I wouldn't have believed it."

"It is hard to believe. Everything is changed. Where do you think the sloop went down? I have no notion of its location. There's so much more water in the lake now and so much tree debris." Laroux slapped at a buzzing mosquito near his ear.

"I think it's over there near that floating cedar tree." The captain stood on the roof of the cabin and held a hand over his eyes to shield them from the sunlight. "Unless, I'm mistaken, I think I see the top of the mast sticking above the water. It's there in the midst of branches."

Laroux joined him on the cabin roof. "I see it. Look to the left in the branches – isn't that the red signal flag that Captain Blanc left as a marker?"

"I think so. Let's take the dinghy over there. If *La Bonne Chance* is in the same spot, even if the water is much higher, it should still be easy to raise. The salvagers left their lines on the sloop and they can be retied and connected to the winches. It shouldn't take more than a day at most." He smiled at Laroux.

They dropped the dinghy overboard and, one after the other, they climbed into the boat. Laroux sat in the stern, while the captain rowed the dinghy toward the cedar. There was barely a ripple on the surface of the water and they quickly reached the floating tree.

Both men stood and looked down into the water. It took them a second or two to make out what they saw below. The captain was the first to speak.

"Dios mío! It's a body!"

Father Olivier sat in the patio playing checkers with his landlady's son, Gervaise. He had finished his dinner an hour earlier and now played what had become his three nightly games with the boy. Gervaise was twelve years old and the best checker player in his class at school. "He's clever enough," Olivier told his mother, "to make me struggle for every game I win."

The boy attended the cathedral school. Blanche Lefevre, his widowed mother, prepared the evening meal for the cathedral clergy in exchange for free schooling for her son. Madame Lefevre also was permitted to take home the left-over food for her family. It amused Olivier to think he ate the same food as the priests in the presbytère, their small house behind the cathedral. While they lived in cramped quarters, he had two spacious rooms upstairs in Madame Lefevre's house as well as the use of the enclosed patio that had been built behind the building.

"You can't win now, Father." Gervaise laughed triumphantly. "It's over! I have three kings to your one and your remaining draughts are doomed."

"You're right. Well, you have beaten me two games to one, tonight. But don't expect to be as successful tomorrow."

"Why not? I've got a strategy now that will put you at my mercy. You'll see."

"Is that so? I wouldn't be so certain if I were you, young man. What's our win and loss record?" Olivier knew he was well ahead of Gervaise, but did not know by how many wins. He watched the excited boy as he examined the piece of paper with their win and loss record on it.

"Of the thirty games we've played, you won nineteen to my eleven. But in the last ten, I have won six to your four. You see, my strategy is succeeding." Gervaise beamed with pleasure as he began putting the checkers away in the wooden box on the table. Olivier had given him the set of cherry and oak checkers and matching board.

"Don't boast, Gervaise," said his mother, a tall thin woman with a wrinkled face. She sat at the table sewing while they played checkers. "As I've told you many times before, 'Boast not thyself of tomorrow; for thou knowest not what a day may bring forth.'"

"Proverbs?" Olivier looked at Madame Lefevre.

"Yes, Father. My mother read Latin and seemed to know all the proverbs. She read her Bible every day of her life until her eyes failed. Then, she taught me to read it to her."

Madame Lefevre turned to her son. "It's time to do your chores, Gervaise."

"The boy made a face, but got up and left the room.

Olivier watched him go and smiled. "Gervaise is a very clever lad. You are to be praised for rearing him so well."

"I may have reared him well, Father, but his cleverness is a gift from God."

Olivier nodded. "That's true, but you taught him to read at an early age and now he has knowledge few other twelve-year-old boys possess. I'm glad Gervaise is being schooled at the cathedral. It would be a shame if his mind was not advanced."

"I have hopes he will become a learned man of God like you, Father." Madame Lefevre smiled at Olivier.

"Unfortunately, Madame, I'm not the best example of a man of God. You know why I've been sent away from the cathedral."

Madame Lefevre made a face. "Yes, it was all because of the sacristan. Mendoza is a pompous fool and everyone knows it."

"Now, Madame ..." Olivier held up his hand.

"It's true, Father. The man walks about as if he's a priest and thinks he knows all about Church doctrine. He's constantly prattling about our sinful nature. Most of us ignore him." She flipped her wrist as if sweeping him away like an annoying fly.

"The Sacristan isn't why I must be penitent, Madame Lefevre. I don't blame him at all. I brought it on myself." Olivier sighed. "Let's not speak anymore of it."

"Well, Father, I still say it's my wish that Gervaise will become a man of God like *you*! As it is, the boy adores you and speaks of you all day long. He can't wait for you to come home at night. With his father gone, God rest his soul, I'm so happy you are here for Gervaise."

Olivier blushed. "I am honored and hope I don't disappoint him. He has given me much joy and I look forward to more time with him. He is a delightful boy. During these last difficult weeks with so much suffering in the lowlands, he has helped me find respite from the sadness of my ministry. It is a terrible time for our parishioners, especially the Acadians."

"Has there been any improvement for those living in the lowlands?"

"Oui, merci à Dieu. (Yes, thanks to God). Those people who survived the hurricane now have food and shelter and are rebuilding their homes. We have accounted for almost all of those lost or missing and have performed the last funeral rites for a while – hopefully for a long while! As you can surely understand, it has been very dispiriting to see so many of our people dead and buried." He sighed. "Even if they go to God, it is still terribly sad."

"It is, Father. I'm glad for everyone that the worst is over. Dieu va-t-il (God will it)! What with the two fires and the hurricane, we have had more than our share of misery in New Orleans. Of course, we were spared the worst of the storm unlike those poor people living in the lowlands. It seems they always suffer more calamities than anyone else – the poor souls."

Olivier nodded. "So true! Not only did they lose their loved ones, they lost their homes, lands and fishing boats. As you know, most of the Acadians depend on fishing for the food they eat. Fortunately, many of their boats and pirogues now have been recovered and they are again plying the waters for fish."

"Father, have you heard anything about the sinking of *La Bonne Chance?* I have heard that Monsieur Dumont engaged a salvage company to bring up the vessel."

"Yes, an attempt was made to salvage the ship a month ago. As I understand it, the onset of the storm suspended the salvage and it has not yet been resumed. I know nothing else."

"What a terrible tragedy for the family. Mon Dieu! To lose two young sons at the same time. I see their grandmother,

Aveline Dumont, at the cathedral and the poor soul looks to have aged a decade since their unfortunate deaths." Madame Lefevre put her fingers over her mouth. "Oh, Father, forgive me. I forgot you know her well."

Olivier brushed her apology away with a wave of his hand. "It's true, Madame, the loss of her grandsons has been a terrible ordeal for Aveline. I worry for her. As you know, she has not been well these last few years."

"I've heard she suffers from a weak heart."

"Yes, and that's why I worry about her. She almost collapsed during the funerals. Her nephew held her while the graves were being filled."

"Thank God for Charles Laroux. He's a fine young man and a Godsend! I don't know what the Dumont family would do without him." She saw Olivier struggling to keep his eyes open. "You look exhausted, Father; you should go to bed."

Madame Lefevre felt guilty for keeping Olivier up after eight o'clock, his usual bedtime. By that time, he was asleep, exhausted from his long day in the lowlands. The hurricane had so devastated the countryside that he spent every moment from dawn to dusk helping the survivors. He brought food and clothing to them, helped rebuild their homes and still continued to carry out his duties as the pastor of Santa María. By the time he came home, his strength had been sapped and he did little more than eat his meal and play checkers with Gervaise before going to sleep.

"Yes, Madame, it's time for me to bid you good night."

At first light, two days later, Olivier walked quickly along Chartres Street toward the cathedral. It was the fifteenth of October and, after so many months of unremitting heat and humidity, New Orleans had its first frost of the fall. He smiled, enjoying the chill in the air. Olivier also looked forward to his visit to the cathedral. He had left the church the same day Father Antonio told him of his assignment at Santa María and had not returned since that time.

When Olivier reached the cathedral, instead of entering it, he turned into the Plaza de Armas across from the church. He wanted to see its façade before going inside. He knew the Catedral de San Luis (St. Louis Cathedral) was not a beautiful building; it was at best the most prominent church building in Louisiana. The austere structure could not compare architecturally to the other cathedrals in Spanish America or the magnificent churches of Europe. He had seen many of the Gothic and Renaissance cathedrals in France and Spain and knew the small simple structure had none of their grandeur.

St. Louis Cathedral, in fact, was an unadorned stone church and, with the exception of its tall central steeple, had no distinguishing features. Balanced symmetrically by two lower steeples built on both ends of the building, the central steeple was a slender spire with a cross on top. The steeple stood above all the other buildings in New Orleans and the cross could be seen from afar. Olivier recalled seeing the cross for the first time from the deck of the schooner that brought him up the river and into the port.

As he moved his eyes down from the high cross to the church, it occurred to him that the cathedral's simple appearance was appropriate for the house of God. It confirmed the simple life of the Savior. Olivier nodded, pleased with his insight. He took a last look at the high cross on the steeple and strode to the door. As Olivier walked over the paving stones, he thought of how the steeple and cross reached up to heaven and to God. Olivier smiled and entered the door.

Once inside, Olivier genuflected and crossed himself as he approached the main altar. He paused briefly to look at the painting of *The Sacrifice of the Lamb of God* on the ceiling and then walked to the rear of the church. Olivier saw Bishop Meléndez kneeling in prayer as he opened the door that led to the pastor's office behind the altar. He knocked lightly on the opened door.

"Come in, Olivier, it's good to see you." Father Antonio waved him inside and hugged him tightly. "Sit, sit," he said, smiling warmly. The parish pastor was a Capuchin monk from Spain. His Spanish name was Antonio de Sedella, but the popular pastor of the Cathedral was called Père Antoine (Father Antonio) in New Orleans.

"It's good to see you, too. How have you been? Olivier sat across from Antonio, who pushed his chair out from his desk.

"Oh, I'm fine, except for a bout or two of gout. It's one of the generous gifts of old age." The skeletal-thin pastor wore an old brown habit with a hemp girdle about his waist and wooden sandals. The habit was old and frayed with loose threads hung around his wrists and ankles. He slept in a simple plank hut built behind the cathedral. His only furniture was a plank bed, a small stool and a holy water font. Father Antonio continued to live an austere life for most of the years he served as pastor of St. Louis Cathedral and the surrounding parish.

"You are not that old. Still on this side of fifty?"

"Menteur! (Liar!), you know I'm older, but I won't tell you my age." Antonio chuckled. "You see, I suffer the sin of vanity. And how are you, Olivier? We all know how hard you have worked at Santa María. You must be exhausted."

"I am tired." Olivier sighed. "I'm not young anymore and I can't work from early in the morning until late at night. I just don't have the stamina."

"I know all too well of what you speak. That's another gift of aging."

Olivier nodded.

"You have done much for the poor people of the lowlands. Don't wave away the praise, Olivier. It's true and everyone in the cathedral knows it – even the bishop!"

"Is that true?" Olivier looked doubtful.

"It is indeed. He told me so himself."

"There is still much to be done in the lowlands. The people have suffered terribly." Tears appeared in Olivier's eyes. "It's always the poor who suffer. They're the ones who live on the lands that often flood; they're the ones who live in flimsy houses; they're the ones who lack the needed food and clothing and, of course, they're the ones who get the least help from the king's officials." Olivier's face flushed as he slapped his thigh in anger.

"It's true. Everything you say is true. Well, at least this time, the Church did its part to help the poor … and you led the way, Olivier."

"Father, please tell me why you have called me here. Surely, it is not only to talk about our ministry in the lowlands. Please speak plainly."

"Ah, Olivier, you do know me and my trouble speaking plainly." Antonio reached over and grasped Olivier's hand. "I've missed you here – we all have missed you, Olivier, the priests and parishioners alike."

The parish pastor had always liked Olivier and tried to ignore his drinking. He looked to the educated Dominican for doctrinal information as well as his advice on the daily operation of the parish. He also appreciated Olivier for his leadership and the theological guidance he offered the other priests. Antonio was a self-admitted *simple pastor* and he had used the Dominican as an unofficial assistant pastor. It was Olivier who articulated the instructions from the archbishop of Havana and explained his decisions to the cathedral clergy. Olivier also had been the cathedral's authority on Church philosophy and theology. Antonio sorely missed Olivier and he had spent many sleepless nights blaming himself for bringing the sacristan's complaint to the bishop.

Olivier blushed. "I've missed you, too, Father. But I must say the ministry at Santa María has been fulfilling for me and humbling in many ways. It saddens me so to see the misery of the lowlands people; they have suffered so many losses in the storm. So many of their children have perished, never mind mothers and fathers and the elderly. It breaks my heart." Olivier's voice quavered. "Grâce à Dieu! (Thank God) At least now it's a little better for the poor people."

Antonio nodded. "I'm glad to hear that." He paused to think of how best to express his request to the Dominican. "Olivier, I have asked you here to, ah, make a request of you."

"Yes, Father." Olivier frowned, wondering what the parish pastor would ask of him.

"As you know, the deaths of the Jean Bertin's sons have not been explained; nor has the sinking of *La Bonne Chance* been clarified. I'm sure you also know the sloop was unfortunately destroyed by the storm before a thorough investigation could be conducted."

"That's what I've heard."

"Well, Jean Bertin and Aveline Dumont have come to see me in search of, ah, advice as to what should be done … to find out why the ship sank and the boys drowned. Jean Bertin is certain the vessel was perfectly seaworthy and cannot understand how it could have sunk."

"Didn't Captain Ordoñez explain what happened?"

"No. Since so much of the ship was lost in the storm, he could offer no explanation."

"I see." Puzzled, Olivier frowned again. "Why then did they come to you?"

"For advice. The family is terribly distraught as you know and they asked me if I could suggest someone who could look into the sinking and come up with an explanation and, ah, I …"

Olivier sighed. "Mentioned me."

Father Antonio's face reddened. "Ah, yes, I immediately thought of you and, without thinking, I mentioned your name. No sooner had I spoken your name when Madame

Dumont said you were the one she hoped I would suggest. In fact, she said you were the only one with mind enough to find the explanation. As you know, she is *quite* outspoken."

Olivier nodded. "Aveline is indeed. Well, I must say it's an intriguing assignment. But, not only am I ignorant of how to proceed in such an investigation, I can't possibly spare the time. You know how busy I am at Santa María."

"I know Olivier. You need help and financial assistance."

"I do, especially since Santa María needs repairs which I confess I have neglected since the storm. Even though the church withstood the worst of the winds, there was considerable damage and the building is in dire need of carpentry and repairs of all kinds. The church actually needs a total renovation. You know our situation. Father Etienne sent you a list of everything the church needed before he retired. So, now that our people are finally recovering from their terrible losses, I must attend to the church repairs."

Olivier stopped speaking and studied Antonio's face. The parish priest frowned, looking appropriately concerned, but Olivier suspected something other than Santa María's physical state was on his mind. He also suspected whatever was on his mind involved him in some way.

Antonio nodded. "That's certainly understandable, Olivier, your attention to the people of the lowlands was your first priority. But, now, as you say, the people there are finally recovering and the church building must be your next concern. It's in a deplorable state, not only because of the storm, but because of our neglect. That's why I told Jean Bertin you were probably too busy at Santa María to be available at this time."

"I'm glad you explained why."

Antonio held up his hand. "But then it occurred to me that young Father Francis – I'm sure you remember him; he's the Irish lad who arrived from Spain last summer." Antonio saw Olivier nod his head. "Anyway, Francis needs experience in parish work – especially with the poor and, with a bit of guidance, he would make a fine assistant pastor at Santa María. The lad also could relieve you of enough of the hard work at Santa María to permit you to take on this assignment. I have a memory of you telling me he was quite clever and a hard worker."

"Francis is a clever lad. But, as you say, he has little, if any, parish experience so how could he be of much help as an assistant pastor? What's more important is that he knows little, if anything, about the Acadians or the lowlands? I doubt he has ever gone ten steps beyond the city walls, if he has even ventured outside the cathedral."

"At this time, I'm thinking less of the parish's spiritual mission in the lowlands and more about of the hard work needed to improve Santa María's physical state. Like you, Olivier, I too am anxious to see Santa María serve the Acadians as a fully functional church. Young Francis certainly looks robust enough to do some of the hard work and he'll quickly become acquainted with the Acadians while there working with them. Forgive me for speaking so candidly, Olivier, but you look exhausted and obviously could use the help of another man – a much *younger* man whose strength and stamina could relieve you of much of the hard work needed at Santa María."

"I see. So he would relieve me of the hard work that has at last flattened my stomach."

Antonio laughed. "Exactly, Olivier. I want to see if you will become one of those fat monks, who now seem to be everywhere you go in the Spanish colonies."

Olivier cocked his head to the side as he looked at Antonio. "So, Father, I take it you want me to carry out this very unusual assignment to please the Dumont family – one of the cathedral's *most generous* benefactors."

"Yes, that's quite correct." Antonio smiled. "A parish priest is not only the pastor of his flock, he must also be constantly aware of the needs of his …"

"Fattest sheep!" Olivier grinned mischievously.

"Yes, indeed." Antonio returned the smile. "However, do keep in mind that some of that fat can be applied to the costs of renovating a deserving little church in the lowlands."

Ah, Father, I think this poor colonial parish may be but a stepping stone to Rome. Have you thought of a future in the Vatican?"

"You know better, Olivier. I have no such ambitions. I'm just a poor church mouse who knows where the cheese comes from here in New Orleans and how to acquire some of it for the Church's numerous needs."

"What about the bishop? What will he think of this assignment – one that is unlikely to help me with my need for humility?"

"The bishop need not concern you, Olivier. *I am the pastor of the parish and I alone will decide the duties and function of the clergy in this parish."* A muscle twitched in Antonio's jaw as he spoke to Olivier.

Olivier stared at Antonio, surprised at his vehemence. He had never heard him speak so severely. He wondered if the pastor had finally stood up to the bishop and ended his meddling in the parish. One of the Capuchin monks, who often helped Olivier in the lowlands, told him the parish pastor and the bishop had exchanged angry words and now only spoke to each other out of necessity with polite formality. The Capuchin said the two men often passed by each other in the cathedral "without even a look, never mind an acknowledgement or token greeting."

"Yes, Father, with the help of young Francis, I'll take on the assignment. I'll look into the death of the two boys and avec l'aide de Dieu (with God's help) find out what happened to them. The Dumont family deserves to know why they died. Their wealth is irrelevant. I assume I have your permission to conduct this investigation as I see appropriate."

"Yes. The authorities seem to have finished their inquiry,

leaving you free to conduct the investigation as you deem necessary."

"What about the body of the girl who was found entangled in the ship's mast lines?"

"The magistrate's men are still trying to identify her. No one seems to know her or has reported her missing. So, that leaves you free to investigate the ship's sinking."

"Good." Olivier nodded. "I assume it will be appropriate to cite your authority should anyone inquire about my efforts in this assignment."

"Yes, Olivier. I only ask for your *discretion* as you go about the investigation. After all, I don't want this assignment to interfere with your struggle with the sin of pride." Antonio's smile turned into laughter. The two priests laughed until they had tears in their eyes.

They were still snickering when the bishop walked by on the way to his own office. He frowned in disapproval and held a finger up to his lips to quiet them. They looked at each other and continued to laugh as the bishop passed the doorway.

"The cathedral is not a place for merriment," Meléndez thought as he entered his office.

CHAPTER THREE

NEW ORLEANS: OCTOBER 26 – NOVEMBER 4, 1799

He waited until his eyes adjusted to the darkness and then entered the kitchen on tiptoes. Moonlight coming through the window gave him enough light to avoid walking into the table or chairs and he could clearly see the closed door to the pantry. He walked step by step trying not to make any noise. At the table, he stopped abruptly when a floorboard squeaked. Pausing for a few seconds to make sure the sound was not heard, he continued on tiptoes to the pantry.

The family's dog came into the kitchen as he reached the pantry door. The dog wagged his tail and limped over to be petted. Still waging his tail, he rubbed his head against the man's leg. The man leaned over and scratched the dog's head. When he stopped a few seconds later, the old dog shambled away into the dining room.

The man spent only a moment in the pantry and then silently left the way he had come. This time he stepped over the squeaking board. In the doorway to the dining room, he looked all around before leaving. Nothing moved in the room not even the dog, now sleeping soundly on a wide pillow that served as his bed. He was gone as the downstairs clock struck midnight.

Francis left the cathedral before matins. The red-headed priest was awake before dawn and on his way to Santa María when the first sunlight appeared on the eastern horizon. A damp mist lingered over the streets as he strode hurriedly toward the San Carlos gates. He carried his few possessions in a haversack over his shoulder.

Francis hurried, fearful that Father Olivier might leave the church before he arrived. The parish priest told him the Dominican spent most of his day in the lowlands and often would leave Santa María immediately after morning Mass. Francis was excited to meet Olivier and begin his first ministry as assistant pastor of Santa María Church. Though he tried to resist it, he felt a flush of pride that he had been made an assistant pastor after only six months in the parish.

He had been the first of the new Capuchins to be given a ministry in a parish church. The other five Capuchins who had come with him from Spain remained at the cathedral taking turns giving Mass and hearing confessions. The rest of their time was spent doing menial chores and running errands for the pastor as well as the other priests. None of them had yet been permitted to give a sermon on a weekday morning, never mind on Sunday.

Francis had never spoken to Father Olivier alone, though he had been among a group of novices when the Dominican lectured them on church history and Christian theology. Listening in rapt fascination at the time, Francis had been in awe of the man and his vast knowledge. But the blunt-spoken priest also frightened him. Francis never dared to offer an opinion or even ask Olivier a question at one of his lectures. He had seen what happened to those foolish enough to articulate a rhetorical question or try to impress him. They would slink away with flushed faces or even tears after a sharp-tongued rebuke from the Dominican. Those few who dared challenge him suffered a worse fate. They would be questioned in the Socratic method and left speechless and ridiculed by the time Olivier had finished with them.

A few of the younger Capuchins were pleased when the bishop reassigned Olivier to Santa María. "He got his deserved comeuppance," said one young priest who had made the mistake of trying to flatter the Dominican. Another agreed, "What with pompous priests like Olivier, it's no wonder the order was all but destroyed during the French Revolution."

The other Capuchins had mixed impressions of Olivier, respecting him for his knowledge and criticizing him for his caustic comments. Those who supported him said the smug sacristan deserved the Dominican's tongue lashing for his pretense to knowledge he did not have. Old Father Luke, who rarely spoke at cathedral meetings, praised Olivier at a clerical assembly in front of the bishop. "We've lost the most intelligent and well-informed priest I've seen in my forty years in this parish all because of the pretentious sacristan. Everyone knows it was about time someone put the sacristan in his place for posing as a priest." No one at the meeting said anything about Olivier's drinking.

Whether for or against him, the clergy missed Olivier. They missed his moving lectures and insights into Christian thinking and theology. "Olivier was a veritable fountain of facts and we have no one to replace him," Father Bernard told them at the meeting. Francis had been one of those who nodded in agreement and he had wondered if he would ever see him again. Now, to his surprise, he was on his way to work with Olivier. Francis increased his pace, almost running, in anticipation of discussing his responsibilities with him before Mass. Arriving moments later out of breath, Francis found the church completely empty. Except for two lighted candles on the altar, he saw no sign that anyone had been in Santa María that morning.

An old Acadian woman entered the church as Francis crossed himself before the altar. He noticed her when he turned around and she nodded to him. Francis was about to ask her where he could find Father Olivier when she put her hands to her ears and shook her head. She then held a finger up to her lips and pointed to his mouth.

"Ah, you can read lips." Francis spoke to her in French, moving his lips slowly so she could understand him. "Do you know when Father Olivier will arrive?"

She smiled, showing him the few teeth in her mouth, and held her gnarled fingers up for him see. The old woman shook her fingers to emphasize what she wanted him to see.

Baffled by her gesture, a frown appeared on his freckled face. He stared at the deaf woman.

She shook her hand and again held it up her fingers in front of him.

Then Francis saw what she wanted him to see. The forefinger and thumb of the hand she held up was separated by a tiny gap. "Ah, you're telling me he's coming soon."

She nodded and mimicked someone paddling a canoe.

"So, he's coming by canoe."

The woman nodded and gestured for him to go outside. Finished with him, she turned away to get a broom from the corner. As Francis left, he saw her begin to sweep the dirt floor.

Olivier arrived a few minutes later with Gervaise walking beside him. Olivier greeted Francis in front of the church, welcomed him to Santa María and introduced the boy to him.

"We're going to look at the wreckage of *La Bonne Chance*. You are welcome to join us, or do you want to stay here?"

Olivier gestured to the church.

"Won't there be parishioners here during the day?" Francis looked puzzled.

"Not usually. Most Acadians come in the evenings. They're out fishing during the day, beginning before daylight. It's not like the cathedral where people come at all times of day."

"What about the women? I assume they're not out fishing."

"No, they're at home mending the fishing nets and maintaining their vegetable gardens. They're also tending to the children, of course."

Francis looked back at the church. The door was open and he could see the old woman still sweeping the floor. He returned his eyes to Olivier. "I'll join you, Father."

"Good. Leave your haversack in the church. Let's be on our way then before it rains this afternoon. I'm not sure how long the good weather will last."

Francis looked up at the morning sky, now sunny and cloudless. The morning mist had already begun to disappear beneath the sun. Not understanding, he frowned.

Olivier nodded. "Yes, even though it's a sunny day. A fisherman's mother I know said there would be thunderstorms this afternoon and she's yet to be wrong."

Olivier waited while Francis put his haversack inside the church and then led the way to the bayou. Francis and the boy walked behind him. The tall priest strode ahead with his beaked nose pointed forward and his long arms swinging in unison at his sides.

Francis smiled as he watched Olivier walk. "It's as they say in town," he thought, "Father Olivier looks like an eagle taking flight from the ground."

The bayou was twenty-five yards away and, following the fast moving priest, they reached it quickly. In the water, a cypress pirogue was tied to a cedar on the bank. Gervaise held the line as Olivier and Francis got into the pirogue. Olivier motioned Francis to the middle of the boat as he went to the stern. Gervaise untied the line, threw it to Francis and jumped into the bow.

Moments later, they were gliding through the wooded marsh. They soon lost the sun as the boat moved beneath a canopy of overhanging trees and vines. At first, it was easy paddling since the pirogue followed the same course as the current, but later they faced the lake's rushing outflow and had to dip their paddles deeper and faster into the water. Olivier steered, while his two companions paddled. They passed a number of big alligators and turtles on the banks and in the water, but none of them appeared to look in their direction. Two water snakes swimming alongside the pirogue seemed similarly indifferent to them as they passed paddling hard.

It took them a little over an hour and a half to reach the lake where the sloop had sunk. Olivier waited until they had entered the lake before telling Francis about his assignment. They were both too busy to talk. Francis concentrated on paddling, while Olivier had to be constantly alert as he steered the long canoe through the circuitous channel cluttered with downed trees and broken branches. Once in the open lake, where the pirogue was left to drift freely on the slow-moving current, Olivier told Francis about the unexplained sinking of *La Bonne Chance* and his assignment to discover what happened to the ship and why the Dumont brothers had drowned.

"Do you think the sloop is still intact?" Francis was still panting from all his effort. He gestured wearily to the fallen trees and branches that littered the shores as well as the water.

"I don't know, let's hope so. I don't know what I can do if it's broken up under water."

There was still a thin layer of fog over the water when they arrived. They let the pirogue continue to drift and waited for the sun to rise above the trees and burn off the mist. It was gone a few minutes later as sunlight brightened the sky and Olivier pointed to a mass of branches and trees they could see in the water near the eastern shore.

"There's a marker on one of the pine trees in the water. I spoke to the coastguard captain yesterday and he told me to look for a red flag which will show us where the ship went down."

"I see it." Gervaise pointed to a huge pine tree. It had been uprooted and lay on the shore and in the water. The tree was about fifty feet in height and more than half of it was in the lake.

"I can't see it yet, but I trust your young eyes, Gervaise." Olivier exchanged a smile with Francis, who could not see the red flag either.

They reached the tree with the marker and Gervaise tied the bowline to a floating branch. Olivier tied the stern line and nodded to the boy. Gervaise leaned over the gunwale and dunked his head down into the water. Opening his eyes and looking down he could see one side of the sunken ship, but nothing more.

"It's there, at least what I can see of it." Gervaise dried his face and hair with one of the three towels they brought with them. "You're right it's cold, but not too cold …"

Olivier shook his head. "No, it's too cold. We'll wait, Gervaise. I'll not have you catch your death of cold. Let's drink our tea and wait until the sun warms the water."

Gervaise went into the lake two hours later. He dove down to the wreck wearing his long winter underwear. The boy resurfaced three minutes later. Olivier timed his dive below with his pocket watch. He anxiously rubbed his hands together until the boy's head appeared in the water. Olivier instantly pulled Gervaise out of the lake and began toweling him off, rubbing the thick towel over his head and upper body. Francis, waiting with a woolen blanket, then wrapped it around the boy. Gervaise tried to speak, but he could do little more than stammer through his chattering teeth. Olivier handed the boy a warm cup of tea he had kept in the sun and told him to drink every drop.

"You are not going down again, Gervaise." Olivier saw him shiver beneath the blanket. "No, and don't make a face. It's too cold this time of year. I regret letting you dive down the first time. Now, take off your wet underwear and put on the dry clothes we brought with us. I also want you to cover yourself with the blanket."

The priests looked away while Gervaise changed his underwear. Then, Francis put a dry towel over the boy's hair and rubbed it vigorously. He saw him make a face.

"Father Olivier is right, the water is too cold today."

Gervaise looked at Olivier with pleading eyes. "It'll be warmer later on. We only have to wait a while, Father."

Olivier shook his head. "We're finished for today. Now, get dressed."

"Let me tell you what …"

"Get dressed and then you can tell us what you saw."

Gervaise dressed hurriedly while the two priests resumed their seats. Olivier would not let him speak until he had dried his feet and put on his stockings. Impatient to tell them what he saw, Gervaise looked up after he stepped into his shoes and fastened them.

"There's only one piece of the ship's hull on the bottom. I think it's the part of one side and the deck where the mast sticks up. I think I saw the top of the cabin, but I'm not sure; it was some distance away."

"Good boy, anything else?"

Gervaise shook his head. "No, Father, nothing."

"Well, let's be on our way then. Without finding the whole ship, there's nothing else we can do. Unfortunately, it probably means the Dumont family will never know what happened to their sons or why the sloop sank."

"That's sad." Francis shook his head.

"It is." Olivier exhaled his breath loudly. "Let's start back."

Olivier made sure all the lines had been untied and he gestured for Francis and Gervais to begin paddling. They paddled the pirogue away from the floating trees and circled around toward the outlet from the lake. As they neared the opening, Olivier steered the canoe along the shore to avoid a partially sunken tree he had seen when they entered the lake. They stopped paddling as the pirogue caught the outlet current and moved quickly. Gervaise stood in the bow looking out for submerged branches or limbs that might breach the thin bark hull.

The boy suddenly held up his hand. "Stop!" he shouted turning to the others. "There's a wrecked ship over there." He pointed his finger toward the wooded shore they were passing on the starboard side of the pirogue. "See it there – it's lying behind those trees."

Olivier immediately shifted the paddle he used as a rudder and tried to point the pirogue toward the shore. Gervaise and Francis paddled as hard they could, but the rushing current kept the boat from turning. The water roiled all around them as they struggled with all their strength. Seeing their exertion, Olivier joined them paddling furiously. It took time, but by digging their paddles deep into the water, they finally managed to point the bow toward the shore. Their arms aching, the three of them slowly moved the seemingly reluctant boat out of current and into the shallows. Everyone then jumped into the water and pushed the pirogue onto land. After one last push, they splashed through waist-deep water to the shore. Exhausted and panting, Olivier and Francis sat on the trunk of a fallen tree. Gervaise collapsed on the sand and lay on his back.

The men had rested only a few minutes, when Gervaise stood up and led them through a copse of small cedars to an open area full of tree debris. There they saw what remained of a ship lying on its side against one of the oak trees that survived the storm. It was little more than the three-sided shell of a ship. Most of the interior, the entire starboard side of the hull, the roof of the cabin and decking were missing as well as the masts and all the rigging. The bow and stern had both been flattened, but were still discernible. On the port side, the majority of planks were gone and most of those still there were smashed and splintered. Only the live-oak keel looked totally intact, though dented in a number of places from bow to stern. The black painted word *Chance* appeared on a broken board and told them they had found the sloop.

Francis shook his head. "What a wreck! The ship looks like it was struck by a giant's fist and broken apart. There are pieces all over the place."

Olivier nodded. "Well, at least we have something to examine."

"Yes, but not much." Francis bent over and squeezed water from the hem of his habit.

"No, there's not much left, but it's all we have. So, let's go over the entire ship and see if we can find anything that suggests why it went down. We have three sets of eyes to examine it, so we should be able to find something telling if it's there."

They spent all morning and much of the afternoon going over the wreckage of *La Bonne Chance*. They looked at every part of the sloop. Olivier began at the bow and Francis the stern and, passing each other, they met on the other side where the port side wall had been. Gervaise examined the interior which was now open to the light. They finally finished their inspection at three o'clock as the sky darkened and a bank of black clouds appeared overhead. Moments later, the first shafts of lightning lit up the lowlands and they heard thunder in the distance. They were in the pirogue paddling away from the lake when rain began to fall.

"You do have a splendid view of the river from your porch, María Adela. It's especially scenic this time of year with all the trees in color and the river running fast and looking blue for a change." Olivier turned from the railing as María Adela handed him a cup of tea. "Thank you."

"It is a beautiful view. Now that I have the porch, I don't know how I could have lived in New Orleans so long without it. The breeze alone makes this house worth every peseta I paid for it, especially in the intolerably hot summers."

"Wasn't it as hot in St. Augustine?" Olivier sat in a cane chair across from María Adela.

"It was, but, at the time, I was a child and never noticed."

Olivier nodded. "Ah, yes, the blessing of youth's indifference to weather."

"Well, Father, how do you like Santa María?"

"It's a well-built little church – that's why it survived the storm, though, of course, there was a lot of damage inside as well as outside. It will take a good while to repair everything, but I have been promised financial assistance by the parish pastor. The parishioners are courageous and hard-working people. With their crops ruined, they now depend on hunting and fishing for food." He sighed. "They've suffered so much."

"It has been awful for them and I know you've worked hard to help them recover. I've heard you now have an assistant pastor to serve them as well – a young Capuchin."

"Yes, an Irish youth named Francis. He's a clever and diligent lad. Father Antonio has assigned him to Santa María so I'll have the time to look into the sinking of *La Bonne Chance*. I suppose you have already heard about it." Olivier sipped his tea.

"Yes, Aveline told me. Have you found anything yet?"

"I'm not sure. I'll discuss what I found with Jean Bertin in the morning."

"Are you at liberty to tell me what you have found?"

Olivier paused before speaking. "I think it best for me to talk to Jean Bertin first."

María Adela smiled. "I understand, it's a matter of confidentiality."

"Yes and, as I've said, I'm not sure I found anything of importance. I don't want to say or mention something that turns out to be easily explained."

"Did you know that everyone is sick at the Dumont house – except Aveline and the two girls? They escaped the illness, Thank God! "

Olivier frowned. "No, I didn't know. What kind of sickness?"

"Some kind of food poisoning. All of the servants are sick as well. Lucille, their oldest servant, is gravely ill – she has convulsions, a high fever and looks to be frothing at the mouth."

"Mon Dieu! That's terrible! So everyone is sick?"

"Yes, even Charles Laroux who ate dinner with the family two nights ago. That's when it happened. Alain, who is still here – he sails to France next week, is also very sick. Poor lad has been trembling and vomiting for hours."

"How did Aveline and the little girls escape the sickness?"

"Gracias a Dios, the girls were with Aveline that night. She had a party for them, hoping to bring them some joy and take them away from the sad house after the funerals. Their school friends were there as well as Jean Bertin's man, Tristan Surette, dressed as a bear. "

"Do they know what brought on the sickness?

"They think the rice everyone ate that night had become moldy and sickened them all. They had ragout de poisson (fish stew) for dinner and it was served over rice."

"Why do they blame the rice for the illness and not the fish? That's what usually makes people sick." Olivier finished his tea and María Adela refilled his cup.

"One of the servants ate the stew without the rice and never got sick. Also, what was left of the stew was given to their old dog, Romeo, and he hasn't shown any ill effects from it. The dog never is given rice, because it makes him give off a bad odor." María Adela smiled.

"You mean a dog fart, don't you?" Olivier grinned.

"Yes, Romeo is never given beans either."

"Anyone look at the rice? I assume it's been thrown out."

"Yes, Aveline threw it out. She's there now nursing everyone in the house. She said it's like a hospital there. Aveline said the rice smelled musty so she immediately threw it out. They use their old outhouse to dispose of such things."

"Did she say anything else about the rice? How it looked?"

"No, but you can ask her yourself, Father. She will be here any minute. Her driver was here earlier and told me Aveline would be visiting at three o'clock and that's five minutes from now. Would you like some fresh tea? It's being brewed now for Aveline."

Olivier nodded.

María Adela went into her upstairs sitting room and pulled on a cord in the doorway to the stairway. Olivier heard a bell ring downstairs and, a moment later, he heard her talking to someone at the bottom of the stairs. He recognized the voice of Renée Latour, the Acadian woman who had worked for María Adela all the years she had lived in New Orleans.

By the time María Adela had returned to the porch, she and Olivier heard voices below and soon Aveline Dumont appeared in the doorway. A little out of breath from hurrying up the stairs, she embraced María Adela and shook hands with Olivier, squeezing his hand.

"It's good to see you, Father." Aveline had tears in her eyes as she sat in a chair beside Olivier. Aware that she still held his hand, she nodded her thanks and released it.

"It's good to see you, too, Aveline. María Adela tells me, you and your family have had an awful time. I hope everyone is doing better now."

"Yes, except for Lucille. I fear for her life. Father Antonio has been to see her several times and one of the Capuchin monks is with her now." Aveline held a handkerchief to her eyes. "Mon Dieu! Haven't we suffered enough? First, the loss of our boys and now this – sickness." She sighed and dabbed her eyes with her handkerchief.

Renée arrived carrying a silver tray and matching tea pot and silverware. The tray also held cups and saucers, napkins and a half dozen assorted chocolate and fruit pastries. Smiling, Renée walked by Olivier and made sure he saw the chocolate pastries she knew he liked.

"Thank you, Renée, please join us," said María Adela.

Renée bowed to everyone "Thank ya, Madame, but I mus be leevin' now. My motha is havin her seventieth birthday ths afernoon." She bowed again and left the porch.

Aveline watched Renée leave. "You're fortunate to have such a devoted servant, María Adela. She's also a very good baker. Don't you agree, Father?"

"How could I disagree?" Olivier smiled and put down the chocolate pastry he had half eaten. "She knows I have a sweet tooth, especially for chocolate."

"So I see. Jean Bertin won't be able to meet with you tomorrow. He's still too sick and will let you know when he's up and about. I expect it will be later in the week."

Olivier nodded. "I certainly understand. Please tell him I wish him a quick recovery. Tell me, Aveline, what makes you think it was the rice that made everyone sick?"

"It was the smell and look of it. I didn't know for quite a while. When I brought the girls home the following morning, I spent most of the day tending to the sick. Everyone was so sick! I went from room to room trying to care for them. The doctor was already there when I arrived and he told me what to do."

Olivier nodded. "Who was the doctor?"

"Doctor Messier. I sent the girls to my house, where they will remain until Paulette feels better. Anyway, when I discovered that Germaine, the upstairs maid and Claude, the coachman, ate only the fish, I suspected the rice."

"Why didn't they eat the rice?"

"It was all eaten at dinner. Then, when Claude told me that old Candide, who never gets it in his food, was fine I thought the rice was spoiled. It's happened in the past, but usually in the summer, especially when it's humid."

"How is the rice stored?"

"It's kept in the pantry in a covered container that holds five pounds. The family uses it up so quickly that the container is seldom full. It was about half full when I looked at the rice."

Aveline made a face remembering its appearance.

"What did it look like?" Olivier finished the pastry and sipped his tea.

"I have never seen rice look so … *disgusting.* It had an oily greenish-yellow look and the stench was absolutely revolting." Aveline twitched her nose. "I can still smell it – ugh, a musty, mousey odor. It made me retch and it was all I could do to keep from vomiting."

"Didn't the cook notice the color or smell when she prepared it?"

"I asked Evette that very question. Poor thing is pale as a ghost and sick in bed at home. Evette said the rice looked perfectly fine when she scooped it into the cooking pot. She did say the rice had a stronger odor than usual, but she thought the addition of a few too many Acadian spices made it seem that way."

"Was the addition of Acadian spices usual when she prepares rice?"

"Jean Bertin likes the rice spicy and Evette tries to please him. He's been that way since he was a boy. My husband was the same; he always added chili sauce to my cooking."

Olivier frowned and looked down at the river. A three-mast schooner was sailing south toward the Gulf of Mexico.

"What are you thinking, Father?" María Adela saw the pensive look on Olivier's face.

"I am wondering if insects got into the rice in the fields during or after the storm. If so, they might have deposited something poisonous in the rice. It's also possible that a poisonous plant's flowers or leaves could have been mixed into the rice during the storm."

Aveline nodded. "Other families are probably suffering the same sickness as ours."

"That's true." Olivier looked at Aveline. "I'll ask Dr. Messier in the morning."

Olivier talked to Dr. Messier before his office hours the following morning. It was a clear day without a cloud in the sky. Rain had fallen most of the night and everything green glistened in the first light.

Olivier left Santa María after morning prayers and, walking leisurely, he arrived at the doctor's house at seven thirty. The physician lived on Calle D'Orleans only a block away from the Dumont mansion. Olivier entered the front gate and saw Dr. Messier at the side of his house pruning his grape vines. The bald, plump man was on his knees trimming dead leaves from the lower vines. He had apparently already finished pruning the upper vines tied to a lattice arbor.

The physician smiled when he saw Olivier and rose to shake his hand. "I haven't seen you for a while, Father. How do you like Santa María?"

"I'm quite content there."

"Good. Of course, I'm not at all surprised. I'd think any ministry away from that medieval bishop would be better."

"How are they doing?" Olivier pointed to the vines that already had been pruned.

"I see, no comment about *Torquemada* (the infamous Grand Inquisitor of Spain, 1481- 1498), eh?" Messier's eyes twinkled as he smiled at the priest. "I understand, Father, and will say no more about the *esteemed* bishop. The vines aren't doing well and it's their fourth year. The humidity and insects in New Orleans seem to stymie all my attempts to produce a good crop of grapes. I'm beginning to think I'll never get any wine from them." He grimaced. "It annoys me since I paid dearly to have the seedlings brought over from Burgundy."

"I've not heard of anyone who has had a good crop of grapes here."

"No, it's this hot humid climate – so unlike the wine country of France. Well, Father, I will not bore you further with my prattling about grape vines. I'm sure you didn't come here to hear me complain." The physician cocked his head to the side as he looked at Olivier.

"I've come to speak to you about the sickness that struck the Dumont family."

"Ah, yes, the food poisoning. It almost killed them all and likely will kill the elderly woman in the next day or so."

"You mean Lucille?"

"Yes, I saw her last night and, sad to say, I haven't much hope for her." He frowned. "She will need all our prayers, I fear."

"The poor soul. We have prayed for her at Santa María as well as the cathedral."

"Good. Mon Dieu, I've never seen anything like it in all my years here as a doctor. An entire family struck down by contaminated rice!"

"You are certain it was the rice."

"Oh yes, I saw and smelled it – some was left overnight in one of the dinner dishes. I'm almost certain it was contaminated by Spotted Water Hemlock. The plant's roots are fleshy and produce a greenish-yellow oil that's very poisonous. The substance smells musty or mousey. It's quite unforgettable." He made a sour face. "You only have to cut open the base of the plant and that foul odor will quickly reach your nostrils."

"Isn't Spotted Water Hemlock a marsh plant?" Olivier had heard the plant occasionally poisoned animals that grazed along stream banks or in swamps.

"Yes, but it also grows in roadside ditches and pastures. It has purple mottled or striped stems and small white flowers that grow in clusters. You can't miss it in the lowlands."

"I've seen the plant in the lowlands – it's all over there and the Acadians warned me to stay away from it. Is it possible the flowers or portions of the plant contaminated the rice crop during the storm?"

Doctor Messier shook his head up and down. "It's quite possible and I have advised the governor's officials to inspect all the stored rice in the city. Any of it harvested since the storm could be contaminated. I certainly don't want to see this sickness become a plague."

"Have you heard of any other similar poisonings?"

"None so far, remerciez un Dieu (thank God), but I'm worried there will be many more to come. The other physicians in the city are likewise concerned. I, of course, immediately sent word of the poisoning to all of them. If I had the authority, I would order all the rice purveyors to carefully examine their stores for signs of the plant. I would also urge every family in New Orleans to do the same before eating any rice."

"I'll see to it that such a warning is given at every church service for the next week. I'll go directly to the cathedral after our talk and tell Father Antonio. I'll also warn my parishioners at Santa María. The storm might have dispersed the Hemlock all over the lowlands."

"Good idea, Father. We must take every precaution possible. We certainly don't want the sickness and death that such a plague would bring to New Orleans."

"I have one more question, Doctor. Since the color and odor of the water hemlock are so distinctive, how was it possible for the Dumont's cook to miss seeing or smelling it? Apparently Evette scooped it out of the container and only noticed what she called a *strong odor*, which she attributed to the spices added to the rice."

Messier rubbed his chin. "I can think of three possible explanations. Evette simply missed seeing the greenish-yellow color of the hemlock because it was not on top of the rice. The oil might have soaked into the rice. Or if on the top layer, she might have mistaken the color for the spices added to the rice; basil and dried mustard are common spices added to rice and would account for both the green and yellow coloring. The spices would also diminish the odor of the poison. Of course, she may well have seen and smelled the hemlock at the time and ignored it. If that indeed happened I could easily understand her unwillingness to admit it."

Olivier nodded. "Those are all plausible explanations. Thank you Dr. Messier. Let's hope there are no more poisonings in New Orleans." He made the sign of the cross.

Olivier walked away thinking about the tragic misfortunes of the Dumont family. "Two sons drowned and most of the family poisoned – all in such a short time." He stopped to count the days. "It's not been less than three months since *La Bonne Chance* sank and now a strange poisoning that almost took the lives of the entire household. It seems much too coincidental." A frown creased his forehead as he continued walking toward the cathedral.

Olivier spent a half hour with Father Antonio. He gave him a brief account of the trip to the lake, the discovery of the sloop's wreckage and his unsettling conversation with Dr. Messier. The parish pastor was shocked to hear about the poisoned rice and ended their meeting to notify the cathedral priests of the need to warn the parishioners of the peril. Olivier left as Father Antonio beckoned one of the Capuchin novices to his office.

"We must notify every church in Louisiana of the possibility of poisoned rice," Olivier heard him say as he walked away.

The bishop stood in the doorway of his office as Olivier left Antonio's office. He nodded and greeted him politely. "Good morning, Most Reverend Bishop." The bishop nodded and said nothing until Olivier came abreast of him.

"What brings you here to the cathedral, Father Olivier? Isn't morning Mass held at Santa María these days?"

"I've come to see the pastor. The parish faces a possible peril." Olivier told the bishop about his conversation with Dr. Messier.

"I see. We must indeed warn the community. A plague must be avoided at all cost."

"That was Dr. Messier's concern. He has notified the king's officials to that end."

Bishop Meléndez nodded and then looked inquiringly at Olivier. "How is it, Father, that you had such a conversation with Dr. Messier? It seems you are here and about town these days. I have seen you in the cathedral on more than one occasion. I would think you have more than enough to do at Santa María?"

"I now have the able assistance of Father Francis." Olivier wondered if the parish pastor had told the bishop of his investigation into the sinking of *La Bonne Chance.*

`The bishop's eyebrows rose. "When was Father Francis assigned to Santa María?"

"He's been there almost a fortnight; I assumed you knew about his assignment as well as mine – my new assignment for the Dumont family." Olivier had to keep himself from smiling. It was obvious the bishop had not known about either and, though regretting it later, he enjoyed seeing the Spaniard caught unawares and uncomfortable. Olivier saw the bishop clinch his teeth and narrow his eyes.

"What assignment do you have other than serving as pastor of Santa María?" The bishop glared at Olivier, his face now flushed in anger.

"Father Antonio has asked me to look into the unfortunate deaths of Monsieur Dumont's sons. He came to the pastor in search of someone to conduct an investigation and Father Antonio suggested I might be of assistance. The pastor thought it important to assist Monsieur Dumont in consideration of the generous contributions he and his family have made to the Church."

"I see." The bishop's face remained flushed.

"Father Francis was assigned to Santa María to serve as assistant pastor and help me in the work of the church. Father Antonio decided it would be a good opportunity for the young priest to get day-to-day church experience, while I spent some of my time on the investigation."

"What about the needs of the suffering parishioners there after the storm? I would think your presence at Santa María is far more important than any service you *could possibly provide* for the Dumont family – their generosity notwithstanding."

"I am present at Santa María when most of the parishioners come in the evenings and only gone during the quiet time in the middle of the day. Remercier un Dieu, the worst is finally over in the lowlands. Of course, there is much yet to be done and with the youth and strength of Father Francis, we are making more progress than any one priest could achieve alone."

"Is that so?" The bishop glared at Olivier. "Even with

you away at all times of day? That doesn't add up to two priests serving at Santa María. On the contrary, it indicates the priests are simply taking turns officiating at Santa María. Tell me, Father Olivier, when will you be finished with this *secular assignment*? It hardly seems appropriate for a priest in the service of God."

"Oh, it's too soon to tell, Most Reverend Bishop. I've only just begun."

Exasperated, the bishop struck the door with the palm of his hand. "Your responsibility is to Santa María and not to the Dumont family. Make sure you finish this secular matter as soon as possible. Is that understood, Father Olivier? "

"Yes, Most Reverend Bishop." Olivier barely managed to keep from smiling again.

"Keep in mind, Father Olivier, one of the purposes of your assignment to Santa María was to dedicate yourself to the humility your priestly office demands. You do remember that, do you not, Father Olivier?"

Olivier nodded. "Yes, Most Reverend Bishop. I am definitely aware of the need for that dedication. Father Antonio reminded me of it the very day he assigned me to the investigation. I recall every one of his words."

"Oh, what did he say?" The bishop stared at Olivier, suspicious of what he would say.

"Father Antonio said, 'I don't want this assignment to interfere with your struggle with the sin of pride.' It seems to me that you passed his office as he uttered those words."

The bishop scowled at Olivier. He remembered the two priests had been laughing loudly as he walked past the pastor's office.

"I trust you are feeling better now, Monsieur Dumont. I've heard what a terrible ordeal your family suffered this past week." Olivier sat across from the Jean Bertin in his office.

The spacious office, situated in a two story building on the corner of Real and San Pedro streets, looked more like a home study than a place of commerce. Ceiling to floor bookcases full of leather-bound books, written in a variety of languages, lined two of the walls and a large still-life painting by Jean Baptiste Chardin hung on a third wall. Jean Bertin's veneered mahogany desk stood beneath the painting and beside a marble-topped table that held a decanter of port and another of sherry. Elegant mahogany furniture, similar in color and style to the desk and table, filled the office and gleamed from daily polishing. Everything in the room was illuminated by light from a tall window that took up most of the east wall.

"I'm feeling better, but, alas, poor Lucille is in a coma and we now fear the worst." Jean Bertin looked haggard and his face had little color. "Thank God, the rest of the household has recovered. My nephew, Charles Laroux, is the only one still sick and home in bed."

"Father Antonio has mentioned Lucille's name in prayer the entire week."

"God help her." Jean Bertin sighed loudly. "The poor woman had the smallest portion and yet has suffered the worst from the poisoned rice. It must be her age."

"Probably so, la malheureuse femme (the poor woman)."

"It's hard to imagine how a little rice could almost kill us all. I've heard that our family appears to be the only one to have eaten the contaminated rice."

"Apparently, but it may be too soon to tell. Of course, after the church's warning, every family in the city is now examining their rice. The king's officials also have been inspecting the stored rice throughout New Orleans. Hopefully, they will find the source of the poison."

"So, they still don't know how the hemlock contaminated our rice."

"No, Monsieur." Olivier shook his head. "None of the

inspections have turned up tainted rice at the food market where your family purchased the rice. Naturally, that was the first place the officials inspected. In fact, no sign of hemlock has been found anywhere in town so far."

Jean Bertin shook his head. "Peculiar, very peculiar! Well, Father Olivier, what have you found at the wreck of *La Bonne Chance*?"

Olivier pursed his lips. "I found three peculiarities which, perhaps, could be explained to be unimportant, *if* your family had not almost perished from food poisoning."

"What do you mean?" Jean Bertin frowned. "Are you suggesting the sloop's sinking and the poisoning are somehow related?"

"Perhaps. I'll tell you what was found and then we can discuss that possibility."

Jean Bertin sat forward and stared at Olivier. "Do continue, Father."

"Before I say anymore, I must ask about the repairs and renovations made on *La Bonne Chance*. I understand the Laroche brothers made several renovations on the sloop before your sons took it out for the first time."

"That's correct. The sloop was refitted and renovated. Marcel Laroche told my nephew Charles the sloop was perfectly seaworthy. He and his brother, Pascal, took it for a trial sailing all the way to the gulf. They said the vessel performed extremely well during the voyage."

Olivier nodded. "That's what they told me. They also said you requested new decking and a stronger cabin door."

"Yes. There was some dry rot in the stern so we had new decking laid down while *La Bonne Chance* was out of the water. We had a new cabin door installed because the previous one had been broken open and our sea charts stolen. A stronger and thicker door was therefore installed – it was more than an inch thick to obstruct any such entry again."

"It certainly was well built. The door and most of the

framework were still attached to the sloop even after it broke up in the storm. There were iron rings on the door and framework so I assume the door was locked with a crossbar. The crossbar, of course, is gone

Jean Bertin nodded. "We had crossbars installed on the cabin door and the storage-hold hatch. The bars were held in place by padlocks – of course, only when the ship was moored and no one was aboard. We were determined not to be robbed again."

"I understand."

"You said the sloop 'broke up in the storm.' Is there enough of it left to be rebuilt?"

"I doubt it. What remains of the sloop lies on shore near one of the outlets of the lake. It's not much more than a three-sided shell of a ship and looks like a shipwright's drawing of the side of a vessel, without masts or rigging. The starboard side is completely gone as well as the cabin roof and much of the planking on the port side. The bow and stern are hardly recognizable. We found a board with the *Chance* painted on it, so we, of course, knew the wreck was your ship."

"I assume the storm battered the sloop and threw it up on land."

"Exactly. Two other observers accompanied me and together we thoroughly examined the wreckage. We were there almost all day looking at every remaining board of the ship."

"What were the three peculiarities you found, Father?" Jean Bertin was not interested in the details of the examination; he wanted to hear what Olivier had discovered.

"The first was a one-inch-diameter hole in the planking at the bow. It was located in the second plank above the keel. Most significant, the hole was not made by some piercing object during the storm. It was made by a drill with the marks of the drill still evident in the wood."

"Were there any other holes? I can't imagine one hole of

that diameter sinking a ship of that size overnight."

"We found no other holes, but most of the planks that abutted the keel were missing and, though we looked all around the area, we could not find any other outer planking."

"Are you certain the hole had been drilled and not pierced by some other pointed object? I would think there could be any number of other explanations for it."

"I'm certain. We pried a piece of the board with the hole in it from the ship and took it to the Laroche brothers. Pascal Laroche said it was a drilled hole. He demonstrated how the hole was drilled into the hull and said there was no purpose he could possibly imagine for such a hole in the hull."

Jean Bertin frowned. "What were the other peculiarities? Were they also in the hull?"

"No, Monsieur, we found them in what remained of the cabin. The port side was still intact after the storm as well as the stout cabin door and the framework around it."

Jean Bertin raised an eyebrow.

"The first oddity we noticed was that the inside of cabin door was badly damaged. There were a number of cracks and dents in the wood suggesting it had been battered from within. The damage to the door also suggested it was closed and could not be opened as the ship was sinking. It's therefore obvious that your sons tried to break through the closed door to escape the flooding cabin. I think they used the butt of a musket to batter the door. That assumption was confirmed by the *La Bonne Chance's* manifest which lists two muskets among other essential items stored aboard. Captain Ordoñez showed me the manifest you gave him."

"A flintlock musket was stored beneath each bunk. I wanted my sons to be able to protect themselves from whatever threatened them." He had tears in his eyes as he spoke.

"I understand, Monsieur Dumont. Would you like me to continue at another time?"

"No. Do continue, Father."

"What remains unclear, however, is why the cabin door was closed. It was a hot summer night – a time when every window in New Orleans was wide open. That itself is baffling! Yet, we know the door was closed because that's how the divers found it." Olivier did not mention that the divers had to open the door to retrieve the bodies of his sons. "But even though closed, your sons should have been able to slide it open. We slid the door back and forth several times and, even after the ship's destruction and so much time under water, the cabin door moved – not easily, but it moved. The Laroche brothers made certain both top and bottom grooves were wide enough to accommodate the inevitable warping of the wood in the door."

"Are you saying my sons should have been able to open the cabin door even if stuck?"

"Yes, unless the crossbar was in place and locked."

"But surely the bar wasn't on the door when you saw the wreck."

"No. But it could have been locked in place until the ship sank and then removed. *La Bonne Chance* lies in shallow water. Captain Ordoñez said the sloop was down no more than eighteen feet – an easy dive for almost anyone. Of course, we don't know the cabin door was barred with certainty. I mention it only because of the last peculiarity we found."

Jean Bertin bit his lip. "I see, continue, Father."

"As we looked over the remaining side of the cabin, we saw that the hinges on the two porthole covers were bent."

Jean Bertin frowned, looking puzzled. "Bent?"

"Yes. The portholes could not be closed because of the bent hinges on the storm covers. So, if water surged over the deck it would also pour through the open portholes into the cabin."

"How did that happen? Were the hinges bent when the ship broke up?"

"No, not according to Pascal Laroche. I took one of the

hinges to him and, after studying it for a few seconds, he said the scrapes in the metal were made by a pair of pliers. He showed me how it could have been done and the type of heavy pliers needed to bend the hinges."

"I see." Jean Bertin paused to think about what he had heard. "So, if someone drilled holes, obviously more than one, in the hull and bent the porthole hinges to let water stream into the cabin from above and below and then barred the cabin door – Mon Dieu, mes garcons ont été assassins! (My God, my boys were murdered)!"

"We can't say that with certainty, Monsieur Dumont, but I'm afraid it looks that way. To be sure, you should tell the magistrate what we have found." Olivier paused as Jean Bertin closed his eyes and collapsed into his chair. His arms dangled down by his sides. Olivier rushed over to hold him up when he appeared to be falling out of the chair. Seconds later, Jean Bertin opened his eyes and blinked several times. He took a breath and sat up in the chair.

"I'm fine now." He nodded his thanks as the priest poured him a glass of wine from the decanter on his desk. He looked at Olivier. "So, it seems someone has marked my entire family for death. It's obvious now the sinking of *La Bonne Chance* and the hemlock poisoning are indeed related. It seems my family has some unknown enemy who seeks to murder us all."

"It appears so, unless other similar poisonings are reported in New Orleans. If there are others, an attempt to kill your family alone would seem less likely."

"Less likely or not, the poisonings that followed the sinking of the sloop are suspicious." Jean Bertin sighed. "It's too suspicious to be coincidental."

Olivier nodded. "I agree. I urge you to tell the magistrate about it. He should be told of our findings and the likelihood that the sloop was deliberately sunk."

"No, Father, I'll speak to the governor."

CHAPTER FOUR

New Orleans: November 5 – 30, 1799

Jean Bertin went to see the governor on the following day. A prominent member of the French community, the wealthy colonist was given the first appointment of the morning at nine o'clock. Government House stood on Orleans Street five feet from the corner of Borbón Street. No more than a ten-minute drive from his office, Jean Bertin ordered Tristan Surette to drive him there to arrive at the precise time of his appointment. Without any traffic that morning, his two-horse carriage reached the gates of Government House one minute before the scheduled meeting.

Government House was a three-story stone building which served the governor as both his home and office. Rebuilt after the fire of 1794, the house's architecture revealed the straight lines and simplicity that characterized many of the mansions built in the late eighteenth century. Peaked dormer windows on the third floor and stone capitals centered above the main entrance and lower windows appeared as the only visible ornamentation on the front of the house.

Jean Bertin admired the building as he briefly stood on the top step of the carriage. "It's simple and utilitarian as a house should be – like mine," he thought. "All that embellishment of the past was excessive, never mind expensive." Jean Bertin shook off his coachman's hand of assistance and, as the cathedral bells ran the hour, he stepped down to the road.

One of the two guards at the gate guided Jean Bertin into the governor's property and led him up the stone walk to the house. Another soldier opened the front door and bowed to him as he entered the building. He was then ushered into the governor's office.

Governor Casa-Calvo got up from his desk and smiled warmly as he went to greet Jean Bertin. The governor was a tall, slender man with the erect posture of a soldier who had served thirty-five years in the Spanish army. He had intense black eyes and a long nose marred by a sword strike that left a long scar from the bridge of his nose to his left ear. He had lost most of his hair and the little that remained above his ears was a mixture of black and gray. His thin mustache and sideburns matched the fringe of hair on his head.

"Bienvenue, Monsieur Dumont. I am glad to meet you again." The governor, given the noble title of Marqués de Casa-Calvo three years earlier, stood before him in an army uniform. Decorated with gold epaulets, it was a striking uniform with a dark blue jacket, white breeches, a light blue sash and black boots.

"My pleasure, Your Excellency." Jean Bertin bowed his head.

"Please sit." The governor gestured his guest to a chair with a brocaded seat cover. He sat across from him in a matching chair. "I know it's quite early in the day, but would you per chance enjoy a glass of Rioja? A new case arrived yesterday from Cadíz."

"Yes, thank you. A half glass please."

The governor nodded to the young orderly, who sat in a chair next to the door. "Arana, a half-glass of wine for Monsieur Dumont and a full one for me. Also s'il vous plait bring some of the croissants you purchased at the bakery this morning."

For a few moments, the two men talked about the French Revolution, the wars in Europe and the devastation caused by the late September storm. They had finished their first glasses of wine and were sipping their second as they talked. The governor sighed as their conversation turned to the death and destruction in the lowlands.

"It has been a terrible time for those unfortunate people. I'm told it will take weeks, if not months for the survivors to recover from their terrible losses. Well, Monsieur Dumont, I'm sure you haven't come to talk to me about this terrible tragedy. How may I assist you?"

"No, Your Excellency, I've come to speak to you about a much more personal matter – a matter that requires a thorough investigation – the murder of my two sons." Jean Bertin told the governor about the strange sinking of *La Bonne Chance* and the later findings in the wreck that indicated the sloop had been deliberately sunk.

The governor rubbed his chin. "Were those the findings of the magistrate? I don't recall hearing of such an investigation, though, of course, I heard of the terrible loss of your two sons." I presume you received my letter of condolence."

"I did indeed, Your Excellency, thank you. No, those were the findings of Father Olivier, whom I asked to investigate the sinking and the death of my sons. It was he who discovered the hole drilled in the hull and the bent hinges on the porthole covers."

"A priest investigated the sinking?" The governor frowned in disapproval.

"Sí Señor. After the sloop sunk, I asked Captain Ordoñez

y Rosas of the guarda costas to investigate the sinking – at the time, it lay in only eighteen feet of water. The captain suggested we bring *La Bonne Chance* up and look it over, but the salvage was stopped by the storm. Then the sloop was lost until Father Olivier found its wreckage on land that bordered the lake."

"I see. Before Father Olivier found the wreckage, did Captain Ordoñez y Rosas conduct a search for the lost sloop?" The governor wanted to know if the coastguard captain had carried out the responsibilities of his office.

"Yes. The captain and my nephew went to the lake and found wreckage where the sloop had been when it sank. That's when they found the body of that unfortunate girl."

"Ah, yes, the unknown girl. She still has not been identified. Please continue, Monsieur."

Jean Bertin briefly closed his eyes and nodded to show his concern for the girl. "Captain Ordoñez sent an Indian diver to the bottom and he saw part of the cabin roof, scattered pieces of wood and the ship's mast and anchor lying there. What was left of the sloop's hull had been thrown on shore into a thick stand of trees. Father Olivier said it was easy to miss. In fact, the wreck could only be seen if a small ship or pirogue took a shallow course close to shore as it sailed out of the lake."

The governor arched an eyebrow as he looked at Jean Bertin. "So, Monsieur Dumont, the hole in the hull and the bent porthole hinges are the findings that make you think your sons were murdered. Is that correct?"

"Yes, Your Excellency. The Laroche brothers, the carpenters who refitted the sloop, said the hole had been drilled into the hull and the hinges bent by pliers. Neither, they said, had been brought about by the ship's sinking or the storm. They were made by a man with tools and there was no good purpose for them. None at all. They certainly didn't improve the sloop's sailing."

The governor made a face. He disliked sarcasm.

"There's another related incident as well. Ten days ago, my entire family almost perished from poisonous hemlock; the only family in this city of 15,000 people to be poisoned by tainted rice. The one and *only* family! What's more, Your Excellency, that singular incident follows the murder of my sons three months ago. It therefore seems clear to me that a murderer has marked my family for death. Also, sad to say, my oldest servant has already died a horrible death as a consequence of the poisoning. Lucille Chastain died in my wife's arms three days ago."

Jean Bertin told the governor his suspicions despite Olivier's warnings against it. He had advised him not to mention the assumption that the cabin door was barred to keep his sons from escaping the sinking ship. The priest also told him it would be a mistake to bring up the poisoned rice and the possibility that an unknown murderer had tried to murder his family. Olivier warned Jean Bertin that the governor would be dubious of such baseless claims.

"With only two specific findings to prove *La Bonne Chance* was sabotaged, the governor may well be doubtful of the deliberate sinking alone," he had told him. "The assertion, then, that the food poisoning was purposeful, I think, might make him wonder if you are mad."

At the time, Jean Bertin had agreed with Olivier. But, once he arrived in the governor's office and found him so welcoming, Jean Bertin changed his mind and told him everything. He knew it was a mistake as soon he saw the concerned look on the governor's face.

"Monsieur Dumont, are you saying someone here is plotting to murder everyone in your family?" The governor tilted his head to the side and stared at Jean Bertin.

"Yes, Your Excellency, that's exactly what is happening. The murder of my sons was his first step, the poisoning the second and God knows what will be his next attempt."

Casa-Calvo nodded, still staring at Jean Bertin. "What is it then, Monsieur Dumont, you would wish me to do in this matter?"

"I would hope, Your Excellency, you would assist in the investigation of the murders of my sons and the poisoning of my family. It is my hope that an official investigation will end in the arrest and execution of the murderer. In the meantime, I intend to hire a team of men myself to guard my family in the future."

The governor sighed and shook his head slowly up and down. "That would seem to be a sensible plan for their protection. As you request, I will speak to the magistrate about initiating an investigation."

The governor sighed as Jean Bertin left his office. "The man is befuddled," he thought. "Undoubtedly the consequence of the loss of his two sons. It's understandable, of course. Qué triste, pobre hombre! (How sad, poor man)!"

The attempt on Charles Laroux' life took place on the fourteenth of November. He was on his way home when someone suddenly struck him from behind and left him for dead on the ground. A bloody staff lay beside him.

"Thank God for Monsieur Guidry. If he hadn't been walking close behind me I would surely have been killed." Charles Laroux sat in in the magistrate's office in the Cabildo, his head bandaged in white gauze. A red spot stood out on the bandage where blood still seeped from his head wound.

"Would you like another glass of rum, Monsieur Laroux?" The magistrate, Major Carlos Castañedo Obregon, was a short, stout man with thick gray hair and similarly colored sideburns. He noticed that Laroux' left hand trembled as he finished his rum and placed the empty glass on the desk. His other hand was bandaged and he held it flat against his chest.

"No, thank you. I'm fine now." Laroux sighed loudly.

"Have you recovered enough to tell me what happened, Monsieur?" Castañedo stroked the end of the closely cropped beard that covered his chin.

"Yes, I think so." Laroux reached up and, with his first two fingers, gingerly touched the red spot on his head.

"The wound appears to have stopped bleeding. Is it still painful?"

"It feels better." Laroux sighed again. He was tired and wanted to go home. Laroux had already told the account of his assault to the magistrate's assistant after he arrived at the Cabildo. Now, he had to tell it again to the magistrate, who had left his dinner at home and returned to his office to interview him. But it was better to repeat it now rather than spend more time tomorrow.

"We can wait until tomorrow to talk if you wish. I'll be here all day."

"No, Magistrate, I'll tell you everything now, while it's still fresh in my mind."

Castañedo nodded and waited for him to begin.

"Laroux once again touched the spot on his head. It had begun to ache and he frowned. "I was walking home – as you probably know, our offices are situated on San Pedro at the corner of Real Street. My house is on Borbón Street between San Luis and Conti Streets in the middle of the block – on the north side of the street."

"So, I assume you walk up San Pedro to Borbón Street."

"Yes, I closed the offices at six o'clock; Monsieur Dumont left a half-hour earlier as is his want. After leaving the office, I proceeded toward Borbón Street. I was walking slowly."

"Were there other people walking along with you?"

"Yes, but not from the office. We have only one clerk

and he leaves at five o'clock. I'm the last to leave and, as usual, the streets were full of people. It's the customary closing time and there were people on all sides of me."

"Were the street lights already lighted? The lower-street lamplighter lights the Conde Street lamps at five o'clock – in the winter." Castañedo smiled. "Though he's known to be tardy."

"Yes, he is all too often. When on time, he reaches San Pedro a few minutes before six o'clock. The upper-street lamplighter begins at five o'clock as well; he begins at the corner of Borbón and Hospital Streets, but, by the time he has lit the lamps on the side streets, he doesn't reach the corner of San Pedro and Borbón Street until after six o'clock."

"So, Borbón Street was dark when you reached it."

"It was, though there were lights burning behind me as the lamplighter followed me onto Borbón Street. But it was dark ahead of me – quite dark."

"Were the streets still full of people?"

"No, there were not as many on Borbón as on San Pedro."

"Did you notice anyone following you?"

"No, Magistrate. I saw no one unusual. To be candid, I was unaware of anyone around me; I had business matters on my mind. But I do recall a man rushing ahead of me as I came to Conti Street. He wore a dark cloak, but he swept beside me and was quickly gone into the darkness ahead."

"You were walking on the north side of Borbón Street at the time – the side where your house is located?"

"Yes. The assault happened in front of the empty lot near the corner of San Luis Street. It's too narrow for a substantial house and has remained empty for years, if not decades. The lot is between Monsieur Hebert's house and Monsieur Guidry's mansion on the corner."

"I know the lot."

"Yes, of course. Well, as I walked beside the lot, I heard the sound of someone running toward me. But, by that time of day, I could not see who was approaching. It was too dark to see much of anything and, then, before I took my next step, I was struck senseless." He made a face, trying to remember what followed. "The next thing I knew, I was lying on the ground and Monsieur Guidry was speaking to me. I don't recall what he said. I do recall being carried into a house and put on a bed, my aching head gently placed on a pillow. By that time, I was aware of my surroundings. I knew I was in Monsieur Guidry's house, and recognized Madame Guidry, who was cleaning my wound with a wet cloth. I remember her holding a cold compress on my forehead. Soon afterwards, Dr. Broussard arrived and he tended to me. It was the doctor who bandaged my wounds. He instructed me to go home to bed, but I thought it best to report the incident while I still remembered it. I've heard that many people with head wounds often forget what happened to them. It was Dr. Broussard who brought me here."

"Do you know what happened to your hand? Did you try to fight off the assailant?"

"I don't think so. I didn't have the time, he struck so quickly. Dr. Broussard believes my hand was cut when I fell to the ground. He also thinks I was struck twice, once on the head and then on the neck. It's his opinion I was initially struck on the head and then on the neck as I was falling. He suspects the second blow was probably aimed at my head, but missed as I fell to the ground. If Monsieur Guidry had not happened upon the assault, I'm certain I would have been killed. It would have been easy to break my skull while I lay prone on the road."

"Indeed. Monsieur Guidry is here now waiting to take you home. I met him in the entry room as I came to speak to you."

"Did he see the man who attacked me?"

"No, he only saw you stagger and fall to the ground. But another man, Monsieur Douet, walking a few paces behind him thought he saw someone dart away into the darkness."

"I know Monsieur Douet, he lives across the street from Monsieur Julien Guidry."

Castañedo nodded. "He helped carry you into Monsieur Guidry's house. I will speak to him tomorrow and, hopefully, he will remember more than he told Monsieur Guidry. Monsieur Douet also retrieved your hat and the staff that was used to strike you on the head."

"Where did he find it?" Laroux ran a finger over the crease in his hat. A large blood spot was inside beneath the crease. He hoped it could be removed. It was his favorite hat.

"Lying beside you on the ground. The assailant apparently dropped it immediately after striking you. Monsieur Guidry said he thought he heard the staff clatter to the ground. The road is partially paved in front of his house and the empty lot."

"Yes, I heard at one time that Monsieur Guidry thought of buying the lot and turning it into a garden. At that time, he extended the paving from his house to include the lot."

"Well, Monsieur Laroux, I have no more questions for now. Thank you for coming into the Cabildo and waiting for me. Be assured that we will do our utmost to arrest the villain who attacked you. For now, I'm sure you would like to go home and sleep." Magistrate Castañedo stood and bowed. "Do you need assistance, Monsieur Laroux?

"No, I'm fine." Laroux bowed and left the room.

The magistrate watched him slowly walk away. "Poor fellow looks a little unsteady," he thought. "So, now it appears there may well be a plot against the Dumont family." He recalled how dubious he had been when the governor told him about Dumont's certainty that a murderer intended to kill everyone in his family. Castañedo sighed. "A thorough investigation will now be necessary. The Dumont family will rightfully demand it."

Giraud Douet went to the Cabildo on the following morning. A young attorney from the magistrate's office was sent to Douet's home to request his presence at an interview. Douet was asked to come at his convenience.

"Thank you for coming to speak to me, Monsieur Douet." Magistrate Castañedo smiled and stood politely as the French colonist entered his office.

Over his twenty years in the king's service, the magistrate had employed his warm smile, solicitous manner and soft-spoken speech to calm the people he interviewed. Most of those who came to his office would later comment on how easy it was to talk to him. "Magistrate Castañedo is so considerate and such a well-mannered man," they would say. The magistrate was especially considerate of the wealthy and prominent members of the community.

Others of the lower and poorer classes, including Acadians, foreign immigrants, Negroes and Indians, did not have the same impression of him. To those people, who all too often found themselves forced to answer his impatient questions, Castañedo was a hard unsmiling man with harsh speech and a contemptuous sneer. His answer to those who inquired about the difference in his interview methods were asked, "Tell me, Monsieur, who are the people found to be guilty of most of the crimes in New Orleans?"

"I assume you want me to tell you about the assault on Monsieur Laroux." Douet, a tall dour looking man with what appeared to be a permanent frown, sat down in the chair facing the magistrate. His voice had a nasal quality and he pulled at his nose repeatedly.

"Yes, Monsieur Douet, I would appreciate your telling me all you recall about it."

"I don't have much to tell you. Monsieur Guidry reached Monsieur Laroux before me. I did little more than help him carry Laroux into his house. I left soon after Doctor Broussard arrived." Douet grimaced and then blew his nose into a handkerchief. "I've had this damned catarrhe all week. I can't taste food or smell anything. Of course, that at least spares me the smell of this fetid city."

"That's too bad." Castañedo nodded sympathetically. "Winter catarrhes do seem to go on endlessly. Monsieur Douet, please tell me what alerted you to the attack on Monsieur Laroux?"

Douet looked annoyed. "Nothing alerted me to the attack on him. I didn't see it."

Castañedo smiled. "What did you see, Monsieur?"

"I was walking a few steps behind Monsieur Guidry on Borbón Street when I saw him start running. He shouted something about a man being assaulted and I followed him. I ran, too, though I have a bad back and I was in pain with every step I took."

"Did you see anything ahead?"

"I saw a man lying on the ground – perhaps fifteen paces ahead."

Castañedo smiled warmly. "Did you see anything or anyone else?"

"No, not clearly. I think I saw someone running alongside Monsieur Guidry's house, but I'm not certain. It could have been a man in a cloak, but I'm not at all certain." Douet shook his head and scowled. "My eyes are full of mucous from this damned catarrhe and I can't see anything clearly. Anyway, it was already dark at the time."

"Even if you didn't see him clearly, do you have any impression of the man in the cloak? Was he short, tall, slender?"

Douet shook his head. "I don't know – I'm not even sure I saw a man in a cloak."

"If you recall something more about the man, please notify me, Monsieur Douet." The magistrate gave up trying to elicit more information about the man in the cloak.

"There's nothing more I can tell you about him." Douet again blew his nose loudly.

"Monsieur Douet, please tell me what happened when you reached Monsieur Laroux."

Douet frowned. "What do you mean? The man was lying senseless on the ground."

"Did you see anything else?"

"What else was there to see?" Irritated, Douet's voice had a rasping tone. "Nothing was there except the man's crushed hat lying beside him."

"His hat was lying near his head?"

"Yes, it was lying there upside down and I could see blood inside."

"Was there blood anywhere else?"

Douet sighed in exasperation. "On his head, of course."

"Anywhere else?" Castañedo smiled again, though he felt the urge to grasp Douet by the shirt front and shake him until he spoke courteously.

"There was a trickle on blood running down his face and into the collar of his shirt."

"Was there any blood on the ground?"

"None that I saw. Of course, there was blood on the head of the staff that had been used to strike him down. The staff was a thick tree limb stripped of its leaves."

"Ah, I see. The limb was lying on the ground near Monsieur Laroux?"

"Yes, a couple of feet away. It seemed obvious that whoever struck Laroux dropped it as he left. I would imagine he ran when he heard Monsieur Guidry shouting from behind him. Laroux probably owes his life to Monsieur Guidry."

The magistrate nodded. "So it seems. What happened next?"

"As I *already* told you, I helped Guidry carry the man into his house – despite the pain in my back. We must have carried the man a hundred paces and the pain was excruciating."

A month before Christmas on a cold windy afternoon, Olivier walked into New Orleans to see Jean Bertin. It was one of those bitterly cold days when few men ventured into the streets even if bundled up in layers of clothing. The cutting wind seemed to find gaps and moth holes in the heaviest of wool cloaks and coats and hats were of no use that day. Even the best of hoods were incapable of shielding a street-walker's eyes, lips and nose from the wind. Even in a heavy cloak that fell to his ankles, Olivier shivered as he hurried through the San Carlos gates and strode up San Pedro Street. He walked bent forward, his hooded face focused on the road and his numb hands hidden in folds beneath the cloak. Olivier looked up as he finally neared the doorway of Dumont's building. His eyes blurred by tears, he sighed in relief when Tristan Surette opened the door to his first knock and let him into the office.

Moments later, Olivier was seated next to the spacious fireplace where a stack of burning wood warmed the room. Jean Bertin and Charles Laroux sat across from the priest, the young man to his right where he could keep the birth mark in the left side of his face out of sight. The men held brandy glasses and patiently waited for their visitor to warm himself before speaking. Rubbing the circulation back into his hands, the Dominican smiled to show them he felt better. He nodded his thanks when Laroux handed him a glass of brandy.

"Thank you, that will help." Though he wanted more, Olivier politely sipped his brandy.

"It's certainly bitter cold out there. You look frozen, Father. I would have understood it, if you waited for another day to come here. I thought I saw snowflakes this morning when I rode into the office." Jean Bertin looked from Olivier to his nephew.

Olivier nodded. "I didn't realize what a stiff wind was blowing when I started out from Santa María. I thought it would warm up when I saw the sun break through the clouds, but I was wrong. I saw snow, too, it was snowing when I arrived at Santa María this morning."

"See, Charles, I told you it snowed this morning." Jean Bertin smiled triumphantly and pointed a finger at his nephew. "Charles and I had a wager if and when it would snow this year. I said there would be snow falling by the end of December and he scoffed at the possibility." He laughed. "Snow was predicted in the farmer's almanac; I read about it last summer."

Laroux shook his head. "So it was. What can I say? Well, Uncle Jean, isn't it time to tell Father Olivier why we asked him here?"

"Quite so, Charles." Jean Bertin sipped his brandy and looked at Olivier. "I am asking for your assistance once again, Father. As I'm certain you know our situation is unchanged. My family remains at risk and the magistrate's investigation has turned up nothing. After the murder of my sons, the poisoning of my family and the attempt on my nephew's life, no one has been arrested and nothing has been done. It's been four months since the murder of my sons, a month since the poisoning and eleven days since Charles was struck down and almost slain." Jean Bertin's face reddened. "He was brazenly attacked on a city street only a block from his home."

Olivier nodded.

"What's this city coming to? It's been one tragedy after another. What with two terrible fires, only six years apart, that almost destroyed New Orleans. The first one burned down four-fifths of the buildings and this building was one of them. Dieu merci, my home was spared. The second consumed more than 200 buildings, including the newly built fortifications. The losses from the fires amounted to some 4,000,000 pesetas. Isn't that correct, Charles?"

"It was almost 3,000,000 pesetas, Uncle Jean."

"Yes, of course. Then, there have been the storms and floods – the autumn storm almost leveled the lowlands. And let's not forget the plagues. Not only Malaria and Yellow Fever, but Leprosy as well. And now these murders. Has God forsaken us, Father?"

"No, Monsieur Dumont. All peoples and cities suffer calamitous times. And with God's help, we, as His children, persevere and hopefully will live more righteous lives."

"There's not much righteous living here in New Orleans. Not with all the gambling and prostitution, never mind the drunkenness. I understand the Spaniards counted the city's taverns and found there to be at least one *licensed* tavern on every block; the ratio was a tavern for every seventy-one people and that doesn't include all the illegal places where cheap products are sold. A Boston trader I know told me in his city the ratio was one tavern for every 694 people. Quelle différence! (What a difference!) Of course, we French don't frequent such places, do we?"

"No, Uncle Jean, we drink our wine quietly at home. We never spend time in those filthy shacks where the common people wallow in cheap beer and taffia (colonial rum) and run amuck about the city streets drunk and disorderly."

"The drunkenness in this city is a disgrace." Jean Bertin grimaced. "Thank God, that's not the manner of the educated class."

Olivier nodded and then looked down at the Persian rug on the wooden floor. The priest knew he had no right to nod in agreement. He had spent much of the previous night drinking in his bedroom. He finally fell asleep around midnight after drinking three bottles of wine. Olivier recalled telling Gervaise he was sick when the boy knocked at his door to tell him breakfast was on the table. It was the third time he had drunk himself to sleep in Madame

Lefevre's house; it was also the third time he had lied to Gervaise as well as his mother. "How can I, of all people, talk of righteous living? I'm a hypocrite. God forgive me," Olivier prayed as he took the second glass of brandy that Charles Laroux handed him.

"Well, Father, I hope you will help us. The murderer must be found and arrested as soon as possible. If he's not found soon, I fear he will kill one or more of my family. The attempt on Charles' life has made me hire another three armed men to protect us. Two men were already in my employ, one here with me and the other at home. Now, I have assigned three men at home to safeguard my family – my mother and her servants are now also with us. The other two men accompany me wherever I go. I wanted to hire two more to guard Charles, but he has refused to be guarded." Jan Bertin frowned at his nephew.

"I'm armed and wary." Laroux opened his blue suit-coat and showed Olivier a holstered pistol on his waist. "I'll not be surprised again."

Olivier nodded and returned his eyes to Jean Bertin. "I take it, Monsieur Dumont, you want me to resume the investigation."

"Yes, Father, I have much more confidence in you than any of the Spaniards. It wasn't until the assault on Charles that they believed my family was in peril. Neither the governor nor the magistrate paid any attention to me when I told them of your findings at the wreckage of *La Bonne Chance*. As you suspected, they also doubted the apparent poisoning of my family. Even now, though they finally believe my family is in jeopardy, they have done little to find the fiend who seeks to kill us all. It's undoubtedly because we are French. I'm certain it would be quite different if we were a prominent Spanish family. Well, so much for Spanish incompetence and indifference to French concerns. Yes, I would appreciate your help, Father."

Three days earlier, Olivier had been locking the church's door for the night, when he saw Tristan Surette approach on horseback. The big man dismounted, bowed his head to Olivier and handed him a note requesting a meeting at Jean Bertin's office. Olivier knew instantly he would be asked to continue the investigation. With that in mind, Olivier decided to help Dumont only if he offered to pay for the needed renovation of Santa María.

As Olivier hurried to the wealthy man's office that afternoon, he realized a bluntly stated bargain – his help for the renovations might well fail. The experienced man of commerce would probably see his part of the arrangement as too costly and look for someone else to carry on the investigation. There probably were any number of better suited men in town to investigate the attacks on his family. In all likelihood, they would also charge less to do his bidding.

It also would be inappropriate for a Dominican to ask for money, even if for a pious use. His monastic training forbade such practices. It would not be as unseemly for a parish priest to do so, especially if he was serving as a pastor of a church. Pleas for contributions were common practices of the parish priests. Father Antonio, a monastic priest himself, apparently had little or no guilt for the money he requested. "But what about a Dominican serving as a pastor?" Olivier shook his head. It still did not seem appropriate. "How then," he wondered, "could a bargain be struck with Jean Bertin Dumont without my request for his financial support?"

Olivier wished he knew the man better. He had heard Dumont was quite thrifty, some said stingy, though he and his family had been generous patrons of the cathedral. It was his contributions to the Church that had prompted the pastor to ask him to look into the deaths of his sons in the first place. But, according to María Adela, Jean Bertin's generosity was due to the urging of his mother, who had always been a prominent supporter of the cathedral. Jean Bertin, however, had never given anything to Santa María, despite his extensive land holdings around the church. Much of the sugar cane he milled was grown in the lowlands. Yet, Olivier knew, he had never stepped inside the church, never mind donated even one peseta to Santa María. It was clear his Christian charity did not extend beyond the doors of the cathedral.

A block from Dumont's office, Olivier suddenly realized how he would induce the rich man to support the church's renovation. It would be done without asking for one single peseta. Olivier stopped in the street and raised his head, letting the frigid wind strike his face and bring tears to his eyes. The realization had come to him as he recalled his mother saying, "You can lead a horse to water, but you can't make him drink." It was then that he knew exactly how to approach the shrewd businessman.

In the office, Jean Bertin frowned when Olivier did not immediately respond. "Did you hear me, Father? I said I would appreciate your help."

"I heard you, Monsieur Dumont. Forgive me, I have been preoccupied with a number of problems at Santa María. The sad state of the old church has been on my mind day and night. I can't seem to think of anything else."

"I see." Jean Bertin looked sincerely concerned.

Olivier made a steeple with the tips of his fingers and put them to his lips. "I would like to help you, Monsieur Dumont, but at the moment I'm engaged in the renovation of Santa María. The church was badly damaged by the tempest and, now, after assisting our parishioners rebuild their homes, we are working hard to put the building back in order. It needs so much repair, hard work and more money than our poor parishioners can afford after the storm. I fear the renovation won't be completed until well after Christmas and perhaps not until Easter. Unlike the cathedral in town, we don't have any wealthy benefactors to help support our church." Olivier sighed and put his empty glass on the table beside his chair.

Jean Bertin cocked his head to the side as he looked at Olivier. He said nothing for a moment and exchanged knowing looks with his nephew. He then pointed to Olivier's empty glass and waited while his nephew refilled the brandy glasses.

"Do you have any notion of the cost of the church renovation, Father? I inquire, though I'm sure you haven't yet thought of how much it would cost." Jean Bertin's eyes twinkled as he spoke to Olivier.

Olivier shook his head from side to side. "No, I'm not at all sure of the total costs. The church needs a new door and roof, windows and, of course, a thorough white washing – three thick coats at least after the mold is scrubbed away. Oh yes, the rigging of the bell needs to be repaired as well."

Jean Bertin nodded, a slight smile on his lips. "Is there anything else Santa María needs to make it serviceable for the lowlands people?"

"The church could use new benches, the others were badly damaged by the storm; some were broken and others water-soaked. The altar and confessional are serviceable, but in need of a good bit of carpentry – if they can be repaired. They also smell of mildew which I'm not sure can be cleaned away."

"Tell me, Father, are there any other *needed* repairs or renovations at Santa María?" The tiny smile remained on Jean Bertin's face. He watched as Olivier, his lips pursed, looked up to the ceiling trying to recall if he had forgotten anything.

"No, Monsieur, nothing important that occurs to me at the moment." Olivier managed to keep a straight face, though he wanted to laugh out loud. He knew Jean Bertin was aware of the bargain he had in mind and, though no mention of it would be made, Olivier also knew Dumont would pay for the church's renovation. The only question was how much he would donate.

Jean Bertin nodded his head. He immediately understood the priest's unspoken proposal and admired how shrewdly Olivier had presented it to him. Now, he had to decide if the clever priest was worth the cost of the renovation. Of course, money had little importance if his family could be protected and the murderer arrested. Jean Bertin recalled it had been Olivier alone who discerned how his sons had been cruelly killed and, following the hemlock poisoning, it was the priest again who warned him about a plot against his entire family.

"Yes," he thought, "the clever Dominican is well worth whatever it costs to renovate the church." Jean Bertin suddenly decided to offer him more than he could have ever imagined. It would be an amount that would easily cover the most costly renovation of Santa María and leave money to spare. "Forgive me, Father, if I ask you something you haven't yet considered, but do you think 10,000 pesetas might adequately cover the costs?" Jean Bertin smiled broadly.

Olivier nodded slowly. "I think that amount would be adequate." It was much more than adequate, he knew, and would allow him to transform the tiny church from its shabby state to be the best looking country church in Louisiana. It would also be a source of pride for the church's destitute parishioners and hopefully encourage the attendance of those of them who rarely if ever came to Santa María. Olivier felt a surge of warmth in his stomach.

"Well then, Father, if we were to offer a donation to Santa María in that amount, do you think you might find the time to assist us in the investigation? I've already spoken to Father Antonio and he approved your taking time from Santa María as long as Father Francis agrees to serve in your behalf while you are away. I trust he will agree to the arrangement since it would give him the opportunity to serve more often as pastor of the church."

"Yes, I would think so." Olivier and Jean Bertin both smiled.

"I trust that means you will help us." Jean Bertin reached out to shake Olivier's hand, but the priest shook his head.

"Before we finalize our agreement, Monsieur Dumont, I want to make certain it is clear to both of us. I will assist in the investigation as you request, but it must be understood at the outset that I cannot promise to find the murderer you seek. I'll do my best, *but* I cannot assure you of success in the investigation. Nor can I tell how long it will take no matter the outcome. Finally, our agreement must be approved by the parish pastor before it goes into effect."

"I understand and accept those forewarnings, Father." Jean Bertin reached his hand out again and this time Olivier shook it.

"Bon. It's settled then." Later, he would chuckle as he spoke of Olivier to his nephew. "He's a clever one that Dominican; it's apparently true what they say about them. But pious or not, all these priests certainly know how to elicit money, don't they?"

Jean Bertin raised a hand as Olivier stood to leave. "One more matter, Father. I want to assure you that I am *not* seeking indulgences for any of my sins. This donation will be offered simply to help Santa María continue its pastoral mission for the suffering people of the lowlands. I mean that sincerely." Jean Bertin's smile had disappeared and was replaced by a tight-lined mouth and the severe look of a stern parent who had scolded his child.

"I'm very glad to hear you say that, Monsieur Dumont. Your unselfish concern for your fellow man is the essence of the Savior's teachings." Olivier spoke the same words he heard the pastor say to a benefactor of the cathedral a month ago. He knew the words were not true, they were the deceitful words of a shameless flatterer. Dumont donated the 10,000 pesetas because he wanted him to continue the investigation. He would never have given the money otherwise.

Olivier thought about his conversation with Jean Bertin as he hurried into the cold wind outside. He was pleased with the donation he had gotten for Santa María, but critical of what he had done to get it. "What have I become?" he asked aloud. "A manipulator of men, a flatterer, a liar and a hypocrite! I've become a typical secular priest. After all my many years condemning the Church for its crass materialism and manipulation of its unaware parishioners, I'm now one of its pastors in mind as well as manner." Disgusted with himself, he let the cold wind under his hood to freeze his face.

"I've little to tell Jean Bertin now after a fortnight of effort. The murderer left nothing – absolutely nothing of his presence in the family's poisoning or the assault on Charles Laroux. He's like some phantom who flies unseen through the night." Olivier shook his head, declining the second cup of tea offered by María Adela.

They sat in the upstairs porch now that the period of intense cold had gone. It was mild again in New Orleans and a light breeze blew warm air off the river. Flushed from the hot tea, María Adela fanned herself.

"Have the Spanish officials been helpful?" She grimaced. "How about the magistrate? I understand he is one of the Spaniards who treats the French with respect. They say he speaks French as well as any of the colonists here."

"Castañedo has been very helpful. I've known him since I arrived here in New Orleans. I baptized his third child, Rosa María, my second week in the cathedral."

"How did he help you?"

"We spent the best part of one afternoon discussing the plot against the Dumont family. The magistrate admitted he initially doubted there was a plot against the family. The attack on Charles Laroux, of course, changed his mind."

"What about the murders of Jacques and Matthieu? I've heard at first Castañedo didn't believe they had been murdered. Nor did he believe the family's rice had been poisoned even when it was well known that no other family in the city had tainted rice."

That's true, but it wasn't entirely his fault. He had not heard of what we discovered in the wreck of *La Bonne Chance* until after Laroux was attacked. The governor never informed him of the findings Jean Bertin described to him in his office. Governor Casa-Calvo believed Jean Bertin was mad from grief and had imagined there was a plot to kill his family. For that reason, he saw no need to tell the magistrate."

"The *superior* Spaniards! They would have believed Jean Bertin if he spoke Spanish."

"Perhaps. Anyway, Castañedo *was* busy investigating the poisoned rice at the time of the assault on Charles LaRoux. Spaniard or not, he's a diligent magistrate."

"Is that so? Did he find anything of importance?"

"It's what Castañedo didn't find that's important. Not one grain of rice in New Orleans was tainted – none except the rice that poisoned the Dumont family. Of course, that suggests the hemlock was put into the rice sometime between the time it was purchased and then eaten. The magistrate learned that Evette, the cook, purchased the rice a week before the deadly meal was served. Therefore, the family ate at least six evening meals, which usually include rice in some form, before they were poisoned. The hemlock could have been put into rice at any time in that week, but it's more likely the rice was poisoned the day or night before everyone was sickened."

"Why do you say that, Father?"

"Because of the hemlock's color and smell. Remember how Aveline described it to us. She said it was a disgusting greenish-yellow and smelled musty or mousey."

María Adela nodded. "I remember it. She said the stench made her retch."

"Exactly. If the hemlock had been put into the rice much earlier, the awful odor would have alerted anyone who took the cover off the container in which it was stored. The longer the hemlock was in the rice, the worse it would have smelled. After speaking to Dr. Messier, who treated everyone poisoned, the magistrate concluded that the must have been put in the rice the night before the next day's evening meal – at the earliest."

María Adela made a face. "That makes sense, I suppose."

"Despite your reluctance to credit the magistrate with sound reasoning, María Adela, you know it makes sense."

She smiled sheepishly. "The rice probably was poisoned the night before. I don't think it could have happened during the day. Lucille, Dieu ait son âme (God rest her soul), supervised the kitchen every day from noon until the last plate was put away after the evening meal. If she left the kitchen for any reason, one of her helpers would make sure nothing was touched. Lucille was very fastidious and would shoo away anyone who entered uninvited – even Paulette."

"What about the children? Didn't they come into the kitchen for sweets?"

"Yes, but only at four o'clock, when most of the food preparation was finished. Lucille never lets them in until that time in spite of their complaints. Of course, that afternoon the girls were with Aveline. Thank God!"

"That means the rice was not poisoned during the day. I assume the kitchen helpers are above suspicion?" Olivier rubbed a rough spot on his chin he had missed shaving that morning.

María Adela laughed. "Denise and Thérèse! They're

young girls, both under fourteen. They ate the rice, too, and were as deathly ill as everyone else. I saw the poor things myself when I went with Aveline to the house to help. It was the next afternoon after your visit when Aveline told you what had happened."

"So, who could have tampered with the rice the night before it was cooked? Was there anyone else in the house that evening with the exception of the Dumont family?"

"Only Charles Laroux. Poor lad, he was poisoned along with everyone else in the house and almost died. He usually eats once a week with the family and he was unfortunately there to eat the tainted rice. Aveline told me Charles suffered more than anyone else from the poison, of course, with the exception of Lucille. He lay feverish in bed for almost a week and Jean Bertin feared for his life. Then, only days out of his sick bed, he was struck down in the street."

"I met Charles Laroux a few days ago myself and the young man looks deathly pale. We were both walking along Chartres Street when I saw him coming toward me. His head was still bandaged when I spoke to him. After I inquired about the attack on him, he reluctantly admitted he continues to suffer headaches."

María Adela frowned. "I'm not surprised, Father. He was struck with a thick limb."

"He was indeed. The staff was more than two inches in diameter."

"Well, Father, what does our very knowledgeable magistrate say about how the hemlock was put into the rice? What are his conclusions now after all his interviews? He interviewed everyone in the house – no one was excluded, not even those poisoned."

"There is only one conclusion that can be reasonably made, María Adela, as I'm certain you know." Olivier spoke sharply. He was irritated by her sarcasm and continuing criticism of the magistrate. "Someone outside the house must have entered the kitchen to poison the rice – most likely the night before. Castañedo's conclusion was based on the fact the family's servants, with the exception of Tristan Surette, were the only ones in the kitchen during the day the dinner was prepared. And they were all poisoned, one of them fatally. Surette, of course, has been with the Dumonts for twenty-five years and the magistrate thought it unimaginable that he would be the poisoner. Besides, he was there in the kitchen only briefly to get flour for the cake Adeline was baking for the girls' party. It's therefore obvious the murderer somehow got into the house. The only question that remains, then, is how he managed to do it."

María Adela shook her head from side to side. "I have no idea."

"Since the front door is always locked – that's what Jean Bertin told the magistrate – is it at all possible that the back door might have been left open that night – either by error or when someone went to the outhouse?"

"No, definitely not!" María Adela made a face. "Everyone in the house uses a chamber pot at night. The back door is *only* open during the day when the servants come and go into the garden. If an intruder got into the house, I don't know how. Jean Bertin locks his house up like a jail at night, even before he hired those ruffians to protect the family. It began last year when someone broke into his office and stole some gold coins and a pocket-watch he kept in a locked chest. The chest had recently arrived from Paris and the thief or thieves broke it open with a bar of some kind. Jean Bertin was furious and swore his home or office wouldn't be robbed again."

"Was that before or after *La Bonne Chance* was robbed?"

"Several months before. The theft of the sloop's charts made him even more cautious, if that's possible. Since then, every building Jean Bertin owns has been under lock and key; a few like the imports storage building and sugar mill are even double locked. His own house as well as his mother's house each have a day and night guard now as well as two locks on all the doors. After what's happened, his caution is quite sensible, of course."

"I assume the locks and sentries were not in place before the poisonings." Olivier sat back in his chair and stretched out his legs, crossing them at the ankles.

"No, there were locks on the front doors of both the houses, but the back and side doors were latched with sliding bolts. Now, locks have been installed on them as well."

"What about the windows?"

"All the windows on the first floor are barred."

"Does the house have a watchdog?"

"No. The family dog, Candide, is a twelve-year-old sheepdog, who does little more than eat and sleep these days. He used to growl at strangers, but now he'll lick anyone who gives him a morsel of food. A pat on the head will get the same results. Candide spends all his time near the kitchen and would welcome anyone he saw with a wag of his tail."

"Well, it's obvious that someone got into the house that night and poisoned the rice. The only possible way would be through one of the doors. Unless one of the bolted or locked doors was left open, the intruder must have had a key to gain entry into the house. I will need to know how many keys were made for the locked doors and where they were kept in the house. Since Jean Bertin was so cautious, I would think he had one set of keys with him at all times."

"Would you like me to ask Paulette about them, Father?"

"Yes. I spoke to her at length after the deaths of her sons, but I now hesitate to approach her and bring up painful memories. The poor woman has suffered so much already."

"I'll be with the family on Saturday. I'll speak to Paulette then. Is there anything else you suggest I ask her?"

"Not for now, thank you, María Adela. The attempt to poison the Dumont family is the only event that can be investigated. I have nothing else. There is no more to be done with the wreckage of *La Bonne Chance* and the vicious attack on Charles Laroux has provided nothing to examine. The magistrate interviewed the two men who were near Laroux when he was assaulted. But neither of them saw the attacker clearly and he left nothing behind except the staff which he used to strike his victim. He vanished into the shadows leaving only the vague impression of a man in a dark cloak." Olivier grimaced. "That's why I have little to report to Jean Bertin."

"You can only tell him what you have found, Father. He'll have to accept that for now." María Adela spoke sternly. "With all his wealth, Jean Bertin has become accustomed to getting what he wants, when he wants it without waiting. Well, now he will have to be patient, a trait that even his mother says has not been his since childhood."

"Patience is hard for all of us, though surely harder for those accustomed to having their wants met immediately. Jean Bertin donated 10,000 pesetas for the renovation of Santa María, of course, with obvious expectations. Though unspoken, I'm certain his generous donation was only given in return for my continued investigation. He donated the money with the expectation that I would find the man who has apparently marked his family for death. I made it clear to him that I could not promise such success and we shook in agreement."

"Then, Father, why are you concerned?"

"Because I believe Jean Bertin still has that expectation despite the agreement. After what we found at the wreck of *La Bonne Chance*, he expects me to find the murderer. With that in his mind, he heard what he wanted to hear when we made our agreement. His money is now being used to renovate Santa María and I'm certain he expects progress in the investigation as a result."

"So, Father, you fear you have made a deal with the

devil." María Adela smirked.

"That's too strong a statement, María Adela, though I admit there's some truth in it."

CHAPTER FIVE

MOSQUITO CREEK AND NEW ORLEANS:
DECEMBER 3 – 15, 1799

He left the little village of Mosquito Creek (Crique de Mostique) in the late afternoon of December third. It was already getting dark when he rode his horse north toward New Orleans. He rode slowly, watching for potholes and washed-out portions of the mud-packed path. Many a rider had been crippled when his horse tripped in one of the holes and threw him to the ground. Holding the reins, he leaned over the left side of the horse's neck and scrutinized the path ahead. The horseman knew he had another mile of careful riding before the rutted pathway would meet the main road that ran alongside the Mississippi River.

He exhaled in relief when he rode out of a copse of trees and saw the river road fifty or so feet ahead of him. "The worst is over," he said aloud, "I'll be home in two hours and a half." He had reached the hard road just in time. The upper rim of the orange sun had dropped beneath the tree-line on the other side of the river and only its last light lingered in the western sky. Without the worry of a fall on the road, even in the darkness, he now could push his stallion to a fast trot the rest of the way to New Orleans.

Despite the cold wind in his face, he felt warm and comfortable. His time in Mosquito Creek had gone exactly as he had hoped. The girl, Suzanne, was no more than twelve years old and quite comely. Madame Villièrs swore the girl was still a virgin and said she had only three monthlies in her life. He believed the Madame, she had never lied to him in all the times he had come to her house. Still, he was relieved when Suzanne bled after he pierced her maidenhead. The girl also cried, but that was to be expected. Virgins always cried and he habitually paused after his first few thrusts to hear their weeping. It was another sign of their virginity.

He had demanded virgins in his initial conversation with Madame Villièrs. He refused to accept any others and that was why he rode once a month all the way to Mosquito Creek. In his search for a place where young virgins were available, he found the Villièrs house to be the nearest and most reliable of those he had visited. Each month, Madame Villiérs made sure she had two new girls available for him to make a selection. For that reason, he willingly took the four-hour long journey to the village even at a fast trot. In bad weather it took much longer and after the summer storm, he had spent six hours on the road returning to New Orleans.

`It was three years since he first rode to the out-of-the-way house in Mosquito Creek. He had arrived at midmorning when there were no other visitors at the house. His visit lasted only an hour and, after agreeing to financial arrangements, he left Madame Villièrs a sizeable deposit and rode back to New Orleans. The twice written and signed agreement was finalized with the touch of two glasses of wine. Each of them kept a copy of the agreement, which he had signed with the name of Molière. The madam smiled when she saw the name of the famous dramatist written on the agreement.

In addition to financial arrangements, the newly signed agreement included a number of Molière's stipulations that were to be strictly followed by Madame Villièrs. She was required to provide Molière with a young virgin to be selected from two girls brought before him each visit for his inspection. His selection would be scheduled one afternoon every month for a year from the date of his first visit. At the time of each monthly selection, the date of the next one would be scheduled. Missed visits were lost and could not be exchanged for later dates. Despite his protests that necessities of business or inclement weather might prevent him from making the scheduled visit, Madame Villiérs vehemently demanded that stipulation in their agreement. He smiled, recalling he had only missed one visit in three years.

Molière did not dispute her stipulation for long since he had his own list of demands. His most important stipulation was that Madame Villièrs make certain the selected girl was a virgin. Secondly, the girl had to be specially prepared for him. He wanted her to be scrubbed clean and well-groomed in every way. Her hair would be thoroughly washed, brushed and lightly perfumed with a flowery fragrance; her teeth similarly cleaned and her fingernails trimmed short, but not polished. He also wanted the girls breath freshened with a mint tea rinse. He had mentally listed the special preparations he wanted during his first journey to Mosquito Creek.

To keep her breath as fresh as possible, the selected girl was not allowed to eat anything until after he left her. Once his selection was made, the girl would await Molière in a room away from the noise of any other activity. She would wear a silk gown he brought from New Orleans. After their time together, the girl was instructed to bathe him in a tub full of warm fragrant water.

At their first meeting, Molière told Madame Villièrs. to

state her price and, when she suggested a costly amount, he raised it by half. He counted out enough gold coins to cover the cost of six visits and handed them to her.

"Here is a binding deposit, Madame Villièrs." His face was fixed and granite hard. "I'm paying you dearly, so you won't be tempted to alter our agreement. I will honor my part and I *expect* you to honor yours. I trust that is satisfactory."

Madame Villièrs nodded her head several times. She looked into his staring eyes and felt a shiver of fear run down her back.

Molière did not tell her his reasons for the special preparations he required. He lived in dread of getting the great pox (syphilis). As an eleven-year-old boy, he had seen the misery of his favorite uncle, who lingered for years with its symptoms before he died in excruciating pain. The memory of his uncle's suffering remained in his mind all through his youth and, as a grown man, he vowed to avoid it no matter the temptations. He had been told the pox was a woman's affliction and could only be avoided by bedding virgins.

Driven by lust, he had bedded an adult woman only once in his life. It happened a week after his fifteenth birthday. The woman, Lys Latour, was a thirty-year-old seamstress who knew no man would ever marry her. She had a shortened leg and limped in an ungainly way that left her without suitors. Her parents were attending a cousin's confirmation at the cathedral when he went to her house and knocked on the door. His mother sent him there to pick up a torn dress the seamstress had repaired. He had gone to the Latour house on other occasions and always was told to wait outside, but this time she invited him inside and told him to wait in the living room.

The room was dimly lit with the shutters closed and only one oil lamp burning on a low wick. Becoming impatient, he walked around the room and looked at the old paintings on the walls. They were portraits of unsmiling people from the past, whom he thought must be family ancestors. He guessed the family must have once been wealthy when living in France. There was also a portrait copy of the French king, Louis XVI, on the wall.

Absorbed in his examination of the family portraits, he did not see her return to the room. Lys entered silently on bare feet and stood behind him, waiting for him to see her. She wore only a thin nightgown that revealed her naked body.

He turned, suddenly aware of her presence behind him. He stood in shock and stared at her body, his eyes fixed on her dark nipples and the triangle of black hair between her legs. He immediately became erect and watched in wonderment as she approached him. She moved step by step slowly, her breasts cupped in her hands. A foot from him, she lifted the gown over her head and dropped it to the floor. She took his head in her hands and pressed his mouth and lips to her breasts moving them back and forth across his face.

"Suck them, suck those nipples, boy! Lick them, Oh yes, lick them. Don't stop!"

She pushed him to the hard floor and sat astride him, rubbing herself against him. She moved off him momentarily, hurriedly unbuttoned his breaches and pulled them down with his underwear. He lay there not knowing what to do, except to lift his buttocks off the floor as she yanked the breaches down to his thighs. Then, she was over him, her legs apart, her knees pressing against his hips. She cried out as she guided him into her body and paused with her eyes closed.

Seconds later, she opened her eyes and, while staring down at him, she began slowly to move up and down. She held her hands out as if in pain and moaned loudly as she moved faster and faster over him. He had already exploded inside her when she reached a frenzied pace, her body trembling. Then she screamed "Mon Dieu!" and collapsed on top of him, kissing his face and lips. She lay on top of him the warmth and wet of her body her flowing over him.

Afterwards, he ran home and immediately took a bath. He felt filthy from being with the woman and scrubbed his body with a rough cloth. Terrified he would get the pox, he scrubbed his member until raw and bleeding and then shuddered in pain when he pulled on his underwear. Crying in despair, he dressed and tried to put the memory of what had happened out of his mind.

But try as he might, he could not escape the vivid pictures of her in his mind's eye. Nor could he escape the animal sounds she made and the feeling of her sweaty body on him. He could still see her trembling flesh and frantic eyes; he could still feel her wetness that seemed to spread out over his stomach; he could still hear her grunts and groans. The more he thought about his time with her, the more it disgusted him. He felt nauseous recalling her slobbering tongue kisses and the smell of garlic on her breath. The rank smell remained with him for days afterwards,

On the way home, he vowed never to be with another woman again. If he did not die of the pox, he would avoid women the rest of his life. He would become a monk and live secluded in a monastery. A year later in the heat of July, he changed his mind when he had an unexpected encounter in the woods with a thirteen-year-old Indian girl. They swam naked in a fresh-water pond and then lay together in a nearby clearing among the pine trees. The girl was a virgin and he felt clean and exuberant after being with her.

His many attempts to find her again unfortunately failed and he spent the next three years in vain looking for another young girl like her. There were only older girls and women available to him, but they never aroused him. In fact, their eager willingness and nudity only disheartened him and left him flaccid and incapable of bedding them.

Then, sometime later, in a gentlemen's club, he overheard a group of members discussing the various houses of women accessible in and around New Orleans. Although the men spoke in low voices, he did hear them mention several brothels where virgins were occasionally available for a much higher price than the other women. Excited by the possibility of finding a young girl, he spent the next six weeks visiting the so-called *best brothels* in New Orleans and the surrounding towns.

His search, however, failed and, disappointed, he almost gave up looking for the virgins he sought. Despite the claims of the houses he visited, there were few *really* young girls and even fewer virgins among the scores of older girls and women he saw. The occasional young girls he did eventually view were usually sullen, unkempt or simply unattractive to him. Following weeks of futile searching, he finally heard about the Villièrs house and the young girls who lived there.

He learned of the house from a merchant he knew from Baton Rouge. The merchant was married, but always enjoyed the company of a much younger woman when he came to conduct business in New Orleans. On one of his visits, it was on the fourteenth of September, 1796, the merchant appeared with a lovely and *very young* girl on his arm. He would never forget the day, a Tuesday, because it so altered his life. The next day after finishing their business, the merchant told him the girl was a thirteen-year old virgin from the Villièrs house in Mosquito Creek. The merchant had hired the girl from Madame Villièrs for his four-day stay in New Orleans.

A week later, he rode down to Mosquito Creek to meet Madame Villièrs and look over the girls in the house. By that time, he was desperate to be with a woman, even if not a virgin. He could think of little else during the day and his mind was full of images of beautiful girls lying beneath him. At night, he found relief rubbing his member against a piece of rabbit fur an old trapper had given him. But his insatiable desires inevitably returned with the daylight and, on the way to his office, he had to control a sudden urge to seize a pretty schoolgirl walking in the street.

Since that unforgettable day with the Indian girl, he had been with only one other virgin – a slave girl he had for no more than five minutes on the stinking deck of a fishing boat. He paid the Welsh captain an excessive amount of money for the wretched experience. Then, afterwards, the burly man gleefully told him he had watched the *pitiful performance* from behind the mast. He instantly wanted to kill the captain, but the shrewd man had taken his loaded pistol and sword after they settled the price for the girl and put them on the dock beside the ship.

At the Villièrs house, he was delighted to learn that on occasion the madam did purchase virgins for her customers. She explained that they cost much more, but could be made available for a weekly or monthly payment. The cost, even if exorbitant, was of no concern to him. He was willing to pay whatever it cost to have a new untouched girl accessible every month. After their first meeting, he rode away feeling so pleased he decided to give a donation to the cathedral.

Now, years later, he had more than enough young girls to satisfy his needs. He smiled as he rode toward New Orleans and saw the lighted lamps ahead at the southern gates. There were two girls exclusively available to him in New Orleans as well as a new girl selected every month in Mosquito Creek. Madame Villièrs now chose the girl for him each month; she knew the kind of girl he wanted, a slender girl with dark hair and eyes and a happy face. The new ones always excited him the most, no matter how well the New Orleans girls performed for him. He enjoyed their innocence, naivety and, of course, their virginity and foolish trust in him.

He often wondered where Madame Villièrs got the young

girls. There were no more than seven or eight of the same girls in the house from one monthly visit to the next. They were not only Acadian, Mestizo or Indian girls either. They spoke a variety of languages: English, French, Portuguese and Spanish. The one he took to *La Bonne Chance*, in fact, spoke Spanish. "What was that one's name? María Isabel? All those Portuguese and Spanish girls were named María. Whatever the girl's name, she was a warm little wench and anxious to please and do whatever he wanted. She even knew enough French to speak to him.

She was the one girl he had met outside the house. He told her he loved her and wanted her to live with him in his home. He smiled recalling the kisses she had given him when he told her of his plan to take her away with him. He had hugged her to him and whispered his scheme in her ear. She was to say nothing to any of the other girls, even if one or two of them were her friends. She had to promise and cross her heart not to tell anyone. She beamed when he told her he would come back for her that very night.

As instructed, the little girl waited until the Madame and the other girls were asleep and then slipped out of a window to meet him. He waited in the woods near the white gate and held his finger to his lips to keep her from speaking when she saw him. They walked a long distance down the path before mounting the stallion he had left tied to a tree.

No one in the house heard them ride away and Madame Villièrs never suspected he had anything to do with her sudden disappearance that summer night. She never even mentioned the girl was gone. Madame Villièrs often told him where the girls went after their brief time in her house; they usually spent no more than five or six months in Mosquito Creek. Afterwards, the girls became servants of the wealthy families in New Orleans or were sent to other cities and towns in Louisiana. A few of them were even sent to families in Florida.

As he and the madam became acquainted, they would sit together in her parlor and talk before a girl was brought to him. They talked while her niece, Gisella, prepared the chosen girl for her afternoon with him. Eventually, their time together included lunch and wine. Knowing he usually arrived at noon, Madame Villièrs had a lunch of soup or stew ready when he rode up to the house. She found he preferred fish soup and rabbit stew. In return, he brought a bottle of French wine from New Orleans for them to share with lunch.

Insisting on privacy after his first visit, he paid Madame Villièrs extra to close the house to other customers on the afternoons he came to Mosquito Creek. She readily agreed since most of the men came at night to her house. Thereafter, he came and went without anyone, except the madam, her niece and the girls in the house aware of his visits.

He smiled again, thinking his visits to the house would never become known. He would never be dishonored or lose his gentleman's standing in town. Even if Madame Villièrs became incapacitated or died or the Spanish officials closed the brothel, his monthly visits would never be revealed. He was Molière in Mosquito Creek and Madame Villièrs held their agreement to prove it. If there was ever an inquiry involving the patrons of the house, the officials would not approach him, no, they would have to interview Monsieur Molière. He snickered as his stallion stopped behind a merchant's wagon waiting to enter the city gates.

He followed eight other horsemen and four merchants' wagons into New Orleans. The carriages of three wealthy men had been waved ahead and were entering the city as he joined the line. They moved forward without a pause, while the others had to be identified. Entering the gates, he turned his thoughts to the plan that was on his mind night and day. He nodded perfunctorily to the lone sentry, thinking of what next needed to be done. There were still so many in his way.

Olivier went to see Magistrate Castañedo early in the morning. It was a dark rainy day, the fifth in a row, and almost everyone complained about roof and window leaks and impassable puddles in the streets. "It'll be dry tomorra, but bitter cold by mornin," an old Acadian woman told him after first Mass. Olivier wore a hooded cloak which was soaked through by the time he reached the Cabildo. Inside, he took the cloak off and shook it before carrying it on his arm. He shivered, feeling his sodden neck and shoulders. The cold rain had dripped through the woolen cloak and wet the upper portion of his cassock. Olivier walked carefully avoiding slippery areas on the stone floor, where rain water had fallen from the clothes of earlier visitors to the Cabildo. He brushed his fingers through his wet hair as he reached the door to the magistrate's office.

"Hang your wet cloak on the edge of the door there," Castañedo told Olivier, when the magistrate's clerk ushered him into his superior's office. The magistrate gestured to the clerk. "Ayala, bring us a pot of tea and a towel – two towels."

"Thank you, Magistrate."

Castañedo waited until Olivier had toweled himself off and sipped some of the hot tea before speaking to him. "I hear you have made a number of renovations at Santa María, Father."

"Yes, Monsieur Dumont has made a very generous donation to the church. We've just started and there is yet much to be done."

"Ah, Monsieur Dumont. So, I assume he has asked you to assist him again. I know enough about the man to doubt he donated the money without expecting something in return."

Olivier nodded.

"He thinks we're incompetent, doesn't he?" Castañedo

made a face. "The French have little, if any, trust in us. It's as if we Spaniards seized this colony as a prize in war. Don't they know that France and Spain were allied against England in the Seven Years War? No, they don't know and don't care. Nor do they know Louisiana was *given* to Spain by the French themselves – by Louis XV. Forgive me, Father, I know you are well aware of the history."

"It's true, the French still doubt the sincerity and worth of the Spaniards in Louisiana, no matter the growth and prosperity of the colony."

"It's astonishing since we've now been here since 1764 – thirty-six years! Dios mio!" Castañedo sighed. "Well, there's nothing to be done to change their thinking, now. Maybe, in time? Quien sabe? Tell me, Father, what have you found since you resumed your investigation?"

"Very little – in fact, no more than you."

The magistrate shook his head. "I don't know that there's any more to be found. The man who attacked Monsieur Laroux was not seen clearly by *anyone*. It's as if he appeared like some specter from the dark, struck Laroux with the tree limb and then instantly disappeared. The man who poisoned the rice wasn't even seen! I assume he's the same man who attacked Laroux. And, no one saw him picking spotted hemlock in the woods or mixing it into the Dumont family's rice."

Olivier nodded. "Yes, and no one was seen tampering with the sloop before it sunk."

"Exactamente. It's hard to imagine how anyone could sabotage the ship anyway since it was kept at the family's pier behind a locked gate. The same is true of the poisoning – at night, that house was locked up like a medieval maid's chastity belt. Furthermore, the only keys to the locks were held by Monsieur and Madame Dumont. How then could someone enter the house in the dark of night? During the day, no one except family members and servants came in and out of the house – and it's unlikely one of them poisoned the rice since everyone was deathly ill after eating the poisoned rice. The one servant who didn't eat the rice is an elderly man who has been with the family for thirty years. So, I can't imagine him as the murderer."

"It's baffling, isn't it?"

"It is. It's almost enough to make me believe in demons or ghosts who become invisible at will." Castañedo looked at Olivier and laughed. "Of course, I know better. These murderous acts are the work of a man. But, so far, we haven't found anything substantial to lead us to him."

"What about the girl's body found in the lake?"

"We have no notion of her identity; no one reported her missing. The medical examiner says she was young – well under twenty. But he could say little else because her body had been in the water for so long. It also had been badly mutilated by the fish in the lake. In addition to bites all over her body, she lost fingers and toes and other body pieces. The fish, probably bass, even took the poor girl's eyes and ears and a portion of her nose."

Olivier made a face. "Did the medical examiner think the dead girl was drowned at the time the sloop sank or afterwards?" Olivier shivered as drops of water dripped down his spine.

"He didn't know. That was the first question I asked him. It occurred to me too that the girl might well have been in the cabin with the boys when they drowned. If so, she then must have been missed by the divers who brought up the boys' bodies."

"The divers would have been looking for two corpses, not three, and overlooked her."

"That's exactly what they said when I interviewed them after the girl's body was found. Though hard to imagine in that small cabin, it's possible her body was hidden behind or beneath something in the cabin when they retrieved the boys' bodies. She was a tiny girl." He shrugged. "Then later her corpse floated free when the ship was broken apart by the storm."

Olivier nodded. "That makes sense. The only other possibility is that her body was blown there during the storm. But from where? There's no settlement or Indian village nearby."

"Yes, Father, it's more likely the girl was in the sloop when it sank – especially since she was naked. It appears she was with the two boys for the night. The lake was a perfect place for a ménage à trois." Castañedo held up a hand. "Forgive me, Father."

"No se preocupe (Don't be concerned), Magistrate. I'm neither ignorant nor surprised by the sensual practices of our people. That would also explain why the boys sailed the sloop to that secluded lake in the first place." Olivier toweled the last of the moisture from his hair and neck. His shoulders were still cold and wet, but he knew there was nothing to be done about it until his cassock dried.

"Yes, Father. I initially wondered why the two lads sailed there. The discovery of the girl's body, of course, told me they were not there for fishing." Pleased with what he thought was a witty comment, Castañedo chuckled, hoping Olivier would be amused as well. He was rewarded with a slight smile on the priest's lips.

Olivier nodded. "The discovery of the body also explains why no one in their family was told where they were going. It was obviously intended to be secret rendezvous."

"Exactamente! It's what I would expect any young men to do at their age. Forgive me, Father, I'm not disrespectful of the Church's teaching. I'm quite aware of the virtue of chastity before marriage, but I'm also aware of the lusts of youth. I recall my own youth."

Olivier smiled. "What you say is indeed true, Magistrate. At that age, young men are rarely spiritual in thought. Keep in mind, I once was young, too."

Castañedo returned the smile. "Ah, those long lost days. Well, let's continue. It's the nudity of the girl that convinces me of the purpose of their anchorage at the lake."

"It does suggest a tryst." Olivier held up a hand. "But, before we say any more about it, we must question the plan to sail to that lake. Was it really secret? If so, how did the murderer know about it? It seems to me that he either knew about it earlier or followed the sloop in his own ship. I doubt the latter possibility because the boys would have observed a ship following them – especially during the day when they must have sailed into the lake. But, somehow the murderer knew about their plan to bring the girl aboard the sloop and stay at the lake overnight."

"So it seems. The man knows too much. Not only did he know about the location of the tryst and when it would take place, he knew how to enter Dumont's locked house at night. He also knew when and where to attack Laroux at the end of the day. It's as if he knows everything about the family – what they do and where they go every day."

"Yet, there appears to be no one associated with the family who has such knowledge and would try to murder them. With Dumont's permission, I have spoken to the house servants and I'm certain none of them had anything to do with the attacks on his family. Most of the servants are women anyway and those few who are men have been with the family for more than fifteen years. Besides, they look to be too old or infirm to commit such acts." Olivier sighed.

"It's bewildering."

"It is. I suppose to be thorough, I'll need to interview the superintendents of Dumont's mills and farms as well as all his clerks. There's also that large man, Tristan Surette, who does a variety of tasks for the Dumont family. Jean Bertin also employs a clever young Acadian clerk at his office. His name is Jean-Baptiste Leblanc. He's one of the many

Acadian boys Dumont has sent to school over the years. An admirable act on his part."

Castañedo snorted. "Admirable you say, Father. The schooling costs Dumont nothing. He sends them to the *free Spanish school*, which the French colonists condemn as inferior. They, of course, send *their* children to costly private schools or employ tutors in their homes. As for the Acadian boys, after finishing school, Dumont puts them to work in his various enterprises – of course, at low wages."

"Is that so?" Olivier had heard similar stories of Jean Bertin's stinginess.

"Yes. It's also said that at least two of those Acadian boys are his children. A decade or so ago, Dumont had a young mistress from the lowlands. Yes, it's true! He had the audacity to keep her here in one of his rental houses on Borbón Street. I saw her myself – the girl was little more than thirteen years of age. I don't know what became of her."

"I see." Olivier grimaced, recalling what María Adela had said about Dumont. "With all his wealth, Jean Bertin has become accustomed to getting what he wants, when he wants it."

"That's not idle gossip, Father. Dumont has secluded other girls here in town in the past as well. He foolishly thinks his adulterous activities have been unobserved, but many eyes have seen his comings and goings to that house on Borbón Street. For a number of years, I've been told his weekly schedule included afternoon trysts on Tuesdays and Fridays."

Olivier frowned. He had heard enough about Dumont's debauchery. "Speaking of girls, isn't it unusual for one to be found dead without a mother or father appearing to claim her body for burial? I'm thinking, of course, of the girl found in the wreckage of *La Bonne Chance*."

"It's quite unusual, Father. After the storm, there were

God-knows-how-many children's bodies found in the lowlands and all of them were claimed and identified."

"Then, what makes this girl so unusual? Why hasn't she been identified? She may well be significant to the investigation."

Castañedo nodded. "Since no one in and around New Orleans has inquired about her, we must assume she's not from here. She could have come off a ship, of course, but I think someone would have seen her somewhere on the dock and notified us. As you know, the discovery of her corpse is well known now. The news of death usually travels like the wind in a storm. It's now even known in Manchac and as far away as Baton Rouge."

Olivier frowned. "Do you think the lack of a facial description might have impeded any inquiries about her? I know there isn't much that can be said about her appearance after all the time she was in the water."

"No, I haven't received notices of any lost girls in quite a while. And all the broadsides I sent about her to the towns and villages in southern Louisiana were ignored. Not one reply was forthcoming. I sent them a week after her body was found. I waited as long as possible and then had the girl buried outside of the city. As you know, the Church requires such a burial since we didn't know if she was Catholic."

"So, she remains unknown. That's unfortunate. Knowledge of her name might have helped in the investigation."

"It is unfortunate, Father, but I don't know where else to look for her name."

Olivier saw Castañedo cock his head to the side. "You've thought of something?"

"Perhaps." He held up one finger. "There's one place near New Orleans where a number of unidentified girls currently live and that's Mosquito Creek."

"Where's Mosquito Creek? I never heard of it."

"It's an Acadian fishing village southeast of New

Orleans. The village is small and only noteworthy for its mosquitos and brothel. The villagers allow the brothel to exist there because the owner, a French woman named Villièrs, pays them a percentage of her profits. They don't interfere with her business and, in fact, protect the brothel's operation. They are always watchful for any of my men and warn the Villièrs woman if they see them near the village."

"Ah, yes, I now recall hearing the parish pastor speak of the sinful place."

"The brothel obviously prospers because of the pretty girls who are available there. But it also prospers because Madame Villièrs safeguards the identity of her clients; some I've heard are from prominent families here in town. Her house is also notable for the fine rum, whiskey and wine served there. Many a man from New Orleans sneaks down to the house and it's a four- hour ride there in good weather. It's said the house is full of men on any given night. I've heard the girls come and go – some supposedly virgins, which, of course, adds to the brothel's appeal."

"Magistrate, are you saying innocent young girls are corrupted in that brothel?"

"That's what I've heard, although we've never seen a single girl in the house. Over the years, I've sent as many as six teams of men to Mosquito Creek. But not once have we seen the girls. We would have closed the brothel if only *one* girl was found on the premises."

"Why have none of the girls ever been seen?"

"As I said earlier, the villagers, watch the road for our men. We think they post at least one watcher night and day. So, when the uniformed men are seen, the madam is warned and the girls are hidden, probably among the houses in the village. We have even tried to send men in colonists' clothing and still haven't caught the brothel unaware. Of course, it's the same here in New Orleans. Any number of brothels thrive in this city and we rarely catch them in operation."

Olivier sighed. "I'm not surprised."

"It's the same with unlicensed taverns and gambling dens – no matter how many we close, they reappear like cockroaches after a house cleaning. We can't stop them anymore than we can stop dueling or drunkenness."

"I suppose not." Olivier wondered if Castañedo mentioned drunkenness and taverns as a subtle hint to him that he knew of his weakness for drink. He scrutinized the magistrate's face, but did not see a knowing expression in it. The magistrate was frowning, obviously frustrated by his inability to close down the illegal activities in New Orleans.

"Well, returning to the unknown dead girl, I think a trip will have to be made to Mosquito Creek. We need to know if the girl came from the brothel." Castañedo grimaced. "I don't look forward to the long ride, but I must be the one to do it."

"With your permission, I would like to accompany you."

Castañedo raised his eyebrows. "The bishop will allow it?"

"I will ask Father Antonio, the parish priest. As the pastor of Santa María I am under his authority and it is his decision to make."

"Well then, if permission is granted, we should leave for Mosquito Creek in the next few days. How about Wednesday morning at first light? It would be best if we arrived early – quien sabe (who knows), we might even reach the house before the girls are hidden away."

Lieutenant Palacios Leguía led the way as they left the main road and walked their horses onto the rutted path that led to Mosquito Creek. They dismounted beside a moss covered live-oak and stretched after the long journey. Olivier and Castañedo were saddle-sore from their time on the road and grimaced in pain as they stepped hesitantly down from the horses. The lieutenant, a young man in his early twenties, was barely able to hide his smile as he watched the two older men dismount. He had seemingly vaulted from his saddle to the ground.

They had ridden out of New Orleans in darkness as the first slice of sunlight creased the eastern horizon. The night lamps still burned and provided more than enough light for them to trot through town and leave through the southern gates. It was a mild morning and they rolled up their coats and tied them behind their saddles. An hour into their journey, they stopped for a few minutes and drank the last of the lukewarm tea they carried in their canteens. By that time, bright sunlight flooded the river valley and they rode three-abreast on the hard road. Few riders were out that morning and they only occasionally had to form a single line to pass carriages or wagons headed toward New Orleans. They had even been able to gallop freely for a few miles over a stretch of hard-packed mud beside the river.

"Well done." Castañedo looked at his pocket watch. "We reached this road to the house in less than three hours. Of course, that's what my watch says; my backside and legs tell me my watch is broken and it took much longer."

"Mine tells me it took *much* longer!" Olivier grimaced again as he stretched out his legs.

Castañedo pointed down the path to Mosquito Creek. "Lieutenant, let's walk the horses a little distance. It's still early, only eight o'clock; we have plenty of time. You lead the way."

Fifty minutes later, they rode through the tiny village and up to the big clapboard house on the creek. The brothel stood at the end of the village some two hundred yards from the last house on the street. It was a two-story wooden building that had been recently renovated with a new cedar roof and outside planking. The freshly cut cedar still retained its distinctive odor. A new oak door also had been installed and painted dark brown. The trim around the second floor dormers and all the window frames were painted the same color.

There was not a sound to be heard in or about the house when they rode up to the gate. It appeared as if empty or everyone was still asleep. The little village had looked asleep as well and not one of its residents had come outside as they rode along its only street.

Castañedo smiled at Olivier as they looked back at the village. "Mosquito Creek is not a ghost town. Look at the smoke coming up from the chimneys. There are women and children in every one of these houses. They just won't show themselves while their men are gone. The men have already left for the day; they're out on the bayous fishing. Girls from the brothel probably are also inside some of them."

Olivier nodded and dismounted after the magistrate. The lieutenant, already standing on the ground, took the reins of the horses and tied them to posts nearest the front gate of the house. There were twelve posts lined up along the fence.

Castañedo pointed to the posts and chuckled. "It seems that Madame Villièrs has a lot of visitors to her house. I *wonder* why? Well, let's announce ourselves, though I'm sure everyone in Mosquito Creek knows we're here. They knew it as soon as we turned off the main road."

The magistrate opened the gate and Olivier and the lieutenant followed him on the stone path to the house. Madame Villièrs answered the door on the second knock. She stood there in the doorway dressed in a long dark blue dress. Olivier thought she looked like one of the many motherly women he had seen over the years in church, a stout woman with graying brown hair and a fleshy heart-shaped face. She wore no makeup.

"How may I help you gentlemen?" Madame Villièrs spoke softly in what Olivier knew was Parisian French. He recalled her pronunciation from all the years he lived in Paris during his youth and novitiate. For a moment, he felt nostalgic for the great city he had once known so well with its magnificent churches, hundreds of carriages and crowds of people. A memory of his last visit to the Cathedral of Notre Dame passed through his mind as he turned to the magistrate.

Castañedo coldly nodded to the woman. "We are here to speak with you. I assume you are Madame Villièrs, the owner of this house."

"I am." She crossed her arms over breasts.

"I am Major Carlos Castañedo Obregon, the Cabildo Magistrate of New Orleans, and this is Lieutenant Palacios Leguía, my aide at the Magistrate's Office." Standing straight as a ship's mast, his chin pointed out, he pointed to the mustached lieutenant and then formally bowed to Olivier. "And accompanying us is Father Olivier of the New Orleans Cathedral Parish."

"I see. Welcome Magistrate, Father." She nodded to the lieutenant. "Please come in and sit in the parlor. I'll have my niece Gisella bring us some tea."

For the first few minutes, Castañedo waited patiently while everyone engaged in polite conversation about the high prices of food and the cold weather. They also talked briefly about the new cedar planking and its expected longevity. Then, as if on a cue he heard in his mind, the magistrate brought up the reason for his visit. He held up his hand and interrupted the lieutenant in the middle of a story about a burro he had seen stuck that morning in an ice puddle.

"Pardon me, Lieutenant, but I think it's time to tell Madame Villièrs why we are here in her house."

"Yes, sir."

Castañedo paused to thank the hunchbacked woman, introduced as Gisella, for the cup of tea she served him. He then waited while Gisella handed everyone a cup of tea and set a plate of pastries on a low table in front of them. She smiled as they thanked her and then left the room. Olivier was the first to take a pastry and the lieutenant immediately followed him. Castañedo smiled, but did not reach for one.

"Madame, we know the nature of this house." Castañedo held up his hand again to stop her from protesting. "Please Madame be patient and listen. We are well aware of the business you conduct in this house – according to our records, it has been in existence some seventeen or eighteen years. But we are not here to obstruct your business nor are we here to close the house. Those are not our intentions. We are here on another matter entirely."

Puzzled, Madame Villièrs cocked her head to the side and frowned.

"We are here to ask you some questions concerning the death of a young girl near New Orleans. We think she might have come from this house."

"Do you indeed, Magistrate? Pray tell me what makes you think the girl came from this house in Mosquito Creek? A girl found dead near New Orleans?" Madame Villièrs spoke in a tone edged with sarcasm. Her lips curled into a sneer as she looked at him and leaned back into her high-backed chair.

The magistrate stared at her and said nothing for almost a minute. When he did speak his face had hardened and a muscle twitched in his jaw.

"I will permit no disrespect, Madame Villièrs. If you dare speak to me in that tone again, you will pay for it. I expect you to answer my questions respectfully and truthfully. If not, I will see to it that this house never operates again. Is that understood?"

Madame Villièrs narrowed her eyes as she stared at the magistrate. She said nothing, but it was apparent from her curled lips that she doubted he could carry out his threat. She sipped her tea and studied him over the rim of her cup.

"Make no mistake, Madame, I will do what I say. If you foolishly think your prominent clients in New Orleans will prevent me from closing the house, as in the past, you are mistaken. No matter what they say to the governor, I will find a way to end your business in this village. All I have to do is inform Bishop Meléndez of your *immoral* activities here and he will not only excommunicate you and your whores, but he will also threaten to excommunicate the men who visit the house. I'll even tell you how it will be done without knowing any of their names."

Madame Villièrs looked down at the floor, her face contorted to keep from crying. She did not want him to tell her how the house could be closed. She always knew it was possible and had worried over the years that a narrow-minded magistrate one day would do it.

"I'll station a couple of my uniformed men on the road to Mosquito Creek for a week or two and get the name of every rider heading to your house. I'll then forward the names to the bishop. We shall see then how many men will be willing to frequent this house thereafter. If you think you can defy me …"

"What is it you want to know, Magistrate?" Madame Villèrs spoke softly, her face now pale, her eyes wet.

"We know you keep a number of young girls in the house. Though I'm certain they are well hidden at the moment, we know they are here. It's indeed the reason so many men journey such a distance to Mosquito Creek six evenings of the week. Is that not true?"

Madame Villièrs sighed and then nodded. "It's true."

"How many girls are here at this time?"

"There are nine now. One of the girls left yesterday." Madame Villièrs dabbed her eyes with a white lace handkerchief.

"How is it that these girls come to your house, Madame?"

She sighed loudly. "They are girls no one wants. Orphans, whose families deserted them or who died at sea or in the plagues, stowaways who arrived hidden and starved in ships, beaten children who fled from drunken fathers, beggars from Europe who saved up only enough coins to pay their way here, young widows and unwanted wives who were sold from man to man and eventually discarded. Shall I continue, Magistrate?"

Castañedo frowned. "No, that's quite enough." He nodded to Olivier who signaled his wish to ask the madam a question.

"Madame Villièrs, has not the Church provided sanctuary for such girls? What about the Ursuline Convent? I understand hundreds of girls are schooled there."

"Not the poor homeless girls who come to this house, Father. Most of the convent girls have families who make annual donations. Many are boarded at the convent, I've heard as many as a hundred, and another hundred or so come to school daily from the city. But unfortunately few, if any of those girls, are penniless orphans, who are seemingly everywhere on the streets of New Orleans."

"What about the orphanage? I know it's small, but surely it serves some of the girls of whom you speak." Olivier did not want to believe that destitute girls had come to the brothel because there was no place better for them to live in New Orleans.

Madam Villièrs shook her head. "The orphanage is in the home of Monsieur Beaurosier and much too small to accommodate all the girls who need help. He's a well-intentioned man, but it's said that the children run amok there and the boys are cruel to the girls. There have been girls in the house who once lived in the orphanage and fled here to escape the cruelty. There are none here at the moment."

Olivier exhaled his breath loudly. "It's said the girls come and go from here. How long do they stay here and where do they go when they leave."

"None stay more than four months,. Many are hired as servants in wealthy homes in New Orleans. The families have heard about the girls situations, and they notify me when they are need of servant girls. I teach the girls good manners and appearance and how to serve the needs of a household. So, they are much desired."

"So, Madame Villièrs, are we to believe your house is a girls' school for servants rather than a house of prostitution." Castañedo smirked as he spoke to her.

Madame Villièrs gave the magistrate a sharp look. "It's both.. The girls earn their keep, learn to perform house duties here and leave with pesetas in their purses. Even if they leave without arrangements for future employment, the girls have money to support themselves, at least, for a while."

"I assume the families in New Orleans pay you a fee for providing them with servants." The smirk was still on Castañedo's face. "So, you profit in two ways from the use of the girls – one, as putas (prostitutes) in your house and two, as a paid alcahueta (pimp) of servants."

"Yes, Magistrate." Madame Villièrs' face reddened.

Olivier interrupted Castañedo's questioning. He worried his combative manner might make her unwilling to help them identify the drowned girl. "Madame, you said many girls became servants in New Orleans. What about the others?"

"Some left for New Orleans without the benefit of prior arrangements. I'm not certain what has become of them. Others left with men who promised marriage or other arrangements, some as their mistresses. A few continue their lives as they did here. I saw one of them in the market the last time I went to New Orleans."

"Does that account for all the girls who left the house?" Olivier watched as she held a finger on her cheek and stared.

"With the exception of two," she replied after a moment's pause. "One was taken away by an older brother who had made his way as a carpenter's apprentice in Manchac. The two of them, as children, had come to New Orleans together as stowaways and he had vowed to come get her when he found work."

"And the other girl?" Olivier exchanged looks with Castañedo as the madam recalled what had happened to her.

"That girl ... what was her name? She disappeared one night after everyone was asleep. She was the only girl to leave without a notice of any kind. Ah, I remember her now her name was María Isabel Mendoza – a Spanish girl. None of the other girls knew where she had gone. In fact, they were surprised she left."

"How could she possibly leave this remote place without help? She would need a horse or carriage. I can't imagine her walking to New Orleans, can you?" Castañedo stared at her.

"I don't know how María Isabel left Mosquito Creek. She obviously had help. When I found her missing the next morning, I assumed she left with one of the men she had spent time with the previous day. But I had no notion which man it might have been."

"Why was that? Were there *so* many men with her the previous night?"

"No, as I recall there were only three. One in the afternoon and two at night."

"Only three!" Castañedo scowled at her. "Do you recall the names of the three men?"

"No, but even if I did, the names they use are seldom their real names. Many of the men are gentlemen and, since they don't want their family names or titles revealed here, they use false names – if they use any names at all."

Castañedo nodded. "That's understandable."

Madame Villièrs did recall the name of the client who had been with María Isabel in the afternoon. It was Molière, but she dismissed him as the man who might have arranged to leave with the girl. She knew his ways. He came early in the day, usually at noon, and left well before evening. He followed that schedule on each monthly visit and always wanted a new girl.

"I don't suppose you know when the men who were

with María Isabel left that night?"

"I do know. The men *all* leave at midnight – that's when I close up the house. A villager with a lantern leads them out to the main road. The path to Mosquito Creek is full of holes. It's difficult to ride during the day; at night it's perilous. More than a few drunken men have fallen from their horses at night. One hit his head on a large rock and died."

Olivier asked softly, "Madame, do you remember when María Isabel disappeared from the house? The month?"

Madame Villièrs replied without a second's hesitation. "It was last summer in August – sometime around the middle of the month."

Castañedo asked, "So, María Isabel told no one where she was going – not you, not any of the girls. Nor did she reveal the name of the man who took her away. She must have been excited and told someone – surely, she had a close friend here, someone with whom she shared secrets?"

"She did have a good friend, Magistrate, it was the girl who shared a bedroom with her. The girl was Spanish, too. Her name was Ana Luisa. But she swore to me that María Isabel told her nothing and I believed her."

"Did Ana Luisa tell you anything about a man in particular who pleased María Isabel?" The magistrate now spoke politely to Madame Villièrs.

"No, but ..." The madam held up her forefinger and paused to remember. "Ana Luisa did tell me she saw María Isabel climb out the window that night and run to the white gate where someone stood waiting. She awoke when María Isabel climbed out the window. The window in that bedroom is over a storage shed in the back and only a few feet from the top of the shed. So, the girl climbed out the window to the shed and then jumped to the ground. Ana Luisa got out of bed and stood by the side of the window, watching María Isabela run away. It was a moonless night, but she did see her reach the white gate."

"Ah, a man was obviously waiting for her at the gate?" Castañedo glanced at Olivier.

"I believe that's what she said." Madame Villièrs studied the magistrate's face. "You're thinking María Isabel was the girl found dead in the lake, aren't you?"

Castañedo nodded. "She might well be the girl. Tell me, Madame Villièrs, do you have any notion where Ana Luisa went after her time here."

"She's a servant in New Orleans. I can look and tell you the family she serves. Please pardon me a moment."

Madame Villièrs rose from her chair holding her back. She grimaced as she left the room and walked into the hall. Seconds later, the men heard keys jingle as she opened a locked door to a room down the hall. She returned a few moments later with a faded green ledger under her arm. She stood in the parlor entrance and leafed rapidly through the pages. At what appeared to be the middle of the ledger, she stopped and studied a page of notations. She looked up at Castañedo.

"Yes, here it is. Ana Luisa Ibáñez is in the service of Madame Aveline Dumont."

Olivier met the bishop at the cathedral the next afternoon. The priest had been to see the parish pastor and was adjusting his cloak to face the cold outside, when Bishop Meléndez came into the church. The bishop's nose and cheeks were rose-colored from his walk to the Cabildo.

"Well, Father Olivier, how are the renovations now proceeding at Santa María?" At foot shorter than the Dominican, he had to look up at him.

"Very well, Most Reverend Bishop. We were able to complete the reconstruction of the steeple while the mild weather lasted. We expect to whitewash the outside of the church during the next warm spell. God willing!"

"I see. What about the interior?" The bishop rubbed his cold hands together.

"The furniture makers, Miguel Gómez and Alfonso Pérez, have already been contracted and are now busy building the new altar and benches. Father Antonio made sure we were given low prices for the work."

"I trust their work has not disrupted church services? We must not permit any pause in religious activities – especially in this depraved parish."

"No, Reverend Bishop, the work is being carried out in the carpentry shops. Santa María continues to serve the lowlands people as always – without any interruption."

The bishop made a face. "I've never seen such a profligate place in my life – of course, with the exception of Paris. What with the widespread adultery, drunkenness, prostitution and miscegenation, I often wonder if prayers to God will ever help this community."

Olivier had seen the same sins in other cities in America and in Europe. Despite the bishop's claim that Catholic life was less sinful in Spain, he had seen similar immorality in Cádiz and Madrid. It was also said that Paris actually had less sin after the revolution, though the Church had been dissolved and its land holdings seized by the Jacobins.

"I fear this colony is God-forsaken and lost. Do you know they sing sacrilegious songs at the dinner table in this city? At the best of homes! I tell you, sensuality and criminal activity are everywhere about us. Why I have seen prostitutes brazenly walking about the streets and in the food markets. I'm sure you have seen them as well. I am sickened every time I leave the cathedral. If it isn't such appalling sights, it's the stench of rotten fish that's wafted up from the river markets. You can't even walk the few steps to and from the Cabildo without the urge to vomit up your meals." He pressed his lips together. "If that's not disgusting enough, wherever you walk in this foul city you see discarded garbage, dead animals and human waste in the streets. You must hold your nose and cease breathing for the time it takes to hurry pass such filth." The bishop sighed in exasperation.

"I've heard the governor has urged the Cabildo to clean up the city."

"It's about time if they actually do it." The bishop sighed. "Well, Father Olivier, what of all your *secular effort* for the Dumont family? Are you still so engaged?"

"I've spent less time on the investigation lately. There has been little progress."

"Is that so? I thought I saw you in the company of Magistrate Castañedo yesterday – in the afternoon. You were riding into the city through the San Carlos gate."

"Yes, Reverend Bishop, I was with the magistrate yesterday."

"I suppose it involved the Dumont investigation?" The bishop glared at Olivier.

"Yes, Bishop; the magistrate is involved as well."

"As he should be. Isn't it his responsibility to maintain order in this sinful city? Though God knows, the man does little or nothing to stop the drunkenness and conspicuous prostitution everywhere about us." The bishop stood frowning with his hands on his hips.

Olivier said nothing.

"Surely, he should be the one to investigate the deaths – not you, a man of God. For the life of me, I cannot understand why the parish pastor has assigned you to this task."

"Father Antonio thinks the renovation of Santa María is well worth my meager effort for the Dumont family." Olivier sighed. He had heard enough of the bishop's complaints.

"Meager effort you say. I've heard that Father Francis is seen much more at Santa María than you these days." The frown remained on the bishop's face.

"No, I hold morning Mass and evening prayers when the Acadians return from fishing each day. Besides two baptisms in November, I've administered all others at Santa María and conducted last rites for all the parishioners we've lost."

"I see. Father, what brings you to the cathedral today?" The bishop held his eyes on the Dominican as he took off his cloak and folded it over his arm.

"I've come here to give Father Antonio an account of my activities yesterday." Olivier hoped to avoid telling Bishop Meléndez about his meeting in Mosquito Creek with the madam of a brothel. Even though approved by the parish priest, he knew the bishop would be outraged.

"And what activities were those?"

Olivier carefully chose his reply. "I accompanied the magistrate to an Acadian village called Mosquito Creek. We went there in search of information relating to the investigation." Olivier silently prayed the bishop would not question him further and he turned toward the door.

"Who or what could be in that tiny town that would assist in the investigation?"

"We went there to try to identify the girl whose body was found in *La Bonne Chance.*"

"I see. Was the girl's family from Mosquito Creek?"

"No, Reverend Bishop." Olivier crossed his arms over his chest. He knew now there was nothing more he could do or say to keep the bishop from learning about the meeting.

"Who there then would know such information?" Bewildered, the bishop frowned.

"A woman named Madame Villièrs – she lives in Mosquito Creek."

"Why would the Villièrs woman know about the girl?" Meléndez frowned. "Villièrs! I've heard that name before. Why she's the owner of that degenerate house of girls. Madre de Dios! The house of prostitution I've been trying to close for months." The bishop's face turned crimson and his whole body shook in uncontrolled fury. He pointed a trembling finger at Olivier and shouted in a thunderous voice. "What in God's name were *you* doing there?"

CHAPTER SIX

NEW ORLEANS: DECEMBER 16 - 20, 1799

The next evening, Olivier and Francis closed Santa María an hour early, at seven o'clock, and went to the house of María Adela Boudreaux. She had invited the two priests to dinner and an evening of Flamenco guitar music. Olivier heard the last confession at six-thirty and, when no one else entered Santa María in the next thirty minutes, he put out the candles and locked the door. Outside, Francis kneeled on the ground and prayed before the new wooden cross erected on the steeple. They left Santa María carrying their cloaks. The cold morning had given way to a mild evening with a balmy breeze blowing in off the river.

At dinner, an itinerant musician from southern Spain played his guitar and sang Flamenco songs from Granada. The guitarist, a stick-thin man named Marco Aquino, stopped over in New Orleans on his journey to Mexico City. María Adela heard him performing in the plaza and hired him for the evening. Aquino played for two hours and then left to board a ship sailing that night.

After the guitarist had gone, María Adela ushered her two guests into her parlor and they talked for the remainder of the evening. The priests sat beside each other on a soft white settee, while María Adela sat across from them in a matching chair. Before taking her seat, she handed each of them a glass of cognac.

"I see it's a Rémy Martin." Olivier raised his glass and nodded his head in a silent toast to her. He then downed half the brandy.

"Yes, it was imported from Paris before the revolution began."

Francis followed Olivier's lead and nodded to her as well. "Madame Boudreaux, I want to thank you for the delicious meal. I've never had such tasty food before."

"The poor lad is from Ireland, which is all too well known for its bland food." Olivier smiled at Francis, who made a face. "It's true and you know it, Francis."

María Adela interrupted him. "I'm glad you enjoyed the dinner, Father. Don't pay any attention to him, he thinks the French are the only good cooks in the world." María Adela turned from Francis and looked at Olivier. "How is the renovation of Santa María proceeding?"

"Slow, but sure. With good weather, we should be finished by Easter. We need more mild days like today. I intend to ask the bishop to hold Easter Mass at Santa María. His presence would please our people." Olivier sipped the last of his cognac.

"Do you think he will accept the invitation after what happened? His outburst has been reported all over the city. I can repeat every word he shouted even though I wasn't there."

"Who knows? He's furious with me and Father Antonio. He accused me of dishonoring the Church and said it was blasphemous for me to even enter a brothel, never mind speak to the madam. I don't know all that he said to Father

Antonio, but they haven't spoken to each other since he stormed into the pastor's office that day."

"I heard he shouted so loudly that everyone in the cathedral heard him. A woman I know said his shouting interrupted her confessional and she was told to return the next morning."

"I'm not surprised. His face turned beet-red and I feared he might have an apoplectic fit there in the cathedral doorway. He shouted until he was hoarse and the effort so tired him he had to lean against the wall to steady himself." It occurred to Olivier that not so long ago the bishop had criticized him for shouting in the cathedral.

María Adela nodded. "That's what I heard. It's said he kept shouting, 'What audacity!' You arrogant Dominican! You think you know everything and can do anything you want.'"

Olivier sighed. "That's my memory of it, sad to say."

María Adela refilled Olivier's glass. "Are you concerned about his threat to report the incident to the bishop of Havana?"

Olivier shook his head. "Not on this charge. Father Antonio will speak for me if I'm to be interviewed by a church council. But I doubt it will come to that end. Bishop Echevarria of Havana is not at all like Bishop Meléndez." Olivier finished his second glass of cognac.

"Well, Father, after all the trouble over the meeting, did you learn anything worthwhile from the madam. What was her name? Oh yes, Madame Villièrs."

"She was quite helpful. We think the drowned girl was one of her young prostitutes – a Spanish girl named María Isabel Mendoza." Olivier told her about the girl's disappearance and Ana Luisa Ibáñez who saw her steal away that night.

María Adela stared at Olivier, a look of surprise on her face. "I knew that girl – she was one of Aveline's servants last summer."

"So the magistrate has discovered. But, unfortunately, she

left Madam Dumont early last month and no one knows where she went. Like the Mendoza girl, she left without notice in the middle of the night. The magistrate is looking for her and we hope she's still in New Orleans."

María Adela bit her lip and looked at Olivier. "I saw her at the plaza market. It couldn't have been more than three weeks ago. She was there with someone I know. Now, who was it? Let me think – it will come to me."

After a few minutes of silence, María Adela shook her head unable to recall the person. "Let's continue talking, I'll think of it." She saw Olivier looking at the Rémy Martin bottle and stood to refill his glass.

"No, thank you." Francis shook his head when she pointed to his glass. "My dear mother would say, "Forgotten thoughts often can be recalled if you move your mind to another subject."

María Adela smiled. "My mother said something similar." She looked at Olivier. "Well, Father, what of your checkers contest with young Gervaise?"

"It's half over. We've now played twenty games and Francis has joined us. What are the current totals, Francis?"

"You've won eight, Gervaise seven and I've won five. It's far from over and I expect to win. We have wagered an hour of slavery – each of the losers will serve an hour of slavery for the winner. They will do whatever tasks the winner decides – he will be the master."

María Adela laughed. "I hope you both lose and Gervaise wins. It would be interesting to see what tasks the boy devises for you. He's a clever boy."

Olivier smiled as he raised his glass. "He is quite clever and I expect he would be quite imaginative if we lose to him – which is quite possible."

María Adela suddenly clapped her hands together. "I know who was with Ana Luisa at the market. It was that crippled man who raises hogs north of the city. You know the man who has that decrepit wagon that tends to break down in town. I don't know his name."

Olivier nodded. "Ah, the man who talks to himself. I've always thought the poor soul was a bit mad. So, you saw him with the girl – are you sure it was Aveline's former servant?"

"Yes, I was shocked to see her. She sat in the wagon with his hand on her shoulder."

A day later, on a sunny, but brisk morning, Olivier and Francis rode to Daniel Ménard's hog farm. The farm was located seven miles northwest of New Orleans and the ride on the hard packed dirt road took an hour and a half. Olivier asked the young priest to accompany him when Castañedo was unable to join him. The magistrate, in pursuit of robbers who had murdered two merchants on the road to Baton Rouge, authorized Olivier to interview the girl in his place.

Olivier and Francis left Santa María after morning Mass. It was a day when the Acadians celebrated the birthday of their oldest elder, a man eighty-years old, and Olivier knew the entire community would attend the celebration. There would be endless eating, drinking and dancing from noon until late at night. Santa María had also been scheduled for interior carpentry that day.

The priests smelled the hog farm before they reached it and the odor became stronger as they neared the road that lead to the pens. Mènard's farm was situated in a pine forest and his log house had been built on the bank of a fresh water stream that flowed into the Mississippi River. Surrounded by trees, neither the house nor the hog pens could be seen from the road.

They rang the rusted bell on the gate and, after a few minutes, a young man walked out of the woods toward them. He was a dark-skinned man with a beaked nose and long black hair tied behind his head. As he came closer they realized he was an Indian. He wore a colonist's woolen coat, but the leather leggings and moccasins were commonly worn by Indians.

"What brings you out here, Fathers?" He spoke perfect French and made no effort to be deferential to them. He stood unsmiling with his hands on his hips.

"I am Father Olivier and this is Father Francis. We are from the cathedral parish and we would like to speak to Monsieur Mènard. He is the owner of this property, is he not?" Olivier spoke softly with a smile on his face.

The Indian did not return his smile. He spoke succinctly. "He is and I am his son. What is your business with him?"

"What do they want?" A shout from the woods stopped Olivier before he could respond.

They turned to see a bearded man in an old horse-drawn wagon approach them. It was Daniel Mènard and sitting beside him was a young girl who Olivier assumed to be Ana Luisa Ibáñez. The wagon reached them a moment later and Mènard nodded recognizing Olivier.

"Ah, Father Olivier. I haven't seen you in quite a while."

"No, Monsieur Mènard." Olivier dismounted and stood by his horse.

"I see you've met my son, Honorè. This is Ana Luisa." He pointed to the small dark-haired girl beside him. "She is my son's new wife."

"Madame Mènard." Olivier bowed his head and turned to Francis who had dismounted and now stood holding his horse's reins. "Father Francis, the Assistant Pastor of Santa María."

"Father." Mènard nodded to the priest. "Well, Father Olivier, what brings you out here to our farm? Surely, it isn't to buy hogs for the Church. Father Sebastian was here only a day or so ago to purchase the cathedral's monthly supply – of course, at the usual lowered price."

"No, Monsieur, I'm here to speak to Madame Mènard."

"Is that so? For what purpose?" Ménard's face hardened as he looked at Olivier.

"It relates to her friendship with María Isabel Mendoza." Olivier made no mention of the brothel where the girls became friends. He smiled at Ana Luisa hoping she would see his smile as a sign that he would not speak of the brothel in front of her husband.

"What is it you wish to know about María Isabel?" The girl looked him in the eye. She appeared to be unmoved by the mention of the missing girl.

"I'm here in place of Magistrate Castañedo, who is busy with other matters. We are in search of Mademoiselle Mendoza – she's missing."

"A priest in pursuit of a missing girl with the magistrate's assistance. What is the world coming to?" The elder Mènard gave Olivier a crooked smile.

Olivier's face reddened. "We are working together on a special investigation." It was now clear to Olivier that his earlier impression of Daniel Mènard had been erroneous. The man definitely had all his wits about him.

"How does that involve my wife?" Honorè raised his voice and continued to scowl at Olivier. He walked over to the wagon and held his wife's hand.

"As I told you, it …"

"I met María Isabel at Madame Villièrs house in Mosquito Creek." Ana Luisa looked up at the two priests. "It was last summer."

"I'm glad you …"

"Admitted it, Father? I'm not ashamed of my time there. Madame Villiérs was good to me. She helped me when nobody else would. My father and mother died aboard ship, I had no family, no home in New Orleans, no food, nothing. Madame Villiérs took me into her home; she fed, clothed me and treated me with kindness. I was with only two men before I left the house."

"You don't have to tell him anything, Ana." Honorè kissed his wife's hand.

Ana Luisa suddenly put her hands to her face and wept. Her weeping turned to sobs and her whole body shook. Honorè stood beside the wagon, holding her in his arms and soothing her with his soft voice. She stopped crying a few moments later and dried her eyes with a wrinkled handkerchief her father-in-law handed her.

"Do you want to go home, Ana?"

"No, Honorè, I want to talk to Father Olivier." She looked up at the priest.

"Are you certain?" Honorè turned to Olivier, this time with plaintive look.

"Yes, I must confess my sins and ask God for forgiveness. I'll never find peacc in my heart until I do. Honorè, I must return to the Church and God again."

Honorè nodded and gently stroked her face.

"I love you, Honorè. You know that. You have given me happiness, but I cannot say I am your wife unless we marry in the Church."

"I've told you any number of times I would marry you in the cathedral. Anytime you want!" Honorè frowned, angry that she had spoken of their private life in front of strangers.

"We cannot be married in the cathedral. You are not a Christian and I have not received communion or gone for confession in many months." Ana Luisa looked through red-rimmed eyes at Olivier, her hands clutching the handkerchief in her lap. "I fear I would not be forgiven my sins if I confessed in the cathedral. It's well known the bishop is a harsh man and has spoken very severely against adultery and fornication outside of marriage."

Olivier spoke softly. "Ana, you need not worry, the bishop or any other priest will ask God to forgive you for your sins. You must only promise not to repeat them."

"How can I promise not to repeat them when I'm with Honorè?" Tears again fell from her eyes. "Honorè is not Christian and he will not consent to be converted."

"There are ways, Ana, for you to marry Honorè with the Church's consent."

"Even if he is not a Christian? His mother was Indian and he prefers their ways."

Olivier nodded. "Yes, even then, Ana. You and Honorè can be married in the Church and I promise to make it so." He made a tiny cross over his heart with a forefinger.

"Thank God!" Ana hugged Honorè as hard as she could.

Olivier smiled. "I am the pastor of Santa María, Ana, and I welcome you to our church whenever you wish to come for communion and confession. First Mass is held at six o'clock in the morning, Second Mass at seven and evening Mass at seven o'clock. I trust you know where Santa María is located."

"I know its location in the lowlands." Mènard spoke up and patted the girl's knee. "We will be there in the morning for Second Mass. As you now know, Father, we are a far distance from Santa María."

"Yes, come whenever possible. We will talk of your marriage at that time. Now, Ana, I would like you tell me about María Isabel's last day in the house of Madame Villièrs."

Ana nodded. "María Isabel came to Madame Villièrs' house a few days after I arrived. She came from Pensacola. Her father, mother and younger brothers had died in the plague that killed so many last winter. She went to live with her uncle – he was her father's brother, but his wife was mean to her and she ran away. María Isabel spent the few pesetas she still had on the voyage to New Orleans and arrived last June. She came here rather than St. Augustine because she heard New Orleans was more prosperous and there would be more places where she might find work. María Isabel hoped to become a servant, but no one wanted her. Her appearance hurt her chances. She wore tattered, dirty clothing. All her clothes, except what she wore, were stolen aboard the ship that brought her here. So, she wore the same clothes day after day for a month."

Ana paused to blow her nose. "María Isabel slept in a wrecked ship and begged for food during the day. She finally found some better clothes in a trash bin behind a rich man's house and she wore them thereafter. The clothes were not only cleaner, they were boys' clothes and, once she wore them, the men in the streets no longer bothered her. María Isabel had been attacked several times before, but had always escaped by running away."

"One day, she begged for bread from a woman named Heloise, who had a bakery cart at the edge of the central plaza. I don't recall Heloise's family name." Ana shrugged. "Anyway, Heloise gave María Isabel a split-open bread that couldn't be sold and they talked while María Isabel sat there eating the bread. María Isabel told Heloise all that had happened to her since she arrived in New Orleans and the woman took pity on her. She took her home that night, fed her a good meal, let her bathe in a tub and gave her clean clothing to wear. Girl's clothes! The clothes belonged to Heloise's daughter, a girl two years older than María Isabel. The girl went to school and boarded at the Ursaline Convent."

Olivier was anxious to hear about María Isabel's last night in the Villièrs house, but he held his impatience in check and listened politely. He saw that Honorè and Daniel Mènard also were impatient for her to get to the night in question. Honorè stood shifting his feet and Daniel sat rubbing his big hands together. Only Francis seemed attentive to Ana's every word.

"María Isabel stayed with Heloise for a while and helped her bake and sell her breads and cakes. But the bakery cart made only enough money for the woman's livelihood and the cost of boarding her daughter in the convent. Then, one day, she told María Isabel she couldn't afford to keep her in her house when her daughter came home that summer.

"She told her about the house of Madame Villièrs and the life of the girls who lived there. Heloise told María Isabel that she had lived there herself many years ago. She met her husband in the Villièrs house and he took her away to New Orleans. He was a baker in town at the time. They married and Heloise had a child, but soon afterwards her husband died suddenly of some unknown sickness. She then took up his bakery business."

Daniel patted Ana's arm. "Ana, please tell Father Olivier about the girl's last night in Mosquito Creek. We must feed the hogs and I'm sure the Fathers must return to Santa María."

"Yes, of course, please forgive me for going on so long. Well, María Isabel decided to go to Mosquito Creek and Heloise contacted Madame Villièrs. María Isabel intended to stay there only long enough to earn enough money to buy a push cart and sell goods in the street. So, in August, Madame Villièrs came to New Orleans by carriage and picked her up."

Daniel patted Ana's arm again. "I'll go back and feed the hogs, Honorè. Don't worry I can do it alone. You stay here with Ana." He nodded to the priests. "Forgive me, Fathers, but I must be off." Honorè lifted Ana out of the wagon and his father guided his horse around and pointed him down the rutted road toward the hog pens.

Ana waited until the horse and wagon had clattered into the trees before continuing her story. "Madame Villièrs placed her in a bedroom with me and we immediately became friends. Madame Villièrs told us we would not meet any men for a while. She said we needed to know what would be expected of us and that would take at least a week." Ana looked at Honorè and saw the grim expression on his face.

"I'll be finished soon, Honorè. I know we must help your father with the hogs." Isabel turned back to Olivier. "A week or so later, María Isabel was told she would be prepared to meet a man who visited once a month. He was expected to arrive at noon. Gisella, Madame's niece, took María Isabel away at eleven-o'clock that morning and she didn't return until three o'clock that afternoon. María Isabel said the man was kind to her. He called himself Molière, but she didn't think that was his real name. She said he grinned when he told her his name."

Olivier and Francis exchanged looks. They realized neither Ana nor Honorè knew of Molière, the famous French dramatist of the seventeenth-century. Olivier thought it odd the man used such a celebrated name to hide his identity.

"Ana, was it unusual for the men to use false names in the house?"

"No, it was common from what the other girls said. The men didn't want anyone in New Orleans to know of their visits to the house. Many, if not most of them, of course, were married. The girls said they often used their wives names accidentally when speaking to them."

"I see, please continue."

"María Isabel said the man was pleasant and gentle, except at first." Ana blushed and squeezed Honorè's hand.

Olivier nodded. "Please continue, Ana." He knew she was referring to the breaking of María Isabel's maidenhead.

"When María Isabel returned to the room, she spent the rest of the day with me. There was much activity downstairs, but we remained in our room. Gisella brought dinner."

"Was María Isabel in good spirits that night?"

"Yes, although she wasn't as talkative as usual. For a while afterwards, she lay on her bed without saying anything. I knew something was on her mind. I thought it probably was about the man who had been with her."

"Any notion of what María Isabel was thinking?"

"I think she liked him and hoped to be with him again."

"What makes you think that?"

"I just know – girls know those things. I could see it in her eyes."

Olivier raised his eyebrows. "I see. Did she say anything about liking him?"

"No. She just said he was considerate and gentle."

"Please tell me about her appearance. Did she look different in any way after being with him that afternoon?"

"No, she looked the same."

"How would you describe her?"

"María Isabel is petite, smaller than me. She doesn't have much of a bosom." Ana blushed again. "She's very pretty with big brown eyes and a clean complexion. No pimples."

"What about the man who was with her? How did she describe him?"

"She said very little about him – except that he gave her a big bonus."

"Do men usually give the girls bonuses?"

"Yes, but not as much as Molière. He gave María Isabel *thirty pesetas!* That's more than what the girls usually get from Madame Villièrs for their share of the price the men pay."

"What do the men usually pay?"

"They pay fifty pesetas, though some men pay more for certain ..." This time, the red in her cheeks spread to her neck. Ana Luisa closed her eyes and hugged Honorè again.

"That's enough." Honorè glared at Olivier. "She's answered enough questions."

"No, Honorè," Ana Luisa touched his cheek. "I need to remove all these memories, all of them, out of my mind. I must be free of them so I can have peace in my heart."

"Are you sure you want to continue, Ana? Olivier saw the pain in her eyes and he felt sorry for her. "You can say it all in your confession at a later time."

"No, Father, I have so much to confess – I want to rid myself of some of it now while you are here. It hurts now, but I'll feel better later. Madame Villièrs gave the girls twenty five pesetas, half of what the men paid her. The girls also got extra pesetas from the men. But Molière gave María Isabel more pesetas than any other girl had ever gotten."

"I see. Did she describe his appearance?"

"No, Father. That's what was very odd. She said very little about his looks. We always talked about the men we saw. We would stand by the sides of the front hall window and watch the men ride up to the house. Afterwards we always talked about them, whether they were good-looking or not." She looked at her husband. "Girls always do that, wives do not."

Honorè made a face, but said nothing.

"María Isabel said nothing about his face, hair ... eyes?"

"No, and when I asked her to describe him, she would only say he had clean white teeth." Ana smiled, showing her own white teeth.

Olivier and Francis laughed and Honorè even smiled.

"Why do you think she said so little about him?"

"I think he told her not to say anything about him to anyone in the house. I thought he worried his reputation would be ruined if his visit to the house was known. That's why he used the name, Molière, and gave her so much money."

"Did any of the other girls see him in the house?" Francis spoke up for the first time.

"No. We were told he demanded privacy and paid Madame Villièrs many pesetas for it. Only the Madame and Gisella ever saw him."

"What about the girls he …" Francis blushed.

"They were sent away soon after their time with him."

"So, no one saw him except Madame Villièrs and her niece, Gisella?"

She nodded. "Gisella told the girls that Madame Villièrs had lunch with him every time he came to the house. Madame Villièrs or Gisella could tell you all about him. I did see Molière leave from the front hall window. María Isabel pointed him out to me when he mounted his horse. He was the only man in the house that afternoon and he left early – not long after María Isabela came back to our room."

"But you didn't see his face, did you?"

"No, I saw only his back as he mounted his horse. I was standing behind María Isabel at the window. I do remember he wore a dark hat and suit. He looked like one of the lawyers you see in the city. I'm sure he was a gentleman."

"Could you tell if he was short or tall? Fat or thin?"

"I didn't notice, I was trying to see his face."

"Did you notice anything else about his appearance?"

"I do remember he wore beautiful boots. They were a reddish brown color."

"Cordovan?"

"I think so."

"What about his horse? Do you recall his color or size?"

Ana shook her head. "There was nothing unusual about him – he was big as I recall, so he must have been a stallion. He might have been a chestnut color."

"How about the saddle? Do you recall its appearance?"

She shook her head. "I was looking at him as he mounted the horse."

"So, it was still light when he left."

"Yes. He left four or five hours before the first men began arriving that night."

"That was eight or nine hours before the house was closed for the night?" Olivier saw her nod her head.

"During the week, the house stays open until ten or eleven o'clock. It's open much later on Saturday night – sometimes until midnight. The house is closed all day Sunday. Everyone goes to the little chapel in Mosquito Creek. A monk usually performs Mass at ten o'clock."

"That would be Father Jerome," said Francis. "Every Sunday, he spends the day riding to a number of the little villages south of New Orleans. I've heard he goes to as many as eight or nine that day."

Olivier nodded and turned to Ana Luisa. "What happened that night – the night when María Isabel left the house? Tell me all you can recall."

"We went to bed when all the noise downstairs stopped. I seem to recall hearing the last horse trot away. Of course, we both went to the outhouse before going to bed."

"Did you see if all the horses were gone when you went to the outhouse?"

"No. The outhouse is behind the house and we went downstairs and out the back door. We had to stand in line and wait behind several other girls."

"So, you don't know if all the horses were gone."

"I do know because all the downstairs candles were out and there was no light coming from under Madame Villièrs' rooms. She and Gisella have their rooms downstairs. Since it was dark downstairs, I knew all the men were gone."

"I see, please continue. You both went to bed afterwards."

"Yes. I usually fall sound asleep as soon as I put my head on the pillow. That's before I met Honorè." Ana blushed and squeezed Honorè's hand.

"But not that night?"

"No, I stayed awake worrying what would happen to me when I would be with a man."

Ana kissed Honorè on the cheek. "Fortunately, when it happened I was with Honorè."

Olivier paused, watching Honorè and Ana Luisa embrace. He spoke when she turned to face him. "You lay in bed thinking, but not moving."

"Yes and I had my eyes closed. I opened them when I heard María Isabel get out of bed. I saw her dressing quietly, trying not to wake me. There was just enough moonlight coming in through the cracks in the shutters to let me see her moving about. I didn't say anything."

"The shutters were closed because of mosquitoes?"

"Yes, some hot nights there were clouds of them and

they got under the mosquito nets no matter what we did. So, we closed the shutters even though the room felt like it was on fire."

Olivier nodded, knowing it happened to even with the tightest of woven nets. "When María Isabel was dressed did you see her pack her possessions?"

"Yes, she put some things in a twine bag – I couldn't see what they were. She then went to the window and opened the shutters as quietly as possible. But one of them squeaked and she looked at me to see if the sound awakened me. She waited a moment to see if I moved and when I didn't move, she climbed over the sill and hung down to the shed roof. The roof is right under the window of our room. She didn't make a sound dropping to the roof and then reached up to close the shutters. She was just tall enough to reach the shutters with the tips of her fingers."

Olivier kept silent, hoping her long story would end with a description of the man.

"I got up then, went to the window and watched her though the crack where the shutters come together. I saw her go to the edge of the roof and hang down to the wood pile that stands at the side of the shed. From the wood pile, I saw her run across the yard. It was a cloudy night, but there was a little light from the moon now and then. I saw María Isabel meet someone near the gate – a man I thought. I didn't see him clearly, he was in the shadows. Then clouds covered the moon and I saw nothing else. They were gone when the moon came out again."

"Did you see any part of the man? His clothes or boots?"

Ana shook her head. "I saw nothing else, not even them walking away. It was much too dark. A few seconds later, I heard a horse riding away in the distance."

Olivier sighed, disappointed she had not described the man María Isabel met that night..

"I've no more to tell." Tears trickled down her face.

"I never saw María Isabel again."

"We didn't learn a lot, did we?" Francis looked over at Olivier as they rode away.

"Not nearly as much as I had hoped."

"At least, we know a little about the *one* man who was with María Isabel before she left the house that night. He certainly has gone to all lengths to keep his identity unknown. Calling himself Molière is interesting, isn't it?"

"Yes, the name tells us he is educated and quite clever. Perhaps, too clever for someone simply seeking the intimacy of a young girl for an afternoon each month. His efforts to remain unknown make that clear. He could be a man of distinction who fears public embarrassment if found to be a customer of the brothel, but somehow I doubt it. What is most telling about him is that he was the *only* man María Isabel encountered before she left the house."

"And, Ana said María Isabel liked him. It seems to me if she left with a man, he would be the likely one. There was no one else she knew. Ana said she had no family left or friends, except the baker woman in New Orleans, who she sent her to the house in the first place."

"True. He does seem the most likely one to have taken her away. But the time he left the house poses a problem with that possibility; he rode away some nine hours before the house was closed that night. Where would he go to wait so long? If he waited in or near Mosquito Creek, he would have been seen by someone. I doubt that happened, but I'm sure the magistrate will send a man down there to find out. If he didn't wait in the village, where else could he wait?"

Francis shook his head. "I don't know of any other villages for miles around that remote little town. So, where could he go to wait for her? The woods? I can't imagine a well-dressed gentleman sitting in the woods waiting nine hours to pick her up. Certainly not in the summer with the clouds of mosquitoes buzzing about, never mind the biting flies everywhere in sight. I shudder thinking about it."

"I can't imagine it either. It would be foolhardy and the man is no fool. Yet, he remains the most likely one to have taken her away. It's possible he found a place to wait nearby that's unknown to us – a place indoors. From what we've heard about him, I think Monsieur Molière is certainly crafty enough to have found a way to wait all those many hours for María Isabel."

"Madame Villièrs and her niece, Gisella, should be able to shed much more light on the man. They both have seen and spoken to him."

"Yes and now Magistrate Castañedo must return to Mosquito Creek and interview them. Even if they only know the man as Molière, they can describe him."

"You think María Isabel was the girl found in the wreck, don't you?"

"Yes, I do. The girl didn't just vanish into thin air."

"No and she was the only unidentified girl found after the storm." Francis regretted saying what was obvious.

Olivier nodded. "There's another fact we know that makes me think María Isabel was the drowned girl. Madame Villièrs said that María Isabel disappeared in the middle of August – the same time as the sinking of *La Bonne Chance*."

"That's more than a coincidence."

"It is indeed."

The priests rode along without speaking for the next hour. They passed through a forest of leafless trees. Near the edge of a swampy area, they saw a herd of deer foraging for grass on the forest floor. A mile further, they reached the flat farmlands that produced most of the corn, grains and vegetables that fed New Orleans. The fields, in February, were empty of all growth except for the dried-up corn stalks still standing after the autumn harvest. Within sight of the city walls, they saw a female bear and three cubs cross an empty field and enter the woods. The bear turned to look at the riders as she waited for her cubs to move ahead into the brush.

Francis spoke to Olivier when they entered the long line of horsemen and wagons slowly passing through the gate beside the San Fernando guard tower. The gate opened onto Orleans Street and the center of the city and usually had more traffic than any other entrance into New Orleans. They talked freely since they were moving in line between two closed carriages and could not be overheard.

"Do you foresee any problems with the marriage of Honorè and Ana in the Church? He's an Indian and I didn't hear him say he was willing to be converted. In fact, the opposite, he seemed unwilling from what Ana Luisa said."

"I don't think that's a problem. I expect his love of Ana Luisa will make him willing."

"What about the Church, Father? I know Catholics can marry Protestants, but what about Indians who are pagans?" He noticed a soldier looking down at them from the guard tower.

"The same Church rules apply for marriage to pagans as to Protestants. A non-Catholic must agree, in writing, to the rearing of the children in the Church and the continued Catholic worship of the Catholic spouse. Think of the thousands of Spaniards who married Indians after the conquest of America. There've been countless numbers of other Catholics in the past who married pagans. St. Augustine's mother, St. Monica, in fact was married to one."

"That's true, though she later converted. How are such marriages performed? There must be Church doctrine on the subject."

"There is Church doctrine. As I recall, the bishop's permission is required for marriages to Protestants. For pagans, I think a bishop's dispensation is also required."

"So, Bishop Meléndez would be involved." Francis smiled as he looked over at Olivier. "How then would you perform the marriage? Do you think the bishop would permit them to be married in the cathedral – with you officiating?"

Olivier exhaled his breath. "No, I'll have to ask Father Antonio to perform the marriage. But I will be in attendance and perhaps assist him."

"Do you think the bishop would permit such assistance?"

"That would be Father Antonio's decision. He is the pastor of the parish and he will be the one to decide how and who conducts the ceremony. Even though the pastor is the bishop's delegate in the parish, he possesses a number of exclusive powers the bishop can never change or limit. Blessing marriages is one of them. Father Antonio therefore can conduct the marriage of Honorè and Isabel as he wishes. The responsibilities of pastors are stated in the proceedings of the Council of Trent and you should re-read them if you've forgotten them, Francis."

"Yes, Father." Francis turned his face away and grimaced. He was angry with himself for saying something to Olivier without thinking it through. It was the fourth time he had been chided by the Dominican and, after each incident, he had vowed it would not happen again.

"Besides, in the last few weeks, it appears Father Antonio has asserted more authority in the parish. At least, that's what I've heard. I believe it began with his decision to have me assist Monsieur Dumont in the murder investigation. His assertion of authority, of course, has resulted in controversy with the bishop."

"That's not surprising."

"No, it's not. Old Father Luke told me they barely speak to each other these days. After my trip with the magistrate to interview Madame Villièrs, the bishop again reprimanded Father Antonio for permitting my *secular efforts* for the Dumont family. He apparently accused him of contributing to my blasphemy and the dishonor of the cathedral parish. I was told Father Antonio responded bluntly, telling Bishop Meléndez that he was in charge of the parish and would not be beholden to him. According to Father Luke, he angrily shouted, 'You can dismiss me if you so choose, but you cannot tell me how to lead this parish.' I spoke to Father Luke yesterday when I went to the cathedral to inform Father Antonio of this trip."

"Is there a chance Meléndez will dismiss him?"

"I doubt it. Father Antonio is well liked here as well as in Madrid. It's said the king was involved in his appointment to the cathedral parish. Bishop Meléndez is not similarly supported. He serves in New Orleans only temporarily until the return of Bishop Peñalvery Cárdenas and I don't think he would take such a rash action. The pastor's dismissal would very probably lead to a lengthy investigation and a resulting delay in a new appointment for him. It's well known that Meléndez is waiting for a placement as a permanent bishop. He has been overlooked in the past and I don't think he will take any risks that could possibly cost him an appointment. I've heard the archbishop in Havana now has him in mind for the next opening."

"That makes sense." Francis nodded to the sentry as they entered the city.

Olivier made a face as they reined in their horses on the other side of the gates. "L'aide de dieu, ce qu'une odeur. (God help us, what an odor.) When will the Spaniards ever clean up the city. Some days it smells worse than Mènard's hog farm."

"It surely does. I'll be glad to leave the city and return to Santa María."

New Orleans was considered one of the worst smelling cities in America. In addition to the stench of the sewage in the streets, refuse dumped along the river levee left a pervasive odor that lingered everywhere in the city. There was no escape from it. The awful odor hung in the air in all seasons, though it worsened in the heat of the summer when discarded foods and dead animals rotted in the sun. The *Orleans smell*, as the colonists called it, only disappeared during and immediately after high-wind storms, when fresh air flowed through the city to everyone's delight. Light winds off the river had the opposite effect. The stench would intensify when the wind blew over the refuse in the levees and force people to walk the streets with handkerchiefs held tightly over their noses. Only the wealthy residents with their two and three-story houses built with high balconies on higher ground evaded the worst of the odor that blighted the city. On some days, however, even they suffered the *Orleans smell.*

"Francis, I'm going to leave you when we reach the Cabildo. I must tell the magistrate what we heard from Ana Luisa. I also want to tell Jean Bertin what we know now."

Francis watched Olivier as he dismounted and led his horse down Orleans Street. Even with the horse in tow, the priest strode ahead with his usual gait; his beaked nose jutted forward and his long arms swinging out in the manner of a big bird flapping his wings as it starts to rise into the sky. Francis smiled, seeing a man across the street flap his arms mimicking Olivier.

It was only a few minutes after one o'clock when he rode past the rutted wagon road to Mosquito Creek. He held his pocket watch up in the moonlight to see the time. The ride from New Orleans had been uneventful. He had not passed another rider on the road and the moon's light let him see well enough to urge his stallion to a fast trot. He dared not push his horse to a gallop in the dark, but he still had managed to reach the road to the village in three hours. He did not count the twenty minutes spent feeding and watering his stallion at the one stop he made.

The bitter cold was the only part of the journey that bothered him. Even bundled up in layers of woolen clothing, he felt cold the entire way. The hood and muffler he wore protected his mouth and nose, but the frigid wind seemed to cut into his forehead as he rode. Squinting his eyes in the sharp wind, he could barely see a few feet ahead of him. The faster the horse moved, the colder he felt. His hands bore the brunt of the wind. He had to hold the big horse's reins the entire trip and his rawhide gloves were not thick enough to keep out the cold. Even though he continually changed hands on the reins, he could hardly move his fingers by the time he reached the road to Mosquito Creek.

The man dismounted at the turn-off, but, instead of taking the rutted path to the village, he led his horse eighty-five feet farther down the river road. He had estimated the distance and sighed in relief, seeing the large water oak that marked a second and hidden path to Mosquito Creek. Even in the darkness, he could make out the oak's lowest limb, thick as a man's thigh, sticking straight out toward the road.

"Ah, there it is," he said to himself. "The path is just to the right."

He had found the hidden path by chance on one of his monthly trips to Mosquito Creek. Preoccupied with thoughts of the new girl he would soon possess, he had ridden a short distance past the turn-off to the village. When he realized his mistake and turned back, he saw two boys approaching him from the river. The bigger of the boys carried a woven bag full of fish, while the other carried their fishing poles over his shoulder. Expecting the boys to pass him on their way to Mosquito Creek, he waited to talk to them. But, instead of passing him, they crossed the road before reaching him and entered the woods beside the large water oak.

He had waited a few minutes and then led his horse though the woods following the path the boys had taken. A half-mile away, he arrived at a huge live oak which had a treehouse built on an upper limb close to the trunk. The house stood some twenty feet up the tree and could be reached by climbing steps that were nailed at intervals for the boys' use. The steps looked to be left-over pieces of the logs used to build the tree house.

Neither of the boys was in the house and he assumed they had taken their catch home. At the time, he had walked his horse along the path from the treehouse to Mosquito Creek. It was a shorter route to the village, but a portion of the path narrowed to two feet as it passed through the water-soaked marshlands that lay alongside the creek. He walked cautiously aware that alligators and venomous water snakes could be anywhere in the vicinity. Moments later, he emerged out of the woods near the creek, only a short distance south of the brothel. Its cedar-shingled roof was clearly in sight when he followed the path toward the village.

Thereafter, he took the path rather than the rutted road to the house. He varied his return route to the river road depending on how much rain had fallen before his visit. If the ground was wet to the touch, he left through the village. He did not want to take the risk of leading his horse through the marsh when the path was narrowed by encroaching water.

Now, months later in the darkness, he walked his horse into the woods toward the huge live oak. He moved slowly with only shafts of moonlight lighting the way. Near the base of the live oak, he tied the stallion to a slender sapling and trotted the rest of the way through the marsh to the creek. There was no reason to worry about dangerous reptiles on that frigid night.

He came out of the woods and paused trying to see the house from where he stood on the bank of the creek. But it was too dark to see it even in the moonlight.

He could see his pocket watch and was pleased to find that he had spent only forty-five minutes reaching the creek. He knew it would take him less than ten minutes more to walk to the rear of the house. Everything was proceeding as he had planned. He exhaled, seeing his breath puff out in front of his face.

"Now, if only my hands would warm up," he thought. After tethering his horse, he had walked with both gloved hands stuck deep in his pockets. He could now move his fingers, but they felt stiff and clumsy.

No light appeared anywhere in the house when he reached the back door. He stood on the stoop, listening for the slightest sound from within. He heard nothing, but waited longer to make certain no one was moving about inside. Still cautious, he kneeled and held his ear to the door for another few minutes. He heard no sound inside.

Still kneeling, he quickly took off his gloves and pulled his knife from the sheath beneath his cloak. The door had to be opened before his cold fingers became too numb to hold the knife. His hands trembled, but he managed to push the knife blade into the thin crack in the door frame where the door was bolted. He left the knife blade in the crack and rubbed his hands together. He rubbed until he felt warmth seep first into his palms and then his fingers. His fingers had to be flexible enough to work the iron bolt out of the hole that locked it in place. The knife blade had been inserted behind the end of the bolt and the next step would be to turn the slender blade carefully to push the bolt out of the hole. He had to apply the precise amount of pressure to push the bolt – too little pressure and the bolt would not move, too much and the blade would snap. If the blade snapped, he would not be able to get into the house quietly.

His only recourse then would be to break a window and climb in over the sill. He shook his head in frustration, knowing the risks of breaking a window. The noise surely would awaken one of the girls, if not everyone in the house. In that event, he would have to contend with not only the girls and Gisella, but Madame Villièrs, who kept a loaded pistol in her bedroom. Even if he then escaped without being seen or shot by the woman, all his plans would be undone. Yet, one way or another, he had to get into the house and do what was necessary now. It could not be delayed and had to be done that night.

He leaned forward so his eyes were almost even with the knife handle. He used his left hand to steady the knife in the door jamb and readied his right hand to turn the handle. He blew out his breath and turned the knife handle to the right. The bolt did not move the slightest bit. A second try turning harder did no better. He sighed and rubbed his hands together again.

His fingers were becoming numb again and he knew if the iron bolt did not budge in the next few seconds he would be unable to continue. He gritted his teeth, gripped the handle tightly and turned it much harder. He could feel the blade bend as he turned it, but still the bolt did not move. Once more, he rubbed his hands, first, together and, then, on his woolen cloak. He sighed and with both hands held tightly on the knife handle, he twisted the blade hard and quickly. He heard the shrill sound of metal striking metal and thought the blade had snapped. But, then, he realized with relief that the bolt had abruptly shot out the hole and struck against the metal stop where it remained when not engaged.

A moment later, he stood still in the kitchen, listening for the slightest sound. He heard nothing. There was not a sound in the house, not even the crackle of logs burning in the parlor fireplace. It occurred to him that he had not smelled smoke from the fireplace when he walked up to the house. He put his cold hands in his pockets and hoped they would warm up now that he had finally gotten inside. The house was not as warm as he had expected, but certainly much warmer than standing in the freezing weather outside. He had plenty of time and he intended to stand there until his hands were warm and his fingers moved freely.

A little later, he took his hands from his coat pockets. He shook them from side to side and wiggled his fingers to make sure they were flexible. He then moved toward the doorway leading into the hall and downstairs interior of the house.

The hall ran the entire length of the house from front door to back door with three rooms on each side of the first floor. Entering the back door, he stood in the kitchen which was the first room on the left side of the hall. A spacious dining room with a long oak table was situated next to the kitchen on that side followed by an equally spacious sitting room, which opened up to the vestibule and the front door. Across the vestibule, there was another smaller sitting room with a fireplace on the right side of the hall. The girls used that room as a parlor during the day before visitors arrived at night. Madame Villièrs used the second room on the right as both a bedroom and office and it remained locked at all times during the day. Gisella slept in the last room on the right near the back door and across from the kitchen.

His eyes already adjusted to the darkness, he took a step into the hallway when he heard someone, obviously one of the girls, walking down the stairs. The boards squeaked as she came down and he retreated to the kitchen and flattened himself against the wall in the darkest corner of the room. He heard the girl's steps as she walked down the hall and approached the kitchen. He could see the light from the candle she carried; the outer edge of its light reached a little way into the kitchen. It made a half-circle on the floor. He stood still not sure what he would do if she walked into the room where he stood.

"Where's she heading," he wondered. "Outside to the outhouse? No, it's too cold, she would have used a chamber pot. In here for something?" His stomach tightened as he pictured her seeing him as she entered the kitchen.

Then, she stopped in front of Gisella's bedroom. He heard her open the door and softly call out to Gisella. She whispered trying not to awaken Madame Villièrs in the next room.

"Gisella, the fire's out. We're freezing upstairs."

He could not hear Gisella's reply, but he did hear her moving about the room. Moments later, she came out of her bedroom and walked down the hallway with the girl. He then heard noise from the parlor and assumed the two girls were stacking kindling and logs in the fireplace. A sudden thud and a hiss of annoyance told him one of them had dropped a log on the floor. When he heard the sound of metal scraping on stone, he knew Gisella had started the fire and dragged the safety screen in front of the fireplace.

The next sound he heard was the girl climbing the stairs to her bedroom. Then, Gisella returned to her room and closed the door. He waited a few minutes before moving. When he did move, he bent down and removed his shoes. The wooden floor was cold, but he knew stocking-feet would be less likely to make noise than shoes. He waited for what seemed like a half hour and once again went into the hallway. At Gisella's door, he listened briefly and, hearing nothing, he eased open the door. It creaked slightly and Gisella stirred in her bed and spoke.

"Is that you again, Marta?" She sounded irritated.

He made no reply and ran to her bed, an iron bar in his

hand. In the darkness, the sound of her voice led him to her. He banged his knee hard against the bed frame and winced in pain.

"What in God's name are you doing, Marta?" Wide awake, Gisella sat up in bed.

He could just see make out the vague outline of her head in the darkness and he swung the bar in an arc that caught her on the left ear. The force of the blow knocked her down on the bed. He sheathed the bar, which he carried in a sword's scabbard and withdrew his knife from its case on his belt. Leaning over her body, he turned her head away from him, felt for her neck and slit her throat.

CHAPTER SEVEN

NEW ORLEANS: DECEMBER 22 – 30, 1799

In the early morning of December 22, the magistrate rode to Santa María and dismounted outside the church. He had timed his trip to arrive as Father Olivier finished Mass. Castañedo peeked in through the crack of the partially closed door and saw the church was half full. He then turned away and leaned against the wall on the right side of the door.

It was a cool sunny morning and he inhaled the clean fresh air of the lowlands. "What a relief to be free of the stench of New Orleans for a while," he thought. "Dios mío, the governor has to clean up the levee or we'll all die of the foul air." He grimaced, knowing the governor was more concerned about the new nation north of Louisiana and the defense of the colony.

He turned to see the door opening and parishioners starting to come out of the church. A few of them nodded to him, but most walked by with only a glance in his direction. Castañedo knew most of the Acadians hated him and he admitted to himself that they had good reason for their hate. He had punished them harder and more often than any other people in New Orleans. They were indifferent to Spanish authority and did whatever they wanted, generally ignoring the laws of the colony. They governed their own towns and resisted the continued attempts of New Orleans officials to make them submit to Spanish regulations and taxes. He sighed, thinking of the countless number of times his officers had raided their unlicensed taverns and gambling dens.

A few moments later, Olivier and Francis walked out of the church with an old woman. She was telling them her troubles and the priests stood in the doorway patiently listening to her complaints. Her frowning daughter waited beside a horse-drawn wagon. Finally, the old woman nodded in agreement to Olivier's advice, made the sign of the cross and let Francis guide her to the wagon. The young priest walked step by step with her to the side of the wagon and then helped her up into the seat beside her daughter.

Olivier watched the old woman hobble to the wagon, her hand clutching Francis' arm. He then saw the magistrate and greeted him with a handshake. Olivier gestured for them to go inside the church, but Castañedo shook his head.

"It's a little cool, but there's plenty of sun and I would prefer to sit outside."

"As you wish." Olivier signaled to Francis to join them.

They walked to a wooden bench situated on the bank of the nearby bayou. Olivier and Castañedo sat facing each other on the bench and Francis sat on a tree stump across from them. The stump had been cut from a downed tree and served as a stool.

"I'm glad you want to sit outside, Magistrate. It's the

first pleasant day we've enjoyed in quite a while and the sun's warmth feels good." Olivier saw Francis smile in agreement.

"It does. I've been cooped-up like a chicken during the freeze and I relish the fresh air down here in the lowlands. I see the church has been whitewashed. It looks much better." The magistrate pointed to Santa María which now gleamed in the sunlight.

"It does look good, doesn't it?" Olivier smiled. "It's our hope the final renovations will be finished by Easter. There's only a little work left to be done outside; the steeple bell needs a bit of adjustment – it's not hanging plumb with the floor. After that's fixed, the carpenters and painters will finish working inside. They have assured me that everything will be finished before Easter, but Francis and I are keeping our fingers crossed." He looked at Castañedo waiting for him to speak of his reason for riding down to Santa María.

The magistrate took off his hat and ran his hand through his hair. "Well, Father, I have to tell you that Madam Villièrs and her niece, Gisella, are both dead. Murdered. I heard about their deaths yesterday morning and spent most of the day down in Mosquito Creek. I rode home in the dark last night."

"Mon Dieu!" Olivier crossed himself and saw Francis do the same. "When?"

"They were murdered in the early morning on the twenty-first. A lad, no more than ten or eleven years old, rode from the village to the Cabildo and told us of the killings; the boy was sent since all the men had already gone fishing for the day. It seems, one of the girls found the bodies when she awoke that morning and then ran to the nearest house in the village for help."

Olivier exhaled loudly.

"The girl, her name's Nina, found the niece's body first

since she was not in the kitchen at seven thirty. It was Gisella's practice to make breakfast at that time. Nina went to awaken her and found her dead. Her throat had been slit. It was a terrible sight for the girl."

"I should think so. What about Madame Villièrs?"

"She suffered the same fate. Each of them was struck on the head with a hard object of some kind and their throats were slit with a knife. I don't know which of them was killed first, but I suspect the niece since her bedroom is located closest to the back door. That's where the murderer entered the house."

"The door wasn't locked?" Francis looked at Castañedo, his eyebrows raised.

"It was locked with a sliding bolt – it was always locked! Madame Villièrs instructed the girls to only open it in the morning when they emptied their chamber pots."

"Then, how did he manage to open the door?" Olivier stared at Castañedo.

"He inserted the blade of a knife into the door frame and pushed the sliding bolt out of its lock. We saw the marks in the doorframe left by his knife. We assume he got into the house late at night and no one heard him come in. Once inside, he went about the killings without concern. Everyone was fast asleep. It seems he killed them both in the same manner. Each was struck on the head to make sure there was no outcry and then he slit their throats. It was over in no time."

Olivier sighed. "Was there anything about the murders that seemed unusual?"

"There was one odd thing. Both of the victims were found with their faces turned to the right, even though they were struck on different sides of the head. The niece was struck on the left side and her ear was flattened as a result. Madame Villièrs was hit on the forehead. Their skulls were cracked where they were struck."

"Are you saying the murderer needlessly slit their throats?" Olivier frowned.

"Yes. There was no need for him to use his knife; they were already dead or dying. He hit them with great force with some sort of heavy implement – possibly an iron bar." Castañedo raised his hand above his head and brought it down with a loud smack on the wooden arm of the bench. "That's how hard he struck Madame Villièrs."

"In the darkness, he may not have known how hard he had hit them."

"Perhaps. But I think it more likely he wanted to make sure they were dead. Probably, so they could never reveal his identity." Castañedo nodded, certain he was right.

"Why do you think the murderer went to the trouble of turning their faces to the right?

"We wondered that, as well. Lieutenant Palacios Leguía, who accompanied me to Mosquito Creek, suggested what I think was the reason. The lad is cleverer than I have credited him. He suggested the murderer slashed their throats from behind so he wouldn't soil his clothes with blood. In that manner, he would leave little, if any, trace of blood on his person. The only blood spots he left were where he wiped his knife on their bed sheets."

"He is fastidious, isn't he? I don't suppose he left either of the instruments of death in the house?" Olivier shook his head, knowing what Castañedo's answer would be.

"No, Father, he left nothing! He's much too cunning. I'm sure he's the same man who drowned the Dumont boys and the girl – what was her name?"

"María Isabel Mendoza. Let's not forget he's also the man who attacked Charles Laroux and attempted to poison the entire Dumont family."

Castañedo nodded. "These murders make me certain the man who calls himself Molière is the man we are seeking. When last we talked, Father, you already had come to that conclusion and now I too am certain. It's obvious he murdered the two women to make sure they would not identify him. I wish now I had interviewed them the morning after you told me what the Mènard girl said about Molière."

"It couldn't be helped, Magistrate. At the time, you were preoccupied with the capture of the road robbers, who thankfully are now in custody." Olivier smiled at Castañedo.

"Verdad (true), but it still bothers me. Now, I'm left wondering how we'll identify him. It's not enough to know he's a well-dressed gentlemen who wears dark clothes and looks like a lawyer. I don't know a lawyer in New Orleans who wears anything other than dark suits."

"If Ana Luisa's memory is to be trusted, we also know the man has cordovan boots and rides a chestnut stallion," added Francis.

"Yes, Father, but God knows how many gentlemen in town wear cordovan boots and ride chestnut stallions. They are both as common as drunken Indians – well, almost."

Francis raised his hand. "There can't be that many gentlemen in New Orleans who wear dark suits, cordovan boots, and ride a chestnut stallion at the same time."

Castañedo looked at the young priest. "That's a good point, Father."

Olivier smiled, pleased to see Francis praised by the magistrate. "What about the brothel ledger? We saw it, when we were there. Madam Villièrs' kept it in her bedroom."

"It's gone, Father. He broke into her dresser to get it. Still, to be sure, I looked all over the house." Castañedo shook his head. "He took the ledger, assuming he was mentioned in it."

Olivier nodded. "I should have known better. That

diablo (devil) is much too clever to leave the ledger there to be found. I assume he knew about it from the many times he talked to Madame Villièrs in the parlor. He probably saw it on one of his visits to the house."

"That's what I think. At one time or other, he must have seen her write something in the ledger and once aware of its existence, he would expect her to keep it in the locked bedroom."

"That would be the logical place for her to safeguard it."

Castañedo clucked his tongue. "Well, with Madame Villièrs and Gisella murdered and without the ledger, I'm at a loss as to what next can be done to find this fiend."

"What about the last girl he was with in the house? She could identify him – that is, if she's alive. I assume you asked the remaining girls which of them was with Molière." Francis leaned forward, his elbow propped on his knee.

Castañedo frowned as he moved his eyes from Olivier to Francis. "Of course, I inquired about that girl, her name was Catarina Fonseca. She was Portuguese. Unfortunately, she's dead, but not by his hand. She was struck by a venomous snake one early morning on her way to the outhouse. The girl went there to empty her chamber pot and was struck twice on her left ankle. It happened on that unseasonably warm day, a week or so before the freeze. They thought the snake, probably one of those large water snakes, was warming itself in the sun when she either stepped on it or walked too close. The girl would not have seen it since they're brown and blend into the dead leaves."

"Fille pauve! (Poor girl!) May God grant her blessed peace." Olivier sighed. "I don't suppose any of the girls in the house saw him when he was with Catarina Fonseca."

"No, nor did the Portuguese girl. She told the other girls that the room was too dark to see his face. The shutters were completely closed and a black piece of fabric covered the only window in the room. Catarina said he had a thick head of hair and spoke softly. She said his kisses were soft as well. The girls told me she could offer no other description of him."

"Too bad! That's of little help. By the way, what has happened to the remaining girls? Where are they now? I should have asked about them immediately."

"Tranquilo, Padre (Be calm, Father), they're fine. The girls, now eight in number, are in the Ursuline Convent and there they will remain until the Mother Superior finds suitable homes for them. It's also possible some of them might stay in the convent."

"Good. I'm glad to hear that. Mother Marguerite will take good care of them."

"That's my expectation. Unfortunately, none of the remaining girls have any knowledge of Molière. Several were new to the house and the others never saw him, though they had heard about him. It's very disappointing."

"It is indeed. That means there's no one left at the house now who can identify him. It's possible one of the men who went to the house in the past year might have seen him, but it would be difficult, if not impossible, to find such a man." Olivier looked at Castañedo, hoping he might disagree with him.

"Not without the ledger and that's gone, I'm sure, forever," Olivier nodded, certain Molière had taken the ledger.

"My men also inquired about the village and no one there took note of the night visitors to the house. They were only concerned when a drunken man or two made noise riding through the village late at night. They're early morning people who are off fishing before dawn."

"Wasn't it Molière's routine to ride to the house about midday and depart before dark?"

"It was, Father, and we asked the villagers about the one man who rode once a month to the house at midday. Most of them had no recollection of such a man, but a few may well have seen him and don't want to admit it. They're a religious people, always crossing themselves for one thing or another. The villagers try to ignore the 'goings-on' at the Villièrs house as one old Acadian woman told me."

"They were not too religious to accept money from the brothel." Francis's face turned red as he spoke. "The villagers received payment from Madame Villièrs for allowing the brothel to exist in Mosquito Creek. I suspect they also were paid for fetching food and other goods from New Orleans. They must have provided other services at the house as well. What hypocrites!"

"It's true, Francis, they *are* hypocrites, but I fear so are we all in one way or another." Olivier sighed. "Piety is all too often wished rather than achieved. It's a struggle for even the clergy to live a pious life. It is for me, is it not for you?"

Francis made a face and then reluctantly nodded.

Castañedo listened and made no comment until Olivier turned to him. "Well, I can only say I've never been equal to that struggle and long ago gave up trying!" He laughed and the two priests joined him.

"Well said, Magistrate." Olivier still smiled.

"There was one man who recalled a rider in the past, who rode now and then through the village at about midday. The poor fellow is crippled and spends much of his time sitting outside looking at the squirrels in the trees. I spoke to him myself as we left the village. He said the rider hadn't come through the village in a long time."

"That's odd, isn't it? We know Molière was a regular visitor each month so why wasn't he seen? Could the crippled man describe him? What's his name?"

"No. His name is Edgard and he said the rider looked much like the other men who rode through the village. There was nothing distinctive about him." Castañedo frowned. "If Edgard's memory is accurate it appears that Molière, for some unknown reason, stopped coming through the village on his monthly visits to the house. Yet, we know he continued to make the trip which obviously means he must have come another way."

"What about the use of a boat on the creek to reach the house?" asked Francis.

"No, Father, the creek doesn't reach the Mississippi River anywhere near the house or the village. I sent men in both directions along the creek looking for another entry point to the river, but they found nothing. So, now I'll order another search north and south along the river road."

"So, for the moment at least, we're stuck." Olivier rubbed his chin.

"It seems so, Father. Do you have any thoughts on the matter, Francis?"

"I suppose it would be useless to alert the sentries at the city gates to look out for a well-dressed man with cordovan boots riding a chestnut stallion in or out of the New Orleans."

Castañedo made a face. "I fear it would be futile. The sentries are barely able to control the road traffic coming in and out of the city. They are definitely not the best of our soldiers. The sentries have even been known to let outlaws into New Orleans – well-known outlaws they were warned to arrest if they saw them. These days, there are all too many such soldiers in the Spanish army. God help us, if this city is ever attacked."

Olivier and Francis exchanged looks. They were surprised to hear Castañedo criticize the Spanish army. Most Spaniards usually found fault with the predominantly French colonists, but never the Spanish officials or army.

"It's also likely that such an alert would reach the ears of Molière." Castañedo continued unaware of their surprised looks. "It seems there is no administrative decision that's not known almost immediately to everyone in this city. As we all know, there's no such thing as a secret in New

Orleans. News of every plan or policy we make seems to reach the streets within hours, if not minutes, after they're made." Exasperated, he exhaled his breath loudly.

"Do you think that's how the murderer learned of your plan to interview Madame Villièrs a second time?" Olivier stared at Castañedo.

"I don't know – possibly. I suppose a number of people knew about it. Whom did you tell beside Dumont?"

"Only Dumont, his nephew, Charles Laroux and Father Antonio. But I told a few others about my interview with Ana Luisa, which included the information that Madame Villièrs and Gisella could describe the mysterious man from New Orleans. Mon Dieu, did I lead the killer to them?" Olivier slapped his forehead.

Castañedo reached over and placed his hand on Olivier's knee. "You're not the only one who talked about your interview with the girl. I did the same, Father. Everyone in my office knew about it and God knows whom they told."

"I did it, too!" Francis exclaimed. "I told my Capuchin brothers about it the next night when we met for our monthly supper together. It was the main topic of the night."

Olivier was not relieved to know the others had also spoken of it. There were tears in his eyes. He feared his pride again had led him astray. Olivier knew he had been proud of his talk with Ana Luisa and pleased with all the information about the brothel she had shared with him. Though he had understated his role in her revelations when later describing them, he knew pride was strongly present in him at the time. And, while he no longer felt guilt for the terrible deaths of the two women, Olivier knew he faced a lifelong struggle with the sin of pride. It occurred to him that the murders and the guilt he had felt might be God's warning to him – a warning that foretold what he would suffer if he did not cleanse himself of sin. He gritted his teeth, hoping he could hold back his tears.

Castañedo saw the tears welling in Olivier's eyes and looked away so as not to embarrass him. He waited a moment and then changed the subject. "So, it's obvious Madam Villièrs and Gisella were killed to prevent them from identifying the murderer. The ledger was taken for the same reason. Unfortunately, now I am left without a sensible direction to take to find and arrest him. Have you any suggestions?"

Olivier sighed and turned his mind to the magistrate's problem. He raised his forefinger. "I think I might know a way to not only identify the murderer, but capture him."

"Tell me, Father."

"Let me ask you a couple of questions first, Magistrate. Is it true that Madame Villièrs' valuables have not yet been found? That's what is rumored in the city."

"Yes, that's true."

"What about her private papers? Have they been found?"

"No, I assume her papers are hidden with her valuables, probably in a safe-box secreted under some loose floorboard, behind a wall or buried beneath a rock in the woods. We have no notion where they are concealed." Castañedo stared at Olivier. "Do you think the woman's cache might be used as an enticement to lure him back to her house – where we can seize him?"

"Yes, Magistrate, but I think her private papers, not her valuables might bring him back to the house. Since the murderer appears to be a man of means, I doubt her money or jewelry would interest him. But if the contents of her papers are unknown and missing, then they might be used to entice him. It would only require a rumor spread about town saying a search of the Villièrs house had not produced her will, deed to the property and other business documents. It would be the phrase *other business documents* that could attract the murderer's attention and possibly worry him." Olivier smiled. "And, hopefully, the phrase will suggest that a copy of the brothel ledger or other means of identifying him might be among the documents."

"Yes, that would definitely bring him back to Mosquito Creek. He would return to find and destroy any of her papers in the house."

"Exactly. That's why he killed Madame Villièrs and Gisella and took the brothel ledger from her office."

"Castañedo pursed his lips. "Yes, Father, such a rumor might indeed lure the murderer to the house. It might be our only chance to capture him."

"The murderer, of course, will be suspicious of the apparent existence of other business documents. He's much too clever to be easily fooled. If the scheme is to succeed, he must be convinced Madame Villièrs kept other records which were hidden away with her valuables. If not, he'll ignore the rumor and never go near the house."

"How then do we convince him? Obviously, the rumor must come from someone whose veracity is well known."

Olivier and Francis sat silently thinking.

"Ah, I have it!" Castañedo's eyes glistened as he rubbed his hands together. "I have a source for the rumor and it's based on truth."

"Francis, please bring us one of the bottles of French wine Madame Boudreaux gave us a week ago. I'm certain there's at least one left." Olivier nodded his thanks to Francis as he stood. "We are fortunate to have such a generous friend," he told Castañedo as the priest hurried away.

"Father, are you acquainted with the licenciado (lawyer), Alvaro Montoya Gómez?"

"No, I'm not."

"Montoya Gómez is an elderly man who has only a few local clients left these days. But he's a close friend of the governor and still counsels him. Well, he came to see me several days after our interview with Madame Villièrs; he heard about the interview from the governor." The magistrate paused as Francis returned with the bottle of wine and two glasses.

"Where's your glass, Francis?"

"I'm not thirsty, Father." The young priest was breathing hard. He had run to and from the church so he would not miss what the magistrate had to say.

"Please continue, Magistrate." Olivier spoke after Castañedo had taken his first drink of wine and smacked his lips, pleased with the taste.

"Montoya Gómez told me he had some information about Madame Villièrs he thought I should know. She had come to talk to him in early December. Her visit concerned a will which was confidential and could not be discussed with me. But during the conversation, she inquired about the cost of storing her private papers in his office safe. Madame Villièrs instantly agreed to the amount required and told him she would return with the papers sometime after the first of the year. At that time, she intended to sign the will he contracted to prepare for her."

"I assume Madame Villièrs had not yet returned to sign the will when Montoya Gómez came to speak to you."

"No, Father, the will is still unsigned and in his possession. But that's not why he came to talk to me; he came to inform me Madame Villièrs planned to close the house sometime this spring and return to France with Gisella. She intended to place the remaining girls in good homes and leave before the storm season. Montoya Gómez told me Madame Villièrs' intentions to be helpful. He had heard the bishop's sermons urging the parishioners to demand the closure of the *house of abysmal sin* as he has called it. The old lawyer knew I would be relieved to know the brothel would soon be closed and the problem of its existence resolved. Of course, the murderer has resolved that problem much sooner for me."

"Indeed. What a good man. So, all lawyers are not the villains they are said to be."

"No, and Montoya Gómez is one of those lawyers deservedly well regarded here in New Orleans. So, now with his information, a *truthful* rumor can be spread throughout this city. It would say the disposition of Madame Villièrs' house cannot be made because her private papers have not yet been found and are believed still to be in Mosquito Creek." Castañedo frowned. "I wonder if that's enough to lure the murderer to the brothel."

Olivier rubbed his chin. "Shouldn't something be included saying the deed to the house is among her papers and is needed for its eventual sale?"

"That statement definitely should be included. It's not only true, but would make the rumor more believable."

"I assume you have thoroughly searched the house for her papers."

Castañedo nodded. "We are still looking. Lieutenant Palacios Leguía and two men are there now. The men are replaced at night by two others who guard the house. An unoccupied house would be a free bazaar for looters and thieves, especially with talk in the streets of piles of gold and silver coins hidden there."

"A very good precaution. May I pour you another glass of wine, Magistrate?" Olivier had finished two glasses, while Castañedo had drunk less than half his first glass.

"No, Father, I have a sour stomach this morning." Castañedo made a face. "It's obvious her papers are stored with her money. For a while, I thought the murderer had taken them along with the ledger. But when I remembered seeing the ledger in her hand, I knew it alone fit in the locked drawer in her dresser. It's much too narrow to hold anything else. The ledger is about an inch thick and the drawer is little more than that in depth; it's also the only locked drawer in the dresser. All the others hold clothing and inexpensive jewelry."

"She obviously hid all her official documents and valuables someplace else in the house." Olivier poured the last of the wine into his glass and took a sip to keep it from overflowing. "We can't be certain the murderer left without her papers, but it doesn't seem likely. No matter how many lengthy conversations and lunches they shared together, Madame Villièrs was much too prudent to let him or anyone else know where such important possessions were hidden. I'd be surprised if even her niece, Gisella, knew their location."

"I agree, Father. The woman was no fool." Castañedo gave Olivier a wry smile.

"No. I suggest that we try to repeat the rumor to the same people we told about the interview with Ana Luisa Ibáñez."

"Exactamente!" Castañedo looked back and forth at the two priests. "We should repeat the rumor and say nothing more. Any embellishment might make it less believable."

Olivier and Francis nodded simultaneously.

"I must now make plans to seize the man if and when he goes to the Villièrs house. It's more than likely he'll go at night, but I'll have to station men there during the day as well. The men would have to be well hidden and perhaps wait for days. Some of them, of course, will be in plain sight since he would expect the house to be guarded and knows we are trying to find the woman's hidden valuables. My God, where will I find so many men?"

"I don't envy your effort, Magistrate. You are dealing with a very clever man who may well suspect a trap. I wish you well."

"Thank you, Father. I know he's clever and so I must be even cleverer." They all stood and walked to the post where Castañedo had tied his horse.

The priests watched the magistrate mount his horse and ride away. They walked to the church in silence. Olivier turned to Francis as the younger man held the door open.

"What's on your mind, Francis?"

"I don't think the magistrate is fully aware of the exceptional mind of the murderer. His success so far suggests a cautious man who plans for every unforeseen possibility. If he does go to the house, which I doubt will happen, I think he will be prepared for whatever trap has been laid for him. He's much too clever to be fooled, never mind captured by the magistrate's men. I fear for those involved in this scheme."

Olivier nodded. "I understand your skepticism, Francis. Like you, I think he will suspect a trap has been laid for him. But I also think he will come despite his suspicions. He will come because the risk of his identity being revealed by some record among her papers is too much to chance. It is then my hope the murderer will make a mistake and underestimate the magistrate."

"But, Father, the murderer may already have her papers. He might have found them the night he murdered her. In that event, he certainly won't be lured to Mosquito Creek."

"That's true. But the magistrate has to assume the murderer didn't find her papers. It's his only hope now to capture him. What else is the magistrate to do?"

Francis shrugged his shoulders. "So, it's a gamble."

"It is! Let's hope he goes to Mosquito Creek and the magistrate captures him. He's intelligent, and may well catch the cunning fiend. I certainly hope so for everyone's sake."

He walked into the woods and tied the big draft horse to a leafless oak only a few yards from the road. The horse nudged his arm and he gave him a piece of sugar; he had three more pieces in his coat pocket for the return trip. There was not a sound to be heard in the woods, but he stood still for a long time before stepping quietly away from the horse. His eyes adjusted to the darkness while he waited. He had followed the advice of the old blind Indian, known as the *Seer*, and ridden south on the fourth day of the new month. The Indian told him that night would be cold and clear with a three-quarters moon. He smiled, thinking the *Seer* as usual was right. It was quite clear and "Remercier Dieu!" (Thank God!) not nearly as cold as the last night he had come to the house.

He hesitated beside the horse, thinking of what lay ahead. He had carefully planned for the night, but there were many unknowns in his scheme that troubled him. His previous plans had no unknowns and he had anticipated almost everything that happened. That was why they had worked to perfection. But, this time, he was going to the house without such certainty and that worried him. He had no notion of what to expect or how many men he might find guarding the place. As he stood in the silent woods, a foreboding of disaster made him suddenly shiver in fear and he wished he had not come. He sighed, letting out a long breath and the mood passed. He knew there was no other alternative. He had to be there to free himself of worry.

He had always known there were risks to his trip to Mosquito Creek. For a week, he had debated whether or not to make the long journey. The rumor of Madame Villièrs' hidden money and private papers might well be true, but he wondered if the contents of those papers would be worth the risk of capture. They might not mention him at all – in fact, they might not mention any of the brothel's clients. There also was the possibility the hiding place where she put them would never be found. The crafty old woman might have hidden everything somewhere outside the house in a safe-box where no one would ever think to look for it.

She was sly, that one, and could have hidden it anywhere. She was so stingy, she would do anything to safeguard her money. That's why she kept records of those who frequented the house. If anyone threatened to close the brothel, she only had to speak to one of her prominent visitors from New Orleans and that would be the end of it. A word to the governor was all that was needed despite the bishop's incessant complaints about the brothel's existence. Her clients knew she would not hesitate to expose them if her livelihood was endangered. Their identities would be revealed even if they had used false names. That mean old woman would let no one threaten her income or know where she concealed her money and jewelry.

He had seen the ledger's contents and that was why it had to be destroyed. The madam had recorded the men's names, whether false or not, and their physical descriptions. She also had included their particular practices with the girls. He recalled shivering when he read what she had written about him. It was ultimately what made him risk the perilous trip to the house. The possibility that a second such ledger existed which mentioned him was too much to bear. He had to go to the house again. He could not take the chance the magistrate's men would find it, especially since he had heard they were tearing the house apart searching for her valuables.

He moved carefully trying to avoid stepping on broken branches or twigs that would snap loudly underfoot. The moonlight gave him enough light to see a few feet ahead of him as well as to the left side where the trail to the treehouse lay hidden in the trees. He walked parallel to the path, some fifteen feet away so he would not be seen. He knew it was likely the magistrate's men had found the treehouse and the boy's path that ran from the river road to the creek. If aware of it, they would have posted a sentry somewhere along the way to watch the path. The treehouse would be the best place for such an observer to stay hidden and watch for someone entering the woods from the road. Its height offered a view of a long portion of the path in the moonlight.

Creeping stealthily, it took him almost three-quarters of an hour to reach a spot opposite the treehouse. He had to move through soft muddy marshlands that hindered his pace. Much of the area around Mosquito Creek was usually wet or water soaked from rain and frequent runoffs of the Mississippi River. Even though he could not see the boys' house from where he stood, he recognized the oak in which it was built. It had the thickest trunk on the path. He crept quietly on his hands and knees toward the tree and crouched down behind a cluster of thorny brambles. He kneeled in wet sand ten or so feet from the tree. From that position, he could look up and see the outline of the treehouse as well as the dark opening of its doorway.

Initially, he saw nothing to suggest anyone was inside the house. But he knew a sentry could be there, sitting or lying on the wooden floor. The little building was no more than four feet in height, which was high enough for the young boys who built it, but not for a grown man. A man would not be able to stand inside without bending his head. Out of curiosity, on one of his journeys to the brothel, he had climbed up to the doorway and looked inside the house.

Now, as he studied its dark doorway, he pictured a man sitting cross-legged on the floor looking down at the path. From that height in the moonlight, a watcher could see a long way, at least a quarter of a mile, toward the creek. Even lying on the ground, much of the trail stood out through the leafless trees.

He grimaced unsure of what he should do. From the treehouse, the narrow path was the only way to the brothel. Sinking sand lay on both sides of the path which stood on ground only a few inches above the wetlands. If he went off the trail anywhere ahead, he would risk walking into water, sucking muck or even quick sands. The only other route to the brothel was the road through Mosquito Creek, which he assumed the magistrate had carefully guarded. No one was in sight when he passed the turnoff on the river road, but they were probably well hidden nearby.

Despite his worries, he knew the path through the marsh was the better of the two routes to the brothel. With luck a watcher might not see him if he crawled slowly and quietly along the path. The man might not be paying careful attention to his assignment. He could be bored or even dozing. Seemingly endless time spent staring out into the darkness would weary anyone. The night sentries, he knew, were assigned twelve-hour shifts beginning at eight in the evening and, if one of them sat in the cramped tree house most of that time, he would have been already on duty for more than five hours. He nodded, thinking that was a long time for any man to watch for movement on the path and remain alert in the darkness.

He stared at the doorway, wondering if he should risk sneaking out onto the path toward the creek. "No," he thought, "It's much too uncertain and dangerous. He might see me as soon as I venture onto the open path and sound an alarm. Or worse, the man might shoot me down as I try to escape." All the magistrate's men were armed and he assumed they had been ordered to shoot anyone approaching the house on sight.

"It's that damned Indian's fault," he hissed though gritted teeth. "Damn him, he deserves to be strangled! He should have warned me the moonlight might expose me on the path."

He recalled standing above the Indian who sat cross-legged on the ground against a tree. The old man took a thin stick from the bag he wore over his shoulder and used it to draw a circle in the dirt. He then mumbled something unintelligible and sketched a small stick-man inside the circle. He pointed a shaking finger at the circle and told him the moon would light his way.

He made a face. "Of course, the old fool didn't think to tell me the moon would light the way for everyone else as well as me."

Annoyed, he was about to return to his horse when he heard a sound from the treehouse. Uncertain of what he had heard, he stopped breathing briefly to listen. He raised his head with his left ear pointed upward toward the treehouse. Then, he heard it again even louder. It was a man snoring. He smiled when another snore followed. He waited only long enough to hear two more grating snores and then crept out onto the path, never looking up at the house. There was no need to worry now, the sentry was fast asleep. His snoring could still be heard as he hurried away. He straightened up when he reached a bend in the trail, where he could not be seen from the treehouse, and ran to a line of pines that bordered the creek.

He stood behind a tree and waited for a time, looking for other sentries. He saw none, but stayed within the woods, moving silently from tree to tree as he proceeded to the back of the Villièrs house. He moved slowly one step at a time, stopping and listening every few steps for any sound that would suggest a sentry was near him. But he heard nothing. He finally saw the outhouse ahead of him, but he remained hidden in the trees to the far side of it.

He saw no one standing or sitting anywhere near the rear of the house, but he suspected at least one sentry would be on guard somewhere outside in back. It would be a hidden spot where the door and windows would be in sight as well as the old dilapidated shed that stood behind the building. He scrutinized the area in the moonlight, but saw no sign of a hidden sentry.

He waited in the woods behind a huge live oak. He

would not move until he knew the hiding place of the outside sentry; it would be foolish to do otherwise. Time passed and he still waited in silence. He held his pocket watch up to the moonlight and saw that it was three-thirty. "I can't wait much longer," he thought. "I've only three more hours of darkness left." He knew when he left New Orleans there was no way of knowing how long it would take him to reach the back of the house. It was one of the unknown problems that made his plan perilous.

More time passed and he was beginning to feel cold. He was wearing layers of clothing to keep warm, but the intense cold seemed to penetrate everything he wore. Like the last time, his fingers had begun to feel numb even with his hands in woolen gloves and stuffed down in his pockets. His toes also were becoming numb despite heavy socks and flannel-lined leather boots. His face, especially his cheeks felt frozen and he found it an effort to move his jaw. The wool hood he wore was of little help since he constantly exposed his face to look about for a sentry's movement. After more than three hours in the frigid night air, he knew his body could not take much more of the cold.

He decided to wait another half hour and, if the outside sentry did not reveal himself, he would leave. Fifteen minutes later, there still was no sign of the man. He frowned in disgust. At four o'clock, he told himself to wait five minutes more and, when that time came, he turned away from the house and started moving toward the path. He had reached the next tree on the way when he heard the back door open up and then close. The sound of the door latch snapping into place seemed especially loud in the silent night.

A bearded man came outside, a fur hat in his hand. He stopped outside to adjust the hat so it covered his ears. The man was dressed warmly in a heavy outer coat and he went toward a live oak beside the outhouse. Another man appeared from behind the tree and the two sentries met near the back door. They talked for a few minutes, shared a laugh and then separated as the man from the house walked over to the live oak and the other sentry entered the back door.

"Ah, they exchanged places," he said to himself. "They're probably on two-hour shifts here as well as in front of the house." Knowing exactly where the new sentry stood, he moved quietly through the trees to come up behind the live oak.

The sentry stood lighting his pipe when he was struck on the back of the head. He fell to the ground with blood running from the wound. A second blow with the iron bar killed him. It was over in seconds with only the soft thump of the bar striking the man's head.

He waited awhile beside the man's body. He doubted the attack on the sentry had been heard, but he waited there in silence to make sure. Several minutes later, he ran to the left side of the shed where the oak firewood had been stacked. He flattened himself against the wall in the shadows that fell from the roof.

Once again, he waited awhile before moving. When he eventually did move, he stepped back from the wall looked up at the window above the shed. It was the bedroom window that María Isabel had used to leave the house in the summer. He stepped a foot or so away from the building to see it better. A dark cloud passed briefly over the moon and he had to wait until the light returned. He looked up quickly when the moon finally reappeared and then immediately pressed his body back against the wall. He had moved out of the shadows for only a second, but it was enough time for him to glance up and see the half open window.

He snorted, thinking the open window was an obvious trap. "Only a fool would climb up to that window; there's surely a sentry there watching the back of the house," he thought. For a moment, he worried he might have been seen when he stood out in the moonlight, but his worry was quickly gone. He knew no one at the window could have seen him from where he stood at the side of the shed near the house.

He turned to the stacked logs beside him and bent over to look at the middle of the pile. The firewood was only five layers high and he assumed at least two other layers had been taken to burn in the fireplace. He took off his gloves and ran his hands over the top of the logs. They were dry to the touch. He then carefully removed two logs from the middle of the third layer of the pile. It was difficult to pull them out from the pile without disturbing the logs above, but he managed it even with cold and numbing fingers. Proud of his success, he smiled, remembering a similar childhood triumph when, with deft fingers, he had won a game of pick-up-sticks.

The memory dismissed, he turned his mind to what next had to be done. He took the six oil soaked rags from the leather bag that had been tied on his belt and placed them on top of the woodpile. Then, one after another he gently pushed the rags into the space he had made in the middle of the woodpile. He paused a few moments while he rubbed his hands together, hoping to remove the numbness from his fingers. His fingers were still a little numb when he stopped, but he decided finish what he came to do and warm his hands later. He took three cotton balls from his coat pocket and nestled them in the oily rags. From his other pocket, he withdrew a piece of quartz flint and short length of steel. Feeling his fingers stiffening again, he hurriedly scraped the quartz flint against the steel.

Only two scrapes were needed and sparks ignited the cotton tinder and, within seconds, the rags were also on fire. A moment or so later, yellow flames began to appear both above and below the burning rags. The fire then spread quickly. Stored more than a year under the shed's overhanging roof, the logs were thoroughly dry and, once the flames reached them, they began to burn. The flames at the center of the woodpile were already leaping up the shed wall. He waited only long enough to see the back wall of the brothel beginning to burn and then disappeared into the woods. Watching from the darkness, he saw the shed implode and disintegrate in the blaze. .

Fueled by the cedar siding, the flames had reached the upstairs windows by the time an alarm was shouted. The sentry sitting beside the open window had fallen asleep and did not see the fire until a flare above the window sill awakened him. He instantly shouted *fire*, but it was too late. By then, the wooden house with its new cedar siding and roof could not be saved. In moments, the entire structure became a roaring inferno that no amount of water from the creek could put out. No one even made an attempt to go for water.

The magistrate's men could only watch the fire as it consumed the house. They stood away from the heat in the road that went into the village. Many Acadians also stood outside watching the fire. There was little said as the flames consumed the building. The burning roof soon fell into the interior of the house and, one by one, the four standing walls toppled into the blackened ruins below. One of uniformed men later said the brothel was engulfed in flames and completely gone in less than an hour. "It was," he declared loudly, "a sign of God's displeasure with the sinful practices that went on in the house."

He left when the entire back wall of the brothel was ablaze. He moved quickly through the woods, striding from tree to tree toward the tree-house trail. A little more than half-way to the path, he saw a heavy man running to the fire from that direction. He assumed the man was the sentry who had fallen asleep in the treehouse. The man had either heard the shouted alarm at the burning building or seen the flames shooting into the sky above the trees. He stopped behind a tree and watched as the treehouse sentry passed him. Panting loudly, the portly man carried a long rifle in his hand.

He did not move until the sentry's panting could no longer be heard. He then turned to run down the trail when he saw another man, this one carrying a lantern, hurrying toward him. Startled, he moved back behind the tree as another uniformed man armed with a rifle ran past him. This man, slender and fast afoot, ran rapidly without a sound.

"Much too close a call!" He exhaled a long breath, realizing the magistrate had stationed a second sentry somewhere along the path. "Probably near the river road," he thought, thankful he had entered the woods well below the trail to the treehouse.

It took him only a few minutes to run down the path and find his hidden horse. He led him through the trees much farther south before leaving the dark woods. He wanted to be far away from the path before removing the thick pads that muffled the sound of his hooves on the road. A satisfied smile on his lips, he mounted the big horse and set out for Point de Roche. The trip was uneventful and he saw no other rider on the road. He still felt cold, but the events of the night occupied his thoughts and he only occasionally felt the cold or numbness in his hands and feet. He reached Point de Roche a half hour later.

He spent another few minutes harnessing his draft horse to the wagon and he was on his way before first light. He had left the wagon among a number of others at the Indian village on Point de Roche. The Indians traded furs and hides to northern merchants who hired Acadians to transport their purchases to New Orleans.

There was no rider or other wagon on the road when

he set out from the village. With a light load of deerskins, he drove his wagon swiftly north toward New Orleans. At the turnoff to Mosquito Creek, while passing two heavily-laden timber wagons, he looked to the east and saw a thin trail of smoke rising above the trees where the brothel had stood. There was also the distinct smell of burning wood in the early morning air.

He exhaled his breath. "Well, that's one problem solved," he thought, "unless she kept her papers in an iron strongbox." That possibility worried him briefly and then he dismissed it. He assumed any written records in an iron box would be ruined by the heat of the fire. Relieved, he sighed and saw the first beams of sunlight stream through the trees ahead of him.

CHAPTER EIGHT

NEW ORLEANS: JANUARY 2 – 18, 1800

"The fire destroyed everything. If there was a second ledger hidden in the brothel, it was undoubtedly burned along with everything else." Olivier threw up his hands.

He sat in Jean Bertin's office three days after the fire. The magistrate told Olivier all the grim details earlier that morning. Leaving the Cabildo, he met Charles Laroux by chance in the street and accompanied him to his uncle's office.

Olivier told them what he knew of the fire as they drank tea and ate an assortment of pastries brought into the office by Tristan Surette.

Jean Bertin listened carefully, his eyes focused on Olivier's face. "Did they find any of the woman's money in the ruins? I've heard she was thrifty and saved every penny. It's said she hid all her wealth in that old house."

"Not yet. They've been looking ever since the fire went out. They have to dig through the charred remains of the building. The fire consumed most of the timbers and only the stone foundation remains intact."

"Her coins would also be intact, no matter where they were in the house. I'd be looking for an iron chest or strongbox, if I were the magistrate's men. You know, similar to the chests they use to carry bullion in ships." Jean Bertin nodded, agreeing with himself. "That would be the most sensible place for her valuables, including a second ledger if there was one."

Olivier shook his head. "Nothing has been found as yet. The magistrate thinks they'll be done with their search by tomorrow. He was there all day yesterday supervising the work."

"That old house was a tinder box only waiting for a dry spell and a spark or two. It's too bad, I've heard Madame Villièrs had two of François Boucher's paintings displayed on the walls of the brothel. Those nudes were worth a pretty penny. Boucher has been dead for thirty or so years and his work has gone up in price every year since his death."

Charles Laroux nodded and Olivier suspected both of them had visited the brothel. He saw them exchange knowing looks. Olivier spooned sugar into his cup and took a sip of the tea. He did not want to be caught staring at them.

"So, it's another incident of Spanish incompetence." Jean Bertin shook his head. "They not only let the murderer get away, they let him raze the house and all the valuables in it. God save us from these Spanish fools!"

Olivier said nothing. He knew any words spoken in defense of the magistrate would be scorned by Jean Bertin. The Frenchman, like most of the other colonists, blamed the Spaniards for every misfortune that happened in Louisiana. It did not matter whether it was their fault or not. "It's a wonder," he thought, "they don't blame the Spaniards for the summer storms that flood the city and the lowlands."

"They never even sighted him?" Charles Laroux filled Olivier's half-full cup. "Surely, one of the sentries got a glimpse of him?"

"No, he was never seen and the house was well guarded."

"How well guarded?" Jean Bertin grimaced in disgust.

"The magistrate deployed eight men in and around the house; four of them were soldiers loaned to him by the commandant of the garrison. All of them were well hidden and out of sight. Outside, there were two men stationed along the rutted road that runs through Mosquito Creek to the brothel, two more men on a path south of the house, one in a treehouse built by Acadian boys and another near the river road. Two of his men were also inside, one watching from an upstairs window in the front of the house, the other from a window at the back of the house. There were also two other sentries – a man hidden outside the front door and another, Rafael Portillo, outside at the rear of the house. Bènissez son âme! (Bless his soul.) He was the murdered man."

Jean Bertin threw his hands out to the side. "Mon Dieu! Yet, with *all those men*, they never even glimpsed him? Astonishing! They must have all been drunk or sleeping on the job."

"No, Monsieur Dumont, they were attentive. To make sure, the magistrate rotated them every two hours. The outside sentries were also well-hidden in the woods."

"That's hard to believe since the outside man was killed before he could utter a sound. If he was so well hidden, how did that happen?"

"The magistrate thinks the murderer was in the woods behind the house and saw the four o'clock sentry rotation – that's when the inside and outside sentries changed places at the back of the house. That would also explain why the fire started at four-fifteen."

"Why then was it that the inside man in the back didn't see the fire start from the upstairs window? If he was watching for the murderer coming from the south, I assume that's where he would be stationed." Exasperated, Jean Bertin exhaled his breath loudly.

"That's where he was stationed and he was the first one to sound the alarm. But, by the time he saw the flames, the fire was racing up the rear wall of the building. It reached the cedar siding in seconds and the whole house was ablaze as the sentry ran downstairs. As you said, the old building was a tinder box and it went up in flames so fast the men inside barely had time to escape with their lives. One of the men ran outside without his coat."

Jean Bertin frowned. "The magistrate should have anticipated the murderer would try to burn the house down. He should have taken other precautions."

"He did. He put down bear traps all around the house at five-foot intervals. They were hidden beneath the dead leaves that still lay on the ground. Somehow, the murderer was able to set the fire without stepping into one of them. It's a wonder how he did it, especially since there were two traps in front of the firewood pile, where the magistrate thinks the fire was started."

"Those traps were not sprung?"

"No, not one of them. After the fire, they had to be carefully removed before the ruins could be searched. The magistrate mapped their location so none of his men would accidentally step into one of them while on guard duty."

"Is it possible that one of the sentries foolishly talked about the traps in town?"

"No, the magistrate didn't mention the traps until the men were given their instructions at the house. And, once assigned to guard duty in Mosquito Creek, no one was allowed to return to New Orleans. Only Lieutenant Palacios Leguía, his first officer, went to and from town and those trips were made to bring food and drink to the sentries."

"It seems the fiend heard about them somehow – unless he was just lucky."

"I don't think he heard about it from any of the magistrate's men. Castañedo took every possible precaution. He even went to Baton Rouge to buy the bear traps so no one would know he had them. At this time, at least, it looks like the murderer was just lucky."

"If so, he has the devil's own luck."

Laroux held up his hand. "Father, didn't you say the magistrate stationed two sentries on the river road to New Orleans?'

"Yes. One sentry stood behind some trees on the north side of the turn-off and the other stood some thirty feet south of the turn-off – just off the road in the woods. The second sentry's position was beside the entrance to a path the magistrate's men found following the murders of the madam and her niece."

"A path? Where did it go?"

"The path extends from the river road to the creek. It passes through thick woods and a marsh into a bramble covered field bordering the creek. From the field, the Villièrs house can be easily seen during the day. Incidentally, we now know the murderer took the path to the brothel. Fresh horse dung was found near the path's beginning at the river road."

"So, both sentries could still see the river road even though hidden in the woods?"

"Yes, they were looking for an intruder to take either the turnoff or the path toward the Villièrs house. The sentries were warned the intruder could be riding or leading his horse."

Laroux frowned, looking puzzled. "Then, why wasn't the man seen on the road from New Orleans? He had to ride or walk past both sentries to reach the path to the creek."

Olivier frowned. "I don't know. I asked the magistrate the same question and he had no answer for it. There were no lone riders on the road that night. There were the usual wagoners on their way to and from Point de Roche in the afternoon, but no horsemen. Earlier that day, a party of seven Indians rode past the turnoff and, at midday, four Acadians trotted by, but none by himself. The murderer somehow also passed a sentry on the path unseen. He was stationed in a child's treehouse about a hundred yards from the river road."

"So, he passed three sentries unseen." Laroux held up three fingers. "He passed the man stationed at the turnoff to Mosquito Creek, the one at the beginning of the path off the river road and the man in the treehouse. That last one surprises me most of all. How could the sentry miss seeing him moving along the path far below him? One would think the man is invisible."

Olivier nodded. "It surprises me, too. Lieutenant Palacios Leguia told me a long portion of the path can be seen from that height. The house is twenty feet up in the tree. After the fire, he climbed up to see for himself. The path was visible that night because of an almost full moon. So, it's hard to understand how the sentry in the treehouse missed seeing the man on the path."

"The sentry was probably asleep or drunk … or both!" Jean Bertin threw up his hands.

Laroux nodded in agreement. "I've one more question, Father. Why does the discovery of the horse dung make the Spaniards so certain the murderer used the path to reach the brothel?"

"The dung was found in the woods several yards away from the road. It was also evident from the trampled ground that the horse had been tied there for quite a while"

"I see. So, they think the horse was left there for his escape after he set the house afire."

"Exactly. How he initially rode the horse to that place without being seen is unfortunately unknown." Olivier grimaced. "Of course, it's easy to explain his escape. He simply waited while the sentries ran to the fire, and then rode off into the night."

Jean Bertin blew out his breath. "In other words, he outwitted the incompetent Spaniards and probably laughed about it all the way home."

His jaw clinched, Olivier stared at him.

"I don't suppose the magistrate spent any nights down

there in Mosquito Creek." Jean Bertin gave a knowing look.

"As a matter of fact, he did. He and his first officer alternated night duty at the brothel. On the nights he supervised the house watch, he was there from five in the afternoon until eight the following morning. However, he was not there on the thirtieth, the night of the fire."

Jean Bertin sneered. "How convenient."

Olivier stared at Jean Bertin. "The magistrate arranged their schedule so he would be in charge of the watch on New Year's Eve, leaving his first officer free for the night's festivities in New Orleans. He wanted the young man, who is unmarried, to enjoy the celebration."

Jean Bertin frowned, ignoring Olivier's explanation. "So, the damned murderer remains unidentified and he has eluded the Spaniards pitiful attempts to capture him. He burned down the brothel and, with it, the madam's business records that might have named or described him. He's now murdered my two sons, my servant and struck down Charles here almost killing him – and the Spaniards have no notion who he is."

"He's also killed a *Spaniard*, a man with a wife and four young children; the oldest only eight years old." Olivier spoke sharply, his face flushed. He had heard enough of Jean Bertin's criticism of the Spaniards. He was also tired of the man's selfish concerns and his indifference to the suffering of others.

"Yes, of course, the Spanish soldier as well." Jean Bertin saw Olivier's anger and tried to mollify him. "What bothers me is the murderer's contempt for the Spanish authorities. The diable thinks he is superior to them. In fact, he's thumbing his nose at them."

"That may be, but whatever his regard of the authorities, the killing of Rafael Portillo was a callous act. He struck the soldier with great force, *twice*, to make sure he was dead. The man's head was split open in two places."

Jean Bertin nodded, looking sad. "That's awful. What's Castañedo planning to do now?"

"For now, the magistrate is concerned with the death of Raphael Portillo. I expect he'll return to the investigation after the soldier's funeral."

"So, what do you now suggest, Father?"

"I'm stymied myself, Monsieur Dumont. I must think about it for a while. But, for the next few days, I must tend to the parishioners at Santa María. Many have lost their children and parents to the plague. I'll also be occupied with the funeral for Rafael Portillo. The magistrate has asked me to officiate at his funeral on Friday."

Jean Bertin frowned. "I must say, Father, I had hoped to see more, ah, progress in this investigation by now. It's been six weeks since we made our agreement and it appears we are no closer to capturing the fiend who has taken the lives of my sons and almost killed my nephew. In fact, he appears to be farther from our grasp than ever. The murder of the Villièrs woman and the destruction of her house certainly showed us that."

Olivier looked at Jean Bertin, but said nothing.

"By now, Father, I expected some indication you were at least near or on the trail of the murderer. Instead, you now say you are *stymied* and *must think about it for a while*. I find that disappointing to say the least, especially since I met my part of our agreement immediately and donated 10,000 pesetas to Santa María." He looked at his nephew. "And I'm told the renovation is now near completion."

"There is still much to be done, but the renovation *is* near completion." Olivier paused and stared at Jean Bertin, looking into his eyes. "Monsieur Dumont, I must remind you of the agreement you mentioned. At the time, I said, *'I will assist in the investigation as you request, but it must be understood at the outset that I cannot promise to find the murderer you seek, I'll do my best, but I cannot assure you of success in the investigation nor can*

I tell you how long it will take no matter the outcome.' Do you recall those words?"

"I do, but …"

Olivier spoke firmly. "There were no *buts* Monsieur Dumont, that was the agreement we made and it remains in effect now and for the future – unless, that is, you wish to end it."

Jean Bertin's mouth dropped open. He was dumbfounded to be both interrupted by the Dominican and contradicted. The priest had even lectured him. Accustomed to deference, fear and obedience, he could not find the words to respond to Olivier.

"As to your donation to Santa María, let me remind you of exactly what you said that day. *'Father, I want to assure you that I am not seeking indulgences for my sins. This donation will be offered simply to help Santa María continue its pastoral mission for the suffering people of the lowlands. I mean that sincerely.'* Those were your words and I thought your contribution to the church was appropriate since you were and still are the largest landowner in the lowlands."

Jean Bertin was still too stunned to speak. He gaped at Olivier and turned his eyes to Charles Laroux as if seeking his nephew's confirmation that he'd heard the same words.

Olivier stood, nodded to both men and left the office.

Two weeks later, Olivier left Santa María later than usual in the darkness. He had stayed an hour after the church's closing time to counsel an Acadian couple whose young son had died the previous week. The chest-cough plague had killed the boy and nine other children. Though sick for days, the adults had survived the sickness, but not the young or very old who seemed to suffer especially high fevers. Francis had been one of those struck down with the plague and he had been sick in bed for almost a week. Earlier that afternoon, he had sent word with another Capuchin monk that he would be back for morning Mass.

It was a cold moonless night with snow flurries and Olivier walked with his wool cloak wrapped tightly about his shoulders. The walk to María Adela's house took him thirty minutes and he was whisked inside seconds after he knocked on the door. María Adela's maid, Renée, handed him a glass of brandy as soon as he removed his cloak. He smiled appreciatively and drank down half the brandy.

"Ah, thank you, Renée, that's just what's needed to warm the cockles of my heart. I'd appreciate another when you have the time."

She smiled at him. "Yes. Madame Boudreaux is sitting in the living room by the fireplace. She's still feeling low."

Olivier found María Adela sitting on the couch staring into the fire. Her eyes were red and she clutched a wrinkled handkerchief. She stifled a sob as he bent to pat her shoulder.

"I can't stop thinking about her, no matter what I do." She looked up at him with tears filling her eyes.

Olivier nodded and sat in the chair across from her.

"Aveline was my closest friend. I met her a week after I moved here. She was with me all the months of Antoine's illness – she helped nurse him until the day he died. I miss her so!"

Olivier reached over and took her hand, squeezing it softly.

"What bothers me most is that I was not with her at the end."

"You couldn't be there, María Adela. She died peacefully in her sleep, un Dieu reposent son âme (God rest her soul). There was nothing anyone could do; it was her heart as you know."

María Adela sighed. "I know, but I never even had the time to tell her how much I loved her; we were as close as any sisters could be." María Adela released Olivier's hand, covered her face and wept openly. She bent over as sobs wracked her body.

Olivier immediately went over to her. He sat beside her and gently rubbed her back.

"Thank God, I was with her all Christmas day," she said through her tears.

"You were with the Dumont family that day?"

María Adela nodded. "I went with them to Christmas Mass at the cathedral and stayed with them all the next day. Aveline and I played endless games with the girls all that afternoon. She sobbed again and pressed her face against Olivier's chest.

He put his arms around her and held her without speaking.

María Adela's sobs subsided a few moments later and, after drying her eyes, she took Olivier's hand and held it tightly.

"Thank you, Father. You've been a Godsend through everything. I'll never forget your eulogy for Aveline; thinking of it still brings tears to my eyes." She sighed and, raising her head from his chest, turned to him. "We should speak of something else. What has the bishop said to you of late? Surely, he's pleased with the renovations to Santa María."

Olivier resumed his seat in the chair across from María Adela. "I haven't spoken to him for quite a while. He has been very ill with the plague. It seems he's suffered longer than most people and has only recently been well enough to leave his bed."

"What is the state of the renovation at Santa María?"

"The renovation has been suspended during the long cold spell. There's no carpentry work of any kind in town. I expect the carpenters will resume their work by the month's end or earlier if warm weather returns."

María Adela paused as Renée came into the living room carrying a bottle of brandy on a tray. She refilled Olivier's glass and looked inquiringly at her mistress. María Adela's glass, still half full, stood on the table beside her.

"No, thank you, Renée, I may have another glass after dinner. We'll eat at eight o'clock if that suits you, Father?" María Adela nodded her thanks to Renée who turned and left the room.

"Yes, thank you."

"Has there been any progress in the investigation? When we last talked – after the fire, you said the search for the murderer was at a standstill."

Olivier frowned. "I fear that's still the situation. The magistrate hasn't the time now to do much about the investigation. He has been in pursuit of the American pirates who seized the schooner *San Antonio*. He's also facing an official inquiry into the unfortunate death of Rafael Portillo. As you know, the commandant loaned the soldier to him for temporary sentry duty at the Villièrs house. The governor is steadfast in his support of Castañedo, but the commandant wants him cited for dereliction of duty. His charge is based on the magistrate's absence from the house on the night the soldier was killed. He has threatened to protest to Havana if the governor doesn't hold an official inquiry into his death."

María Adela made a face and shook her head from side to side. "What foolishness! So typical of the Spaniards; they must find someone to blame for any failure. I assume you have been busy at the cathedral as well as at Santa María."

"Yes, many priests have been sick with the plague, including Father Antonio. I was very busy last week. But now, remerciez un Dieu (thank God), most of them have recovered. I've been at Santa María alone these past two days since I'm no longer needed at the cathedral."

"What about Father Francis?"

"He has been sick, too, but now is better. I have heard he expects to return to Santa María in the morning. Now, I will have the time to continue the investigation."

"So, Jean Bertin still wants you to continue with the investigation. I heard you put him in his place. Good for you!"

María Adela smiled for the first time that night.

"That's not what happened? Who told you about my meeting with him?"

"Paulette. She laughed when she told me and said, 'Jean Bertin is too arrogant these days and it's about time someone let him know it. I'll thank Father Olivier the next time I see him.' Of course, that was before Aveline's death."

Olivier shook his head. "I did not remark on his behavior. My comments to Jean Bertin concerned the agreement we made in November. I simply reminded him of its provisions, which he *apparently* had forgotten." He saw María Adela smile at his emphasis of the word apparently. "At our meeting, in November, I told him I could not assure him of success in the investigation or inform him how long it would take. Then, at our recent meeting, he expressed his impatience with the time spent without result and said he was disappointed with the investigation's lack of progress. So, I informed him he would either have to accept the agreed terms of our agreement or terminate our arrangement. That was the extent of my comments and I left thereafter."

"I'm sure he didn't like what you said – especially after his donation to Santa María."

"That may well be, but the next morning, he sent Charles Laroux to Santa María to make amends. Laroux said Jean Bertin was in low spirits that day, thinking about the loss of his sons, and that's why he was out of sorts at our meeting."

María Adela smiled again. "Do you believe him?"

"It doesn't matter what I believe. What matters is that I will continue the investigation. I want to find this fiend; he must be arrested and executed. The entire community is at risk as long as he walks the streets. He's a cunning and vicious killer and *must* be put to death. I know those aren't the words a priest should utter, but such a man, one who has already slain so many people and imperils the lives of others cannot be allowed to live out his life."

"If and when he is arrested, why not imprison him?" María Adela studied Olivier's face.

"There would always be the risk of his escape and other killings that might follow."

"Would you think the same if it was determined he was unsound of mind?'

"No, of course not. But this man is not mad, he knows exactly what he's doing. We may not know his intentions, but it's certainly obvious he's intent on killing the Dumont family. We also know he'll stop at nothing to keep his identity unknown and has already killed three people to that end. There also may be any number of others he has killed in the past. I fear this man is a fiend, perhaps a satanic creation, who must be exorcized from our world as soon as possible."

María Adela nodded. "So, Father, I assume you have a plan in mind to find him."

"Yes, but it's one with only a minimal chance of success. I will be interviewing the last girls to live in the house. I think I told you they're now at the Ursuline Convent. It's unlikely they know anything helpful, but I must ask them anyway. As they say, I can't leave any stone unturned. The magistrate agreed with me and has urged me to talk to them. Father Antonio also agreed and asked Mother Marguerite for her permission to let me to speak to the girls. I received word of her approval in a note yesterday. The prioress said I could interview them briefly in the presence of one of the sisters."

"That surely will keep them safe from you, Father." María Adela smiled and then, seeing the shocked look on his face, she laughed out loud. "I was only joking."

"I should have known. You do enjoy embarrassing your friends." Olivier smiled as he shook his finger at her. He was pleased to see María Adela laugh again after so long a time of grieving. She still had a smile on her face as they both sipped their brandy.

"I haven't decided yet whether to speak to the girls one

by one or in a group. Apparently, there are five there who might have information. None of the other girls taken into the convent had any knowledge of the *afternoon gentleman* as he was called by the girls. What do you think would be best approach to them?"

"I think you will learn more if you speak to each girl alone. They might well hesitate to speak openly in the presence of the other girls. It also would be better if the nun wasn't there in the room. I'm certain her presence will limit what the girls would say. I suggest you ask Mother Marguerite if she would allow the sister to sit beside the door outside the room rather than inside. I've always found her to be reasonable and I think she would be willing to make that decision if you explain your reasons."

"Yes, that makes sense. I'll do as you suggest."

"What else do you plan to do?"

"I must speak to those girls who lived in the house at the time María Isabel disappeared. As many of them as possible. I'm hoping they're still in town and can be found. Apparently, a number of them were working as servants as of last August. Madame Villièrs said she routinely moved the girls in and out of her house. It seems four months was the extent of their service in Mosquito Creek. The girls who didn't leave with men or family members within that time were sent as servants to private homes in New Orleans. You, of course, know of Ana Luisa."

"Yes, Aveline told me her background when she hired her last summer. The girl served her well for a time." María Adela took a deep breath, thinking of Aveline. She pressed her wet handkerchief to the fresh tears that filled her eyes.

Olivier waited while María Adela dried her eyes. "Madam Villièrs spoke of the practice as if she were providing *new opportunities* for the girls, but it benefitted her much more than the girls. It was a clever scheme to make more money. The madam was paid to teach the girls to be servants, while they simultaneously worked in the brothel. She profited in two ways employing the girls and, in so doing, offered her customers at least one fresh young face a month."

"It was a clever scheme. What a greedy woman!" María Adela made a face. "Now, I certainly understand her need to keep a copy of her business records. She wanted to make sure her house wouldn't be closed. With who-knows-how many influential men in town recorded as customers in those records, the crafty woman knew her brothel was secure. She had them under her thumb. They feared exposure and would never permit anyone to close the house – not even the governor! There might even have been prominent Spaniards who frequented the house from time to time; that's a rumor that's now circulating around town since the brothel was destroyed. It makes sense, of course, men are the same – English, French or Spanish! "

"I don't know who frequented the brothel, but I assume there were enough influential patrons to keep the house open despite the bishop's repeated demands to close it. So long as it flourished, its patrons were secure from exposure and Madame Villièrs became a very wealthy woman."

"It's said she wanted to return to France with her niece and live comfortably from the profits of the house. So, the hidden papers assured her of that future no matter what befell the ledger she kept in her dresser."

Olivier nodded and drank the remainder of his brandy. "María Adela, I want to tell you something you must keep in strict confidence." Olivier saw her nod her head. "We're not sure there was a second ledger. We used that rumor as a ruse to bring the murderer down to Mosquito Creek. We hoped to trap him when he went to the house. But, alas, that plan failed and cost the life of Raphael Portillo."

"What is it they say? Something like 'the best-laid schemes o' mice an' men'?"

"Unfortunately those words are all too appropriate."

Olivier exhaled his breath. "It was my suggestion to lure the murderer to the house."

Seeing Olivier grimace sadly and she changed the subject. "Tell me, Father, how do you intend to approach the girls who were in the house last summer when María Isabel disappeared?"

Olivier sighed. "I don't know! I don't even know where the girls are now. Without the madam's ledger, I don't where they went. If Madame Villièrs spoke the truth some were sent to wealthy homes where they became servants. That's what happened to Ana Luisa Ibáñez when Aveline took her into her home … " Olivier paused worried that María Adela might be upset by his mention of her friend's name, but seeing her nod in agreement, he continued … "but I have no notion who hired any of the others and where they might be living."

"I may be able to help you, Father. I'll inquire among the women I know in town as well as in the cathedral. I recall Aveline telling me she took Ana Luisa because a number of women had spoken highly of the girls from Mosquito Creek."

"Thank you. I know of no other way to find this fiend and he must be found. He now has murdered seven people and nearly killed Charles Laroux."

"Seven? I thought it was six."

"Seven – the two Dumont boys, Jacques and Matthieu, Lucille, María Isabel, Madame Villièrs, Gisella and Rafael Portillo."

"My God! I forgot poor Lucille." María Adela put a hand over her mouth.

Three days later, at first light, Olivier walked from his rooms on San Felipe Street to the Ursuline Convent. It was a pleasant walk in the unseasonably warm weather that New Orleans had enjoyed for the week. The two-story stone convent, finally completed in 1750, stood on the corner of Condé and Ursulinas Streets, four blocks east of the cathedral. A plain unadorned building, the balcony over the entrance was the convent's only noticeable feature.

The heavy door opened immediately after his first knock. One of the older nuns ushered Olivier into the convent and led him to a small room just to the right of the front door. The room was sparsely furnished with a table and four hard wooden chairs. All the walls had been recently whitewashed and the smell of fresh paint still lingered in the air. An elaborately carved crucifix hung on the wall facing the doorway and a dark portrait of a grim looking nun hung on the wall next to the door. Olivier assumed the woman was either the founder or one of the first prioresses of the Ursuline Convent. The third wall had nothing on it and two tall windows took up most of the fourth wall. Both windows were shuttered, but one was half open.

Politely asked to wait for the prioress, Olivier sat in the chair beneath the portrait. He looked out the open window, but saw nothing of interest in the courtyard. A few leafless trees stood outside along with the withered remains of the summer's flowers. The cold winter had killed all but the hardiest plants in the city.

Olivier only had time to give the bleak courtyard a glance when the prioress entered the room. Mother Marguerite genuflected before the crucifix and crossed herself. The prioress then turned to Olivier who had risen when she appeared. She gestured for him to be seated and sat in the chair across from him. A severe looking woman with striking blue eyes, the prioress sat with her hands clasped together on the table.

"Good morning, Father. Welcome to our home and school." She looked at him coldly, her mouth set in a tight line.

"Good morning Mother Marguerite. Thank you for

permitting me to visit the convent." Aware of the stern expression on her face, Olivier knew her words of welcome were no more than a perfunctory statement. Marguerite's manner puzzled him. He had never met her before, though he had seen her at Mass in the cathedral.

Mother Marguerite nodded, her unsmiling face without expression. "I trust this meeting room will be adequate for your interviews, Father." She went on without waiting for his reply. "I expect the interviews to take no more than two and a half hours – that allows you a half hour to meet with each girl. Sister Helene, whom you have met, will bring the girls to you, one at a time, and, she will sit outside the door during your interviews; that is as you requested. When you have finished your interviews, which should be at the time the cathedral bells ring the hour of ten, she will see you outside. I expect that covers everything."

"Thank you, Mother Marguerite, it does."

"Au revoir, Father." The prioress rose and left without another glance at him.

"Au revoir." Olivier cocked his head to the side as he watched her leave the room. "She certainly made no effort to be cordial," he thought. "It's clear she only allowed me to interview the girls because of the pastor's request. I suppose she's heard of the incident at the cathedral and views me with criticism, if not contempt." Olivier felt his stomach tighten. It saddened him to know the Ursuline prioress was one of an increasing number of townspeople in the diocese who regarded him with disapproval. Unfortunately, it was not his first experience with disapproval. He had faced it before in other dioceses. Invariably it always involved his pride and drunkenness. He sighed wearily and looked aimlessly out the window.

Olivier stood to greet the first girl brought into the room. Sister Helene introduced the girl, Sylvie Dubois, to him and withdrew from the room. The girl was tiny and thin and had an almost colorless face. She smiled shyly and, following his pointed finger, sat in the chair across from him. She looked down at the table until he spoke softly to her.

"Sylvie, thank you for coming to talk to me." Olivier smiled, hoping to calm any fears she might be feeling.

Sylvie nodded, but said nothing. She held her hands over her stomach and continued to look down at the table, avoiding his eyes.

"Do you know why I asked to speak to you?" Olivier smiled again.

"Yes, Father. You are looking for the afternoon gentleman. They say he killed Gisella and Madame Villièrs." This time Sylvie looked at him.

"Yes, Sylvie. I am hoping you can help me identify him. He must be found, arrested and, of course, punished for those murders." Olivier saw no reason to tell the young girl about his other murders.

"I never seen him. The madam made us stay in our rooms while he visited the house. The only one to see him was the girl he was with."

"Did any of the girls try to see him anyway – out of curiosity?" Olivier grinned. "I'm sure everyone was curious."

Sylvie nodded, a tiny smile on her face. "There was those that peeked."

"Did any of them see him?" Olivier knew she was one of the girls who had peeked.

Sylvie shook her head. "No, he spent all his time downstairs. We was all upstairs behind closed doors. Madame Villièrs sat in a chair at the bottom of the stairs to make sure no one tried to come out of the rooms to look at him. And when she went somewhere else, then Gisella was there sitting in the chair looking up the stairs."

"Did one or the other sit in that chair the entire time he was in the house?"

She shook her head. "No, the Madame would greet him

at the door and invite him into the parlor when he arrived. They would talk there awhile and eat lunch. We sometimes heard them laughing. That's when the girls peeked."

"So, they were very friendly."

Sylvie shrugged.

"Yet no one saw him even when they peeked?"

"No, Gisella was serving them lunch and coming in and out of the downstairs hallway. She would look up the stairs to make sure we were in our rooms. It was only when Gisella was in the kitchen preparing the food that one or two of the girls would dare leave their rooms. They would tiptoe down the stairs – usually no more than a few steps down from the upstairs landing. They could hear some of what he said, but they never seen him."

"So, he never came upstairs."

"No, Father."

"Where did he spend his time with the girl?"

"In Gisella's room."

"The bedroom that was next to the kitchen and the back door?"

"Yes, Father."

"I see. So that's why none of the other girls saw him. They would have had to come down at least half the stairs to get even a glimpse of him going into Gisella's room. But with Madame Villièrs or Gisella sitting at the bottom of the stairway or walking about the hall that was not possible."

Sylvie nodded.

"Was he ever seen entering or leaving the house?"

Sylvie shook her head. "Then, Gisella would make sure we was all in our rooms. On the day he was to come, Gisella would come upstairs and send us all into our bedrooms – sometimes more than an hour before he came. But we would always know when he arrived when we heard the front door open and close. It squeaks loud."

"Was he ever seen riding up to the house or leaving? The

girls in those front bedrooms could look out the windows and see anyone approaching the house from the road."

Sylvie shook her head. "He was never seen that way. I was in a front bedroom, the one near the stairway, and I looked out the window, trying to see him the whole time we was in our rooms. But I never seen him. I only knew he was there when the door squeaked."

"What about the girls whose bedroom windows faced out the back of the house? Did any of them ever see him come or go?"

"No, Father, they didn't see him neither and they looked like we did."

"Didn't the girls who were with him ever speak about his looks – or maybe tell the other girls what he said or did?"

Sylvie shook her head. "He gave them money to say nothing. It was more money than a girl could earn in two months."

"Even with all the money, didn't they say something about him that you heard?"

"He scared them, too, so they wouldn't say anything about him. I shared a bedroom with Suzanne and he scared her something awful. He told her would hurt her 'in ways she could not imagine' if she ever told anyone anything about him. He said he would find out if she dared say anything and he would hunt her down wherever she was."

"When was Suzanne with him?"

Sylvie paused to look out the window. "It was early in December, I think."

"Sylvie, how long were you in Madame Villièrs' house?"

"Nine weeks and he came to the house two times while I was there."

Olivier smiled, knowing the girl had anticipated his next question. "So, he came to the house about once a month."

"Yes, that's what the other girls said. We knew when he was coming to the house. That day the Madame made us clean the downstairs extra good and she would cook a special lunch for him. We could smell it."

Olivier was about to ask another question when Sister Helene tapped at the door. They both turned their eyes to the door. Sylvie stood and smiled shyly at Olivier.

"I have to go now, Father."

"I know, Sylvie. Thank you for speaking to me." He returned her smile. "So, Suzanne said nothing else to you – nothing at all?"

Her hand on the door handle, Sylvie turned and nodded. She opened the door and Olivier saw Sister Helene there with another girl. Sylvie closed the door and he heard the muffled sound of them talking outside. A moment later, Sylvie stepped back into the room. She spoke softly.

"There's one thing I forgot to tell you, Father. I don't know if it'll help but, a week after he had gone, Suzanne started to tell me about him. We were talking in bed before going to sleep and she said, 'There's something about him …' but she stopped and would say no more except, 'I'm afraid he'll find me, Sylvie. There's evil in his eyes. He scares me.'"

"Thank you, Sylvie." Olivier saw her reach for the door handle. "Do you know where Suzanne went when she left the house?"

She shook her head and left the room.

Olivier interviewed the four other girls and left the convent precisely at ten o'clock. The prioress did not return to bid him farewell. As he left Olivier thanked Sister Helene for her help and dropped three silver coins in the collection box.

After supper that night, Olivier told Francis and Madame Lefevre about his interviews in the convent. Francis now ate his evening meal with Olivier three nights a week. They talked at the kitchen table while Madame Lefevre finished sewing a shirt she had made for Gervaise.

"The first girl, Sylvie, told you the most, Father." Madame Lefevre looked up from the sleeve she was stitching together.

"She did indeed. But, little Marie Moreau gave me the names of the three girls he was with before Suzanne. She had been in the brothel since September. Poor little thing has been sick for most of that time. She's little more than skin and bones."

"I'm sure the sisters will fatten her up." Madame Lefevre shook her head with certainty.

"The sickness at least spared Marie from the sin in that house," added Francis, a look of satisfaction on his face.

Frowning, Madame Lefevre shook her head vigorously up and down. "Her sickness was a blessing, Father Francis." She clucked her tongue. "The poor child was spared – surely a sign of God's love." She turned to Olivier, her sewing needle poised above the shirt. "Did Marie know where those girls went after leaving the house?"

"No, and it'll be difficult to find them especially since Marie only knew their first names. None of the other girls I interviewed knew their family names either. One of them thought the girl he was with in November had the name *Lavasseur*, but she wasn't certain."

"At least we now have the sequence of the girls he was with, from María Isabel to Suzanne." Francis counted them out on his fingers. "María Isabel in August, Felice in September, Jeanne in October, Valarie in November, and Suzanne in December."

Olivier nodded. "There are five then who can identify him. Let's hope at least one of them is still in New Orleans. If what Madame Villièrs said is true, we have a good chance of finding one of the girls here. She said, 'Many go to wealthy homes in New Orleans where they are hired as servants.'"

Francis snickered. "Well, we shouldn't have any trouble

finding one of the girls – there are only about two hundred wealthy homes in the city and who-knows how many others outside on the plantations." Seeing a scowl on Olivier's face, Francis stopped speaking.

"You're right, Francis, it will be exceedingly difficult, but I know of no other way to find this fiend – that is, *unless you have a better suggestion."* Olivier stared at the young priest.

"No, Father, I do not." Francis regretted his sarcasm and looked down at the table.

"We'll also have the help of María Adela. She intends to speak to the women she knows at the cathedral as well as her other acquaintances about town."

"Father Antonio also might know some of the families who took in the girls." Worried about Olivier's look of disapproval, Francis now tried to make amends by offering a suggestion. "Surely, the girls accompanied the families to confession and communion now and then."

Olivier nodded. "I spoke to Father Antonio yesterday after Estelle Laroux' funeral. He had indeed heard their confessions and given them communion in the past, but not recently. The pastor did not know their names nor those of the families who had taken them into their homes. But even if Father Antonio had such knowledge, he could not have revealed it to me for fear of breaking the seal of confession." Olivier saw Francis nod in understanding.

Madame Lefevre spoke up interrupting Olivier. "Poor Estelle – she suffered such a long painful illness. I truly hope she finds the peace in heaven she so richly deserves."

"I pray she does. Everyone says she was a good woman." Olivier sipped the hot tea he now drank every evening after supper. He found it helped him sleep and kept him from waking up once or twice in the night. He also had been drinking less of late and, though he doubted tea was the reason, Olivier continued the nightly practice with that in mind.

"Estelle was indeed, Father, and not an insulting word

was ever said about her. The poor soul, she lived so long in the shadow of death. At least, she died knowing her son, Charles, has become a well-respected businessman and gentleman in and about town."

At that moment, Gervaise walked into the room with a checkerboard under his arm. He had a wooden box of checkers in his hand. After eating supper, Gervaise had gone into the next room to do his nightly studies.

"Well, who will dare challenge the current champion?" Gervaise stood grinning at them, his head cocked to the side and his free hand on his hip.

CHAPTER NINE

NEW ORLEANS: FEBRUARY 2 – 17, 1800

The sky was overcast when Olivier left Santa María after Mass on the misty morning of February second. He had an appointment at eight thirty and he hurried to make it in time. His head thrust forward, his arms flapping at this sides, he went quickly through the San Carlos gate and, once inside the city, turned up Bienville Street to reach Borbón Street. A moment later, he sighed with relief when he found the residence of Fernando Jiménez only three houses from the corner. The large white clapboard house, three-stories high, stood behind a stone wall. Catching his breath at the wrought iron gate, Olivier looked at his pocket watch and saw he had arrived only two minutes late.

A little girl, no more than ten years of age, skipped down the stone walk to the gate. She stood up on her tiptoes to unlock the gate and struggled a moment to withdraw the bolt from the door jamb. She curtsied and smiled up at him with big brown eyes.

"My name is María Rosa Jiménez, welcome to our home."

Olivier patted her gently on the head. "Thank you, María Rosa, I'm Father Olivier." He smiled, amused at her prepared greeting. Olivier knew her mother had taught her the welcome and he recalled his mother teaching him a similar greeting when he was a boy.

María Rosa led Olivier to the house. She curtsied again as he passed her and went inside. Olivier waited while the child closed the door and then followed her into a parlor which was to the left of the entry hall. He thanked her as she ran to her mother who stood waiting in the room.

"Welcome to our home, Father Olivier." Señora Sofía Jiménez greeted him with a smile and bowed slightly, closing her eyes.

Señora Jiménez, a slender dark-haired woman, was dressed in black out of respect for her father who had died two months earlier. Olivier had never met the man, but knew he had come to New Orleans in 1766 and served as an aide to the first Spanish governor of Louisiana. He had heard the man had suffered a long painful illness before his death.

"Sientase, por favor (Please sit)." She gestured to a green and yellow flowered settee that stood facing the front window and turned to the child.

"Mama." The little girl, standing by her mother's side, looked up at her.

"Yes, you can go play now, María Rosa – but be nice to your little sister."

María Rosa nodded, curtsied once again to Olivier and scampered off to the rear of the house. "Here I come," she shouted running down the hall, "ready or not."

Señora Jiménez smiled at Olivier. "María Rosa is a very curious child – she wants to see everyone who comes into the house. But, once her curiosity is satisfied, she loses all interest in the visitor, and she only wants to return to whatever activity that was interrupted."

Olivier nodded and returned her smile.

Señora Jiménez sat in a chair across from him. The chair had the same colored upholstery as the settee and was situated beside the window. Señora Jiménez leaned to the side and opened the green drapes that hung in front of the window. She adjusted the drapes allowing the morning sunlight to enter the room. A beam of light fell on the floor and brightened the shiny surface of the French provincial desk that stood by the door.

"There, that should lighten up the parlor sufficiently without shining into our eyes. Well, Father …" She paused as a shrill squeal and then strident laughter sounded from the rear of the house. "That's my María Rosa." She sighed. "There are times I think the child's shriek could wake the dead."

"María Rosa is a lovely child – she has her mother's eyes."

Sofía Jiménez blushed.

"Thank you for seeing me, Señora Jiménez. I assume Madame Boudreaux told you the reason for my visit."

"Yes, Father." The color gone from her cheeks, Sofía Jiménez sat with her hands in her lap. "María Adela and Aveline, God rest her soul, have been my closest friends for many years. María Adela told me you are looking for a few of those unfortunate girls from Mosquito Creek." She made a face.

"Yes, Señora Jiménez. We are aware that some of those girls came to New Orleans and became servants in a number of homes." Olivier saw her nod in agreement.

"Yes, Father, that's true. One of them, in fact, served for three years in our home. Her name was Madeleine Petit."

"So, she is no longer with you."

Señora Jiménez shook her head. "She married the gardener's nephew and they left New Orleans last September. I've heard they now reside in Baton Rouge. Madeleine was a lovely little girl and a great help to me. It's a wonder after what the poor girl suffered at that appalling house in Mosquito Creek. I must say I was quite pleased to hear it burned to the ground.

And, forgive me, Father Olivier, when I admit I shed no tears when that *dreadful Villièrs woman* was struck down. She took advantage of those unfortunate girls." Señora Jiménez stuck out her chin, certain of her righteousness.

"Señora Jiménez, may I ask how you came to employ Madeleine?"

"I heard about the girls from a friend who had taken one of them into her home."

"Was that friend Madame Dumont?"

"No, it was Madame Trudeau. Aveline got a girl much later – it was last summer when I told her how satisfied I was with Madeleine. Unfortunately, the girl – Ana Luisa was her name, left her after only a couple of months. She slipped away this past November in the dark of night. The ungrateful girl left Aveline when she was sick in bed."

"What made you decide to take in one of the Mosquito Creek girls?"

"Aimee – Madame Trudeau was pleased with the girl who came to her home and told me about the necessary arrangements. Of course, we took her in to give her a better life."

"I see and what were those arrangements, Señora?"

"We were required to pay the woman fifty pesetas for the girl's service."

"Did you select the girl?"

"Dios mio, no! Neither my husband nor I went near Mosquito Creek. We would never set foot in that sinful house or speak to that horrid woman. All the necessary arrangements were made by our attorney, Juan Fernández Moreno. He met with the woman, prepared a contract and had a physician examine the girl before she was brought into our home."

"What was the nature of the contract?"

"I don't know the particulars, Father. You will have to ask my husband about them. I do know the contract, más or menos, declared that we would receive a healthy girl of not more than seventeen years of age for the payment of fifty pesetas. It stated the girl would be trained in the ways of house service before she came to us and would serve us for three years. If we found the girl unsuitable, we could return her for a full refund; the agreement gave us thirty days to assess her suitability. " She frowned. "Oh yes, we were required to pay a deposit of ten pesetas until a girl became available. It seems we were fifth on the woman's list to receive one of the girls and, four months later, Madeleine arrived at our home. She came to us in August of 1796; it was at the end of the month; I don't recall the exact date. Señor Fernández Moreno brought her here to our home," she hastened to add.

"Of course." Olivier paused, hearing another shriek from the rear of the house. The scream was followed by the sound of loud sobbing.

Señora Jiménez shook her head. "Their play always seems to end up with one of them hurt – usually the little one, Carlotta. She's only six. Please continue, Father, the minder will see to them."

Olivier nodded. "Tell me, Señora Jiménez, what were Madeleine's wages during her three years in your home?"

"Madeleine was given her own room, new clothes, all her daily meals – she ate with the children. She also benefitted from the education we provided for our children. She was present while the French tutor taught them their lessons. He came mornings Monday through Thursday and Madeleine missed only Tuesday, on our market day. That's when she went with me to carry the food sacks to and from the carriage. Madeleine could not read or write when she came to us, but she could write her full name when she left."

Señora Jiménez was aware of Olivier's frown as she spoke. "Madeleine, of course, accompanied us to the cathedral on Sunday mornings – and then, of course, she was free to enjoy herself in that afternoon and evening."

"So, she served without wages."

"Yes, Father, we paid for three years of service and

Madeleine signed the contract to that effect. She signed willingly, there was no coercion of any kind."

"I understand, Señora. How old was Madeleine when she signed the contract and entered your service?" Olivier cocked his head to the side as he looked at her.

Her face reddened. "She was almost fourteen."

"And still a child," Olivier thought angrily. The young girl signed a contract she couldn't read that bound her to three years of unpaid service, with the exception of a tutor's lessons three mornings a week. He gritted his teeth to hide the disgust he felt for the practice of child-servitude and the opportunistic people who employed it to get years of free labor. "So, Madeleine signed a three-year contract to serve in your home as an indentured servant."

"Yes, but it was a short time for such service. As you know, children of immigrants often serve as many as seven years here in New Orleans. Only adults serve as few as three years; most serve five years. Our gardener, Maximillian, has a five-year contract and has only one more year of service left." Certain she was right, Señora Jiménez stuck out her chin again.

"I assume Madeleine finished the three years of service before her marriage."

"Oh, yes, she met her obligation to the exact date and day of her arrival. Madeleine was an honorable girl."

Olivier nodded. "An honorable girl indeed!" He knew there was no point criticizing the woman. He wanted information and it would be foolish to antagonize her.

Señora Jiménez held up a thin finger. "One more thing, Father Olivier. Madeleine may have been young, but the girl was old enough to realize she would be far better off in our home than … doing what she did in that house for that horrid woman."

Olivier nodded again. He wanted to say, "You're right, Señora, Madeleine was better off, she exchanged a house of prostitution for a house of indentured service." Instead, he asked, "Do you know any other families who have taken girls from Mosquito Creek? We are trying to find as many of the girls as possible."

Señora Jiménez smiled. "Yes, Father, I know several others. I'll make a list for you." She rose from her chair and walked to the desk. "Please excuse me, Father," she said, turning her back to him. Removing a scented piece of paper and a silver quill from the center drawer, she spent a minute writing the names.

Olivier rose and watched her finish writing out the list.

She handed him the list. "There are six families here whom I know have had girls from Mosquito Creek. I am sure there must be others, but these are the families I know."

"Thank you, Señora Jiménez. I am grateful for your assistance." Olivier took the list she handed to him and turned to leave.

"Por nada, Padre. I trust the fall of that house will end the servitude of such girls in the future." Señora Jiménez stood with her arms crossed over her chest.

"I would hope so." Olivier studied her. "Tell me, Señora, since you were so satisfied with Madeleine's service, did you seek another girl from Mosquito Creek?"

Señora Jiménez' sighed. "We did and we were again put on a waiting list."

Olivier nodded and turned to the door. Outside, he looked back at the house, a frown on his face. "Ah, yes, Señora, a good indentured servant would be well worth the wait and the fifty pesetas to pay that *horrid woman*. Where else could a trained servant be obtained so cheaply?"

Two weeks later, on a cool but sunny February morning, Olivier and Charles Laroux rode along Real Street in one of the Dumont family carriages. Tristan Surette sat outside, driving the two-horse carriage. With the windows open, sunlight streamed into carriage warming them and lighting the interior. They were heading to the home of Monsieur Marcel Laurent, who lived on Tolosa Street, where many of the wealthy families owned luxurious mansions.

Laurent's large mansion stood on a spacious lot with high stone walls surrounding it. The house was located in the middle of the block between Real and Condé Streets. As the carriage turned into Tolosa Street, Laroux told Olivier the names of the families living on the block. He pointed out the orange tile roof of the Laurent house as soon as they entered the street. It was the tallest building on the block.

"The families on this street are all descendants of French nobility and are prominent in New Orleans even though the revolution in France has destroyed much of the aristocracy there. According to Madame Jiménez' list, it appears that only the Laurents and Fortiers have had girls from the Mosquito Creek. The other families on this street have their servants brought over from France. They won't hire anyone who can't speak French."

Olivier nodded, grateful for Laroux' knowledge of the local families. Following his visit to Señora Jiménez, he had learned the names of eight more families in addition to the six she had given him. The elderly French woman in the first house he visited afterwards provided him with the other names. With so many families to approach, Olivier was relieved when Charles Laroux offered his help to meet them. He made the offer when the priest went to Jean Bertin's office and showed them the list of people who had taken girls from the Villièrs house.

In a week's time, with Laroux' help arranging interviews and accompanying him, he had spoken to ten families on the expanded list. The families all had acquired girls from the Villièrs and seven of them still served as servants. Unfortunately, none of the girls Olivier had hoped to interview had been found. Felice, the young girl who had been with the murderer in September, had served in one of the homes, but died of the fevers in December.

Now, he could only hope that one of the three other girls who had been with the murderer was still in town. With a bit of good luck, he would find her in the Laurent house. Olivier closed his eyes and prayed silently as the carriage came to a stop. He opened his door and stepped down to the street in front of the house. Standing on a slight hill, the three story structure loomed high above him and Olivier guessed the land beneath it had been raised before its construction. After the devastating fire of 1788, many of the wealthy families constructed their new houses on raised land to protect them from the spring flooding of the Mississippi River.

Olivier and Laroux talked to Madame Laurent on the patio behind the house. She offered them the choice of meeting in the family parlor or the patio and both men chose to talk outside in the warm sunlight. The stone patio was surrounded by a dormant flower garden and a variety of leafless trees. Two massive live oaks still in full leaf stood at the rear of the property. The three-hundred-year old oaks towered above the house and lot.

Olivier looked about approvingly. "It has been awhile since I've spent any time outside and this is the perfect day to do so."

"It is indeed, I quite agree, Father Olivier." Madame Laurent, a thin gray-haired woman, smiled warmly. "Please sit, tea and pastries will be brought outside shortly."

They sat in cushioned chairs which were arranged around a table already set with a white tablecloth and napkins, white plates with painted floral medallions and highly-shined silverware. The tableware had been crafted in Normandy and painted with Brittany blue paint. A carafe of tawny port and two wine glasses had been placed in the center of the table.

They had no sooner settled themselves in their chairs when a white-haired manservant arrived carrying a silver tray.

"Thank you, Daniel." Madame Laurent studied her guests as the manservant poured tea for everyone and placed a variety of petit fours on their plates. Daniel filled the wine glasses and then stood off to the side of the table near Madame Laurent.

"I don't drink wine in the morning, but don't let that influence you in any way."

They engaged in polite conversation for several minutes and then Olivier asked Madame Laurent about the servant girl from Mosquito Creek. "Madame, as you are aware from Monsieur Laroux' letter, we are here to inquire about the girl from the Villièrs house."

Madame Laurent nodded. "You are referring to Valarie, Valarie Poulin?"

"Yes, Madame, that is if Valarie Poulin came to you sometime after November."

"Yes, Valarie came to us just after the first of the year. "Why do you ask, Father?"

'We are looking for a girl named Valarie – unfortunately, we don't know her last name. We only know she was living in the Villièrs house as of last November." Olivier did not tell her the girl had been with the murderer of Madam Villièrs and her niece. There was no reason for her to know about it and he feared the information might affect the girl's life in the house. "If Valarie Poulin is indeed the girl, we would like to talk to her."

"I see. If I may ask, why is that Father Olivier?" Madame Laurent frowned.

Charles Laroux spoke when Olivier paused in search of a suitable answer to her question. "We are trying to learn as much about the Villièrs house as possible – we want to make certain such an appalling place never is established again in the province."

Madame Laurent nodded and looked at Olivier.

Olivier also nodded, regretting it immediately. His nod of agreement to Laroux' lie was likewise a lie. He drank half the wine in his glass. Olivier always prided himself on telling the truth no matter how uncomfortable he felt speaking candidly or how it affected others and, now, here he was brazenly lying to the woman. His stomach tightened and he suppressed a belch that left the bitter taste of bile in his mouth. "Mon Dieu," he wondered, "what have I become."

"Well, unfortunately, whether or not Valarie Poulin is the girl you seek, she is no longer with us. She's been gone for a week now."

"Gone! She left …"

"Yes, Father, Valarie left one night when we were all asleep. We were very sorry she left. Valarie was a lovely, cheerful girl – everyone in the house immediately took to her. The family, the servants, everyone! She was a dear girl … I miss her very much." Her eyes watered and she dabbed a handkerchief to them. "Our children are now grown with their own families and, when Valarie came to live with us, we felt like parents again. In fact, we were thinking of raising her as a daughter before she left." She dabbed the handkerchief to her eyes again. "I know that may sound foolish since Valarie was only with us for five weeks, but my husband and I both thought her to be a girl of good substance."

"She left you a note?"

"No, Father, which is what I would have expected of her. She seemed very happy here with us and I can't imagine why she left." Madame Laurent again wiped tears from her eyes. She held her handkerchief balled up in her hand.

"Pardon me for saying so, Madame, but you don't appear disturbed that Valarie broke the contract made with Madame Villièrs." Olivier finished his wine and Daniel refilled his glass.

"That contract meant nothing to us. We paid that woman, but had no intention of holding the child to three years of service. We told Valarie that the day she arrived; she was free to leave whenever she wished. We took her from that Villièrs woman to give her a new life in a Christian home. We heard about the plight of the girls from Father Antonio and we took the girl to get her out of that awful house. I must say I'm pleased it's gone now, though I certainly don't condone the killings that ended its existence."

"So, Valarie was not required to sign her name to the written contract made between you and Madame Villièrs?" Olivier studied the woman's face.

"No, Father, she did not sign it." Madame Laurent spoke sternly. "We alone signed the contract. Valarie was not bound to us legally. We wanted her to *choose* to stay with us."

"That's commendable, Madame." Olivier looked at her with genuine appreciation.

Madame Laurent was the one woman he had met who paid for indentured service and did not expect it to be fulfilled. All the women he had interviewed previously spoke of their concern for the girls and the need to free them from the brothel, but none before had been willing to give up three years of household servitude. Olivier knew the transfer of girls from the Villièrs house to the wealthy homes in New Orleans had been popular more for the service it offered than for the good Christian works claimed by those involved.

"You paid Valarie wages then?"

"Of course!" Madame Laurent looked indignant. "She was paid the same wages as the other servants – six pesetas a month. Marcel, my husband, says we who have the means should be generous to those who are less fortunate. That's the least we can do as Christians."

Olivier nodded. "Indeed, Madame, you are to be blessed." He made the sign of the cross. Olivier looked at the woman with new admiration. The servants at the Laurent house were paid much more than the typical servant wages in New Orleans. "If only the other wealthy families in town had such Christianity," he thought. He pictured himself giving a sermon on the subject of the need for Christian charity in New Orleans. It then occurred to him that such a sermon would only be meaningful at the cathedral and not at Santa María where most of the parishioners were as poor as servants. His introspection was interrupted by Madame Laurent's next words.

"We also keep a bowl of coins for the servants in the kitchen; the coins are there for them to buy sweets and the personal things they want."

Olivier smiled. "How unlike the Jiménez household," he thought. "So, Madame Laurent, you have no notion of why Valarie left?"

"No, Father, it's bewildering." She sighed and shook her head slowly. Tears again filled her eyes and she again dabbing them with her handkerchief.

Charles Laroux spoke up when she paused. "Madame Laurent, do you know if Valarie had any friends in town – any friends who visited her here in your home or whom she visited elsewhere now and then?"

"No, at least none whom I met or heard about, Monsieur Laroux. I don't recall her ever speaking about a special friend or friends and no one ever visited her. Valarie actually showed little interest in leaving the house at all, other than going to the market with me on Thursdays. In fact, I don't recall her ever going out by herself – so I don't think she had a young man courting her in town. She seemed quite content spending her free time playing with Christine – Christine is the eleven-year-old daughter of our housekeeper, Melisent. She also loved to romp with our Airedale, Vandal, here in the patio."

"Did she have *any* visitors, Madame?" Laroux gestured toward the outside street. "You said Valarie had no friends to your knowledge and 'no one ever visited her,' but did *anyone* visit her while she was in your home."

Madame Laurent put a finger on her chin as she thought

for a moment. “No, Monsieur – none except a young girl who stopped here briefly one morning. It was about ten days ago. She spoke to Valarie for only a few seconds at the front gate. I was upstairs in my bedroom and saw her from the window. I went to the window when I heard the gate open; it frequently squeaks in the winter. Valarie told me the child was looking for our neighbor’s house.”

“Madame Laurent, do you recall the girl’s appearance? Was she Valarie’s age?” “I’m inquiring because you spoke of her as a child,” explained Charles Laroux.

“She was a child about seven or eight years old. I saw her only briefly, Monsieur, but she looked small and thin; I think she was a poor child; her clothes looked shabby.”

“Do you recall the day the child came to your house?”

Madame Laurent paused to look away at the high stone wall that surrounded the property. “It was the first of February. I remember that morning because Valarie and Christine bathed our dog and he sprayed soapy water all over the kitchen.” A look of sadness spread over her face.

“Madame Laurent, did the girl’s visit affect Valarie in any way that you noticed?” Olivier nodded to Laroux, pleased with his questions. The young man rarely asked questions during the interviews, but those he asked were always astute and useful.

“Valarie seemed the same as ever. Do you think the child’s visit might help explain her disappearance?”

“I don’t know. Valarie’s explanation makes me doubtful.”

Madame Laurent nodded.

”So, Madame, there’s nothing to explain her sudden and baffling departure.”

“No, Father, and what’s even more baffling is that Valarie left without taking away any of her personal things. She left with only the clothing on her back. When I went to wake her the next morning for breakfast, her room looked as if she had left for only a moment and intended to return. At first,

I thought she must have been somewhere else in the house. Then, I saw she hadn't slept in her bed. She had taken off the bedspread and folded it on her chair and laid out her night dress on the bed; Valarie was a very neat girl. It looked as if she was preparing for bed and had stepped out of the room for something." Madame Laurent sighed, choking off a sob.

Olivier waited while she composed herself. He looked at Charles Laroux to see if he had any questions for her, but the young man shook his head.

"Forgive me, Father."

"There's nothing to forgive, Madame Laurent. I am sincerely sorry for your loss. Please take whatever time you need, I only have a couple more questions to ask."

Madame Laurent sighed and pressed the balled-up handkerchief to her eyes. She inhaled deeply and nodded to Olivier. "I'm fine now, Father, do continue."

"Madame, did Valarie have keys to the outside doors?"

"She had keys to both outside doors, front and back. Marcel said she went out the back door. The next morning, he found the door keys behind the stoop. That's where we hide the keys, after locking the door, if we are outside at night."

"So, Valarie locked the back door before leaving?' Seeing her nod, Olivier then asked, "Would she have locked the door if she intended to return to her room?"

"Yes. Everyone in the house knows to lock the outside doors at night even if outside for a short time. A couple of our neighbors have been robbed at night when the outside doors were left unlocked; one robbery took place with everyone at home."

"It's possible, then, that Valarie locked the back door, hid the keys behind the stoop and left intending to return?'

"Yes. Valarie was always considerate; she would have followed that procedure."

"What night was it that Valarie left your home?"

"It was the night of February 3. We had a family party for my husband's birthday which lasted until bedtime. We had a ballad singer and a dwarf jester whose antics made us all laugh. Then, a couple of hours after the party ended she was gone."

"One more question, Madame. Did Valarie take anything – anything of value from the house?" Knowing her affection for the girl, Olivier had hesitated to ask her the question.

"No, nothing at all. Valarie would never …" Her eyes watered again and, this time, tears cascaded down her cheeks "The only thing missing from her bedroom was a candle, which our gardener found the next day on the ground by the back door. It was still in its holder."

It had been much easier than expected. The street girl had handed her the note and then left immediately as instructed. For less than the cost of a cheap glass of wine, the girl had given Valarie the message and then was gone. He had ridden slowly by in his closed coach and seen everything, even the puzzled look on Valarie's face when she read the note. He smiled recalling Valarie was one of the few girls at the house who could read and write. At the end of the block, where Tolosa crossed Condé Street, he left the coach and sauntered slowly along Condé Street to the cathedral. Entering the church, he flipped the promised coin to the girl as he walked by her in the doorway. He stood to the side to allow two women pass him and surreptitiously watched the tiny girl scamper away down the street. A half hour later, he left the cathedral and went to his waiting coach, which as his driver had been instructed, was standing in front of the church.

The rendezvous with Valarie also went as planned. Valarie left the house at midnight as the brief note had instructed her. She went out the back door, walked quietly around the side of the house under the live oak's limbs and out onto the stepping stones to the gate. He watched her from the shadows as she unlocked the iron gate.

Valarie eased the locking bolt out of the hole in the wall. At first, the bolt was hard to move, but then it came out abruptly surprising her. She paused to look back at the dark house, hoping the sound had not awakened anyone inside. She sighed in relief when no lights appeared in the house. Still she waited a few seconds before pulling the gate inward. Knowing the grating noise the gate made when opened, she moved it very slowly trying to muffle the sound. She then stepped out into the street and looked from side to side. To her left in the darkness, Valarie saw the hooded figure standing beside the wall and, with a broad smile on her face, instantly went to it, her arms opened for an embrace. The figure came toward her with opened arms as well.

"I don't want to awaken anyone in the house, Suzanne," she whispered, "so we'll have to talk quietly." Four steps away, Valarie realized the figure approaching her was much bigger than Suzanne. She stopped, wondering who it was and suddenly some insight told her she would die.

The weighted stocking struck her head as she raised her hand trying to stop it. Too late, she saw the moving arm in front of her. Valarie fell as soon as she was hit; she lay motionless on the ground her face pressed into the dirt. She was still alive, but unconscious. She had been hit by a glancing blow above the right ear.

He bent over and struck her again on the back of the head. He hit her as hard as he could; there was no sense taking any chance of her awakening and crying for help. This time, he made sure she was dead. He heard her skull crack as the one-pound cannon ball in the stocking hit her. He recalled hearing the sound when Madame Villièrs and Gisella had been killed; it sounded like a musk melon falling to the ground.

It started to rain as he turned to the stone wall where a roll of sailcloth lay on the ground. Seeing a streak of lightning over the house, he ran to the wall, retrieved the sailcloth and rolled it out on the ground beside the girl's body. He kneeled behind the body and was about to push it onto the sheet of sailcloth when he was startled by a sudden explosion of thunder overhead. The thunder was followed by a strong gust of wind that blew dead leaves and dirt toward him where he kneeled. He paused to cover his eyes with his hands, but then turned around when he heard the sheet flapping behind him.

The wind had picked up the sailcloth and it rose like a hot air balloon in the air. He threw himself on the sheet to keep it on the ground and he lay there on his stomach, his arms and legs stretched out over as much of it as possible. He remained motionless on the flapping sheet until the force of the wind diminished and, then, disappeared as suddenly as it had arrived. Once the wind was gone, he got up on his knees to roll the dead girl toward him. In less than a minute, he completely covered her corpse in the sailcloth. As he got to his feet, it occurred to him that the body in the sailcloth looked like a rolled-up rug someone would store in a closet.

He stood in the rain, reviewing his plan and the way it had worked. He smiled pleased with himself. "The first and hardest part of his task is finished," he thought. Another bright flash of lightning took him from his reverie and he knew it was time to tie up the bundle and carry it to his horse. He smiled as he looked down at the rolled up sailcloth. "Little Valarie is no more than a bundle of refuse now," he said aloud, "just a worthless bundle of refuse to be discarded."

The rain increased accompanied by lightning and thunder. In seconds, it became a heavy downpour that deluged the road. He was drenched in the few seconds it took to retrieve the coils of rope he had left at the wall. The rain fell in sheets and heavy drops beat on his head and back as he knelt to tie the rope around the wrapped body. He had to pause for a time when rain water filled his eyes and blinded him. The downpour eventually abated as the storm moved out of New Orleans. A lighter but steady rain remained for another hour, but, by then, he was soaked and its intensity made no difference to him.

His clothes were completely soaked, even his underwear. Unwilling to remove his hood, rain water streamed down his face and neck and ran down his back and chest. It was a cold rain and he shivered when the first drops dripped down his back. Trying to ignore the cold and wet, he went about tying the bundle as tightly as possible. He tied it in four places, above the head, around the neck and waist and at the ankles. The rope was wound twice around each place. He was tying the last of the ropes around her ankles when he heard the clatter of horse hooves on the oyster shell road. He hastily knotted the rope, rolled the bundle against the wall and dropped to the ground next to it. He almost screamed when his face landed in horse dung.

A moment later, a black coach coming from the corner of Real and Tolosa Streets passed him without slowing down. He saw it clearly as a bright streak of lightning lit up the street. The coach's windows were tightly shut and the hooded driver stared straight ahead without a glance to either side. He waited until the coach reached the next corner and then stood quickly to wipe the dung from his face. The steady rain helped him wash his hands as well.

He still smelled the dung, but there was nothing to be done about it. Disposing of the girl's corpse was his main concern for now, not the stench. With a grunt, he lifted the bundle and hoisted it over his shoulder. He then walked toward his horse. His horse was tethered two houses away behind a pile of stone blocks. The blocks were stacked beside the street for the construction of a wall which already stood three feet high.

Valarie was slightly built, but she became heavy when the muddy ground slowed his pace and the walk took longer than he had anticipated. It was difficult to see more than a foot ahead in the dark and he shuffled through puddles and slippery leaves. A short distance from the pile of blocks, he unexpectedly stepped into a washed out ditch and almost fell. Barely managing to stay upright, he twisted his left ankle and staggered the rest of the way to the horse. Soaked to the skin and gritting his teeth in pain, he pushed the bundle up onto the horse's back and secured it with a rope; one end was tied around the saddle, the other around the horse's belly. In agony, he leaned his back against the horse after bending under him to knot the rope.

He paused reluctant to put his left foot in the stirrup to mount his horse. He dreaded the excruciating pain he would feel when he put his weight on the ankle. But it had to be done and quickly. There was no time to waste and other work yet to be finished that night. He gritted his teeth again and mounted the horse, stifling a scream as he swung his right leg over the saddle. Waiting a few minutes for the pain to subside, he urged the horse forward into the rain.

An hour before dawn, he sat in his living room in front of the fireplace, his left ankle and foot soaking in a pail of hot water. He lighted the logs in the fireplace as soon he got home, but he had to wait what seemed like an interminable length of time before the flames heated the pot. When the water was finally hot, he poured it into the pail and washed himself as best as he could standing on one leg. Meanwhile, another pot of water was heating over the fire and, when hot, he added it to the pail. He now sat in a pillowed chair with his eyes closed. He was exhausted and his ankle ached, but at least he no longer smelled the horse dung.

"All in all, it had gone well," he thought, "despite the storm and twisted ankle." He had achieved what had to be done without being seen and nothing had been left behind that could be traced to him – not even the handkerchief used to wipe the dung from his face. It was all because of careful planning. He had left nothing to chance. The note written to Valarie had been penned in Suzanne's large-letter style; a saved love note from the girl had shown him her lettering which was easy to copy. To make sure his stallion was not seen at the Laurent house that night, he had ridden another horse purchased a week earlier from an itinerant trader. The horse was not noticed either so he left him unsaddled and loose for someone to find in the poorer section of the city.

He smiled, recalling his plan for the disposal of Valarie's body and the purchased horse. He rode the horse to the eastern end of the city where the Mississippi River turned south toward the Gulf of Mexico. The streets were silent at two-thirty in the morning and no one was visible anywhere along his way. He rode slowly looking from side to side at the dark houses he passed. He was relieved that no light appeared in any of the windows. The town remained asleep and the horse, fitted with thick cotton pads over his shoes, made little noise as he moved over the roads.

His only concern was the chance of being observed by a sentry on the eastern wall or in the San Carlos guard tower. He took Hospital Street, two streets from the wall, all the way to the wharf. Hospital Street had two broken night lamps in the last block before the river. Avoiding the curious eyes of anyone not asleep at that hour, he leaned over the horse's neck and slowed him to a walk beside the last block of houses.

Dark clouds still covered the moon and it was pitch dark when he reached the old shed on the quay. The weather-beaten building stood beside the berth where he moored his sloop. It had survived the summer storm, though half the roof was lost and had to be replaced. He dismounted, again stifling a scream of pain, and limped to the shed. Standing on his good leg, he took the key from his pocket, but dropped it before he could unlock the door. He swore angrily and struck the wall with his fist. After struggling to bend down and pick up the key, he unlocked the door only to find it was stuck shut. It took him a few more minutes to free the door and then it grazed his bad ankle as it swung open. This time, he could not stop himself from screaming.

Waiting until the pain abated, he looked all about to see if anyone had heard him and was coming to his aid. When no one appeared, he led the horse into the shed and tied him beside his stallion. He then closed and latched the door and groped for the tinderbox and candle holder in the dark. They lay on a stool by the door where he placed them the last time he entered the shed. Quickly lighting the candle, he sat on the stool, took off his shoe and stocking and examined his ankle. It was red and swollen, but fortunately not broken. Despite the intense pain, he felt around the swelling and judged the ankle to be sprained.

After examining his ankle, he returned to the purchased horse. He reached up behind the saddle, untied the ropes holding the body on the horse and let it fall to the ground. It landed with a loud thump. Surprised by the sound, he stood listening for a few seconds. But hearing nothing except the barely audible flow of the river, he dragged the bundle away from the horses. He grimaced in pain, pulling it only a few feet.

The next half hour was spent removing the sailcloth from the body and then tying it up in a woven fishing net. His sore ankle throbbed with every move he made and there were moments when he doubted the pain would allow him to finish the task. He sat on an empty crate when his work was done. After only a minute or two, he wearily stood up and limped over to unsaddle the horse and remove the shoe pads. He knew it was essential to leave well before first light when most of the townspeople took to the streets.

It was a few minutes after four o'clock when he finally left the shed. He rode away on his stallion, leading the other horse by a rope. He headed across the city and, at the foot of Bienville Street, a block from the western wall, he pulled the horse up beside the stallion and removed the lead from his neck.

The purchased horse had done his work well and he patted his rump and left him standing in the street. At the corner of Conti Street, he turned in his saddle and looked back to see the horse grazing on the side of the road.

At home, he felt drowsy and leaned his head back against the chair. He knew that sleep was coming and let it happen. Too tired to get up and go to bed, he decided to sleep in the chair until the morning light awakened him. He carefully lifted his foot out of the hot water and put it on the pillow he had placed on a stool. His ankle was still swollen, but the pain had lessened a little. Tomorrow he would take his carriage rather than walk.

He closed his eyes and thought of the next day's schedule. The morning would be busy, but not the afternoon. After lunch, there would be plenty of time to dispose of Valarie's body. He smiled pleased with the plans he had made.

In his last thoughts, he saw himself sailing his sloop down river. He was on his way to a solitary inlet he knew from many visits made in the past. The tiny inlet, only six miles south of the city, was thirty-two feet in depth and surrounded by thick brush and leafy water oaks. Barely discernible, it's opening to the river could only be seen during the daylight. He had dropped two other bodies in the secluded spot the week before and that was where Valarie would be dropped as well. Bound tightly in the woven fishing net and weighted down with ballast stones, her body would fall speedily to the river bottom. In a week or two at most, catfish, crawfish and the other numerous bottom feeders would devour her flesh. Her bones would then eventually sink into the mud and never be seen again.

He saw his afternoon sailing clearly in his mind's eye. After the rainstorm, he expected a bright sunny day, sparkling water and a fast running river to the inlet. It would all be finished in a matter of minutes. He pictured himself in the stern of the sloop, watching the bound body drop deeper and deeper until it disappeared forever from view.

"Madame Laurent's gardener found the shoe, Father. It was lying on the ground, near the stone wall, to the right of the front gate. It was covered with mud – a brown shoe hard to see."

Olivier sat in the magistrate's office a week after his visit to the Laurent home. One of the magistrate's men had been sent to Santa María to ask him to come to a meeting at the Cabildo. Olivier left the church after Mass and walked through a cold mist into town.

The magistrate nodded. "Her gardener, a Freedman named Isaiah, found the brown shoe yesterday when he was raking leaves at the front gate. He noticed it out of the corner of his eye, the heel stuck up in the air. Until then, Madame Laurent thought Valarie left of her own volition. Knowing that the girl was probably seized forcibly and taken away, she was terribly distraught when I went to see her."

"I'm not surprised. She had become very fond of Valarie; in fact, she and her husband decided to raise her as their daughter. I take it she recognized the shoe as Valarie's."

"She was certain it was Valarie's shoe. She recalled when the girl purchased the pair. In fact, the woman even knew when Valarie last wore the shoes and what dress she wore with them." Magistrate Castañedo raised his eyebrows. "I suppose it's one of those things women notice, but men never see. She said Valarie wore the shoes the night of her husband's sixtieth birthday celebration. February the third."

"The night she disappeared." Olivier studied Castañedo's face. He looked much better than the last time he talked to him. Castañedo no longer faced an inquiry into the death of Rafael Portillo, the soldier murdered in Mosquito Creek. Governor Casa-Calvo held an official hearing on Portillo's death and determined the ill-fated soldier had died in the line of duty. He concluded that Magistrate Castañedo had acted appropriately at the brothel and did not deserve to be cited for dereliction of duty or face an official inquiry. The commandant, though disappointed with the governor's decision, did not complain to his superiors in Havana and the case against Castañedo was summarily closed. Portillo's widow received a sizeable pension.

"So, we can assume Valarie is dead. I expect she was seized by the murderer in front of the house and slain – probably somewhere else." The magistrate exhaled his breath loudly.

"It's what I feared when Madame Laurent told me the manner of her leaving."

"Unfortunately, the shoe was the only item found. We looked all over the area and along the wall. If there was any blood from a wound, it was washed away by the rain. There was that terrible thunderstorm the night Valarie disappeared."

"I remember the storm, it awakened me in the night."

"Well, Father, where does that leave us now?"

"We are left with only two girls we know spent time with him." Olivier shook his head from side to side in frustration. "Unfortunately, we have no notion where the girls might be now. With Charles Laroux' help, I've met and spoken to every family who took a girl from Mosquito Creek. I also have talked to five of the girls still employed as servants. But I've been unable to find the girls who were with him after the murder of María Isabel in August."

"Isn't one of them the last girl he bedded in December? I don't remember her name."

"Yes, that's Suzanne and I haven't the faintest idea where she went. There's also Jeanne who was with him in October. She also has disappeared. We can only hope the murderer hasn't found and killed them both by now."

"Dios mio! The diablo has murdered eight people since August –the two Dumont lads and the girl with them, Dumont's servant, the Villiers woman, her niece, Portillo and

Valarie. He also came close to killing Charles Laroux. God knows how many others he has slain." The magistrate threw up his hands. "He must be found and executed."

"Yes, as quickly as possible. I fear what he will do next if he's not stopped. It's obvious he has no moral limits – he's a truly evil man."

"It's true, he's a monster in our midst. Do you think him mad, Father?"

"I think not. He knows exactly what he's doing. He killed Madame Villièrs, her niece and the other girls to keep them from identifying him. Rafael Portillo was struck down because the unfortunate soldier was simply in the way when he burned the brothel down. The house, of course, was razed to destroy any and all existing records that might identify him." Olivier sighed in exasperation. "He'll stop at nothing to keep from being known."

"What about his attacks on the Dumont family? It seems his murderous rampage began with the two Dumont lads."

"So it did and I don't know why. What could those two young boys possibly have done to deserve the dreadful way he killed them? I can't imagine what it could be, can you?" Olivier saw Castañedo shake his head. "It also bewilders me that he then attempted to poison the entire Dumont family. I don't understand any of it." Olivier put his hands together, entwining his long fingers. "But I suspect the fiend has some scheme in mind and I fear his scheme includes more murders than we have already seen. No, Magistrate, this man isn't mad – he's an evil and all too clever killer who must be stopped."

Castañedo nodded. "Gracias a Dios, the governor doesn't know all of it. He, of course, knows about the deaths of the two boys and the murders of the women and Portillo in Mosquito Creek. But he doesn't know they are all connected and committed by the same man. I dare not tell him, not knowing what might follow. I fear one of his aides might carelessly mention it to a gossip monger and, within a couple of days, everyone in town would know a murderer walks the streets among us. A murderer of eight people! Solamente Dios sabe (God only knows) what then would happen – I shudder to think of it." He shook his head and stared at Olivier. "I'm sure you understand my reluctance to tell him."

"I do, Magistrate. The fewer who know the number of murders, the better. The city has more than enough problems without the spread of fear among the people. Only Father Francis knows all of the murderer's crimes, but you can be assured he will tell no one about them. Of course, Father Antonio knows everything as well."

"I'm not concerned about either of them saying anything." Castañedo shook his head. "What about Dumont? Doesn't he know all the murders are connected?"

"He does, Magistrate, but he won't say anything about it in public. Jean Bertin is worried the murder of his sons might damage his businesses, so he has decided to say nothing more about it. Charles Laroux told me about his change of mood while we were together this past week."

"Why is he worried about such a possibility? It seems unlikely to me."

"Dumont worries his customers might hesitate to deal with him if they know he and his family face the risk of death, especially at the hands of a murderer."

"Ah, I see now. What a greedy man! Money is always on his mind." Castañedo made a face. "What about Laroux? He knows everything, too."

"Laroux won't say anything either; he will follow the lead of his uncle. Besides the lad is still suffering the loss of his mother. You can see the grief he feels on his face. He says nothing about her, but the sadness shows in eyes. He often stares into the distance obviously preoccupied by his thoughts of her. You know the poor woman suffered a long lingering death with constant pain. I'm told it took her almost a year to die after she fell ill."

Castañedo inhaled deeply. "That's awful. Por favor Dios permitió que mí morirme en mi sueño. (Please God let me die in my sleep.)"

Olivier nodded. "It's what we would all ask of God." He crossed himself.

"I suppose Laroux still thinks about his own nearness to death in November."

"He does and he admitted it to me one afternoon last week. I think it's often on his mind, especially when on foot in town. On more than one occasion, I've seen him suddenly whirl about to see who was walking behind us. He carries a pistol as well as a dagger to protect himself."

"I can't fault him for it. If I had barely escaped an attempt on my life, I'd be looking over my shoulder, too." Castañedo stood to end their meeting. "Well, Father, from what you've said, it's essential we find those two girls who can identify the murderer."

"It is. They're the only ones left who spent time with him. Without at least one of them to tell us about him, I don't know what we can do to find him."

CHAPTER TEN

NEW ORLEANS: FEBRUARY 21 - MARCH 5, 1800

Four days later, Olivier found Bishop Meléndez waiting for him after morning Mass. He was initially surprised to see the bishop's coach standing in front of Santa María, but he assumed Meléndez had come to look at the church's renovation. Knowing the bishop's poor opinion of him, he expected a critical, if not a nit-picking, inspection of the building. A week earlier, Olivier had written him requesting his presence at Easter Mass and he thought Meléndez was there to make sure the renovation work would be done before he agreed to officiate.

Olivier was unaware that Meléndez had driven to Santa María well before his own arrival at dawn. It was still dark and an hour before first Mass when the bishop's black coach reached the church and stopped some a distance away in a small clearing surrounded by water oaks. The temperature had dropped below freezing during the night and Meléndez sat bundled up in wool blankets inside his coach. The side window facing the church was partly open so he could see Santa María clearly.

Meléndez ordered his driver to lead the horses to the clearing because it was well hidden and yet offered an unobstructed view of Santa María. The bishop had stopped his coach in that sheltered spot once before in August to escape the merciless heat of the sun. Now, as the first light of morning appeared above the trees, the clearing, though still shrouded in darkness, was the perfect place to see who entered Santa María. Even before the sun had fully risen, the freshly whitewashed exterior stood out in the dawn and he could clearly see the doors of the church.

It was not only cold, it was that damp, bone-chilling cold that seemed to linger over New Orleans all winter. Meléndez shivered now and then even huddled under the heavy blankets he had wrapped around his body. He grimaced, knowing it was the price he had to pay to observe the church through the open window.

Meléndez arrived early to see who would open the church and perform the first Mass that morning. He waited impatiently without seeing anyone approach the church and, as time slowly passed, he began to tap his cold fingers on the window sill. He tapped faster and louder as the sky lightened and the first shafts of sunlight stretched between the trees and touched the top of the bell tower. It was then that he saw the slender bird-like figure of Olivier suddenly appear out of the darkness and stride toward the door.

He sighed expelling a long breath of air. Meléndez had expected Father Francis to open the church in the morning and he turned his mouth down in disappointment. He had gotten up in the middle of the night and, then, sat freezing in this place for God-knows-how-long. All for nothing. Though Meléndez would not have admitted it to anyone, he had made the surprise visit to Santa María in the hope Olivier would not arrive until later, if at all that morning.

The bishop longed to find the *drunken Dominican* guilty of neglecting his parish.

Meléndez assumed Olivier drank copiously at night and undoubtedly was incapacitated in the mornings. How seriously incapacitated the man became, he did not know. He had heard it said that some habitual borrachos (drunks) could drink as many as three bottles of wine without effect. He did not know Olivier's capacity for drink, but he was sure the arrogant priest would be in no condition to officiate at Santa María in the morning. Certain the *drunken Dominican* was guilty of neglecting his parish, Meléndez decided to watch Santa María for three days in a row to see if and when he did arrive. If as he expected, Olivier was absent or arrived late for morning Mass one of those days, the bishop intended to charge him with dereliction of his priestly duties. But now to his chagrin, Meléndez knew he would have to find another way to dispose of him.

The bishop knew he had the authority to remove Olivier from Santa María without cause, but he hesitated to take that action. Meléndez was well aware of the priest's popularity among the local parishioners and he feared a public commotion that might reach the ears of the current archbishop in Havana. He also knew the Dominican had the strong support of the parish pastor, who would not hesitate to protest. If he had been the appointed *Bishop of Louisiana*, Meléndez would not have worried, but he served as Visiting Bishop, a provisional position that would end when Bishop Peñalvery Cárdenas returned from Cuba. More important, he awaited assignment as bishop of his own diocese and he would do nothing to jeopardize that opportunity.

Now, watching Olivier unlock the church doors, Meléndez muttered to himself. He knew no meaningful charge could be made against the priest even with cause and he did not intend to endure another cold morning in the damp lowlands. It occurred to him that he could return to Santa María when the weather warmed, but the prospect of getting out of bed early and sitting in the coach for so long again seemed intolerable. He would have to find another way to make a case for removing the arrogant priest – a case with such clear evidence that no one could accuse him of arbitrary action.

Bishop Meléndez knew he could not charge Olivier with criminal conduct or corporal or spiritual defects which were the most common reasons for removal. Drunkenness was a corporal defect, but he doubted a convincing case could be presented, particularly without the support of Father Antonio. The cathedral pastor would contradict him no matter what case he made against him. Besides, everyone in the Church knew what a pervasive and unresolved problem drinking had become for the clergy. There appeared to be no place without the problem, not even Spain.

"Persistent disobedience" as it was termed in the Church might also be a reason for his removal and there was no doubt the arrogant Dominican had repeatedly disobeyed his orders. He could not count the number of times he had told Olivier to give up the secular effort for Dumont and return to his priestly duties at Santa María. All to no avail! The arrogant priest had paid no more heed to him than if he had been a filthy beggar asking for money in the street. He brazenly defied him, flouted his authority and ignored his orders. He had indeed "persistently disobeyed" him – the Bishop of Louisiana. What audacity! He continued the worldly murder investigation without the slightest pause and even entered a vile house of sin in the process. Yet, despite such willful disobedience, the drunken priest had the parish pastor's consistent support.

His best chance would be to accuse him of *serious or prolonged neglect of duty,* which he knew had been used by the Church to remove troublesome priests in the past. But Antonio again would come to the Dominican's defense and dispute whatever he said about his performance as a parish priest. The pastor also needed to be dismissed from the diocese; he was too permissive of his subordinate's misbehavior and also too worldly for the good of the Church.

If only he had been appointed Bishop of Louisiana and not the *Visiting Bishop*, he would have quickly removed him along with the drunken priest. But he knew his time in Louisiana was now coming to a close. *Thank God.* He had heard Bishop Cárdenas would soon be returning to New Orleans to assume his office again. It was said he would return before the end of the year.

Meléndez closed the coach window. "I'll have to content myself to watch and wait," he said to himself. "The obstinate Dominican may well do something yet that would require more than an official reprimand. His unrestrained pride will undoubtedly lead him to some impious act sooner or later. In the meantime, I must wait patiently for a new posting from Havana. Con la ayuda de Dios (with God's help) I'll soon be out of this miserable colony and in charge of my own diocese – hopefully in Europe." He made the sign of the cross and wondered if it was too prideful to pray for an appointment in Spain.

The bishop waited until the morning parishioners entered the church and then ordered his driver to station his coach in front of Santa María. Meléndez counted the number of people who came for morning Mass and was surprised there were so many – a total of nineteen parishioners. He listed them on his fingers; seven women, five with infants and two of them elderly, four old men, one of them a cripple, a young man and his pregnant wife, an idiot boy led by an adolescent girl, probably his older sister, and four mixed-breed Indians. Meléndez raised his eyebrows as he counted them again in his mind.

"Nineteen!" he thought. "That's only ten or so fewer parishioners than those who come to the cathedral on most mornings. The Dominican is as silver-tongued as Satan."

Olivier saw the black coach as soon as he opened the doors after Mass. He nodded to the bishop and then one by one he bid the parishioners goodbye. Meléndez watched with mounting impatience as the young couple spoke at length to Olivier about the future baptism of their baby. The bishop was sure the defiant priest made no effort to end the conversation; in fact, he seemed to draw out the discussion. Even when the couple finally left, Olivier did not hurry to the coach and apologize for keeping him waiting.

"Welcome to Santa María, Most Reverend Bishop." Olivier bowed his head to the seated man. "Would you like to see the church? There is still much to be done, but I'm quite certain everything will be completed by Easter."

The bishop returned Olivier's greeting with a superior smile. "Not today, Father Olivier. Perhaps, another day if I can possibly find the time."

Meléndez had no intention of ever visiting Santa María as long as the Dominican served as its pastor. He had laughed out loud when he read Olivier's request for his presence on Easter morning. At the time, the bishop had decided to send him a brief statement denying the request, but later he thought it would be better to ignore it until a few days before Easter. Then, he would write a one-line refusal. The thought of that strategy amused him and brought a smile to his lips.

Olivier frowned in puzzlement. "Then, how may I help you, Reverend Bishop?"

The bishop beckoned Olivier closer to him. "Where is Father Francis today?" Meléndez replied, ignoring the question. He spoke softly requiring Olivier to bend down closer to him.

Olivier jerked his head back and turned red in the face. He had seen the bishop's nostrils twitch and realized Meléndez had brought him close to smell his breath. Olivier scowled at the bishop, barely controlling his anger. "Father Francis is in town at the cathedral this morning; he is attending a meeting with his Capuchin brothers."

"I see, so he usually opens Santa María in the morning and holds First Mass."

"No, Bishop." Olivier would not give Meléndez the benefit of his full title. "At times we are both here for First Mass." He did not tell him that they usually took turns in the morning.

"How often is that, Father?"

"It depends on the needs of our parishioners, Bishop."

"What needs take place outside of Santa María?"

"The birth of children, family crises, illness and death, Bishop." Olivier knew Meléndez was well aware of the parishioners' needs outside the church.

"Secular needs then – much like your efforts for Monsieur Dumont." Meléndez gave him a smug smile.

"No, Bishop." Olivier narrowed his eyes as he looked at Meléndez. "The visits we make to our parishioners are as spiritual as they are secular. As you are aware, the parish extends well beyond the church building." He turned and pointed to Santa María. "As priests, we go about the parish reminding the faithful that they are the people of God and instruct them, confirm them and encourage them to a more fervent and spiritual life. We also serve as shepherds, seeking to lead non-believers in the community to the faith by proclaiming the Gospel to them. In addition, of course, we go among the people to contribute the Word of God to their celebrations and give our support to them in times of chaos, sickness and death. We …"

Meléndez' scowled at Olivier. "Don't you dare lecture me on the duties and functions of our parish priests, Olivier. I'm well aware of them! The question is – are you?"

"I am indeed, Bishop." Olivier noted that Meléndez called him by his first name and left out his Church title. He knew it was purposeful to annoy him. "If you are referring to my efforts for the Dumont family, I must remind you that those efforts were requested by the pastor of the parish in which I serve. And, unless I am badly mistaken, one of my duties as a priest is to serve the parish and comply with the pastor's orders. Is that not correct, Bishop Meléndez?" It was now Olivier's turn to smile; he cocked his head to the side and gave the bishop a beatific smile.

Meléndez' face flushed and he glared at Olivier, his brown eyes hard as marbles. "What about my orders? The orders of *your* bishop, the Bishop of Louisiana! It is your duty to comply with my orders – first and foremost!" Meléndez had to keep himself from shouting.

"Yes, Bishop, it is my duty to comply with your orders. Obedesco y me cumplo con sus órdenes." (I obey and comply with your orders.)

"Is that so?" sneered Meléndez, still fuming. "That's not my impression."

"Yes, Bishop Meléndez, I've obeyed your orders – all of them." Olivier spoke in a quiet and calm voice which he sensed infuriated the bishop. "I trust I may continue."

The bishop made no comment as he continued to glare at Olivier.

"I left the cathedral the same day I received your orders from the parish pastor and took charge of Santa María the next morning. It was the morning of August 31, last year. Father Etienne turned over the church keys to me before First Mass and I have served as the pastor of Santa María since that day. According to your instructions, I replaced Father Etienne, whose age and regrettable ill health forced him to retire, and now have I served at Santa María a total of five and a half months.

Also, according to your orders, Bishop Meléndez, I have tried to restore Santa María's meaning in the parish. Your exact words as quoted to me by Father Antonio were, 'The church is in desperate need of renovation as well as the restoration of its meaning in the parish.' With your words in mind, I immediately set to work trying to accomplish both of your concerns – of course, with the help of Father Francis. The results of those efforts have been gratifying. The church building is soon to be completely renovated, while attendance at Santa María services has trebled, if not quadrupled, in number and …"

Meléndez raised his hand abruptly and stopped Olivier in mid-sentence. He suspected the long speech was made to irritate him. He glared at Olivier, a muscle pulsing in his jaw.

"What about your personal failings, *Father Olivier?* He spoke softly instead of shouting at him which he desperately wanted to do. "You were sent here to Santa María to strengthen your moral character as well as to meet the needs of the parish. You do remember those instructions, as well, don't you, *Father*?" Meléndez emphasized his title to remind Olivier of his subordinate position in the Church hierarchy. "I also assume you remember your appalling behavior in the cathedral that prompted those instructions."

"I well recall the incident, Bishop Meléndez." Olivier's stomach churned as he faced the bishop. "Dieu m'aider (God help me)," he thought, "it's hard not to hate this man."

"What about my instructions relating to that behavior?" The bishop's lips curled into a look of contempt. "Did you conveniently forget them?"

"No, Bishop Meléndez, I well remember them. Father Antonio repeated them to me the same day I left the cathedral." Olivier briefly looked up into the sky. He prayed for the strength to endure the bishop's interrogation.

Meléndez assumed Olivier's pause meant he had forgotten his instructions. "What were they then? You seem to remember everything else said to you, that is, what you want to recall."

Olivier looked down at the seated man and calmly repeated his words. "You said, 'Tell Father Olivier that I expect him to use this new assignment to strengthen his moral character and dedicate himself to the humility that his priestly office demands.'"

"That's correct, Father. Now, do tell me what you have done about *those instructions?*" Knowing he had reasserted his authority, Meléndez now spoke as calmly and quietly as Olivier. The smug smile returned as he stared at the priest.

Olivier looked at the bishop, knowing he would lie to him. There was no way to avoid it without receiving a severe reprimand as well as the possibility of a punishment that would lead to his expulsion from Louisiana. He could endure whatever the bishop said to him, but he did not want to be forced out of New Orleans.

Though it had taken him awhile, he had come to enjoy his life in Spanish Louisiana. He had friends inside and outside the Church and was known and generally appreciated about town. Parishioners from the cathedral acknowledged him wherever they saw him, some with smiles or waves and others with cordial greetings. His friendship with Father Antonio especially pleased him as well as the paternal role he played with Francis. He liked the young priest more and more as time passed and it occurred to him that he should be less critical of the lad.

Outside the Church, he cherished his time with Gervaise and María Adela and, of course, Aveline, who sadly now was deceased. There was also Gervaise' mother, Madame Lefevre, who lovingly mothered him along with her son. Some others at the cathedral and in town, including Magistrate Castañedo, likewise enriched his life in New Orleans and made him feel appreciated as a valued member of the community.

Most of all, his time at Santa María had revived his sense of himself as a priest and a man of God. The renovation of Santa María and the restoration of the parish's significance among the struggling parishioners of the lowlands had helped him feel good about himself for the first time in years. He knew he was finally doing what God expected of him. After many uncertain years in the Church, Olivier realized he was best suited to be a parish priest. Instead of serving as an omniscient teacher, seeking the adulation of his clerical students, he knew he belonged in a small unadorned church serving the spiritual needs of the poor, meek and miserable. They were truly the *children of God* and the *salt of the earth* as the gospel of St. Mathew stated.

Olivier knew the discovery of his calling had made him more accessible to the Acadians and, as a consequence, they had come to accept him. Now, he even had their respect and trust. He was greeted with smiles and handshakes wherever he went in the lowlands and was treated as an appreciated guest at all celebrations. Some of the typically taciturn men even had invited him to their family gatherings. But more significantly, he knew he had been fully accepted when they freely discussed their village conflicts in his presence and now and then asked for his advice.

He still drank, sometimes to excess, but much less frequently these days. And, though he had to admit his seemingly inescapable pride still kept him from attaining humility, he was aware of less concern for appreciation and praise. He was a better man and priest here in the lowlands and he would not do or say anything to jeopardize his new joie de vivre (joy of life).

Olivier nodded. "I've kept your instructions in mind, Bishop Meléndez, and pray daily for God's help to strengthen my moral character. I …"

"What else have you done specifically to that end in your daily life?" Meléndez frowned, giving Olivier a skeptical look.

"I have stopped my intake of inebriating drinks …" Olivier said "during the day" under his breath. "Instead of wine, I also have substituted tea to drink with my meals." He knew his unspoken admission was as much a lie as if he had said it aloud.

Meléndez stared directly into the Dominican's eyes. "Are

you saying, Father Olivier, that you have stopped drinking – entirely?" There was disbelief in his voice.

"Yes, Bishop, entirely." This time he had not tried to evade the question; instead, he lied, boldly lied as he looked into the bishop's eyes.

Meléndez made a sour face and shook his head. It was obvious he did not believe him. "What about your need for humility? What have you done about that?"

Olivier smiled. On this subject he could answer the bishop's question truthfully. In fact, he had been waiting for Meléndez to ask him about it.

"Do you find that question amusing?" Meléndez frowned, wondering if the Dominican was mocking him.

"No, Bishop Meléndez, not at all. I smile because I have indeed found humility here at Santa María. It's an unforeseen humility I never could have known in the cathedral or in any of my other previous assignments as a priest. It has come from meeting and knowing the dauntless Acadians who survive here in these harsh lands. I feel small and petty among these people who struggle endlessly to feed their poor families and cope with nature's capricious behavior. They live on courageously with a profound love of God despite the suffering and many troubles that confront them daily. Beside them, I, who have enjoyed a long life free of want with a privileged place in society, find myself not only humble, but of little significance here."

His mouth open in amazement, Meléndez looked up at Olivier. He did not doubt the Dominican's words. He could see the sincerity in his face.

"I see," he finally mumbled.

Olivier smiled again.

"Well …" It took the bishop a full minute to gather his thoughts. "with your devotion to this parish, Father, why then do you still do Dumont's bidding?"

"I must finish my assignment for Father Antonio. He

asked me to see the investigation to the end. And, when it's done, Si Dieu le veut (God willing), I intend to devote myself entirely to Santa María and the people of this parish."

Meléndez sighed wearily. He knew there was nothing to be gained by talking to Olivier any longer. He was tired after rising so early and wanted to return to town for breakfast.

"I'll anticipate a quick conclusion to your secular efforts, Father. I'll also look forward to the devotion to this parish you claim when I see your total commitment at Santa María. Then, I'll know what you said today is more than rhetoric." Meléndez wanted to say *Dominican rhetoric*, but stopped himself worried the priest would report it to his provincial superior in Havana.

Olivier smiled, this time broadly. "I understand, Bishop Meléndez. With God's help, the investigation will be over soon, very soon – hopefully, by Easter, when the parish of Santa María looks forward to your presence at Sunday Mass."

Meléndez studied the priest's face and thought to himself. "That arrogant smile again. I wouldn't be so presumptions if I were you. It makes me wonder about your claim to finding humility here in the lowlands, Father." Meléndez gave a tight-lipped smile and struck the end of his staff on the roof of the coach. Seconds later, the bishop was on his way to New Orleans.

Olivier lost three successive games of checkers, two to Gervaise and the other to Francis. Though he made no excuses, he could not concentrate. He was preoccupied with thoughts about the stymied investigation.

It was now the last day of February and he had found no information about the location of the two missing girls. There had not been the slightest hint of where they might be – if still alive. The investigation was at a standstill. Despite the help of María Adela, Charles Laroux and all the families who had taken girls from the brothel, he had learned nothing new about the whereabouts of Jeanne or Suzanne. A couple of times, he had heard their names mentioned by the servant girls he interviewed, but only one girl said she had met Suzanne in Mosquito Creek. None of the servant girls had ever met Jeanne, though her name had been mentioned by others after she had left the brothel.

Olivier did discover to his satisfaction that a number of the girls who initially served as house servants had eventually married. Some stayed with their husbands in New Orleans, while others moved away to nearby towns and villages in the colony. He also heard that a couple of the girls had reunited with family members and left the city for unknown destinations. Although Olivier was pleased to know some of the girls had prospered, he had not learned anything about what had happened to Jeanne or Suzanne after they left Mosquito Creek. He worried they had suffered the same fate as Valarie.

The magistrate's search for the girls had no better results. He sent men to interview ship captains, dockworkers, shopkeepers, traveling merchants and street vendors, but none of those interviewed had ever seen or even heard of the girls. After leaving the brothel, the two girls had simply disappeared. Castañedo told Olivier the only good news he could tell him was there had been no new killings he could blame on the unknown murderer. There were, of course, still the usual tavern fights, stabbings and drunken brawls over whores that ultimately ended in death, but they were to be expected in the poorer sections of New Orleans

Anxious to spend all his time at Santa María, Olivier became increasingly irritated with the demands of the murder investigation. It was simply taking too long and, without any idea of how to pursue the murderer, he had begun to suspect the man might never be known. More often than not, he found himself tempted to ask Father Antonio to release him from the investigation. But Olivier never made the request, worried it would affect their close friendship. He knew the pastor would readily agree to his request, saying he understood his frustration, but Oliver feared his disappointment would result in a loss of trust in him. The loss of trust might be miniscule, but it would exist nevertheless. More practically, Olivier did not want to alienate Antonio, knowing he would need his future financial help at Santa María. He therefore continued his efforts with the investigation despite his doubts and mounting impatience. But, as the weeks passed and the signs of spring were apparent everywhere about him, he desperately tried to find some means to end the investigation by Easter.

"Gervaise, it's time to do your schoolwork. There will be time enough tomorrow night to play checkers." Madame Lefevre spoke sternly to her son as he crowned a king against Francis. "Now, Gervaise, and don't make a face."

Olivier smiled as Gervaise, who did make a sour face, reluctantly got up from the kitchen table and went to his room. Olivier sighed, relieved the games were over. He now could sip a bit of brandy and talk to Francis.

"You've been preoccupied tonight, Father." Francis poured a glass of brandy for Olivier and half a glass for himself.

"I have, Francis. I hope the boy was unaware of it."

"He was. As you know, Gervaise delights in beating you and he was too ecstatic over his victories to notice your lack of concentration."

"Good, I'm glad. He's a competitive boy, isn't he? I was too at his age. Of course, I still am, though I would like to deny it." Olivier chuckled.

Francis smiled. "I assume you're thinking about the investigation."

Olivier nodded. "I am and my thoughts keep me awake at night. Some nights, I'm awake well past one o'clock, my mind full of plans and schemes that in the morning seem foolish in the light of day."

"Everything depends upon finding one of those missing girls, doesn't it?"

"Yes and try as I might, I cannot think of any other means to identify the murderer. Do you have any suggestions on the matter?"

"What about trying to identify him by his boots and clothing? I know there are numerous well-dressed young gentlemen here in New Orleans, but wouldn't it be possible to compile a list of those men from the tailors in town. The men then could be interviewed to find out if they had the time and opportunity to ride all that distance to Mosquito Creek particularly during the week when the murderer went to the brothel."

"That's a good idea, Francis, a very good idea. There are some 8,000 people in the city, but most of those people are poor. In fact, most are former slaves and along with the Acadians, they probably account for well over ninety percent of the population. I wouldn't think there are more than a hundred families here who could afford to be dressed by tailors."

"That was my thinking, Father. With such a small number, how many young men might there be here who wear tailored clothing or have expensive cordovan boots made for them?"

"Not many. Of course, some of the wealthy men have their clothing imported."

"That's true, but with so many European tailors now in New Orleans – I've seen three of their stalls on San Pedro Street alone, I can't imagine many of the wealthy men would continue to order clothing from abroad. It takes much too long – at least eight to ten weeks. Beside they can be better fitted in town where tailors will make adjustments any day of the week."

Olivier nodded. "I assume boots and shoes are made here, too."

"They are, though the newest women's shoe styles come from Europe. For men's wear, however, the finer leathers are still imported from Europe, but local boot and shoemakers make them here. From what I've seen around town, there are even more shoemakers than tailors in New Orleans."

Olivier nodded. "You're right. We might indeed find the murderer by the clothing and boots he wears. Without any other way to identify him, it's certainly well worth trying. I'll tell the magistrate your suggestion. He could certainly have a man or two interview the town tailors and bootmakers."

"It could be done quickly with a list compiled. It would help if we could speak to Ana Luisa again. Hopefully, she would remember more details of the murderer's clothing. I recall she said he wore a dark hat and suit and looked like a lawyer. It was at the same time she spoke of his beautiful boots, reddish-brown in color."

Olivier smiled for the first time that evening. "Yes, I remember her saying that, too, and she thought his boots were cordovan. Good thinking, Francis. We may yet find the fiend. As you know, I'll be seeing Ana Luisa and Honorè after Mass on Sunday; I'll talk to her then."

"What did Father Antonio say about their marriage?"

"Ah, I'm sorry, Francis, I forgot to tell you about my meeting with him on Monday. My mind must be muddled. Father Antonio has decided to perform the marriage here at Santa María. Surprisingly, he had no difficulty getting the bishop's approval. In fact, Meléndez seemed to be pleased with his decision."

"I am surprised. Do you know what he told Father Antonio?"

Olivier nodded, a slight smile on his lips. "Father Antonio was also surprised, in fact, very surprised. The bishop said, 'We need to bring as many of the pagans as possible into the

Church. That's what we Spaniards did when the New World was settled. That's why today the Indians are Catholic and more civilized in Mexico and South America than in North America.'"

"There is truth to what he said." Francis looked at Olivier to see if he agreed.

"There is, but even if the Indians are more civilized in Mexico and South America, they live no better there than they do here in Spanish Louisiana."

"That's so, but, wherever the Indians live in our colonies, they have the Church and hear the true word of God and not the Protestant blasphemies."

Olivier nodded. "Quite so, Francis, but it was not the bishop's words that surprised the pastor – it was the bishop's instant agreement. Father Antonio has come to expect his criticism or disagreement every time he tells him a decision made without consulting him. Instead, this time, Bishop Meléndez said Santa María was the appropriate place for the marriage since 'there are so many Indians living outside New Orleans'."

"That's true." Francis looked at Olivier, wondering why he had mentioned the comment.

"The lowlands are mostly occupied by Acadians. They are the vast majority of our parishioners, not the Indians! I think the bishop said it was *appropriate* because he didn't want the marriage of a white woman and an Indian held in the cathedral. What is your opinion?"

Francis stared at Olivier, a frown on his face.

"Don't you agree?"

"May I speak frankly, Father?"

"You know I always want you to speak your mind."

"Well, Father, I must say I think you are judging the bishop unfairly. He's certainly not a likable man, but I don't think that comment marks him as narrow-minded. It's possible he thinks Indians are as common in the lowlands as they are elsewhere around New Orleans. The bishop has obviously seen them on his journeys outside the city walls, but I doubt he has knowledge of which area has the greatest number of Indians. Before I came to Santa María, I myself thought they were more numerous than the Acadians in the lowlands."

"So, you think his comment came from ignorance and not narrow-mindedness?" Oliver was surprised that Francis defended the bishop.

"I do, Father. To be candid, I think your conflict with him has made you see him at fault in everything he says or does."

Olivier made a face, annoyed by his comment. "That may be. Well, Francis, do you have any other notions of how we might find the murderer?"

Francis bit his lip, knowing he had irritated Olivier. "I do, Father. I suggest you speak to that girl, Sylvie, again – the one who shared a room with Suzanne. Now that she has been living in the convent a while, she might remember more than when you spoke to her a month ago. It's possible she might have some memory of where Suzanne went after she left the brothel."

Antonio and Olivier sat in the same small room where Olivier interviewed the girls when he visited the Ursuline Convent in January. Mother Marguerite met them at the door and, bowing respectfully, she welcomed Father Antonio to the convent. Olivier received an obligatory nod as she turned away. In the room, she spoke to the pastor and virtually ignored Olivier. The prioress did not even acknowledge him when Sister Helene was introduced. Her eyes passed over him as if he were invisible. She left after a brief conversation with the pastor about the convent's need for additional funding. "Au revoir,

Father Antonio," Marguerite said as she walked away.

"She certainly disapproves of you," said Antonio when Sister Helene had gone out to get Sylvie. "What in God's name have you done to her, Olivier?" The pastor smiled.

"Nothing to my knowledge. With the exception of exchanging greetings with her at the cathedral, I've never spoken to the woman before my visit here. At that time, she treated me as if I were the devil's disciple. Now, she simply ignores me."

"So it seems. It may be that you *are* his disciple and I never knew it." Antonio smiled and then chuckled when he saw the frown on Olivier's face. "Well, now I'm glad I came along as you suggested."

"I doubt she would have admitted me if you hadn't accompanied me. I think ..." Olivier was interrupted by the opening of the door.

Sylvie entered the room and smiled at Olivier. The tiny girl looked much healthier than she did on his last visit. She had gained weight and there was color in her cheeks.

"Good morning, Father Olivier."

"Good morning, Sylvie, it's good to see you." Olivier turned to Antonio. "Sylvie, this is Father Antonio, he is the cathedral pastor and he has come with me to see you."

"Good morning, Father Antonio, I'm glad to meet you." Sylvie bowed and smiled shyly.

"Bless you, my child, I'm glad to meet you, too." Antonio gestured Sylvie to the chair across the table from them. "Please sit with us."

They talked a few moments about the first signs of spring now appearing everywhere in town, the bed of yellow crocuses blooming in the garden and Sylvie's life since she arrived at the convent. The girl spoke at length about her school work and how much she enjoyed learning to read and write. When she finally paused to blow her nose, Antonio turned to Olivier who had sat in silence while they talked.

Olivier waited until she put the handkerchief in her lap before speaking. "Sylvie, as you know, we are still trying to locate the girls who were with you in Mosquito Creek." Oliver did not mention Madame Villièrs or her house; he thought it best not to remind the girl of her life in the brothel. "Since our last talk, we've found most of them or we know where they went – but there are a couple of girls we have yet to locate."

"Did you locate Suzanne? I've been worried about her." Sylvie laid her hands on the table and clasped them together.

"No, not yet. She is one of the girls we are trying to locate." Olivier saw Sylvie's chin tremble and she began to cry.

"I was afraid of that," she mumbled through her tears. "He's killed her."

Olivier reached across the table and patted her hands. "I don't think so, Sylvie. I think Suzanne has gone someplace where he won't find her. That's why we can't find her either."

"Why do you think that, Father?" Sylvie wiped her eyes with her handkerchief, but tears cascaded down her cheeks.

"I just think so. You know how every once in a while you know something before it ever happens. It's one of those things I know, without knowing why. I'm not only certain Suzanne is alive, I am certain we'll find her."

"You're sure he won't kill her?" Sylvie's eyes were wet, but there were no more tears on her cheeks. "How will you stop him?'

"He won't find her; we'll find and arrest *him* first." Olivier smiled at her.

"I've had those feelings, too. Do you think they come from God?"

"Yes, I do. God speaks to us in many ways."

"If we open our hearts, we will hear his words as clearly as bells," said Antonio. "That's what my Mother said when I was a boy and I have never forgotten it. It's true, of course, God's words are heard by those who open their hearts to Him."

Sylvie smiled. "Please tell me when you find Suzanne, Father Olivier. She was like a sister to me – we shared everything. I love her so."

"I will, I promise. Sylvie, try to think back and see if you can recall where she might have gone. A place she knew well or liked, a village where she lived as a child, a place where a friend lived – anywhere she might have mentioned to you."

"She came from somewhere in Canada, but said she would never go back there again." Sulvie shook he head from side to side. "Suzanne hated the cold weather. It made her hands red and rough and gave her cold sores."

"Do you remember if she mentioned any other places she liked or any other places she may have wanted to visit?"

Sylvie shook her head. "Suzanne liked it here, no matter how hot the weather. If she went somewhere else, it would have to be some place warm."

"I see. Did she have friends in New Orleans or a nearby town?"

"No, Father. Suzanne came to Madame Villièrs house soon after the ship brought her to New Orleans. She sneaked aboard one night and hid behind some barrels until the ship landed here. She didn't dare show herself and almost starved; the only food she ate was the scraps the crew left from their meals. She picked through the garbage before it was thrown overboard."

"Mon Dieu!" exclaimed Antonio. "Were there any other stowaways on the ship?"

"I don't think so. At least she didn't mention any others."

"Sylvie, please describe Suzanne," said Olivier. "We don't know what she looks like."

Sylvie smiled. "Suzanne is so pretty, slender as a reed. She has big brown eyes and the whitest skin – not a blemish on it. She has white teeth, too."

"How old is she?"

Sylvie paused to think. "Suzanne will be fifteen in June,

but she looks much younger. I remember Madame Villièrs saying Suzanne looked like she was no more than twelve."

Olivier thanked her for talking to them and blessed her as she got up to leave the room. "If anything occurs to you, Sylvie, anything at all that might help us find Suzanne, ask Mother Marguerite to tell Father Antonio." Olivier knew the prioress would be more likely to inform the parish pastor than him.

"I will, Father, au revoir." Sylvie bowed to Father Antonio, stood and went to the door. She turned and smiled at Olivier before leaving the room.

When she closed the door, Olivier shook his head. "Too bad, she was our best hope."

Antonio nodded. "Sylvie is such a sweet child. I hope, with God's help, she can leave the past behind her."

"I think she has her best chance here at the convent. Well, Father, unfortunately, I think we're finished here. I don't know what else we can do."

"Be patient, Olivier, with God's help … What's on your mind?" Antonio saw the priest cock his head to the side and look at the door.

Olivier stood. "We might learn something here yet." He went to the door and spoke to Sister Helene, who had just arrived to escort them out of the convent.

Antonio, who had lost hearing in his left ear, could not hear what was said, but he saw the sister nod, say a few words and then walk away. "What's happening, Olivier?"

Olivier returned to his chair and looked at Antonio. "It occurred to me that there is one other girl here who knew Suzanne and Jeanne. I forgot about her until a moment ago. Her name is Marie and she was quite ill when I was here in January. It was Marie who gave me the names of the girls the murderer was with from September to December of last year. She was living in the brothel the entire time."

"Did she know them all?"

"Yes, but not very well. None of those girls shared a room with her, but she knew them in the house. Marie is ill with some strange ailment that has deadened her legs and limited her movement. It came upon her soon after she arrived in Mosquito Creek. She was confined to her bed most of the time and the other girls would stop by and comfort her as they went about their daily activities. They took turns bringing meals to her. So, it's possible she knows something that might be helpful. It's not likely, but who knows?"

"I assume Marie's not bedridden anymore."

"No, but she can only walk with the use of a cane."

"How sad! It's terrible to see an innocent child suffering so. It's bad enough to see the suffering of a crippled man or woman. But a child, Mon Dieu"

Olivier nodded. "There must be a very special place in heaven for such children, a place where they surely find the love of God."

"I expect so." Antonio turned to the door as it opened and Marie struggled into the room.

Marie walked with two canes, moving carefully one foot at a time. Sister Helene stood behind her worried she might fall. The priests watched as the crippled girl negotiated her way to the chair facing them. Olivier pulled the chair out from the table and, with a grimace, Marie sat down. She waved away Sister Helene's attempt to help her.

"Bonjour, Father Olivier, how nice to see you again." Marie gave Olivier a bright smile and looked at Antonio.

"It's good to see you, too." Olivier returned the smile. "I'd like to you to meet Father Antonio, he's the parish pastor."

"Hello, Father Antonio. I'm indeed honored, the pastor of the Cathedral himself is here. Ah, Father Olivier, so you needed more authority to get into the convent this time." She giggled and looked up at Sister Helene. "I'll be fine, Sister. Thank you for coming with me. I'll ring the bell when we're done." Marie took a bell from a pocket in her tunic and put it on the table.

Olivier turned to Antonio as Sister Helene closed the door. "I forgot to tell you, Father, Mademoiselle Moreau is too clever for her own good."

"It's the convent. Everyone is so serious. There's almost no laughter, they act as if God has no mirth."

"Indeed He does, Marie." Antonio smiled. "He created humans, didn't He?"

Marie laughed. "I like that. Well, you're not here to talk about my life in the convent. I assume you haven't found the murderer and that's why you are here."

Olivier saw the surprised look on Antonio's face. "I told you she was too clever for her own good and she's not yet fifteen."

"It's not that I'm clever, it's obvious. Why else would you come to the convent, Father? I knew the minute Sister Helene asked me to meet you." She grinned at him.

Olivier nodded. "I suppose it is obvious. No, we haven't found the murderer yet. We are still trying to identify him."

"Is that why you spoke to Sylvie before me?" Marie giggled again. "I did see her leave the sewing room with Sister Helene."

"Yes. As you know, Sylvie shared a room with Suzanne in the Villièrs house and we are trying to find Suzanne – so far without success."

"Is that because she was the last girl with the murderer?" Marie no longer smiled.

Olivier nodded. "We want to speak to Suzanne because she saw him and will be able to identify him." He decided to tell her all they knew about him. Marie was too smart to be fooled and, if the clever girl knew more, she might be able to help locate Suzanne. "Unfortunately, we know very little about the murderer. He's quite cunning and used a false name, Molière, in the Villièrs house. He also made sure he was seen only by Madame Villièrs, Gisella and the one girl he met each month." Olivier hesitated, trying to find a suitable word for fornication to use when speaking to the young girl.

Marie shook her head up and down. "There should be a lot of girls who can identify him. I heard he had been coming to the house for a long time – at least a year or two."

"That's right. But, so far, none of the girls we have found in New Orleans ever saw him. They knew of him, but were not the ones he selected."

"He didn't select the girls. Madame Villièrs selected the girls for him."

"How do you know she selected them, Marie?"

"We all knew who was chosen, everyone in the house. Madame Villièrs chose the girl at least a week ahead of his expected arrival. It was *always* a new young girl and she was primped and specially prepared for him."

"How was the girl *specially prepared*?" Olivier leaned forward on his forearms.

Marie frowned. "She was given special consideration the week before he came. First, the girl was freed from all housework that week. Then, she bathed every day and lay about having everyone else serve her every need. On the day of his arrival, Gisella bathed and perfumed her with a sweet scent he left in the house for the times he came to Mosquito Creek. Gisella saw to it that the girl's hair was brushed and her hands and toe nails cleaned. None of the girls Madame Villièrs selected were permitted to use rouge or face paint. It was said that cleanliness was what he wanted."

"Anything else special about her preparation for him?"

Marie shook her head. "No, nothing that I can think of. Oh, yes, I almost forgot. The girl waited for him without eating or drinking anything except for tea spiced with mint. Of course, you know the girl had to be a virgin. He would accept no other girl. Gisella said he made that demand the first day he visited the house. She said he paid dearly for it, too."

Olivier and Antonio exchanged looks.

"You didn't know that, did you?" Marie smiled, a smug look on her face.

"No." Olivier's face reddened. He was dismayed by Marie's blunt mention of the man's bodily needs. Olivier knew the young girl's ease speaking about such things was due to the time spent in the brothel, but it still bothered him.

Seeing the innocent look on her face, he changed the subject. "Marie, all the girls who were with him in the past are no longer in the city. They may be elsewhere in Louisiana, but as yet we haven't found them."

"Has he killed them all?" Marie's smile disappeared.

"I don't think so. Most of them probably moved away. We know of several who were in New Orleans and later left the city with boyfriends and some with husbands."

Marie brightened and she smiled again. "I'm glad – good for them! What about Valarie? I knew her better than any of the other girls chosen for him? Did she marry?"

"No. Marie, we are particularly interested in Suzanne because she might be living some place near New Orleans." Olivier emphasized the search for Suzanne in the hope Marie would not inquire further about Valarie. "Sylvie told us Suzanne liked warm weather so we're hoping she's still somewhere around here. What do you think?"

Marie bit her lower lip. "I don't know, Father. I know she liked to sit outside, even at midday when the sun was hot."

"When did she come to the house?"

Marie paused and put a finger to her lips. "I think that Suzanne came in November. She sat in the sun in the afternoons, even then. There are still a lot of warm days then."

Olivier nodded. "Some November days are even hot, especially at noontime. Last year the heat lasted until …"

Marie abruptly leaned back in her chair. "I think I might be able to help you find her after all." She slowly shook her head up and down and a wide smile of triumph spread across her face. They looked at the girl, their eyes fixed on her mouth.

"I remember one day when Suzanne brought me my lunch. It was a hot day and her face was pink from the sun. We talked awhile, then she left the room so I would eat my food. Everyone's worried about my weight; they think if they can fatten me up, I'll get better. But I'm getting worse no matter how much I eat. When you were here last, Father, I was able to walk with one cane – now I need two." She sighed. "Well, enough of that! You didn't come here to listen to my complaints." Marie held up her hand, stopping the priests from protesting. "I don't want to talk about it. Talking isn't going to help me get better. Let me continue."

Olivier nodded.

"Suzanne was waiting for me to finish my lunch so she could take the dishes to the kitchen. While I ate, I heard her talking to Rochelle, a new girl from New Orleans. Rochelle didn't stay with us long. She had run away from home and stayed for only a week or two. She was homesick and refused to do what Madame Villièrs expected of her."

"Marie, please tell us what Suzanne and Rochelle talked about in the hallway." Olivier raised his voice, irritated with the irrelevant details she was telling them. He also did not want to hear what Madame Villièrs expected of Rochelle.

"Forgive me, Father, I'll get to the point." The sparkle in the girl's eyes vanished and she looked crestfallen.

"No, Marie, I am the one who needs to be forgiven. I am much too impatient. Please do continue." Olivier looked at Antonio and the pastor nodded his approval.

Marie smiled again. "I understand, Father Olivier. You're in a hurry to find Suzanne and save her from the murderer." She saw him nod."What they talked about in the hallway was Rochelle's home in Natchez. I didn't hear everything, but I do recall she said the house was on a hill above the Mississippi River. Suzanne asked if it was warm there most of the year."

CHAPTER ELEVEN

New Orleans: March 6-10, 1800

Olivier went to see Castañedo the next morning. He headed for his office immediately after morning Mass and left Francis to perform the two scheduled baptisms that day. The sun was already up when he stepped away from the church and a cool breeze blew through the trees. "It's going to be a beautiful day," he thought as a line of brown pelicans flew effortlessly above him toward the ocean. Even walking leisurely through the countryside, he arrived at the Cabildo well before the magistrate. As if greeting the priest, a slender beam of sunlight touched the door as he arrived in front of the building.

Olivier had slowed his usual pace that morning to enjoy the signs of spring he saw on his way into New Orleans. There were orange and yellow wild flowers blooming in the grasslands and the buds of tree leaves had seemingly opened overnight. Some of the trees even had new leaves already formed on upper branches. Olivier recognized the buckeye with its red flowers, the swamp maple and a few of the other common trees, but there were a number of others whose names he did not know. As Olivier neared the San Carlos gates, he smelled the sweet fragrance of something flowering in the air. He stopped, closed his eyes and stood for a moment, inhaling the aroma. "Spring has finally arrived," he said aloud and smiled the rest of the way.

"I can't spare a man to go to Natchez, Father." Castañedo shook his head. "Half my men are sick in bed. They have that chest cough and high fever that's going around and the others are stationed at the governor's house. He's having a reception for another envoy from France. God knows what Bonaparte wants now."

"Isn't this envoy the third one sent from France? Do you know what's happening?"

"Yes, the third envoy! I haven't been told anything officially, but I've heard Bonaparte wants Louisiana returned to France. A man who accompanied the last one told me the Emperor Napoleon has demanded the colony and Spain is too weak to resist."

"But didn't France yield the colony to Spain in 1763 after the Seven Years War?"

"Yes, but now Bonaparte wants it back." Castañedo shrugged his shoulders.

"Of course, he has the armies to get what he wants."

"Exactamente. Well, we can't do anything about such things decided in Europe."

'No, Magistrate, but we can do something here about the murderer. This is our chance to discover who he is and then arrest him. If we don't find him with the help of the girl in Natchez, I fear he will continue killing our people. I know of no other way to stop him." Olivier did not mention Francis' suggestion to use his tailored clothing and hand-made boots to identify him.

Castañedo exhaled his breath. "I know, Father, but, with

so many sick at home, I simply don't have enough men to police the city, never mind send one man off to Natchez."

"This fiend must be stopped. Not only might he resume his attacks on the Dumont family, there may also be others he has in mind. If he's not stopped now, God only knows what he'll do next." Olivier sighed in frustration.

"You're right, Father. How long would it take for a man to go to Natchez?"

"A fortnight." Olivier knew the journey could take even longer since Suzanne's location was unknown. Finding Rochelle in Natchez would be the first task in the hope she knew where Suzanne might be found. Olivier did not want to even think about the possibility that she had not gone to Natchez after leaving Mosquito Creek

Castañedo grimaced. "That's a long time, Father. I'll have to ask Palacios Leguía if we can spare a man for that long. He's in charge of the duty rosters for our men. But, if I were you, I wouldn't hold out much hope that a man is available. Yesterday, he told me there were so few men available for duty he had to serve in the place of a sick man himself for the last four days. Apparently, he spent most of Tuesday night dragging drunks to jail."

"I understand the predicament Magistrate, but I *do* hope he'll find a way to send a man to Natchez. I'm sure you'll tell him how important it is for the community."

"Seguro. (Of course.) Father, if a man can be released to make the journey, can you go with him? You would be the one to find the girl. Most of the men speak only Spanish, which would be a distinct problem in an English-speaking city. Also, none of them have, shall we say, the needed *ingenuity* to find a French girl there, especially without knowing her family's name. The description of Suzanne as a young looking girl with brown eyes and white skin and teeth wouldn't be much help either. There must be any number of girls who fits that description."

"Verdad (True)." Olivier ran a hand through his hair. "I doubt if I can go, Magistrate."

"Because of the bishop?" Castañedo sneezed twice in succession.

"Dios te bendiga. (God bless you)."

"Gracías, Padre. I hope I'm not getting the damn sickness. So far, I've managed to avoid it, Gracías a Dios." He crossed himself. "Palacios Leguía has also escaped its misery so far."

"Con la ayuda de Dios, espero que usted no lo consiga, Magistrado. (With God's help, I hope you don't get it, Magistrate.) Unfortunately, the sickness has spread all over the city."

Castañedo nodded. "What about the bishop? Will he stop you from going to Natchez?"

"No, though he would surely protest such a journey if he heard about it. No, it's just that I have so much to do at Santa María before Easter. There's also the completion of the renovation which must supervised. You can't imagine the details yet to be settled." Olivier saw Castañedo smile. "I'm sorry, of course you can."

"What about Father Francis? Can he go in your place?"

"No, Francis was assigned to Santa María solely to serve as assistant pastor. Antonio sent him to me so I would have time for the investigation." Olivier sighed. "I'm the one to go! It's time we ended this murderous rampage. I'll find Suzanne, God willing, if she's in Natchez."

"I assume Francis can manage Santa María while you are gone. The trip may take longer than a fortnight. Our plans often go awry and take more time than we expect."

"True. Francis will serve the parish as well as I would. I am fully confident of him and I have informed Father Antonio of his competence as well."

"I trust Father Antonio will agree to the journey."

Castañedo worried the Church might blame him for persuading Olivier to go to Natchez. He had too often been criticized by both the bishop and the pastor. Among their other incessant complaints, they held him responsible for the "*excessive number of taverns in New Orleans and the continued existence of houses of prostitution everywhere in the colony.*" They also blamed him for the number of gambling dens that had seemingly appeared in the last year. The bishop even criticized him in a cathedral sermon. He accused him of "*permitting the moral degradation that now pervades the community.*" Castañedo met with the two clerics at the cathedral, but was unable to end their complaints. The magistrate explained that he had closed numerous houses of prostitution, unlicensed taverns, gambling dens and other illegal enterprises in town only to see them reappear in other places. His explanation and vow to carry on his efforts had not satisfied either the bishop or parish pastor. They continued to rail against the moral deterioration of the colony and censured him for the decline.

"Father Antonio is as anxious as we are to see the murderer arrested. Of course, I'll ask his approval, but I'm certain he will agree to it."

Olivier remembered what the pastor said as they left the Ursuline Convent the previous day. "I don't want another girl killed by that man, Olivier. Do whatever you must to stop him."

He made up his mind as he thought of the pastor's words.

"I'll leave Monday morning. There shouldn't be any difficulty finding a ship sailing up-river to Natchez."

"I wouldn't think so. There are ships sailing to St. Louis every day. I'm sure one of the captains would be willing to stop at Natchez even if the port isn't on his route. For a few extra pesetas, of course." Castañedo smiled.

Olivier nodded. "For secrecy, I think it might be better to take such a ship rather than one sailing directly to Natchez. This time, with the exception of Francis and Father

Antonio, I'll tell no one where I'm going. I don't want to risk the girl's life."

"Exactamente. No one else should know your destination. The man I'll send with you will know nothing of your plans. You can inform him en route to Natchez."

"Gracías, Magistrado." Olivier stood. "Let's hope this trip is the beginning of the end of these murders."

It was seven o'clock when Olivier and Francis left Santa María and walked toward town. The sun had set and only a little light remained to show them the path they used to reach the city gates. They took long strides, hoping to get near enough to New Orleans to see the night lamps before darkness closed all about them. They knew it would be a moonless night and hurried to avoid tripping over a rock or something crawling over the path. Francis, who dreaded snakes, lived in fear of stepping on one of the many rattlesnakes that inhabited the lowlands. He looked in every direction as he walked, making sure one of them was not anywhere near.

The early evening was warm and they walked bareheaded through the woods. Without the slightest breeze, nothing seemed to move, not a slender branch or a leaf. A stillness like the time before a thunderstorm pervaded the lowlands. There was not even the occasional squawk of a sea bird flying overhead.

Francis looked over at Olivier. "I forgot to ask you, Father. Do you want me to preside with Father Antonio at the marriage of Honorè and Ana Luisa? It's scheduled for the twenty-second and you said your trip might take as much as two weeks."

Olivier stopped and sighed. "I forgot about the marriage. Thank you for reminding me, Francis." He sighed.

"That would leave only eleven days for my journey, if I leave Monday as planned. I doubt that's enough time for what I have to do. Yet, I promised Ana I would assist Father Antonio at the marriage." He rubbed the stubble on his chin. "I don't know what to do."

"You could re-schedule their marriage."

"I don't want do to that. They've waited a long time and Honorè has attended Mass with Ana Luisa the last few weeks. Let me think about it and I'll decide what to do before I leave."

Francis abruptly turned and looked behind them.

"What's the matter? Did you see a snake?"

"I heard something moving there." He pointed to a group of pine trees they could still see in the dim light. The trees were about fifteen feet behind them.

"I didn't hear anything."

"I did." Francis took a step toward the trees, trying to see better. He was about to walk back to the trees, when Oliver touched his shoulder.

"Let's be on our way. You probably heard one of those wild hogs rooting around in the brush. I've seen several of them recently; they're all over the woods these days."

"I don't think it was an animal, Father. I've had the feeling we've been followed since we left Santa María." Francis walked a few feet away from Olivier and looked again at the trees.

"Followed? Did you see anyone behind us?" Olivier looked where Francis pointed, but saw nothing moving.

"No, but I know someone is back there somewhere. I can feel it."

"Then, let's get into the city before dark." Olivier strode ahead, but glanced back at the line of pine trees. It occurred to him the murderer could now be stalking him as he had Charles Laroux. The murderer must know his role in the investigation and might consider him a threat, a threat to be eliminated. He vowed to be alert from now on, especially when alone.

Moments later, they passed through the San Carlos gate and walked along Conde Street. At the corner of San Felipe, Olivier turned up the street and Francis proceeded on Conde toward the cathedral. He was meeting with his Capuchin brothers that evening.

As Olivier started up San Felipe, he saw only three people walking in front of him. They appeared to be a block ahead. No one was coming toward him. He thought about the murderer stalking him and moved to the center of the street where the faint light of the oil lamps seemed strongest. The lamps lit up the street corners, but left the middle of the blocks in murky light. Aware of how weak the light was ahead of him, Olivier stayed well away from dark doorways and shadowed building facades.

Most of the buildings had been built with overhanging roofs or balconies that sometimes extended as far as three feet over the streets. During the day, especially in the hot summer, the extensions gave welcome shade to pedestrians who walked alongside the buildings, but at night they left the streets below in the dark. The faint light of the night lamps reached no more than a few inches beneath the balconies.

Olivier crossed Real Street without incident, but, as he hurriedly stepped out of the way of a fast-moving coach on Borbón Street, he bumped into a drunken man. The man, obese and smelling of beer, almost fell into his arms. Olivier barely managed to hold the lurching man off as he vomited all over himself. Olivier tried to move out of the way, but he stepped back too late. The vomit erupted out of the man's mouth as if lava from a volcano and struck him in the chest.

"Sorry, Father," he mumbled as another drunken man grabbed his arm and dragged him away. His companion looked back at Olivier and snickered when the fat man stopped to vomit again. "Wot a waste a'gud beer," he said, showing three missing teeth in his smile.

Olivier made a face as he watched the two drunken men careen clumsily down the street. He turned to the street lamp and looked down at his soiled cassock. Disgusted, he mouthed the word "merde!" A soupy yellow stain stood out on the black garment. Thick with chunks of fish and rice, the soupy stain stretched across his chest and waist and dribbled down the right side of his cassock. The vomit also penetrated the cassock and wet his chest and stomach. Worst of all, it stank of fish and beer.

Olivier found a stick on the ground and used it to scrape the vomit off his cassock. He covered his nose with one hand and held the stick with the other. Still the sight of it made him nauseous and he gagged several times. The sickening smell remained after he finished. Olivier dipped his handkerchief in a puddle left from the previous day's rain and wiped as much of the stain from his clothes as possible. The disgusting odor remained, but there was nothing more to be done until he got to his rooms.

Dropping the ruined handkerchief, he hurried along San Felipe Street intent on reaching Madame Lafevre's house as fast as possible. Olivier's only thought was to remove his reeking clothes and he pictured himself sponging his body where the vomit had struck him. He walked hurriedly through the block between Borbón and Bayona Streets and picked up his pace to a trot as he approached the Lefevre house. In the last light of day, he saw the roof line when he was two houses away.

Olivier did not notice the unlit corner lamp at Bayona Street and the impenetrable darkness of San Felipe Street as he hurried on. Nor did he notice that no one else walked ahead or behind him. He was oblivious to everything except the stench of vomit. His only thought was to throw off his foul cassock and bathe himself.

The attacker came at him from the shadow of a building.

He came suddenly without the slightest sound or warning. Olivier felt the searing pain in his left arm before he knew what had happened. He averted the second strike by instinctively raising his right arm up. The attacker, a few inches shorter than Olivier, held his knife up to stab him and, in the darkness, did not see the priest's raised arm.

His eyes were on his victim's neck, where he intended to strike him. "Even if the priest moves back," he thought, "I'll stab him in the chest." Realizing the knife blade might hit bone, he brought it down with all his strength. Too late, he saw Olivier's forearm rise up in front of his face. The attacker's wrist hit Olivier's raised arm and the hard blow numbed his fingers. He lost his grip on the knife and it clattered to the cobblestones. For a second, he stood motionless, shocked at what had happened.

Olivier took advantage of the attacker's immobility and thrust his forearm into the man's face. The blow knocked him back, but he recovered quickly and stepped to the side. Olivier's wrist was wet where he stuck the attacker and he knew his nose had been bloodied. Olivier saw the outline of the hooded figure coming toward him and again he raised his forearm, this time in front of his chest. He intended to use his arm to block the attacker's approach. But, instead of another attack, the man bent over in one quick movement and retrieved the knife. Olivier, too slow to do anything to stop him, saw him rise up with it clutched in his hand.

The attacker now sidled in a circle around Olivier's left side. He crouched like a feral cat ready to pounce on his quarry. Olivier watched him move and turned with him. He matched his movement, step by step. The man circled to the priest's left side where he had been stabbed and would be vulnerable. Even in the semi-darkness, he could see Olivier's arm hanging uselessly at his side. "It's only a matter of a few seconds now and the priest will die," he thought.

Olivier backed cautiously away, making sure he faced the

crouching figure as he moved. His right arm remained raised and he bent his knees lowering his head and chest. He attempted to shrink his height to make it harder for the man to strike a killing blow.

At that moment, the attacker suddenly rushed toward him, knife in hand. Olivier tripped as he tried to turn away from the man and went down on one knee. The fall saved his life. The attacker's knife missed Olivier and he almost fell over the priest's bended knee. He staggered to the side to avoid falling on his victim and, by the time he steadied himself, Olivier was up on his feet facing him. The attacker moved back and forth to confuse Olivier and was poised to rush at him again, when a sudden light lit up the street where the two men faced each other.

A man with a lantern stood in the doorway of the house behind the attacker. He held the lantern in one hand and a pistol in the other. "What's going on out here," he shouted. "You there with the knife. Stop or I'll shoot!"

The attacker instantly sidestepped out of the light and disappeared down the dark street. Olivier heard his footsteps on the cobblestones, but could not see him in the gloom. He was gone before Olivier could see his face. The unexpected light had blinded him and by the time his eyes adjusted it was too late. He only saw the man's back and the hooded cloak that covered his head.

The following afternoon, Olivier and Francis ate lunch with María Adela. They ate in her dining room and she directed the wounded priest to a upholstered wing chair at the head of the table. Olivier's left arm was in a sling and bandaged from the shoulder to the elbow. He rested his forearm on two pillows stacked on the arm of his chair. A bowl of pork stew stood on the table before him. The pork, potatoes and carrots had been cut into small pieces for him.

Olivier smiled as María Adela cut up a dinner roll for him. "Thank you, María Adela, but I can still use my left hand. I was fortunate he missed my neck and only slashed my arm."

"There's no need to aggravate the wound. The less you use the arm, the better."

"I don't want to be a consentido (a spoiled one)."

"Better that than a dead martyr." She gave him a disapproving look. "Now, tell me about the attempt on your life." She poured him a second glass of wine.

Olivier took a large drink of his wine and then described the attack. "I was saved by two coincidental and unusual events, which can only be attributed to the love of God."

"What do you mean?" She looked at Francis for confirmation and he nodded, a look of certainty on his face.

"The first event was accidentally bumping into a drunken man as I crossed over Borbón Street. He got sick as we collided and vomited on my cassock. If that hadn't happened, I would have walked the rest of the way home and been stabbed to death. But, because of the stench of the man's vomit, I ran along San Felipe in a hurry to get home to bathe myself. Since I ran, the murderer misjudged the location of my chest in the darkness and he stabbed me in the upper arm. His knife missed my heart by only a few inches."

"What was the second event?"

"The man with the lantern, Monsieur Roland Colbert, was bolting his door for the evening when he heard the knife clatter on the cobblestones. Wondering what made the noise, he opened the door with his pistol and lantern in hand. The light from the lantern lit up the attacker with his raised knife. He was poised to attack me again and, by then, I was too weak to fight him off. I would have been killed, if Colbert hadn't appeared."

"Why was that unusual? Would not anyone have opened the door if he heard a scuffle outside in the street?" Puzzled, María Adela frowned.

"Yes. What was unusual was his decision to bolt the door at seven-thirty, an hour earlier than usual. His custom was to lock the door just after his children were put to bed at eight-thirty. But last night, he said, 'I had the inclination to close up earlier. It was as if I was told to do it.'" Olivier nodded, a satisfied smile on his face.

"Monsieur Colbert heard the words of God," added Francis. "He was told what to do. There's no question about it! The two events were too well connected to be coincidental. They were the work of God!"

Ah, I see what you're saying, Father." María Adela nodded, though she thought the two events were coincidental and not the work of God.

María Adela did not believe God intervened in human events. The elderly woman had been raised Catholic in Spanish Florida, but, as a young girl, she lost her faith in the loving God proclaimed by the priests. When only fifteen, she witnessed the brutal killing of her family and could not believe a loving God would permit such a massacre. A merciless murderer raped her mother, tortured her father and dragged them, still alive, into a fire he set inside their logwood house. Her two brothers, one a baby, and sister also died in the burning building. María Adela, hiding in the nearby woods, heard their screams as the house became an inferno. Thereafter, she remained in the Church, but never again believed the sermons about the love of God. Instead, while living in the home of a Portuguese physician, she became acquainted with Enlightenment philosophy and chose to be a Deist, believing God made the world, but only set it into motion.

Olivier smiled broadly. "It's not often we see the loving hand of God in our lives, but last night he showed himself and saved my life." He crossed himself. "La louauge est à Dieu." (Praise be to God).

María Adela nodded again, knowing it was a deceitful gesture. She did not believe God had anything to do with Olivier's survival. Monsieur Colbert's sudden appearance with a pistol had surely ended the attack in the dark street, but it was the murderer's missed knife thrust and Olivier's resistance that saved his life. María Adela looked down at her folded hands and said nothing more. "It's better to let sleeping dogs lie," she thought.

"What's on your mind, María Adela?" Olivier saw the pensive look on her face.

"I was thinking it's too bad neither you nor Monsieur Colbert saw the murderer's face. It seems he always manages to escape before anyone sees him."

"True. He's quite cunning, but this time he was lucky. Monsieur Colbert stood behind him and the lantern light only showed a man in a black cloak – a hooded cloak. I faced him, but was briefly blinded by the sudden light and, by the time I could see clearly again, he was gone. It was just his good luck." Olivier sighed and shook his head.

"Did he leave anything that might help identify him?"

"No, but I did see his cordovan boots as he ran away. They were new and shiny as Ana Luisa accurately remembered them." Olivier looked across the table at his assistant. "Francis has wisely suggested the magistrate assign a man to interview the bootmakers in town. A list of the gentlemen who had cordovan boots made for them could then be compiled and the men on the list interviewed by the magistrate. Even if some of the gentlemen are prominent, I would think the governor would permit him to interview them."

"What a good suggestion!" María Adela smiled at Francis.

"It's an excellent suggestion," agreed Olivier. "We know very little about the murderer or how to find him, but the boots give us a good way to search for him."

Francis smiled pleased with Olivier's praise. "Cordovan boots are not uncommon here in town, but even if the bootmakers made a number of pairs, I'm sure they would recall who bought them. There are certainly much less common than ordinary leather boots."

"I've seen a few, now and then, but they were well-worn and muddy," said María Adela. "None have been as clean and shiny as Ana described them. But, even if there were as many as fifty pairs of boots made, I'm certain the bootmakers would know who ordered them. Customers who bought costly cordovan boots would be not only well regarded, but well remembered." She refilled Olivier's wine glass.

Francis leaned forward, his elbows on the table. "Exactly. And I can't imagine it would be difficult to interview even as many as fifty men."

"No it wouldn't be, Francis. The problem is finding men to interview the bootmakers."

"What do you mean?" María Adela looked sharply at Olivier. "Won't *your good friend*, the magistrate, be willing to assign his men to do it?"

"He would indeed, but he has no one available to interview them. Half his men are sick with the chest cough and the others are stationed at the governor's house for the French envoy's reception. I spoke to him this morning and he can't even spare a man to go with me to Natchez."

"What! You can't possibly travel alone, especially after the attack last night. What's that Spanish tonto (fool) thinking? Has he no heart?"

Olivier held up his good hand. "Let me explain, María Adela. Yesterday morning, the magistrate said he would assign a man to accompany me, but, today, he told me there is no one available to go. Three more of his men came down with the sickness overnight. He urged me to postpone my journey until the illness has passed or, at least a week, when several of his men are expected to return to duty. At that time, he promised to send two men with me to Natchez. He came to see me at Monsieur Colbert's house last night – he came immediately after hearing of the attack. The magistrate also rode to Santa María this morning before first Mass to talk to me again. He doesn't want me to attempt the journey to Natchez without armed men at my side."

María Adela frowned. "But you are going now anyway, aren't you? Even with your wound and wearing a sling?"

"Yes, I must go. I fear for Suzanne's life. The girl is doomed if the murderer finds her before we do. There also may be others he has marked for death in town as well. Who knows what he will do if we wait for the illness to come to an end? It could last another month. We can't wait and risk the lives of more of our people, especially since there's now a possibility of identifying the murderer in a week or so."

"I'll go with you, Father. I'll ask the pastor to replace me temporarily at Santa María. I know two of my Capuchin brothers who are experienced enough to officiate in my place."

"No, I must go alone. You are needed at Santa María. Everyone at the church knows and trusts you and I don't want to do anything to disrupt the parish or disturb our people. Besides there are three baptisms next week as well as the confirmation of Jacques Mercier's son. And, as you know, Mercier has asked for you to be present. Francis, you are the only one to perform those sacraments, not a new priest who is unknown to the Acadian community."

"What about the meeting with Honorè and Ana Luisa to plan their marriage?"

"You can plan it as well as I, Francis, you know that. I'll be leaving on Monday morning and should return within a fortnight. With a bit of good fortune, I'll be back sooner perhaps in a week. Though I know neither of you will say anything about my trip, the magistrate urged me to emphasize the need for secrecy."

Francis nodded. "I'll tell anyone who asks about your whereabouts that you are carrying out a mission for the pastor and will return soon. I'll say nothing more."

"Exactly. If anyone wants more information, tell him to speak to Father Antonio."

María Adela shook her head. "I don't like it, Father, you shouldn't be going alone."

Father Antonio waited until Monday morning to tell the bishop about Olivier's journey to Natchez. He spoke to him after first Mass when the priest was already aboard a sloop sailing up the Mississippi River. Antonio spent a few moments watching one of the young Capuchin priests begin second Mass and then he walked slowly to the bishop's office. He did not look forward to his conversation with his superior.

Meléndez had attended first Mass and now sat at his desk drinking tea. The door to his office was open and, peering over the rim of his cup, he saw the pastor appear in the doorway. Swallowing the tea in his mouth, the bishop motioned him to the chair beside his desk.

"Father Antonio." The bishop was surprised to see the pastor since they met and talked earlier that morning. At the time, Meléndez told Antonio the archbishop of Havana had written him of the imminent return of Bishop Peñalvery Cárdenas to New Orleans. The official bishop of Louisiana and the Floridas was expected to return soon after Easter.

"Bishop Meléndez, I would like to speak to you for a few moments. I trust you have the time this morning."

"Certainly, Father Antonio." Meléndez pushed his empty cup to the side. "But before you do, I must speak to you about young Simon's speech problem."

Antonio grimaced, well aware of what was coming.

"I left second Mass because I found Simon's stammering simply too disturbing to bear. I'm sure I am *not* the only one who has difficulty listening to his inept performances. I saw a number of the parishioners with pained faces as he struggled to give his opening greeting. He was unable to even finish 'In the name of the Father' without adding three Fa-Fa-Fa's to Father. I cringed as he stammered. God of all creation! It was a pitiful performance and in the cathedral of all places in the diocese."

"That was the only mistake he made in the greeting."

"You always defend him despite his obvious failings."

"Simon is one of our best young priests. He's not only pious, but very knowledgeable – I think he promises to be an excellent biblical scholar."

"Simon may be pious and shows much promise as you say, but his stammering will turn away our parishioners if he's permitted to speak with any frequency at the altar. In these all too worldly times, when our daily attendance is shrinking, we definitely don't want to do anything to diminish the community's devotion to morning Mass. Surely you agree."

"I understand your concerns, Bishop Meléndez, but I'm sure Simon will improve in time. The lad is just a bit uneasy speaking in front of a large assembly of people. He expresses himself perfectly at the weekly meetings and with his Capuchin brothers. Simon, in fact, is often the one who accurately summarizes what's been discussed during the meeting. I've seen him succeed in that capacity myself despite the numerous statements and opinions expressed. He has a fine mind and, in time, will be a font of information for the entire parish."

"That's what you said about Olivier and let's not forget about the many problems *he* has brought the parish." The bishop glared at the pastor.

Antonio looked at Meléndez, but made no reply.

"So, what was it you wanted to discuss with me?"

"Actually, it's about Father Olivier. I wanted to inform you that I've sent him on an assignment out of New Orleans."

Enraged, the bishop's flushed face contorted into so hideous a scowl that Antonio briefly imagined he had become a living gargoyle. Meléndez wanted to shout "You incompetent fool!" but, instead, he paused and spoke softly to the pastor. "Pray tell me, Father Antonio, what is the nature of Olivier's assignment and where has he gone?"

"It is to seek the identity of the murderer who has killed so many of our people."

In a futile effort to contain his fury, Meléndez exhaled his breath loudly. "I see and why is Olivier, a priest of the Church, on such a worldly assignment – outside this parish? Tell me, Father, what in God's name has it to do with his designated mission at Santa María or the parish at large?" Meléndez sneered. "Or does his assignment involve some grandiose scheme to serve the Church, perhaps, to Christianize the wild Indians of Louisiana?"

Antonio ignored the bishop's sarcasm and answered him calmly. "No, Bishop Meléndez, Father Olivier's assignment is in the service of this parish. There is a pitiless killer loose in New Orleans who must be arrested and executed. He has already struck down as many as ten of our people and may have marked any number of others for death. Since the murderer has not been identified, Olivier is in search of someone who can lead the magistrate to him."

"Why isn't the magistrate making the search instead of the Dominican? Surely, he's the one who should be doing it and not a priest of the Church."

"The magistrate has no available men to make the search. The plague has cost him half his men and all the others are serving the governor during the visit of the French envoy. Under those circumstances, the magistrate asked me if Olivier could make the search and I agreed. I want this bloodbath ended and the parish peaceful again. It must be done before our parishioners become aware of this vicious murderer and the number of his victims. We must do everything possible to prevent panic in the city."

"What about Santa María and the people of the lowlands? Are they not of concern to you as well?" Meléndez glared at the pastor. "I suppose you intend to replace Olivier with Francis, an inexperienced priest whose ordination was no more than a year ago."

"Father Francis *is* experienced. He has been at Santa María since October. I've visited the church twice in that time and observed him performing Mass, presiding at holy matrimony and administering baptism. He performed all flawlessly and I'm certain, with Father Olivier's teaching, Francis has mastered the administration of the other sacraments similarly as well. I've no doubt of his ability to preside at Santa María while Olivier is away for a week or so. In fact, I think Father Francis will be my choice to fill the next available opening in the parish."

Meléndez stared at Antonio, his fingers tapping the top of his desk. "I don't approve of this entire undertaking. It is a civil matter and should not involve the Church or our clergy in any way. Olivier's assignment is plainly outside the prescribed duties of a priest and your decision to dispatch him on it is a misuse of your parish authority. I therefore have no recourse, but to report it to the archbishop of Havana." Confident of such action, Meléndez leaned back in his chair.

Antonio stared at him. "That's fine. You can make your report, Bishop Meléndez. I'll welcome any investigation that follows." He nodded, thinking to himself, "Yes and I'll have some of my own comments to make on the manner of your leadership of this diocese."

Meléndez scowled. "I will do exactly as I wish, Antonio; it's not your prerogative to tell me what to do or not to do.

You have become increasingly impertinent these days. You forget yourself and your position in this province. I am the bishop of Louisiana and you are the pastor of New Orleans under my administration. You may have the authority to preside over the parish, but I have the authority to dismiss you – and without cause."

"Quite so, Bishop Meléndez, but if you take that *reckless* step I think you will regret it." Antonio suspected the bishop would not risk the exacting Church inquiry that would follow his dismissal. At the least, it would mean a delay in the usually slow process of an appointment to another diocese. At the worst, it might mean Meléndez would not be appointed to a bishopric of his own; instead, he might spend the rest of his life as a subordinate or clerical administrator shuffling papers from one Church office to another.

"Are you threatening me? How dare you?" A muscle twitched in the bishop's jaw as he scowled at the pastor.

"No, Bishop Meléndez, not at all." The pastor spoke calmly even though the bishop had called him by his first name without his proper title. "I'm simply reminding you of the problems involved in such a procedure. It is especially arduous under some circumstances." Antonio was subtly reminding Meléndez of his influence at the court of King Charles IV. The king's father, Charles III, had supported Antonio's appointment as parish pastor of St. Louis Cathedral and the Capuchin priest continued to be well regarded in Madrid.

Meléndez stared at Antonio, but did not immediately reply. The bishop was well aware of the monarchy's involvement in the pastor's appointment and, suspecting the king would hear of his dismissal, he knew it would be foolish to confront the Capuchin priest within the Church hierarchy. He therefore decided to pursue a different course of action.

"Whatever I decide to do, Father Antonio, you can be sure I'll be scrutinizing the scheme you have hatched.

You've sent Olivier out of New Orleans not only without my permission, but knowingly against my wishes. So, now, Antonio, *you alone* are responsible for his well-being." The bishop's lips curled into a sneer. "*Yes, you alone, Antonio*! I hope Olivier returns to Santa María without incident, but, if something ill-fated should befall him while carrying out this reckless assignment, you will be called to account. Yes, you can be assured Havana will hear of it."

Antonio nodded, his face now reddened in anger. He noted how the bishop intentionally addressed him by his first name and ignored his clerical title. He also knew Meléndez would be pleased if Olivier's mission ended in failure or was ill-fated as he suggested was possible. Staring at Meléndez, who still sneered, he wondered how such a man with so little compassion could become a bishop in Christ's Church.

"Incidentally, where is Olivier headed? I assume his journey is within the jurisdiction of this colony."

"No, Bishop, Father Olivier is traveling to Natchez." Antonio sighed. He had hoped to avoid revealing the Dominican's destination.

"Natchez! Natchez is in a Protestant land. Dios mío! It's not even in Spanish territory. It's in the United States."

"Yes, Bishop Meléndez, that's where we hope to learn the identity of the murderer." Antonio spoke politely to Meléndez, hoping it might mitigate his criticism.

Meléndez glared at Antonio, his mouth agape. "You – you sent the Dominican into the land of Protestant heretics. How could you?" He pounded his fist on the desk beside his cup spilling tea on his hand.

"There are Catholics still living there. Bishop Cárdenas visited Natchez in 1796, one year after he arrived here in New Orleans."

"Bishop Cárdenas had Church authority to make such a visit, the Dominican did not." Furious, Meléndez hissed his words through tightly clenched teeth.

Antonio did not argue with the bishop, although tempted to point out that Olivier traveled to Natchez on his authority as parish pastor. Instead, he mentioned the provisions made for the priest's stay in town.

"One of our parishioners, a local shipper by the name of Carlos de Mosquera has a brother now living in Natchez and he advised him of Father Olivier's arrival. His brother, Miguel de Mosquera, is also one of the Church's parishioners and invited Olivier to stay in his home for whatever time he needed in Natchez."

Meléndez narrowed his eyes as you looked at Antonio. "I see. So, how were those arrangements made?"

"I spoke to Señor Mosquera a week or so ago after Mass and he was happy to help and immediately sent word to his brother."

"So, Antonio, your plot has been in motion for almost a fortnight and you did not deign to inform me. You never said one word about it." Meléndez pointed a trembling finger at Antonio. "You deceived me and conspired with that arrogant Dominican. Don't deny it," he said, seeing Antonio shake his head. "It's not the first time either. No, it isn't! The two of you have plotted against me time and time again." The bishop's face was beet red.

"No one has plotted against you." Antonio paused while Meléndez used a handkerchief to wipe away the spittle that had appeared at the corners of his mouth. "I intended to inform you of the plan when it was more fully developed. Father Olivier was not scheduled to leave so soon, but the recent attempt on his life hastened his departure. He feared the murderer would kill other innocents if he remained unidentified and at large." Antonio saw the bishop shake his head in disbelief.

"That's no excuse. I should have been informed at the

outset of the planning – weeks ago! You have deliberately deceived me and left me in the dark until now."

Meléndez threw his hands in the air. "Dios mío! You have sent the *drunken Dominican* to a foreign city committed to the Protestant heresy. Who knows what he will do or say in his cups to embarrass the Church!"

"Father Olivier will be in Natchez only as long as necessary. He has taken this trip to save the lives of our parishioners in New Orleans. Many have already been murdered and we are certain any number of others are in jeopardy and we can't wait idly by while the murderer capriciously kills them one after the other."

Antonio did not mention that one of the people in jeopardy was a former prostitute living in Natchez. Nor did he tell the bishop that Olivier was searching for her in the hope she would identify the murderer.

The bishop abruptly stood, shaking his head from side to side. He had heard none of the pastor's last words. Meléndez was too incensed with what he considered to be Antonio's betrayal to listen to anything he said. Antonio's last words were likewise ignored.

"I will take *all* responsibility for Father Olivier's mission no matter what comes of it. That's my pledge to you, Bishop Meléndez."

The bishop stopped shaking his head and glared at Antonio. "I've heard enough, more than enough. Leave me! Leave me, this instant!"

CHAPTER TWELVE

NEW ORLEANS AND NATCHEZ: MARCH 10 – 20, 1800

At first light, the murderer stood among a milling crowd of townspeople at the city dock. The people were watching the departure of three heavily-laden cargo ships. They left the dock one after the other. The first two ships were sailing down river to the Gulf of Mexico and then on to Mobile and Pensacola, while the third was headed north to the river towns of Baton Rouge and Natchez. The murderer left the dock when the schooner, *Santa Teresa*, caught the prevailing cross wind and sailed northward.

He walked to his waiting horse, mounted him and sat thinking of possible solutions to his problem. Olivier had to die, the question was how it could be done. He had watched him board the *Santa Teresa* and knew the troublesome priest was on his way to locate someone to identify him. It had to be Jeanne or Suzanne. All the others had been eliminated.

The problem was how to kill Olivier outside of New Orleans. It had to be accomplished before he talked to the girl or immediately afterward to prevent him from divulging whatever she told him. The murderer assumed the girl would reveal his identity to Olivier and she would have to die as well. Her death could wait a while since she lived so far from New Orleans. "Olivier, however, must be killed as soon as possible," he concluded. "But how can it be done?" He could not leave New Orleans to dispose of him. Fortunately, there were those in both Baton Rouge and Natchez who could be counted on to assist him to that end.

The last light of the day still lit the sky as the *Santa Teresa* approached the Natchez pier. It had been a much longer voyage than expected. Slowed by the river current, capricious winds and delayed at Baton Rouge by the replacement of the mainsail, the ship needed four full days to reach Natchez.

"It's not at all unusual this time of year," the Dutch captain told Olivier.

Once docked at five-thirty, Olivier spent another half hour at the customs house before leaving the pier and walking into town. He found the house of Miguel de Mosquera easily and received a warm welcome from the family. Mosquera, owner of a prosperous sawmill, greeted Olivier with a deferential bow and the customary Spanish expression, "Mi casa es su casa." He did not ask about his bandaged arm. The plump, smiling man, plied Olivier with Spanish wine and his even plumper wife, María Inez, made him a delicious dinner of aroz caldoso de monte (rice with rabbit). It was the tastiest food he had eaten since leaving New Orleans. The evening in the Mosquera home ended much later than Olivier would have wished, but his host's sixteen-year-old son, Felipe, entertained everyone with his Flamenco guitar. At nine o'clock, the three younger children went to bed, but Felipe played and sang Spanish ballads until midnight.

The next morning after breakfast, Olivier and his host talked in the family's living room. Mosquera had planned to take the priest to see San Salvador, the town's Catholic Church, but a heavy rain kept them inside all morning. They sat across from each other drinking Bohea tea. (Chinese black tea).

"Unfortunately, San Salvador is no longer in use, Father Olivier," explained Mosquera. "It's in need of costly repairs and Natchez no longer has a resident priest. We have continually petitioned the Church to send us a pastor, but our requests so far have been in vain. Those same futile requests were made to Bishop Cárdenas when he visited Natchez four years ago."

"Yet, I've heard the sacraments are still performed here."

"They are, Father but not regularly. A Capuchin priest from Baton Rouge comes here now and then and performs them in one of our homes. We take turns as hosts for him."

"Why not in San Salvador? Is the church building unsafe?" Olivier frowned.

"No, Father, but it's full of mold and smells; many of the benches are also broken. The church has been that way for some time and, without a priest, no one wants to put any effort or money into it. Our women refuse to enter the church; they say it's too gloomy and smells foul."

Olivier nodded. "When I return to New Orleans, I'll tell the pastor the situation here. He may be able to provide a priest for the church." Olivier knew Bishop Meléndez had the authority to assign a priest to Natchez, but doubted he would be responsive to any request from him.

"Thank you, Father. Now, what brings you up to Natchez? My brother, Carlos, wrote me of your visit, but didn't tell me it's purpose."

"I am seeking a young girl whose home is here in Natchez. She went to New Orleans for a short period of time last

October or November and then returned home. Her name is Rochelle and she may be fifteen years of age. I don't know her family name or whereabouts. I do know her family lives in a house above the river." Olivier did not mention that Rochelle had run away from home or spent time in a brothel.

"I see." Mosquera looked at Olivier, waiting for him to tell him the reason for his search.

Olivier realized what his host expected of him, but he did not know how much to reveal to him. He was tempted to tell him all about the murder investigation, but his fear for Suzanne's life kept him from mentioning it. Instead, he decided to say nothing about it.

"You may be wondering why I am searching for Rochelle, Señor Mosquera, but, for now, I'm not free to discuss it."

"I understand, Father. Though curious, Mosquera did not ask Olivier any more questions. "It shouldn't be hard to find the girl with what you told me. There are only twenty or so houses on the bluff. Let's begin by asking Felipe if he knows Rochelle. Please describe the girl."

Mosquera listened to Olivier's brief description of Rochelle and then excused himself to leave the room for a few minutes. He returned with Felipe who greeted Olivier with a respectful bow. He stood beside his father.

"Tell Father Olivier what you told me, Felipe," Mosquera urged his son.

"I recall hearing the name Rochelle in the past, but I don't remember meeting her. She would have been much younger than me. I've been away in Madrid until recently."

"Felipe has been studying guitar with el famoso maestro, Dionisio Aguado." Mosquera beamed with pride. "He's been in Spain for two years and has only returned a week ago."

Olivier smiled. "Es un gran honor! (It's a great honor!)"

Felipe's face reddened. "Thank you, Father."

"Tell Father Olivier what else you told me." Mosquera smiled at Felipe.

"I have a friend, Roberto – Roberto Luis Prieto. Roberto is a lawyer and now serves as a clerk in the attorney general's office. I will go talk to him and ask about Rochelle."

Mosquera nodded. "Roberto shouldn't have any trouble finding Rochelle, Father Olivier. She must be included in the last census which was completed in 1775." He looked at his son.

"I'll go see Roberto this morning. Do you need the carriage?" asked Felipe.

"No, Felipe, take it. We will await your return." Mosquera smiled at Olivier. "Would you like another cup of tea, Father?"

It was still raining heavily, when Felipe returned two hours later. His father saw him arrive from the window in the living room. He entered the house after stabling his horse and pushing the carriage into its enclosure.

"Rochelle's family name is Beauregard," said Felipe as he took off his wet coat. "Her father is François Marie Beauregard. I recall Rochelle now, she was a shy little girl."

"I am well acquainted with Monsieur Beauregard," announced Mosquera. "He has been a good customer for years. His house and all his outbuildings have been built with wood from our mill. Monsieur Beauregard owns all those Indigo lands west of Natchez."

Felipe waited until his father had spoken and then told them what else was included in the census record. "According to the census, Rochelle is one of three children – the oldest. She is fifteen. The Beauregard house is located on the bluff."

"I know where it's situated; I've been there a number of times – thank you, Felipe."

Felipe took Olivier to the Beauregard house the next morning. The carriage trip was his second that day. He had driven there earlier to arrange for the priest's visit to the family. Felipe waited in front of the house until Olivier was invited inside and then drove away.

A Negro house servant ushered Olivier into a small sitting room where he stood awaiting Madame Beauregard. The room was furnished with two armchairs, two side chairs, a secretary, a commode and low table. All the chairs were constructed of carved and gilded beech wood and upholstered with a rose-colored fabric. The other furniture in the room featured marble tops and lacquered surfaces of black and gold. Four still-life paintings of autumn fruit adorned the walls. The sitting room looked spotless to Olivier and he smelled the fragrance of a flowered furniture polish when he entered the house.

Madame Beauregard entered the room and bowed politely to the priest. A slight woman, she had light brown hair and green eyes. Madame Beauregard wore a green velvet dress which seemed appropriately coordinated to the rose-colored armchair where she sat. For the first few minutes, she inquired about Olivier's voyage to Natchez and his initial impressions of the town. She also asked him if San Salvador could be restored for use in the community. He responded to her questions, saying his voyage had been too long and the rain had kept him from seeing the city or the church. He told her of his intention to tell the parish pastor about the need for a priest. Madame Beauregard then bluntly asked him the purpose of his visit.

"I would like to talk to your daughter, Rochelle, Madame Beauregard. It concerns her visit to Louisiana last year."

Olivier was unsure what to say to the severe, unsmiling woman. He did not know what Rochelle had told her mother about her brief stay in Mosquito Creek. "Has she told her mother about the Villièrs house?" he wondered. "Has she mentioned any of the girls from the house?" Olivier worried he might say something that would contradict what Rochelle had previously told her mother. Not only might such a mistake result in Rochelle's punishment, it might also result in her mother's refusal to permit him to speak to the girl.

Madame Beauregard frowned. "What about Rochelle's visit to Louisiana, Father, is of concern to the Church?" There was an indignant tone to her voice.

"A young girl from our parish, a friend of Rochelle, has gone missing and we are trying to find her. We are in hope your daughter might know where she went." Olivier held his breath hoping he had made a convincing presentation. "At least I told the truth," he thought.

"I assume, Father Olivier, you are speaking of a friend Rochelle met in New Orleans? I don't recall her mentioning a friend there, but her *journey* to Louisiana was made many months ago." She stared at his bandaged arm, but did not comment on it.

"It was a long time ago. The two girls met in October or November." Olivier avoided her question, but did not lie to her. It was obvious Rochelle had not told her mother about her time in the brothel. Her mother would have been horrified, even if informed her daughter had stayed only a short time and never served any men. As it was, Madame Beauregard preferred to speak, if not think of Rochelle's running away to Louisiana as a *journey* rather than a flight from home. Olivier realized her choice of words was a mother's way of making her child's misconduct less offensive to herself as well as others.

Madame Beauregard pursed her lips. "Well, in that case, I see no reason why you should not speak to Rochelle. Please excuse me a moment, Father." She stood, walked to the doorway and spoke to the manservant. "Joshua, tell Rochelle to join us in the small sitting room."

Rochelle arrived several seconds later. After curtsying and greeting Olivier politely, she sat in a side chair beside her mother. Rochelle wore a dress very similar to her mother's, though of a lighter shade of green. The girl, however, looked nothing like her mother. She was several inches taller, plump and had dark eyes and hair. Unlike her stern-looking mother, Rochelle also had a ready smile and a sparkle of amusement in her eyes.

Madame Beauregard turned to her daughter. "Rochelle, Father Olivier has travelled here all the way from New Orleans to speak to you. He is searching for a friend of yours, whom you *apparently* met there. What was her name, Father?"

"Suzanne. She has gone missing, Rochelle, and we are hoping you might help us locate her. I have been sent here by the pastor of the cathedral in New Orleans." Olivier wanted her to know the search for Suzanne had nothing to do with the Villièrs house.

"Suzanne Lavasseur?" Rochelle smiled at Olivier.

"The girl from Canada?" Olivier assumed Suzanne Lavasseur was the missing girl, but he wanted to make sure before continuing their conversation.

"Yes, Father."

"You didn't know her family name, Father?" Madame Beauregard frowned as she looked at him. She eyed him suspiciously, staring again at his bandaged arm.

"No, Madame Beauregard, we didn't know it. We only knew her first name and where she lived before coming to New Orleans. She arrived on a ship as a stowaway." Olivier did not reveal what happened to her afterward.

"How peculiar. You know very little about this girl and yet you are anxious to find her. Why is that if I may ask?"

"I'm not free to discuss the matter, Madam Beauregard, but I will say it is crucial that we find her soon."

"Crucial for her or the Church?" She scrutinized his face as he answered her.

"It is crucial for her, I assure you." Olivier held her gaze as she stared at him.

"Suzanne is living somewhere around Natchez, though I don't know where." Rochelle interrupted the strained conversation between her mother and Olivier. "She is now married and soon to be a mother."

"When did you last see her, Rochelle?" asked Olivier turning his eyes to her. He held his breath hoping she had seen Suzanne recently.

"A month or so ago. I met her at the market one day when mother and I were shopping. Her husband has a stall there at the market. He's a saddler and makes leather things for horses and draft animals – saddles, of course, as well as bridles and harnesses. He also makes men's boots and belts."

"Do you know his name, Rochelle?"

"Only his first name, Father. It's Richard. I didn't hear his family name when Suzanne told me – there was a commotion when a cooper's work table fell over."

"I see. Can you describe him?"

"He's tall and has dark curly hair and a beard. He's quite handsome." She blushed.

Olivier left a half hour later. He learned nothing more about Suzanne. Rochelle walked with him to Felipe's carriage which was standing in front of the house. Since it had begun to rain they walked beneath her umbrella. Rochelle spoke to him with her back deliberately turned to the front window. She suspected her mother was watching them from the window.

"Thank you, Father, for not mentioning the Villièrs house in front of my mother. She was very angry about my running away and she would be *furious* if she knew where I stayed. If she found out, I would probably end up as Cinderella in the house." Rochelle smiled. "Forgive me Father, I should also tell you I lied about meeting Suzanne in the market. I've seen her several times since she came here to Natchez, the last time was a week or so ago. My mother would not approve – she would say Suzanne is a common girl and not suitable for a friend."

Olivier nodded. "I understand." He stood facing her under the umbrella.

"But I didn't lie about not knowing where Suzanne lives.

I hope she's not in any trouble now." Rochelle sighed, showing her concern.

"Suzanne will be fine, try not to worry. Thank you for your help, Rochelle. It shouldn't be too hard to locate her now that I know her husband's first name and trade. Vous bénisse, mon enfant (Bess you, my child)." He patted her on the head and then climbed into the carriage As Rochelle curtsied, Olivier leaned from the window, made the sign of the cross and said, "Aller avec Dieu, (Go with God) Rochelle."

The murderer heard about Olivier's arrival in Natchez the same morning the priest went to the Beauregard house. A messenger brought the news to him by ship. He disembarked at the dock at eleven o'clock and immediately walked to a tiny two-room house on Bienville Street. It was a short walk and he needed less than five minutes to reach Bienville and turn up the street. The house stood almost hidden behind a much bigger house, but the messenger found it quickly. He had memorized the directions recited to him in Natchez. He was given written instructions as well, but, lacking the ability to read, they were useless to him. His memory had served him well all his life and he had no need to refer to a line of marks on a piece of paper.

Now, at the door of the house, he knocked loudly (he'd been told the occupant was old and hard of hearing). He waited a few seconds and knocked again. This time, he used his fist and banged on the closed door.He waited with the sealed envelope clutched in his other hand.

A white-haired woman opened the door and faced him with sightless eyes. She leaned on a cane. "Yes, how may I help you, Monsieur," she said.

The messenger made no reply as he had been instructed. Instead, he pushed the sealed envelope into her free hand.

He made sure she held it tightly and then turned to leave.

"Ah, yes, I have been expecting this letter," she said as he walked away.

The messenger stayed in New Orleans only long enough to eat a meal and then boarded the next ship sailing north. Since the ship's cargo took up all the space below, he spent the next three days on deck, one day in heavy rain. On the evening of his arrival in Natchez, he received the other half of the payment he had been promised for the delivery.

The murderer picked up the envelope the next morning. Wary of someone seeing him at the house, he looked up and down the street before opening the door. Satisfied that no one had noticed him, he went inside and spoke briefly to the old woman. Moments later, he left and rode to a tavern he occasionally frequented. He ordered a cup of strong tea, sat at a table in the corner and opened the wrinkled envelope. The succinct two-line message, written in French, included no salutation, closing statement or signature.

"The priest with the bandaged arm arrived on the evening of the thirteenth. He will be carefully watched while here. Natchez, March 14."

The murderer made a face. He worried his instructions would not be precisely followed. He had instructed his agent, Louis Parsall, to follow the priest wherever he went and inform him of all his activities and meetings in town. He wanted Olivier to be under his scrutiny every hour of the day. That was the task and the promise of two Spanish escudos (gold pieces) per day had secured Parsall's prompt agreement. But, even with such an exorbitant price for his service, the murderer worried the man might miss something. Despite his reliability in the past – Parsall had always carried out his assignments exactly as instructed, the murderer still worried. The success of this special assignment was essential to everything he had planned for so long. Yet, now to his dismay, he found himself forced to depend upon another man's effort and reliability. He exhaled a long breath in exasperation. There was nothing else to be done.

He then reminded himself that Parsall was more reliable than his agent in Baton Rouge. It was fortunate the priest had sailed there rather than to the other port. Parsall not only completed his tasks efficiently, he never inquired why they needed to be done. In fact, he did as he was told and never asked any questions at all. The more he thought about Parsall the more he realized the man was his best agent outside of New Orleans. He also was in place to do what was needed.

A second report reached the murderer three days later. As he had instructed his agent in Natchez, another messenger was paid to bring the sealed letter to New Orleans. He did not want any one messenger to become familiar with the method of delivery. He was concerned the man, out of curiosity or hope of additional money, might seek to discover who received the envelope. To avoid that possibility, he knew it was necessary to alter the method of delivery – especially if Olivier remained much longer in Natchez. He would take no chances or let down his guard.

"The priest is lodged here with the Mosquera family. He has been driven to the Catholic Church, Mosquera's sawmill and here and there in the family carriage. No meetings of any kind were observed. He made a visit to the Beauregard house up on the bluff. Natchez, March 16."

The second report angered the murderer. He slapped the arm of his chair after reading it. "Damn him!" he shouted. "I told him to tell me *every place* he went. 'Here and there' is of no help to me and the name Beauregard means nothing to me. The damned fool! I'll deduct a coin a day from his final payment for such incompetence." He guffawed. For a fleeting moment, he had forgotten Parsall's final payment would be a one way voyage on the Mississippi River.

Though more informative than the two earlier messages, the third report still lacked the details he had told Parsall to provide. He gritted his teeth, thinking how he would like to choke the life out of the man. When calmer, he knew nothing could be done about the situation. It was now too late to write a letter demanding more information. By the time it reached Natchez, the meddlesome priest probably would be gone. So, he had to rely on Parsall – at least temporarily. He sighed and reread the report.

"The priest went to the Catholic Church and then to the town market. It was not possible to follow him inside without being seen. He was not observed talking to anyone. He returned to the Mosquera house in the afternoon. Natchez, March 17."

Parsall did not tell him that he had not followed Olivier that day. He had been in bed all morning sick to his stomach and plagued by incessant diarrhea and vomiting. Distraught by his illness and inability to carry out his assignment, the attentive agent reluctantly hired his younger brother, Jean-Jacques, to follow Olivier. He did not tell his employer of his sickness nor did he inform him his brother would be watching the priest that day.

Parsall did not intend to hire his brother for the assignment, but no one else trustworthy was available. He did not doubt Jean-Jacques would try to do whatever was asked of him. He always had the best intentions. The problem was that Jean-Jacques was a drunkard, who drank rum every day. He carried a flask of rum with him at all times. Fearful he might find himself without it when he needed a drink, Jean Jacques kept the flask conveniently placed in his right side coat pocket. He would pat the pocket now and then, making sure it was there, and, every once in a while, touch the cork stopper to be certain it had not loosened. Jean Jacques had been drinking steadily since his sixteen-year-old wife and their one-year-old child died of the plague in the winter of 1798. Parsall did not know how much rum his brother drank during the day, but he suspected it was at least half a bottle.

At the time he agreed to watch the priest, Jean-Jacques crossed his heart with his fingers and promised his brother he would refrain from drinking that morning. Standing in front of his brother's bed, Jean Jacques said he would not take "one single swallow until one o'clock." He was certain he could do without rum throughout the morning hours. In fact, he seldom drank at all in the morning, except for a dram of rum after awakening and opening his eyes. It was in the late afternoon and evening when he drank with his friends.

Parsall accepted his brother's pledge and planned to get out of bed in time to relieve him at one o'clock. He assumed his sickness would be over by then despite his wife's skepticism. The brothers arranged to meet across the street from the Catholic Church since Olivier always went there at midday. The priest spent his time in San Salvador scrubbing the walls and floors in the hope the town's Catholics would again open the old church for worship.

Jean-Jacques followed Olivier without incident that morning. Begged not to drink by his older brother, he watched the priest walk about without opening his flask. He was aware of the flask's weight in his coat pocket and, now and then, he heard the rum sloshing around inside. It happened when Jean-Jacques increased his gait to keep up with the fast walking priest. He was not worried about leakage since the stopper had been pressed hard into flask, but the sound of the rum splashing about made him acutely aware of it. Every time it happened, his mouth became dry and Jean-Jacques found himself wishing he could take just a dram to quench his thirst. But remembering his promise to his brother, he resisted the urge and tried to forget about it.

The priest left the Mosquera house at dawn. As was his custom, he went to the river and walked along the bluff as the sun rose in the sky. A bank of broken clouds lay over the horizon that morning and the sunrise colored them in orange, pink, purple and red. The colors covered the eastern sky and, for a few moments, even spread across the river and touched the tops of the trees on the other side. Olivier stood transfixed by the sight and did not move a muscle until the colors eventually dimmed and died away.

His mind occupied with thoughts of his expected meeting with the saddler, he wandered about aimlessly before walking into town. By then, dark clouds covered the sky and a cold wind was at his back. The wind intensified as he hurried on, looking forward to his morning tea. An hour later, Olivier arrived at the *Cat and Fiddle*, where he was the first customer of the day. He usually sat outside drinking his tea, but the increasing cold and threat of rain sent him inside.

The previous two mornings, Olivier sat outside on a weathered chair near the door. He drank his tea outside to keep the town gossips from saying the visiting Catholic priest spent his time in Natchez drinking at the *Cat and Fiddle*. He doubted Bishop Meléndez would ever hear such a rumor, but he did not intend to take any chances. What no one knew in or outside of town was that the tavern's owner, an understanding Scotsman named David McFadden, always added a generous splash of rum to Olivier's tea. It was therefore of no interest to anyone in Natchez that the Catholic priest drank two cups of McFadden's tea and occasionally a third whenever he stopped at the *Cat and Fiddle*.

Jean-Jacques followed Olivier from the tavern to the church. He watched him leave the *Cat and the Fiddle* and walked behind him on the other side of the street. He then waited until the priest entered San Salvador before approaching the building. Jean-Jacques remained on the other side of the street and stood across from the church beside a huge sycamore tree. The tree was ideally situated for him to observe anyone entering or leaving San Salvador. It allowed him to stand there hidden behind its thick trunk and occasionally peek out along the side to see if the church door opened. The trunk also blocked the cold wind that now blew in from the west.

As time passed, Jean-Jacques felt the cold even standing behind the tree. The wind had increased in strength and now seemed to find him no matter where he moved. He buttoned his coat all the way to his throat and pulled up the collar, but felt no warmer. Instead, a cold shiver ran down his spine and he sneezed several times in succession. Jean-Jacques now worried that he might be feeling the first symptoms of catarrh. He wished he had listened to his brother who had urged him to wear a heavy shirt and thick stockings that morning.

Olivier left San Salvador at noon. He walked into the street without Jean-Jacques seeing him. Preoccupied with his worries about suffering catarrh, Jean-Jacques not only missed seeing Olivier leave, he did not hear the squeaky oak door open and close as the priest left the church. Fortunately, Jean-Jacques caught sight of him walking down the street. His white bandage and black cassock made the priest easy to follow and he stepped out from behind the sycamore. He had to wait to cross the street as a horse-drawn wagon loaded with lumber passed him, moving swiftly. Avoiding the spray of dirt and pebbles from the horses' hooves, Jean-Jacques jumped back and then hurriedly strode to the other side of the street. The priest was still clearly in view.

A few minutes later, Jean-Jacques saw Olivier enter the town market. The market was a short walk from the church and he quickly caught up with him. With the cutting wind blowing in from the river, few people were in the street and no one noticed him following Olivier. Again, he found a big tree to stand behind while waiting for the priest. The tree stood across the street, but a half-block from the market's door. Though tempted to follow him inside, Jean-Jacques feared the priest might notice him if, as he suspected, few people would be there shopping at midday. He also worried that someone he knew would speak to him and the priest would leave before he could break away from the conversation.

The longer Jean Jacques stood outside, the colder he became. Shivering incessantly, he kept looking at his pocket-watch as time seemed to slow down between noon and twelve-thirty. By one o'clock, Jean-Jacques knew the temperature had dropped and that was the cause of misery, not catarrh. He hopped up and down, stomped his feet and crossed and uncrossed his arms over his chest, in the hope he could warm himself. But nothing he did helped. And, now, his lower jaw trembled and his teeth chattered along with his shivering. Finally, without any other means to warm himself, he took the flask from his pocket and drank half its contents.

Parsall found his brother at two-thirty. Still feverish and suffering severe cramps along with frequent bouts of diarrhea, he left his sick bed to relieve Jean-Jacques. He took his carriage to the church and, when his brother was not to be found there, he continued along the dirt street to the market. A short distance ahead of him, he saw a group of people standing around someone lying in the street. A man was on his knees bent over the figure on the ground. Parsall grunted in despair, certain the figure lying on the ground was Jean-Jacques.

Later that afternoon, he learned what had happened. Back in bed propped up on pillows, Parsall stared at his brother who stood at the foot of his bed. Jean Jacques, his emaciated face still bruised from his fall, looked down at the wooden floor. Shamed by Parsall's criticism, he spoke softly, slightly above a whisper.

"The c-cold made me do it – I just couldn't take it anymore," he explained, avoiding his brother's eyes. "I had to do something to warm himself and stop shivering. I waited until 1:30 before taking a drink, a half hour later than I promised. I was out in the cold all morning and, by that time, I was chilled to the bone."

"But you didn't just take a drink, Jean Jacques, you drank the entire flask of rum – every drop." Parsall shook his head. "You drank so much you lost your senses and fell to the ground. Townspeople from the market saw you in the street and thought you were dead."

Jean-Jacques grimaced, but said nothing. He had no memory of what happened after he took his first drink and felt the warmth of the rum spread through his body. Jean-Jacques only recalled awakening and finding himself lying on the ground with a red-faced man leaning over him. At first, Jean-Jacques did not recognize the man, who had risen and looked down at him. Then, he realized the man was Monsieur Lavelle, the town tailor.

"You have nothing to say?"

Jean-Jacques turned his hat in his hands. "I have no memory of what happened, Louis."

"Then I'll tell you. I heard the entire account from Monsieur Lavelle. Madame Marceau was the first to see you lying in the street. She was leaving the market and saw what she thought was a dead body in the street. She hurried back into the market and several people followed her outside to see the body. Of course, they soon discovered you were the one lying on the ground and that you were *drunk*, not dead. He said the odor of rum was quite distinct. Monsieur Lavelle told me he had to slap you awake since nothing else he did to rouse you succeeded."

Jean-Jacques said nothing.

"So, Jean-Jacques, what do you have to say for yourself? Nothing? I'm not surprised at all. You not only have failed me when I needed your help on an important assignment, you also have humiliated our family. I can't imagine what our mother will have to say to you when she hears of your despicable behavior."

Parsall knew he had no choice, but to resume his following the priest the next day. Too much time had already elapsed to find the priest's whereabouts that afternoon and his condition would not have allowed him to attempt it anyway. Parsall sighed, knowing there was nothing to be done about it. Unfortunately for the conscientious man, Olivier already had been unobserved for a number of hours and would continue to move about in the same manner the rest of the day.

"Go on now Jean-Jacques," he said, dismissing his brother with a wave of his hand.

Parsall, a Presbyterian of strict ethical convictions, knew he had to deceive his employer in New Orleans. It bothered him, but he believed he had no choice. Parsall was certain the man who signed his letters with the initial M would not tolerate any change of plans. M expected his assignments to be completed exactly as instructed and he included that demand in every contract Parsall had signed. That was the rule and he knew there were to be no exceptions, no matter the reason. Parsall knew everything would be lost if M found out his brother had served in his stead following the priest, never mind that he had failed to watch him the entire afternoon. Not only would he lose the lucrative current assignment, he would also lose his long-standing business in New Orleans. In the middle of the night, unable to sleep, Parsall made his decision. He decided not to mention his brother or the unfortunate events of the day in his report. Instead, he intended to watch the Catholic priest as if nothing unusual had happened the previous afternoon. Far away from New Orleans, Parsall hoped M would not learn of his deception.

Olivier did not know he had been followed his first few days in Natchez. He went about the town completely unaware that his movements were watched from dawn to dusk each of the days in town. Olivier's mind was focused on finding Suzanne Lavasseur and it never occurred to him that the murderer or his agents might be following him to find her whereabouts as well.

On Tuesday, Olivier entered the town market hoping to find Suzanne's husband. He had waited until after lunch when he was told the saddler usually arrived at his stall – he spent most mornings working at home without the inevitable interruptions that limited his production at the market. Olivier immediately saw the curly-haired saddler upon entering the door. His stall was situated in a back corner, but clearly visible from the entrance.

The saddler was rubbing oil on a new saddle when Olivier approached him. He looked exactly as Rochelle had described him. Engrossed in his work, the young man did not look up until the priest's shadow fell across the saddle. Seeing Olivier, he smiled and bowed politely.

"Bon journée, Père. I assume you're the priest who has been asking about me."

"Bon journée, Monsieur Molyneux." Olivier learned the saddler's family name the same day he talked to Rochelle and her mother. Felipe drove him to the town market after leaving the Beauregard house and, when he could not find the saddler there, one of the other tradesmen told him his name. "Yes, I am Father Olivier from New Orleans."

"So I've been told. Everyone is talking about you, wondering why you are here. You are quite a novelty in Natchez." The saddler smiled.

"Apparently." Olivier returned the smile. "I've seen the curious stares, though everyone has been very polite to me."

"The townspeople haven't seen a priest in Natchez in quite some time – and a priest with a bandaged arm from

New Orleans at that. They, of course, assume you are here to open up San Salvador once again." He pointed in the direction of the church. "It's well known you have been toiling every day to clean the church."

Olivier nodded. "That's a reasonable assumption. I would like to see San Salvador open again, but that's not why I have come to Natchez."

"What brings you here to this frontier town, then, Father?"

"I've come to speak to you and your wife, Monsieur."

"I trust you know I am not Catholic."

"I suspected as much, but that's not why I've sought you out, Monsieur Molyneux."

Puzzled, the saddler frowned. "Then why? What do you want of us?" The saddler spoke brusquely, now suspicious of the priest.

Olivier saw the wariness in the young man's frown and knew he would have to tell him everything – everything that had happened in New Orleans and Mosquito Creek. He knew it was essential to earn his trust. Olivier had come to Natchez to save Suzanne from the murderer. He wanted her to identify the fiend, but saving her life was now his foremost concern. Throughout his journey, Olivier had prayed for her survival every time her name came to mind. And, now that he stood before her husband, Olivier knew to save Suzanne he had to persuade Molyneux to take her away from Natchez as soon as possible.

"May I sit?" He pointed to a stool at the back of the stall. "I have much to tell you."

"Of course." The saddler moved the stool a few feet from the sawhorse to where Olivier stood. Veuille vous asseoir, Père (Please sit, Father).

Olivier told him everything that had happened from the murders of the Dumont brothers to the surprise attack in the street that nearly cost his life. He spoke steadily without a pause and his account lasted a half hour. The saddler leaned against the wooden sawhorse while listening. His face contorted as Olivier described the murders. He pointed to the priest's bandaged arm as he finished speaking.

"I assume that's where he stabbed you."

Olivier nodded.

"Well, what's to be done?" Molyneux ran his fingers through his hair.

"I suggest you take Suzanne away until the murderer is arrested. I think it best you leave Natchez and go someplace secret where no one can find you. You must not make the mistake of thinking the murderer will not find you here so far from New Orleans. He is much too clever to be underestimated. I have found you and so will he, probably sooner rather than later. As they say, 'It is better to be safe than sorry.' You must leave Natchez soon! Tomorrow, if possible!"

The saddler nodded. "You're right, Father. That's the only course of action."

CHAPTER THIRTEEN

NEW ORLEANS AND NATCHEZ: MARCH 18 - 30, 1800

Antonio stood in the doorway of the cathedral looking out into the rainy morning. It had rained all night and was still pouring an hour after first light. Seeing rain drops splashing on the hem of his cassock, Antonio closed the door and entered the cathedral. He had intended to visit Santa María that morning and attend Mass. Antonio wanted to talk to Francis and inquire if the young priest needed any assistance. The pastor had not seen him since Olivier's departure ten days earlier and, though not concerned about his performance, he knew it was time to pay him a visit. "After all," he thought, "Francis is quite young and Santa María is his first church position. But, now, with sheets of rain falling, Antonio decided to put off his visit. It would be foolish to take his carriage outside town and risk getting stuck in the muddy road to or from Santa María.

Antonio actually had planned to visit Francis earlier, but he had been much too busy in New Orleans. The week had begun with the death of Marie Moreau. The crippled child had died at midnight on Sunday night. He had been called to the Ursuline Convent a half hour earlier and administered last rites before her death. She awakened from a coma as he stood beside her bed, but only looked about the room momentarily. He thought she smiled faintly when she saw him standing there. Antonio shook his head sadly, thinking how he hated to see a child die. His only consolation was knowing the child would be with God ever after.

Anxious to escape his memory of Marie's death, he turned his thoughts to the unpleasant meeting he had with Jean Bertin on Monday afternoon. He sighed remembering it. The meeting had lasted almost an hour and he had been thoroughly exasperated with him by the time it ended. Antonio found Jean Bertin to be insufferable. The man's blatant selfishness appalled the pastor and it was only with a concerted effort that he managed to keep himself from commenting on it. Antonio hesitated to say anything critical since the Dumont family was a prominent benefactor of the cathedral. The family's generous support of the Church had been the only reason he had requested Olivier's assistance in the murder investigation.

Jean Bertin arrived at his office door unannounced and without an appointment. He had blithely entered the cathedral, opened the closed door to the clerical quarters and walked to his office as if it were a daily routine. Later, upon reflection, Antonio realized the man had no sense of propriety; he simply assumed his position in the community permitted him to do whatever he wished whenever it was convenient to him.

"Father Antonio." Jean Bertin stood in the doorway. "I must talk to you."

Startled, Antonio looked up from the book that lay before him on his desk. He had been reading Alban Butler's, *Lives of the Fathers, Martyrs and Other Principal Saints*. He frowned not understanding how Jean Bertin could have come to his office unannounced.

"Ah, Monsieur Dumont? What brings you here?" Antonio actually wanted to say, "What brings you *uninvited* to my office?" He gestured Jean Bertin to the chair across from him.

"It's the failed search for the murderer of my sons." Jean Bertin sat down heavily in the wooden chair and it creaked under his weight. "The priest you recommended to me has nothing to show for all the money I gave to the church. We are no closer to arresting the murderer than we were last August when he murdered my sons. Eight, no, now nearly nine months have passed without results; and when I queried the priest in January about the lack of results, his only reply was, 'I'm stymied myself. I must think about it for a while.' That's all he could say. Can you imagine it?" Jean Bertin's face was flushed and sweat beaded on his brow. "To make matters worse, the Dominican had the temerity to be impertinent to me in front of my nephew. Of late, he hasn't even deigned to inform me of his recent efforts. Now, he's gone and I have no notion where he went or why. Nor do I know if his journey has anything to do with his assignment for me. His assistant, an uninformed and very unhelpful priest … I believe his name is Francis, ah, Father Francis – he told me to talk to you."

Antonio held up a hand to stop Jean Bertin's outburst. "Calmez-vous, Monsieur Dumont, I can't understand your concerns if you speak so fast."

Jean Bertin nodded. He wiped his brow with a wrinkled handkerchief he withdrew from a pocket in his breeches.

"Now, Monsieur Dumont, let's start at the beginning and go over the arrangements you made with *Father Olivier*." Antonio emphasized Olivier's name and clerical title as he spoke to Jean Bertin. He wanted Jean Bertin to know he was to refer to the priest by his clerical name, not his religious order.

"I don't recall every word in the agreement, but the *Dominican* … Father Olivier agreed to assist in the investigation and find the murderer."

"Father Olivier said he would find the murderer or *try* to find the murderer?" Antonio stared at Jean Bertin as he emphasized the word *try*.

Jean Bertin made a face. "He said he would try to find the murderer, but the arrest of the man was assumed."

"Is that so? Tell me, Monsieur Dumont, are *assumption*s usually included in the contracts you make with other men of commerce?"

"No, Father, but the arrangement I made with the *Dominican* … Father Olivier was not a written contract. We made the agreement in spoken words. The meeting was held in my office a month before Christmas. I remember the cold day as if it were yesterday. My nephew was there to witness the contract." Jean Bertin smiled, pleased with himself. He had quickly come up with a clever reply to the pastor's unexpected question.

"I see." Antonio noted Jean Bertin's smile and stared at him. He then looked through the pile of papers that lay on his desk. Extracting several from the bottom of the pile, Antonio found one which he studied and then passed over the desk to Jean Bertin.

"Tell me, Monsieur Dumont, are these the words included in the *spoken contract* between you and Father Olivier?" Antonio saw Jean Bertin frown as he picked up the paper.

Jean Bertin read the words and nodded. His face which had lost its color reddened once again. For the second time since the contract had been made, he was confronted with the words the Dominican had spoken in his office. "*I will assist in the investigation as you request, but it must be understood at the outset that I cannot promise to find the murderer you seek. I'll do my best, but I cannot assure you of success in the investigation nor can I tell you how long it will take no matter the outcome.*" He leaned over and handed the paper back to the pastor.

"The day after his meeting with you, Father Olivier wrote down the words of the *spoken contract* here in this office. He never forgets what he hears, says or even reads, you know. God has given him one of those exceptional memories that few others enjoy. So, to assure me he had not made an arrangement which I would find objectionable, Father Olivier wrote his words down on that piece of paper." He held it up with the writing facing Jean Bertin.

Jean Bertin turned his eyes away. He did not want to look at the paper again.

Father Antonio visited Santa María the next morning. It was a cold damp day, following an overnight rain. The pastor left the cathedral at eleven-thirty and, walking leisurely, reached the church a few minutes after noon. A young couple was leaving Santa María as he approached the church. Francis had been talking to the couple in the doorway and saw Antonio walking toward him. The pastor smiled and raised his hand.

Following their greetings, they entered Santa María and Francis showed the pastor the new communion table, pulpit and benches that had been made during the renovation. Antonio patted Francis on the back after looking around the interior. He praised the carpentry as well as the other changes that improved the little church's appearance and made it more hospitable. The priests then went to the rear of the building and sat on benches facing each other. Antonio had brought bread and cheese with him and they talked while eating together. The parish pastor also brought a half-full flask of wine which they shared during their meal.

When they finished talking about what had been accomplished during the renovation and what was yet to be done,

Antonio told Francis about his meeting with Jean Bertin. He began by apologizing for gossiping about him. Antonio also criticized himself for his inability to listen to Jean Bertin with Christian understanding. He, then, launched into a scathing critique of the man, scowling as he described his behavior.

"The man is utterly consumed with his own needs and how to achieve them. I doubt he ever thinks about the concerns of others. I think he is completely ignorant or, worse, indifferent to Christ's mission on earth. For whatever reason, he has no thought of the love of others in his daily life. It's as if he considers every interaction, even with Christ's Church, as a commercial arrangement. I'm now sure he viewed his support of Santa María renovation as nothing more than the wages he had to pay for Olivier's investigation. He assumed Olivier was no more than one of his obedient hirelings, who would do his bidding without a word of complaint." Antonio smiled suddenly. "Of course, Jean Bertin didn't know Olivier, did he?"

Francis nodded, a smile on his lips. "No, he did not."

"Well, he now knows better!" He looked at Francis and they both laughed. "Speaking of Olivier, has anyone inquired about him – that is with the exception of the parishioners?"

"No, Father Antonio, no one except Jean Bertin. The parishioners were informed that he would be gone. He told those who attended his last Mass and it was well known by the evening." He smiled. "You know how fast word travels in the lowlands."

It's the same everywhere, Francis, as you will discover in time." Antonio shook his head and crossed his legs. "Incidentally, have you heard anything from Olivier?"

"He sent me a brief message from Natchez. He said nothing about his voyage up river and included only a few words about the Mosquera family. Most of his message concerned the marriage of Honorè and Ana Luisa. He hopes to be back in time for their marriage."

"He wrote me with the same concern. I'll see to it, whether or not he returns in time. I assume he also sent you the same secret message." Antonio saw Francis nod his head. "So, the weather is mild in Natchez and there are signs of the arrival of spring."

"Which means the search for the girl is progressing." Francis smiled.

"Exactly. Now, Francis, tell me about the parish. What are your plans for Easter? I hope the renovation will be completed by then."

Olivier met with Suzanne the same day he spoke to her husband at the town market. He rode in the saddler's carriage to their home and ate a meal with them before leaving in the late afternoon. Olivier talked to Suzanne as Richard packed the carriage for their departure the next morning. The pregnant girl told the priest what she knew about the murderer and he left before sunset, riding again with the saddler. At his insistence, Olivier was left on the road in a wooded area a mile from town. Rain was falling when he stepped down from the carriage, but he walked to avoid being seen in Richard's carriage. He realized his meeting with the young couple might put them at risk – the risk of someone seeing them together and reporting it to the murderer.

Now that he had met Suzanne and Richard, Oliver worried about their welfare. As he left their home, it occurred to him that he might have been followed to Natchez and possibly even to the market where he met the saddler. Though few people were in the market that cold afternoon, he worried a follower had seen him talking at length to the saddler and, then, watched him leave town in Richard's carriage. Olivier chided himself for failing to think of the possibility of being followed and vowed to be more aware in the future. Above all, he wanted the young couple to leave Natchez without the murderer finding them. Though Olivier now knew the identity of the murderer, he could not stop him until he reached New Orleans.

The worry kept him awake for hours that night and occupied his mind the next day when he made arrangements to leave Natchez. He decided to depart on Thursday, March 20. A large schooner, the *Concordia*, carrying wheat flour from St. Louis had docked at Natchez was bound for Baton Rouge. It was scheduled to return north a week later. Olivier found the captain at the *Cat and Fiddle* on Wednesday afternoon and purchased his passage down river to Baton Rouge.

Olivier took the *Concordia* as a precaution if someone had been following him while he was in Natchez. He hoped a watcher would assume he was headed to Baton Rouge because his search for Suzanne in Natchez had been unsuccessful. By that time, he suspected the murderer knew he was searching for one of the missing girls who could identify him and therefore might have had him followed. With those suspicions in mind, Olivier wanted the murderer to think he had so far failed to find one of them. His did not want anyone who had helped him in Natchez to face the murderer's vengeance. He had killed Madam Villièrs and her niece because they could identify him and he would similarly kill anyone else he believed endangered him.

Olivier boarded the *Concordia* at dawn. Though there were five other passengers, he sat by himself amidships. He felt ill and did not want to talk to anyone. His head ached and, after a night of chills, he was hot with fever. Worst of all, Olivier could not stop coughing, each cough leaving him with a stabbing pain in the right side of his chest.

He had slept fitfully his last night in Natchez. Olivier had begun coughing shortly after arriving at the Mosqueras' house at dusk. The coughing worsened during that evening and into the night as the seemingly endless hours slowly passed. In the morning, he spit up phlegm with traces of blood and considered waiting a day or two before leaving town. But, worried what the murderer might do while he waited for his coughing to abate, Olivier knew he had to board the *Concordia* for Baton Rouge. He was consumed with fear that the murderer would kill everyone who helped him in Natchez. With that worry in mind, he willed himself to sit up and then stand, holding on to a bedpost. Once on his feet, Olivier coughed several times, his free hand on his chest where the pain was acute. He grimaced feeling unsteady and fearing he would fall.

Olivier trembled as he took off his night shirt and he almost collapsed on the bed when a wave of dizziness overwhelmed him. He sat on the edge of the bed until the dizziness passed and then stood slowly to dress. Olivier had to lean against the wall to put his cassock over his head. Short of breath, he had to sit down afterward. A few minutes later, after packing his haversack with his few possessions, he straightened his posture and walked carefully out of the bedroom. Olivier wanted to look fully able to the Mosqueras.

The family was waiting for him in the kitchen. They looked him over, instantly seeing his weakness. Señora Mosquera spoke up, ignoring her husband's gesture to say nothing.

"You are in no condition to travel, Father, and you know it," she said reprovingly. "Your face is as white as a ghost's and your red eyes reveal your fever. I heard you coughing in the night. It sounds like pneumonia to me. My dear mother, bediga su alma (bless her soul), died of pneumonia." She crossed herself.

"María Inez, por favor no mas (please no more)." Her husband held up his hand.

She glared at him. "It's the truth and Father Olivier knows it!"

Olivier smiled sadly. "You may well be right, Señora, but I must go." He spoke softly and then coughed three times in succession, each time grimacing from pain.

Despite the family's urging to stay with them until he felt better, Olivier shook his head and politely asked to be taken to his ship. Felipe drove the open carriage with his father sitting beside Olivier, his comforting hand on the priest's knee. They said nothing during the short trip, each of them uncertain of what to say. Olivier waved to them, after unsteadily climbing up the gangplank with the help of one of the ship's crew. Once on deck, he watched Mosquera and his son walk toward their carriage and, when they turned to look at him, he waved for the last time. Olivier then hurried amidships, where he dropped his haversack and sat on the deck. Exhausted, he stretched his legs out and leaned his head back against the mast.

By that time, Olivier could only take short breaths. He opened his mouth wide, hoping to bring more air into his lungs. But nothing helped and he felt dizzy again. Olivier closed his eyes and tried to will away the dizziness. His last awareness was the sudden speed of the *Concordia* as it found the fast-moving current in the middle of the river.

Olivier awoke in a soft feather bed, the blurry-face of someone looking down at him. He blinked his eyes and, when his sight cleared, he saw a smiling woman above him. She spoke to him, but he did not understand what she said. Olivier frowned, trying to remember the words she used and then he went back to sleep.

"Sleep is good for him now," said the bald, bearded man standing beside the woman. He pushed his spectacles up from the end of his long nose. "Let him sleep as long as he wants and only feed him if he asks to eat. Blood-letting is the best treatment for him. The leeches should drain enough blood from him today. I'll be back in the morning to see how he's doing."

"Thank you, Doctor Standish. What do you think of his present state?"

"It's much too early to tell, Mrs. Mitchell. Pneumonia is a difficult illness to treat. Some patients recover after a week's venesection (blood-letting), alas, others never do. It also depends upon how soon the pneumonia is detected and treated. Pray tell me, Mrs. Mitchell, how did the sick priest come to be here with you and Timothy?"

"Timothy brought the sick priest home yesterday. He came off the *Concordia*. It seems he fainted on deck and could not be revived. According to one of the sailors, he appeared to be sleeping, sitting up, until the *Concordia* altered course suddenly and he toppled over on his face. The ship altered course to avoid a huge log in the water. Of course, everyone rushed over to the fallen man and tried to awaken him from his stupor, but to no avail. A froth was then noticed on his lips and, fearing the plague, those who had attended to him immediately moved away. They stood looking at the man from a distance. One man, remained at his side. Meanwhile, one of the crew advised the captain of the situation and he arrived soon afterwards. He also was hesitant to come close to the sick man and stared at him from a distance. It was then, at that very moment that Timothy and our son Jonathon sailed by in the *Good Samaritan*. Hailed by the captain, a Portuguese man, I don't remember his name – it was one of those long impossible-to-pronounce or spell foreign names. That's when they came alongside the *Concordia*."

"So, the ship's captain asked Timothy to take the priest to shore." The doctor interrupted her in mid-sentence. He regretted being impolite, but he was impatient to leave and hoped to shorten one of Elizabeth Mitchell's well known wordy stories. "What a damned fool I was to ask her about the priest," he thought to himself.

"Yes." Mrs. Mitchell frowned, annoyed by the interruption. "The captain told Timothy the priest would be dropped overboard if he didn't take him. The horrid man said he couldn't take the risk of endangering his crew or the other passengers if the priest had the plague."

"I see, so, Timothy took the sick man and brought him home." This time the doctor was able to speak before Mrs. Mitchell began another sentence. "I now must take my leave" he said, nodding to her. "I'll be back in the morning."

"But there's more – much more!" Mrs. Mitchell clucked her tongue in irritation. "The man who had stayed by the sick priest's side on the *Concordia* helped Timothy carry him aboard the *Good Samaritan*. He could not get back aboard the Concordia … the current …"

At the door, Doctor Standish shook his head. "I'm sorry, Mrs. Mitchell, but I've another patient I must see this morning." He turned and hurried out the door.

It was a *bold-faced lie*, as his mother would have told him when he was a boy, but he had to leave the loquacious woman. He could not bear to hear another word from her. She was quite comely and a splendid cook, he knew from the times she brought delicious dishes to the church's suppers, but he did not envy Timothy Mitchell. "No, no, not at all." He could not imagine how the man could tolerate the woman's incessant talking. It would have driven him to despair.

The murderer received two messages concerning Olivier on the following Monday. They arrived after a weekend of worry. He knew the priest had taken passage on the *Concordia* bound for Baton Rouge, on Thursday, March 20, but he had heard nothing about his arrival in that city. The *Concordia l*eft in the early morning and should have reached Baton Rouge by noon, Friday, at the latest. At first, the delay puzzled him, then, it annoyed him and, finally, it infuriated him. But, by

Sunday evening, he was worried.

"Had the priest escaped the scrutiny of his watchers? Had he seen and eluded them, only pretending to board the *Concordia*? Had he disembarked unseen somewhere else before the ship reached Baton Rouge? Had he hidden himself on the *Concordia* and somehow disembarked at Baton Rouge with anyone seeing him?" The questions repeated themselves over and over in his mind. He had no answers and could not escape them, especially when he tried to sleep at night.

He received the first message early Monday morning. It was sent from Baton Rouge and tersely said, "The priest did not arrive here on the *Concordia*." The second message reached him after lunch. It allayed his initial worries, but added new worries to his mind. The blunt message related what happened to Olivier in three sentences. "The priest fell into a stupor and was taken off the ship. It was thought he had the plague and might be dying. He was taken away in a sloop called the *Good Samaritan*."

The murderer crumpled the message in his fist and shouted, "Vous stupide bastard!" (You stupid bastard!) "How does the sloop's name help me find the priest? The owner's name is what I need to know!" His face flushed with fury, he stood in the deserted street beside his horse. He gritted his teeth, picturing Abelard Boyer, the man he had hired to follow Olivier aboard the ship. "Another one who will go to the bottom of the inlet."

He mounted his stallion and turned him up San Felipe Street. Still angry, he thought of how he would kill Boyer. He saw the little man entering the boat house on the quay. Boyer was there to collect his wages for following Olivier. But, instead of the ten silver coins he expected, he would get a weighted stocking on his head. The murderer saw Boyer reaching over to pick up the pile of coins on the table and the stocking striking him just as his fingers touched the top one. It was a fitting way for the fool to die since he had failed to carry out his assignment. There were others who would be paid the same wages for their incompetence. He had a mental list of twelve so far and there probably would be a number more before everything was settled.

An hour later at home, sipping a cup of tea, he had calmed himself and begun to think of the ways he could find Olivier's whereabouts. It initially occurred to him that the clever priest might have already died from his illness, but he knew better than to make such an assumption. It was nothing more than wishful thinking. Even if Olivier was near death, he remained a threat to tell someone what he learned in Natchez. Though he did not know it with certainty, something told him Olivier knew he was the one – the one they all wanted to find. The priest was too clever for his own good. "Yes," he said aloud, "the damned Dominican knows I'm the one."

A sudden shiver ran down his spine and he knew the priest was alive and would recover from his illness. It was as if the chill he felt warned him Olivier would continue to be a threat to him. He must be found as soon as possible and killed. As long as the priest lived, he threatened all his plans and everything he had worked so hard to achieve.

He nodded and thought of two ways to learn the name of the sloop's owner. One would be to tell his man in Baton Rouge to ask the captain and mates of the *Concordia* if they knew the man's name. The second involved Louis Parsall in Natchez. The murderer had not been pleased with his performance while Olivier was in the port city, but he still was his best agent outside of New Orleans. He therefore penned a note to Parsall, telling him to inquire among the shippers and ship captains for the owner of the *Good Samaritan.* As he sealed the envelope, it occurred to him that the dock workers in Natchez knew the ship's owner and for a few pesetas would gladly reveal his name. He was tempted to add that inquiry to his instructions to Parsall, but decided to wait and see what was discovered from the other approaches.

Now calm and quite content, he leaned back in his chair, certain he would soon find the doomed priest. Even if the two agents failed to learn Olivier's location, he was now confident of thinking of other ways to discover his whereabouts. The next morning, two messengers left New Orleans by ship, one sailing to Natchez, the other to Baton Rouge.

On March 30, Antonio received a brief letter from Olivier. It had been written six days earlier and brought to the pastor by the first mate of a schooner carrying a cargo of cotton to New Orleans. The mate, a burly Irishman, arrived at the cathedral after midnight. He knocked loudly until one of the Capuchin novices unlocked the door. Unable to persuade the man to hand him the letter, the sleepy novice went to awaken Antonio. He apologized for disturbing him, relating the messenger's refusal to give the letter to anyone other than the cathedral pastor. Antonio nodded, got out of bed, and with the novice leading their way with a candle, hurried to meet the man.

The messenger waited outside the cathedral while the novice was gone. He stood there in the dark until Antonio, carrying a candle, opened the door and identified himself as the pastor of the church. Following a brief greeting, the man informed Antonio he would have to answer a question before the letter would be given to him. Annoyed, Antonio frowned, but then smiled broadly when he heard the question. He knew both the question and the letter had come from Olivier.

"You are to tell me where Jenne D'Arc was born. Sorry, Father, but that's what I was paid to do." The sailor looked down at his shoes.

"I understand. Jeanne d'Arc was born in Domrémy, in northeastern France."

"That's it!" The Irishman looked up after scrutinizing a scrap of paper he had taken from a pocket. He handed the envelope to Antonio and turned to leave.

"Wait a moment." Antonio reached out and touched his back. "We can offer you some food and drink here before you leave. Please come in, Monsieur …"

"It's McManus, Father, Francis Patrick McManus." He grinned and his eyes seemed to shine as he looked down at the pastor.

Antonio nodded. "Do come in Monsieur. McManus, I want to give you something …"

"No, Father, I must be on me way. My ship is here only as long as it takes to unload the cargo. Don't be worried, I've been well paid to carry the message to you."

Antonio smiled and patted the man's arm. "May God be with you, Monsieur McManus."

He read the message in his office an hour later, when he knew the bishop was praying at the main altar. As soon as the pastor opened the envelope and looked at the writing, he knew the message had not been penned by Olivier. His lettering was small and simple, while the lettering in the note was large and ornamental. He suspected it was a woman's writing.

Reverend Antonio de Sedella, Parish Pastor
Cathedral of St. Louis, King of France

Father Antonio,

As you can see, I am not the writer of this letter. I have been sick with what I have been told was pneumonia, which has temporarily left me with a trembling hand. So, I am indebted to another person to write what is included in this note. That person's kindness and consistent care have brought me through the ordeal of pneumonia and I am for-

ever grateful for all the effort that was put forth for me. I know without it I would have perished. I can only hope that sometime in the future I will be able to show my gratitude in some way.

I will be leaving here when the weather improves. It has been raining here for a number of days and the Mississippi River is a raging torrent. It is also full of flotsam that makes sailing extremely perilous. Only the boldest captains are risking voyages to New Orleans and, I've been told, none are presently boarding passengers on their ships.

Whatever the weather, I expect to return to Santa María well before Palm Sunday. I want to reach New Orleans as soon as possible so I can prepare for the liturgical procession that day as well as the other church activities the rest of Holy Week.

Respectfully Yours in Christ,

Olivier Blanchard, Pastor
Saint Mary's Church
24th of March of the year 1800

Antonio smiled, instantly seeing the word he had hoped would be in Olivier's letter. The English word, *prepare,* told him Olivier's journey to Natchez had been successful. He now knew the identity of the murderer. If any other word had appeared in reference to Palm Sunday, the pastor would have known Olivier had either failed to find Suzanne or she had been unable to identify the murderer. Unfortunately, Olivier alone knew the man's identity.

Antonio reread the priest's message and frowned. There was no mention or even a hint of his name. Puzzled, the pastor wondered why Olivier had not used some biblical passage or Church writing to tell him the murderer's name. With his remarkable memory, he could have referred to any number of texts which would have led him to the name. Olivier had used French history to make sure his message reached him. Why, then, had he not done something similar to reveal the murderer's identity? Baffled, Antonio shook his head and decided to show the note to Francis in the morning. Perhaps, the clever young priest could see something in the message he had missed. It was essential to know the name of the murderer in the event something happened to Olivier.

But, first, he had to inform the bishop of Olivier's location. He sighed, reluctant to speak to Meléndez about Olivier. Antonio knew it was necessary to show him the letter, but he did not intend to tell him about the hidden message that Olivier had included. Instead of the seeing it as the success of Olivier's mission, he assumed the bishop would condemn it as an act of pride.

The bishop had just returned from praying when he saw the pastor standing in front of his office door. His mouth turned down indicating his irritation, Meléndez nodded to Antonio. He motioned him to the visitor's chair, which stood across from him on the other side of the desk.

"How can I help you, Father Antonio?" he asked apathetically. The two priests had not exchanged pleasantries for almost a month.

"I'm here to inform you of Olivier's location and his plans to return to Santa María."

"I see. Where is he then? Has he left the land of Protestantism?" Meléndez would not have admitted it to anyone, but he was disappointed to hear Olivier was on his way back to his jurisdiction. He had hoped never to see him again.

Antonio saw the bishop's frown when he heard about Olivier's travel plans. Instead of saying anything else about Olivier, he handed him the note. He noticed the frown remained on the bishop's face as he read it.

Meléndez stared at Antonio. "So, what was the result of his long journey to the Protestant lands? Unless I missed something reading Olivier's message, there is no statement of success to be seen in it. I can only assume the murderer's identity is still unknown." He snorted and looked at Antonio awaiting his response.

The pastor's face hardened. "God forgive me, but I'm beginning to dispise this man," he thought to himself. His face softened as he smiled in return. "There's a saying I recall from my novitiate which think appropriate at this time. "We must never assume what is yet to take place. Only God knows what is coming to the world of men."

Antonio stood, bowed respectfully to the bishop and walked through the cathedral to the front doors. Outside in the warm sun, he decided to walk rather than ride in the church carriage to Santa María. It was too beautiful a day to dwell on uncharitable thoughts about the bishop.

The pastor reached Santa María thirty minutes later and found Francis sitting outside the church in the sun. He was reading St. Augustine's *City of God.* They talked about the life of the revered saint for a few moments and, then, Antonio handed Francis the message from Olivier.

"Before you read the note, Francis, you should know there is a hidden message in it. The word, *prepare*, tells me he knows the name of the murderer."

"What good news, Father!" said Francis, smiling. "So, you agreed to use that word in the event the note fell into the murderer's hands." He placed Olivier's note on the cut tree trunk that he used for a table.

"Exactly. It was Olivier's idea. He thought of it when we were seeking ways to protect those who helped him in Natchez. After the fiend's murders in Mosquito Creek, we worried he might kill anyone suspected of assisting the search for his identity."

"Yes, of course. A necessary precaution to take."

Antonio nodded. "However, it appears Olivier has taken another precaution that has not helped us end this massacre of innocent people. Unless I have misread his message."

"What precaution is that, Father?"

"Olivier did not give us the name of the murderer in his message. At least, I don't think he did from my reading of it. I need other eyes to read it, younger eyes, so I would like you to look it over, Francis. Tell me if a name or even a hint of one is hidden somewhere in the note."

Francis picked up the note and read it again. He read it a second time, but much more slowly. He shook his head and handed the note to Antonio.

"If there's a hidden message in the note, I don't see it."

Exasperated, Antonio sighed loudly. "I don't understand it. Why in God's name would Olivier tell me he knows the murderer's name *without* telling me what it is?"

"I can offer two possible explanations, Father." Francis waited for Antonio's nod before continuing. "One would be his fear the murderer's status here in New Orleans would prevent his arrest unless Olivier were here to provide the magistrate with the needed proof of his guilt. The murderer is obviously a man of means – his costly clothing and horse tell us that and he will not be easily arrested. The second would be a premature accusation or attempt of arrest might give the murderer sufficient time to escape the city and even the colony. There may be any number of other explanations, but these two stand out in my mind."

"Good thinking, Francis. You are quite right. There may well be many explanations for Olivier's decision to omit the murderer's name from his note to me. I was too quick to fault him. I should have known better. Thank you, my son." He patted the young priest's hand.

Antonio stood up and entered Santa María by himself. He went to the altar and kneeled down to pray. A few minutes later, after crossing himself, he left the church, smiled at Francis and walked back to the cathedral.

"We think he is on his way to New Orleans." Francis was sitting on María Adela's porch after dinner as the sun set in the west. It was a cloudless evening and a cool breeze blew over the river and reached the porch. One of the two chimes hanging from the overhanging roof tinkled lightly. Francis sipped a citrus drink, while María Adela drank brandy.

"Do you think Olivier is returning by ship despite all the debris in the river?" She asked, looking down at a schooner sailing toward the Gulf. Francis had told her about his message, but omitted the information about the murderer.

"I don't know. A number of ships now have arrived carrying passengers, but he hasn't been on them. I can't imagine he would journey overland so soon after leaving his sick bed. I have heard that pneumonia is quite a debilitating illness and those who survive it feel weak for days if not weeks afterwards." Francis sipped his drink.

"I've heard the same. I must say I worry about him whatever way he travels and not only because of his state of being after his sickness."

"You mean because of the murderer's recognition of his danger to him."

"Exactly. The bold attack on San Felipe Street showed us he was worried about Olivier's involvement in the investigation. That's why, I urged him *not* to leave the city. It's obvious he would be more vulnerable to an attack outside the walls than inside. But he ignored my advice and left anyway alone without anyone accompanying him and with a useless arm. God help him if the murderer makes another attempt on his life. Of course, it's well known how stubborn men are and sometimes *stupidly* stubborn." María Adela pressed a handkerchief to her tearful eyes. "Forgive me, Father, but I have recently lost my oldest friend, Aveline Dumont, and I now fear the loss of Olivier."

"I understand Madame Boudreaux. I also fear for Father Olivier." Francis was surprised to hear her refer to the pastor of Santa María as *Olivier* without his proper title, but he assumed her worry about him was the reason for it.

"Well, there's nothing to be done about it now. We can only hope he returns to town in the next few days." María Adela wiped her eyes. "I'm sure there's much yet to be done at Santa María before Holy Week."

"There is and we also have four baptisms and three marriages to perform."

"What about the marriage of Honorè and Ana Luisa?"

"They are to be married sometime in the week before Palm Sunday. As you know, they want Father Olivier to perform the marriage and hope he will return to Santa María in time to do it. They agreed, albeit reluctantly, to have the pastor marry them if Father Olivier is delayed beyond the fourteenth of April. Father Antonio warned them if their marriage is not performed before Palm Sunday, they will have to wait until after Holy Week."

"So, everyone is waiting for Olivier. Those who appreciate him and those who do not."

"Are you referring to the murderer in the latter group?" Francis did not comment, but it bothered him that María Adela again spoke of the pastor as *Olivier* rather than Father Olivier. He frowned, thinking it was much too familiar and improper of her.

"No, though he certainly belongs in that group as well as the bishop." She smiled seeing Francis raise his eyebrows. "Every parishioner in town knows the bishop's opinion of Olivier. After all, he shouted it out in the cathedral, didn't he? The bishop shouted it in the middle of the afternoon when a number of parishioners were in the cathedral for confession and prayer. You surely don't think what he said to him stayed in the church, do you?"

"Of course not." Francis knew there was nothing he could say to contradict her.

"No, Father, I was thinking of another of his foolish critics – *Jean Bertin!* I heard one of his rants yesterday afternoon while visiting Paulette and the girls. In a rage, he went on and on complaining about the arrogant priests and unappreciative Church. Paulette apologized for his outburst and said he vents his spleen, at least every other day when he comes home. She usually takes the children outside until his fury is spent. I can't imagine how many times Charles Laroux has heard his rants."

"I assume his complaints concern the money he donated to the renovation of Santa María and the unfinished investigation of the murder of his sons."

"That's why he's furious with Olivier … Father Olivier." María Adela had seen Francis frown each time she neglected to use the priest's title. "He's also incensed by what he considers to be the flagrant disrespect both Father Olivier and the parish pastor have shown him. He claims they have insulted and even mocked him instead of thanking him for the generous contributions he and his family have made to the Church over the years. 'They take the Dumont generosity for granted,' he said, 'and show too little appreciation.'"

"I can't imagine either of them disrespecting Monsieur Dumont in any way. They would never 'kill the golden goose' as they say. The only problem I know they have with him concerns the agreement he made with Father Olivier. Jean Bertin apparently had some expectations which were not in the agreement. The pastor showed him the agreement made with Father Olivier, but it did not satisfy him. Father Olivier, who has an extraordinary memory as you well know, wrote down every word of the agreement and gave it to Father Antonio for his approval. He gave it to the pastor the day following his meeting with Monsieur Dumont."

María Adela nodded her head knowingly. "That explains it, Father. *Disrespect* to Jean Bertin means they disagreed with him. He's accustomed to everyone's acceptance of everything he says and does. With the exception of his mother in the past and, occasionally, Charles Laroux, no one else would dare to contradict or disagree with him. Even Paulette avoids provoking him, though she ignores most of his demands, especially if it involves the girls."

"Is that why he said they insulted him?"

"Probably. I would guess they either read or showed him the agreement he had accepted. Even if unsigned, it was available as a written agreement Jean Bertin could not dispute. On the contrary, he had to admit it did not include what he assumed and *wanted to* be in it. So, to him, a man who sees himself as superior to everyone else, he was insulted."

"I see." Francis nodded, recalling Father Antonio's criticism of Jean Bertin as "utterly consumed with his own needs."

"He was quite selfish as a child and has remained that way as an adult. His own mother admitted that to me. She had hoped he would leave such behavior behind him when a man ... but, instead, it worsened." María Adela saw Francis grimace and a frown form on his brow. "Ah, so you've also had an unpleasant meeting with Jean Bertin, haven't you, Father?"

For a few seconds, Francis hesitated to respond and, then, seeing her knowing smile, he nodded. "Yes, it happened two days ago in the morning. Jean Bertin arrived at Santa María and rudely interrupted a baby's baptism I was performing. Impatient to talk to me, he strode nosily up and down the aisle waiting for it to end. He deliberately struck his leather heels on the stone floor to make as much noise as possible. The angry father finally ordered him out of the church and threatened to strike him if he didn't leave. His rudeness continued as soon as the couple left and he re-entered the church. Without even a polite greeting or an apology for interrupting the baptism, Jean Bertin demanded to know where *that Dominican* had gone. And, then, when I courteously told him to ask the parish pastor, he snorted derisively and sneered, 'Spoken like an obedient Church minion. You're all the same.'"

"That's how he behaves when his demands aren't met immediately."

Francis nodded. "He stood in the center aisle waving his arms around the church. 'You know,' he said, 'I'm the one who paid for all these improvements here, but I suppose that means nothing now to you or that arrogant Dominican."

"I hope you told him an act of Christian charity does not require acknowledgement."

"I did not respond, knowing whatever I said wouldn't appease the man. Instead, I looked away and saw Charles Laroux standing silently in the doorway. He apparently had accompanied Jean Bertin to Santa María and had just entered the church. Laroux stood there with another man – a large man whom I assume was Monsieur Dumont's driver."

"Yes, that's Tristan Surette. Both Laroux and Surette accompany Jean Bertin any time he leaves New Orleans, which is infrequent. He barely escaped mauling by a black bear as a boy in the woods and has tried to avoid any trips outside of the city as a consequence. Laroux conducts all of the out-of-town business. Did Laroux say anything?"

"No, but to my surprise, he shook his head and frowned. I think, he was embarrassed by his uncle's rude behavior."

"I'm not surprised." María Adela sighed. "I'm sure Jean Bertin has embarrassed him any number of times. Was that the end of the meeting?"

"Yes, except for Jean Bertin's final remarks. As I turned back to face him, he said, 'You there, monk! How dare you look away when I'm talking to you? I do not abide such disrespect! Do you hear me, monk?' He banged his walking stick on the bench nearest him and then left, striking all the benches he passed on the way out of the church."

Francis talked to María Adela until the Cathedral bells

rang at eight o'clock. He then left as a damp mist settled over the city. Too tired to play his usual game of checkers with Gervaise, he stopped briefly by Madame Lefevre's house to apologize to the boy before continuing on his way to the priests' residence. He arrived there a little before nine o'clock and was asleep fifteen minutes later.

Jean-Jacques, smiling broadly, clapped his hands in delight. He now had information that would surely please his brother. It might even make up for his collapse and failure to follow the priest in town. There was no doubt about it, the information would make up for it and then some. Jean-Jacques pictured Louis nodding his head as he told him about the priest and, when finished, saying, "Well done, Jean-Jacques, well done!" He might even give him a bonus for it.

He had acquired the information on his own, without anyone telling him how to do it. He smiled again. It was with his cleverness that the information was known. His brother Louis had nothing to do with it and he should definitely give him a sizeable bonus.

As instructed, he had gone to the city dock to look for the owner of the *Good Samaritan*. Jean-Jacques never saw the ship, but after spending half a morning talking to the layabouts there, he learned the man's name. An old peg-legged sailor named Horace told him Timothy Mitchell owned the *Good Samaritan*. "It's a sound little sloop," he had said. On his own, Jean-Jacques then found out that Timothy Mitchell lived several miles south of Natchez on the east side of the Mississippi River.

He heard about Mitchell from a muscular dock worker called Bigbreed, who toiled from dawn to dusk loading and unloading ships at the dock. Bigbreed, the son of an

English colonist and an Indian mother, spoke to Jean-Jacques when there was a brief pause between loading jobs. After three drinks from Jean-Jacques' flask, he told him Timothy Mitchell was a wealthy farmer who grew cotton, Indian corn and tobacco on bottom land along the river.

When Bigbreed went back to work, another dock worker named Benjamin told him more about Mitchell. Most of what he knew concerned the farmer's comely wife who was rumored to flirt with other men; it was said she gave them the *big eyes*, when her husband's back was turned. Benjamin also told Jean-Jacques about the sick priest taken aboard the *Good Samaritan*. He said the farmer took the priest to his plantation, where it was said he had almost died. According to Benjamin, a physician from Natchez saved the priest's life by a timely treatment of blood-letting and purging (emptying the bowels). He did not know the physician's name.

Jean-Jacques then asked about town and learned that Doctor Standish was the physician who treated the sick south of the city. Once a week, he took his carriage down along the river to see sick people whose families sent riders to Natchez to request his visits. It was well known in town that Standish only visited the homes of patients who could afford his costly charges.

Jean-Jacques went to see Doctor Standish, claiming he suffered from intense back pain. Standish listened to his heart, looked into his eyes and ears, thumped his back in several places and gave him a foul smelling salve for his pain. While engaged in his examination, the talkative doctor also told him all he needed to know about the priest's physical state as well as his travel plans. Jean Jacques only had to mention that he heard the physician had saved a priest's life and Standish spent twenty minutes giving him a detailed account of the event. Jean-Jacques left the doctor's office free of pain and most of the silver coins in his pocket.

The murderer heard about Olivier's recovery at Mitchell's farm two days later. He also heard the priest was traveling overland to New Orleans. Smiling, he clapped his hands loudly after reading the message from Parsall. "Calm! Be calm!" he said to his big stallion, when the horse initially shied away from him. "Everything is quite all right, yes, *quite* all right."

He mounted his horse, still smiling. The troublesome priest was finally within his grasp. Far away from New Orleans, he should be easy to kill. Parsall had carried out his mission perfectly. "Perhaps, he will be spared after all," he thought. "One less to take to the inlet."

He sat in the saddle, thinking about the news he had received. "So, the priest is coming by land. Splendid!" he said aloud, seeing a horseman approaching a block away. He nodded to the rider and continued to think about Olivier's return to New Orleans as the man went by him. "If the Dominican had decided to sail to New Orleans, it would have been much harder to kill him," he thought, "It would have been possible, but with many risks. Now, that he intends to come overland, the risks will be fewer and the opportunities many."

Planning how the priest could be intercepted along the way, he let the horse trot leisurely toward his office. His first concern was to make certain he would be informed if Olivier changed his mind and sailed to New Orleans. Parsall assured him he would be immediately informed in that eventuality, but the possibility still concerned him. Parsall also said the flooded Mississippi was still turbulent and, with rain continuing to fall up river, it was unlikely passengers would be aboard most ships sailing to New Orleans. The murderer heard a similar appraisal of the river's turbulence from a ship's captain that day at the city dock. But, whether Olivier traveled by horse or ship, he was confident Parsall would inform him in time to waylay the priest en route.

The Natchez agent was within sight of Mitchell's house and would notify him as soon as he was certain of Olivier's movements. If the priest was traveling overland, he would ride south, if by sea, he would go north to board a ship in Natchez. Once his route was known, a messenger would be immediately sent to New Orleans on the fastest ship available.

The murderer next considered the likely possibility that the clever priest would suspect he was in danger. If so, he would protect himself in some way – probably with a pistol. But pistols were heavy and hard to handle at an unexpected moment. A pistol would be even harder to use without the help of his left arm, which was bandaged and of limited use riding a horse or steering a carriage. Though the priest was right-handed, that hand would be in engaged holding the reins of a horse as he rode along a road. In such an instance, he would be unable to take his hand from the reins and withdraw an unwieldy pistol from a pocket or holster in time to defend himself. The problem would be same whether he was riding a horse or steering a carriage.

The murderer shook his head from side to side. It was unlikely that Olivier would carry a pistol to protect himself. An accompanying guard was more probable – an armed man, someone from Mitchell's plantation. No one else was available, except in Natchez and, according to what Parsall told him, the priest was planning to leave forthwith before any such arrangements could be made. Therefore, the only man available to him would be one from Mitchell's plantation. He would have to serve the priest as his guard and caretaker. Since Olivier was still recovering from pneumonia, he needed help as well as protection no matter which way he decided to travel. The murderer smiled, wondering what lout or louts Olivier would find to guard him among the inept overseers and field slaves on the plantation.

"The priest is doomed," he said quietly to himself as his horse slowed to a walk near his house. "It's of no matter who accompanies him, he's on his way to death."

CHAPTER FOURTEEN

New Orleans and Galvez: March 31 – April 1, 1800

At noon, on Monday, Father Antonio went to the office of Attorney Sebastián Gutiérrez Carrera, to meet the magistrate. The two-story office building stood on the southwest corner of Borbón and Santa Ana Streets. Gutiérrez Carrera was an elderly lawyer, whose general practice over the last five years had been reduced to real estate law. The attorney greeted the pastor and magistrate, who arrived almost simultaneously, and then left for a midday nap at home. The two officials selected the lawyer's office as a meeting place since neither of them would meet in the other man's office. To do so would have suggested one of them was superior to the other. After a day and a half exchanging messages with unacceptable meeting locations, the two men finally agreed to a compromise. Their meeting would take place in the office of a Spaniard who was a generous donor to the cathedral. They met on the last day of March.

During the message exchange, they also agreed their discussion would only concern the return of Olivier to New Orleans. Their long-standing dispute over the continuing existence of the gambling dens and houses of prostitution in the city would not be mentioned at the meeting. Though the two officials had little appreciation for each other, their concern for Olivier's safety brought them together to protect him as he traveled from the Natchez to New Orleans. Antonio went to the meeting to persuade the magistrate to send his men north to guard Olivier. Castañedo met Antonio to learn the route of the Dominican's journey to New Orleans. He had also received a note from Olivier telling him of his trip, but his message offered no other information.

Seated across from Castañedo in the attorney's office, Antonio told him about Olivier's letter. He related what Olivier had written about his illness and his planned trip to New Orleans, but he did not tell him about the hidden message in the letter or what it meant. The pastor, like most of the French colonists in New Orleans, did not trust the Spanish magistrate. He doubted his competence and hesitated telling him anything that might endanger Olivier's life. The pastor thought Castañedo had mishandled the scheme to capture or kill the murderer at Mosquito Creek. He also blamed him for the death of the Rafael Portillo, the sentry killed by the murderer at the Villièrs house. Now, Antonio feared if he told Castañedo that Olivier knew the identity of the murderer, the magistrate might let the information slip out of his office to be spread about town. In that event, it would soon reach the ears of the murderer and he would certainly intensify his efforts to kill him. Olivier, incapacitated by his wounded arm and the weakness following his illness, was already an easy mark for the murderer.

Worried about such a possibility, Antonio sighed loudly as he looked at Castañedo. "My concern is that the murderer will attempt to kill Olivier as he journeys to New

Orleans. He has already tried once here in town and Olivier will be much more vulnerable on the roads through the northern forests."

Castañedo frowned. "Father Olivier is traveling by land rather than by water?"

"It appears that way. The spring rains have so flooded the river that most vessels sailing south are not taking passengers aboard. A week or so ago, a woman and her child standing on the deck of a schooner fell overboard and drowned when her ship struck a partially submerged log in the river. Since that accident, no ship captain will take the risk of boarding passengers."

Castañedo nodded. "I know of the accident. Is Father Olivier well enough to make that long journey? It's 175 some miles from Natchez to New Orleans and will take at least a week by carriage. After suffering from pneumonia I can't imagine him riding a horse that far. There's also his left arm which is all but useless after the stabbing."

Antonio nodded. "Exactamente. I don't know the state of his health, but I can only hope he is feeling strong enough to make the journey. Olivier is headstrong, however, and no matter his strength I'm sure he is on his way. My concern, therefore, is the possibility of the murderer waylaying him somewhere on the roads between Natchez and New Orleans. I assume Olivier is traveling by carriage and I hope, at least, one able man accompanies him. A man who is strong of arm and carries a pistol and sword."

"That would be my hope as well. We already know of the murderer's strength. Let's not forget he easily overpowered Charles Laroux, a strong young man himself."

"Indeed." Antonio frowned, thinking he did not need to be reminded of how vulnerable Olivier would be if the murderer attacked him.

"There's another problem that concerns me. If Father Olivier is coming overland as you expect, how and where will he procure a horse and carriage? There's also the question of where he will find a man experienced in the use of arms?"

Antonio frowned again. "He has both English and Spanish coins in sufficient number to purchase whatever he needs – whether a horse and carriage or an armed man to accompany and guard him. It is not Olivier's state of being or means of travel that concerns me. Rather it's how he can be located on the roads from Natchez and guarded against a murderous attack. That's my concern, Magistrate! So, what do *you* suggest?" Annoyed, Antonio spoke sharply and there was a distinct challenge in his question.

Castañedo did not like the pastor's tone of voice, but he decided to overlook it. He liked Olivier and would not allow what he perceived to be the pastor's disrespect to affect his decision to help the priest. He paused, staring hard at Antonio, and then answered him calmly without any of the irritation he felt. He spoke in a soft voice only a little above a whisper.

"I'll immediately send two men to Baton Rouge and, if they don't meet Father Olivier on the road there, they will continue northward on the river road to Natchez. The men will be out of uniform so no one will report them as foreign intruders from Louisiana. Two additional men will be dispatched to Galvez. There is a rutted farmers' road from Galvez that bypasses Baton Rouge and meets the river road north of the city. The road has much less traffic, but runs through a thick woods where travelers can be easily waylaid. For years it has been a site where brigands have set upon carriages and riders alike. So, there are two roads where Father Olivier can be attacked in Louisiana, though one is more perilous than the other. Con la ayuda de Dios (with God's help) Father Olivier will be met by one of the pairs of men before such an attack takes place."

Antonio now regretted his sharp tone of voice when speaking to Castañedo. Even though the magistrate had not known Olivier was traveling by land, it was obvious he already had made plans for that possibility. The pastor nodded, smiling in approval, and leaned forward to speak.

"Those plans appear to be exactly what are needed at this time. Thank you, Magistrate, for your assistance."

Castañedo nodded, noting that the pastor had changed his tone of voice and even thanked him. It surprised and pleased him. He raised his forefinger. "Please excuse me, Father Antonio, I want to start the men north immediately. He rose from his chair and left the room.

Antonio heard him open the outside door of the building and shout to an aide outside who had accompanied him to the attorney's office. He could not hear what was said, but assumed the magistrate had given his aide instructions regarding the men to be sent to meet Olivier. Antonio shook his head, again regretting how he spoken to Castañedo.

"Forgive me, God," he prayed, "for my arrogance and intolerance." Instead of the love of God, Antonio knew he had shown Castañedo his meanness and misjudged his good intentions. This was the second instance of his poor judgement recently. Antonio frowned, knowing he had critically misjudged Olivier as well.

Castañedo returned and resumed his seat, facing Antonio. "I have dispatched four armed men to meet Father Olivier. The two riding to Baton Rouge will leave later this afternoon. The men riding to Galvez will leave at first light. I had hoped both would be departing immediately, but my aide informs me that our best horses need to be shod."

"I understand. Thank you again, Magistrate." Antonio bowed his head.

"Por nada. Do you have any notion when Father Olivier left the Natchez area?"

"Unfortunately, no! His letter was dated March twenty-fourth and he said he would leave as soon as the weather improved. Is there any news of the weather up river?"

Castañedo made a face. "I've heard the heavy showers have ended, but light rain is still everywhere along the Mississippi River."

"Must we then assume the light rain is also falling on the river road south of Natchez?"

"Yes, the entire river valley suffers the same weather."

"I see." Antonio smiled and spoke softly, looking at Castañedo. "Well, then, I assume Olivier is already on his way to New Orleans. Knowing him as I do, I'm sure he left as soon as the heavy rains ended. He would be too impatient to wait for the rain to stop completely. I'm certain he wants to return to Santa María before Holy Week, which begins this year on Monday, the seventh of April." Antonio also knew Olivier would be anxious to see the murderer arrested before he could escape from the city.

Castañedo nodded, pleased to see the pastor's respectful manner. "So, Father, we must now try to discover the day of his departure. Did he say anything about the state of his health in his letter? It would help to know if he was still in bed or on his feet."

Recalling the letter's wording, Antonio placed a finger on his lips. "Ah, yes, Olivier said he was 'through the ordeal of pneumonia.'"

"That sounds like he was on his feet or at least near the end of his illness."

Antonio shook his head from side to side. "No, I think not. I now recall Olivier was not the writer of the letter. He said another person was writing his words because he suffered from a trembling hand. From the penmanship on the letter, I suspect the writer was a woman."

"So, that probably means Father Olivier still was bedridden at least part of the day."

Antonio nodded. "I would think so, Magistrate."

"I don't know how long it usually takes to recovery from pneumonia, if such information is known, but I think he would not be ready to take to the road for another week. There's also his wounded shoulder which surely adds to his weakness. What do you think, Father?"

"As I said earlier, I think Olivier is already on the way here. While certainly not robust, he is a determined, if not a stubborn man. My father would have said Olivier has a paving stone for a head." Antonio smiled, recalling the bishop's report of his confrontation with Olivier.

Castañedo grinned. "I like that image of Olivier … Father Olivier. Well then, let's try to determine when he left the Natchez area and where he might be today. The heavy rain ended on the twenty-sixth of the month; that's two days after he wrote to you. So, what do we think a very intelligent man with a 'paving stone for a head' would do? Would he leave the first day after the rain abated or would he wait another day to make sure the heavy rain had actually stopped?"

Antonio shook his head. "That's the question, isn't it? I don't know the answer, but to be best prepared let's assume Olivier left the twenty-seventh."

Castañedo smiled. "That's my thinking too. Now, we need to consider where he might be today on this last day of March. I think he might be either in Baton Rouge or on the bypass road to Galvez by now. Of course, he might have been slowed by bad roads; it's likely the long period of rain damaged the roads. It's also possible other incidents might well have delayed his journey. Wherever he is now, we must hope my men reach him before the murderer."

"Si, con la ayuda de Dios (Yes, with God's help)!" Antonio exhaled his breath loudly. "How long will it take your men to reach him if he has arrived at one of those destinations?"

"I'm hoping they'll reach him in less than two days, Father. The men will be riding our best horses and that's why we are making sure they have new shoes. The roads are poor and the rains have made them even worse. Daylight riding is dangerous and night riding is impossible."

"I understand, Magistrate. I shall pray for their safe journey and, of course, for Olivier as well." Antonio stood to leave. "I am most appreciative of all your effort."

Castañedo also stood and nodded. "Por nada. I will immediately notify you when my men meet Father Olivier."

"Gracias, Magistrate." Antonio stood facing Castañedo.

"Father, there is one bit of information I want to share with you. It's something that affects both of us."

"Oh, what is it?" Antonio frowned, worried about what Castañedo had left for last.

Castañedo sighed. "The governor informed me yesterday that Monsieur Dumont spoke to him and complained about us – both you and me. He accused us of indifference in regard to the murderous attacks on his family. Dumont told the governor that we have been unhelpful, if not apathetic, to the murders of his sons, the murderous attack on his nephew and the attempt to poison his entire family."

"Dieu m'aide, cet homme sera la mort de moi (God help me, that man will be the death of me) No matter what's been done for him it's never enough. He's insatiable!"

"Indeed. We have the same impression of him. No matter what actions we have taken to find the murderer, he ignores or criticizes them to everyone he meets, loudly proclaiming we are incompetent. Instead of meeting with me to discuss his concerns, he refuses to speak to me. We have found more success speaking to his nephew, Charles Laroux. A reasonable and thoughtful man, though a Protestant."

"I'm not surprised. What did the governor say about Dumont's complaint?"

"He told me to contact Monsieur Dumont and try to appease him. His prominence here in New Orleans is obviously his reason." Castañedo grimaced. "The governor, of course, knows of our efforts in pursuit of the murderer, but wants me to satisfy the man somehow so he doesn't continue to bother him. He also told me Bishop Meléndez would be informed of his complaint against you. I'm sincerely sorry, Father, to be the bearer of such information."

Antonio nodded. "Don't be concerned, Magistrate. Thank you for telling me."

"Adiós, Padre."

"Adiós, Magistrado, gracias." Antonio squeezed Castañedo's hand as he shook it.

Olivier left the Mitchells' farm at first light on March twenty-seventh. It was a cold, misty morning with sleet falling and a thin layer of snow on the ground. Bundled up in heavy woolen coats over their nightclothes. Timothy, Elizabeth and their son, eight-year-old Jonathon, waved to him from the open door of their house. They stood there until the wagon disappeared into the trees bordering the rutted track. The track ran two hundred and fifty yards to the main road that extended south along the Mississippi River from Natchez to Baton Rouge.

Two men accompanied Olivier on his journey. One was the young man who had helped the priest when he collapsed on the *Concordia* and carried him to the *Good Samaritan.* His name was Emile LeClerc and he readily accepted Olivier's invitation to travel with him. The long trip to New Orleans included a brief stop in Baton Rouge, the town where he lived and worked as a blacksmith's apprentice. The other man was William Mitchell, Timothy's uncle and co-owner of the farm. William planned to accompany Olivier to New Orleans and then immediately return home in time for the spring planting.

LeClerc had not intended to stay at the Mitchell's farm. It had happened accidentally. In the course of carrying Olivier from the *Concordia* to the *Good Samaritan*, he fell on the deck of the smaller sloop and had been unable to re-board the schooner. Holding the unconscious priest under the arms, the strong-armed blacksmith leaned over the ship's side to lower him to Timothy Mitchell. He had no sooner released Olivier into Mitchell's hands, when the *Concordia* abruptly changed course. The sudden movement of the schooner threw him over the side and down on the sloop's deck barely missing Timothy Mitchell. LeClerc landed unhurt on a pile of sails, but he could not return to the *Concordia*. The two ships, which earlier had been within a yard of each other, had moved too far apart. Left stranded on the *Good Samaritan*, he accompanied Mitchell and his son to their farm.

William Mitchell volunteered to take Olivier to New Orleans, when he and his nephew realized the priest would need help to make the trip. They talked about his condition the first day the sick man got out of bed. He stood, but was obviously very weak. With his wounded arm and weakness from pneumonia, they knew Olivier could not ride a horse or even steer a carriage for the length of time the journey would take. A moment later, after seeing the sick man's obvious struggle to stay erect, William decided he would be the one to go with Olivier. Although he was forty-six and fifteen years older than Timothy, he convinced his nephew that his army experience during the war made him the logical one to accompany the priest.

Still hale and hardy, the gray-haired man spoke forcefully to his nephew. "Keep in mind, Timothy, in the event of brigands attacking the wagon on the roads, I'm the only one here at the farm who has experience with a pistol and sword. I also can be spared for a fortnight or so, but you cannot with your many responsibilities. Hopefully, I'll be back by Easter."

The men rode in a roofed-wagon that Timothy had converted from an ordinary eight-foot long farm wagon. It was designed principally to carry farm supplies rather than passengers, but a removable canvas roof was added to the horse drawn vehicle along with benches for riders when needed. The roof was rounded and supported by wooden hoops that had been steamed and bent into shape so their ends fit into iron brackets installed on the sides of the wagon. The sheet of canvas was stretched over the hoops to cover the entire wagon except for openings in the front and rear. The openings provided entry and exit access and, in front, a place to seat the driver of the wagon. In the rear, the opening usually remained open to let light into the interior.

The covered wagon lacked amenities of any kind for passengers. There were only two wooden benches and neither had padding. The driver sat on the bench in front and, if passengers rode in the wagon, they sat on the one behind him. Timothy made sure the second bench could be easily removed if additional space was needed behind the benches. With the second bench in place, the wagon had twenty square feet of floor space, which usually was enough to carry farm products as well as building supplies and imported goods purchased in Natchez. Extra storage space was also available inside the benches which actually were chests with removable lids.

The three men left the farm with William Mitchell driving the wagon. LeClerc sat behind him and Olivier lay on the blanket-softened floor with bear furs over him. The day was cold and misty with intermittent rain, sleet and snow. Despite the weather, the road south to Baton Rouge was surprisingly smooth and, even with four rest stops where the two horses were fed and given water, the wagon covered twenty-three miles the first day. They finally stopped for the night at five o'clock in the afternoon. Unable to start a fire in the continuing rain, they ate cold food in their tent. Without much else to do in the closed tent, they went to sleep soon afterward.

The next three days on the road passed without incident. They rode beneath cloudy skies that now and then produced a light rain and mist. The mist made it difficult to see the road ahead and the carriage bounced about as its wheels rolled into holes and struck stones along their way. Mitchell and LeClerc shared the driving. Wrapped up in canvas, they remained dry in the rain as the carriage proceeding south along the river.

During the day, Olivier rested on a pile of furs in the space behind the benches. With the carriage rolling over the uneven and rock littered road, it was impossible for him to sleep for any length of time. At night, in a tent they all shared, he slept deeply sometimes as many as ten hours without awakening. Day or night, Olivier never felt the rain inside the covered wagon,

Though the temperature dropped to near freezing on the first night of their journey, they slept comfortably under furs. They also ate well. Elizabeth Mitchell sent them on their way with a roasted leg of pork, two pounds of boiled venison, a roast pheasant, a pound of sage cheese and three breads she baked the night before they left the farm. They drank Pekoe tea, hard cider and now and then drams of rum from a quart bottle William brought with him. He also brought his oak pipe and tobacco for the times they stopped for the horses or after meals. Elizabeth packed everything, including their eating utensils, pans and plates, in the two bench chests.

By the third afternoon on the road, Olivier was feeling stronger. While not restored to his normal state of health, he no longer needed to sleep so many hours each night. For the first time since he had walked aboard the *Concordia*, he left the carriage and strolled about whenever they stopped to feed the horses or give them water. At sunset that afternoon, as Mitchell prepared the evening meal, he was even able to help LeClerc put up their tent and carry all the supplies inside. Afterwards, Olivier collected several piles of firewood and that night he sat by the fire with them until nine o'clock. With the help of his translations, they shared stories of their youthful follies.

Early in the morning on the fifth day the wagon's right front wheel broke after striking a sharp stone. Mitchell was steering at the time and, moving his horses closer to the right edge of the road to give a passing carriage more space, he missed seeing the rock until he heard the iron tire strike it. The sound of the iron tire striking the stone was instantly followed by the wagon's tilt to the right. He swore loudly when he jumped to the ground and saw the wheel. LeClerc and Olivier, instantly following him, climbed down from the wagon and looked at the broken wheel. The wooden rim was split and three of the spokes stuck out of the wheel.

"How close are we to Baton Rouge?" Mitchell asked LeClerc. He spoke slowly, hoping the Acadian would understand the few English words in his question.

LeClerc looked at Olivier and then spoke to him at length in French. Olivier replied and they continued to talk for a few minutes. Mitchell heard them mention Baton Rouge, Galvez and New Orleans, but the rest of their words were unknown to him. Finally, Olivier turned to him.

"Emile says it's ten miles to Baton Rouge, but he thinks he can get another wheel from a farmer whose house is near here. He offers to ride there to see if the farmer will help us."

"Most of us up north have extra wagon wheels. What about here in Louisiana?"

Olivier nodded. "It's the same here. LeClerc thinks the

farmer must have extra wheels and will sell one to us. He expects the man, an Acadian like LeClerc, will take the time to bring it in his wagon. Acadians are known to be very helpful of each other."

Mitchell sighed loudly. "Tell him to do it. I should have foreseen the loss of a wheel and brought an extra one with us."

They watched LeClerc kneel and use the length of his hands to measure the diameter of the wheel. He then quickly unhitched one of the horses from the carriage and, without a stool or request for help, leaped up on the big horse's back. LeClerc smiled at their surprised looks, tipped his hat and urged the horse south toward Baton Rouge.

When LeClerc had ridden away, the two men sat on a downed pine tree that lay along the road across from where their stalled wagon stood. Mitchell smoked his pipe while they talked. The rain stopped during the night and the sun broke through the clouds as they walked across the road to the tree. Five riders passed them going north and, one by one at different intervals, they all stopped to inquire if they could assist them. Each of the riders was thanked for his concern and told a new wheel was on the way. An elegant black carriage, however, went past without a pause and the black-cloaked driver sitting outside did not even look in their direction.

While waiting for LeClerc's return, they discussed the journey ahead of them. Mitchell showed Olivier a hand-drawn sketch he had made from an old army map. The sketch included mileage estimates between Natchez and Baton Rouge and Baton Rouge and New Orleans. The number 100 was written between the first two cities and 80 - 90 between the second two cities.

"I made the sketch the night before we left the farm," said Mitchell, looking up from the drawing. "I have the original map from my time in the war. It's one of the few mementos I have from my youth. I was seventeen when

I fought with General Daniel Morgan's marksman in the Carolinas." He sighed. "It was a long time ago."

"It was." Olivier nodded. "I was a youth living in France at the time. Everyone around me knew about the war and wanted the colonies to be victorious."

Mitchell smiled. "As you know, the French were our allies against the English. It's said we might not have won the war without France's help."

Olivier frowned. "Unfortunately, the France of that time is gone, perhaps forever. In its stead is a godless society with a reckless general leading the foolish people from one disastrous war to another."

Mitchell did not reply, thinking there was little difference between the wars of Napoleon and those of the French kings who preceded him. Instead, he looked down at the map. "Well, it appears that our journey is half over and we have about ninety miles to go to New Orleans."

Olivier nodded. "So it seems if we continue to Baton Rouge and take the main road east toward New Orleans. However, LeClerc said there's a shorter route that bypasses Baton Rouge and proceeds southeast through the pine forests to Galvez. He said it meets this road a couple of miles up ahead. LeClerc described the road as the hypotenuse of the triangle connecting Baton Rouge and Galvez. Its surface is rough in places, but shorter than the main road."

Mitchell thought for a moment and turned to Olivier. "I'm willing to try it if you think you can stand the bouncing about. As you know, the carriage is missing springs."

LeClerc returned three hours later, riding in an old farm wagon. He was accompanied by André Durant, a big, broad-shouldered Acadian, who had long gray hair tied behind his head. Durant spoke less English than LeClerc, but with Olivier's help, introductions were courteously made and greetings exchanged. Mitchell bought the new wheel from Durant and, with LeClerc's help, they emptied the tilted wagon. Then, while the Acadians held up the tilted side, he removed the broken wheel and installed the new one in its place.

It was after one o'clock when the work was done and their possessions were once again loaded inside. They stood outside in the warm sun, drinking from William Mitchell's bottle of rum. Each of the men took a stiff drink from the bottle as it was passed around and then another at his urging. Olivier, who stood last in line, took a third swallow before he stoppered the bottle.

A half-hour later, Mitchell's covered wagon was moving south again. Durant followed with LeClerc sitting beside him in the farm wagon. They parted company at the by-pass road as Mitchell turned his horses southeast toward Galvez. LeClerc watched the covered wagon as it rolled away and disappeared into a dip in the road surrounded by pine trees.

Mitchell and Olivier moved quickly the first hour and a half on the bypass road. Except for occasional creases, pitted areas and easily avoided rocks on the road's surface, their wagon trundled along as if on a city street. Though they rode through a seemingly impenetrable forest with tree branches leaning across the narrow road, the sun's rays still reached them, providing unexpected light and warmth.

The smooth surface ended abruptly at a two-foot wide gully made by the week of heavy rain. Partially filling the gully with stones and tree branches, they moved out again, but much slower than their earlier pace. The roadway was now uneven, littered with rocks of all sizes and shapes and often obstructed by downed tree limbs or large stones which had to be pushed aside. There also were washed out areas that required leveling and gaping holes to be filled. Worst of all, they encountered sinking sands in several places along the road. When their wagon almost rolled into the one, Mitchell left the driving to Olivier and walked ahead of the horses to look for others. He cleared their path of tree debris as he went.

No carriages or wagons passed them moving in either direction, but an occasional rider rode by heading east. They spoke briefly about the state of the road and then went of their way. Altogether they met six horsemen that day. Only two of them, a father and his son, were riding west from Galvez. The older man, a bald, bearded man, told them the roadway would be better some three hours ahead. He suggested that they proceed another couple of hours and, after a good night's sleep, go on to Galvez the next day.

"If you leave at first light, you should arrive there no later than one in the afternoon." The man told them. "Don't eat in any of the taverns in town. Instead, look for Mama Mellete's house – everyone in town knows where it's at and you'll eat some food you won't ever forget!"

They stopped for the night two hours later as the sun began to set above the trees behind them. The wagon was maneuvered into a clearing behind a row of oaks on the north side of the road and the horses were tethered to two young trees close to their campsite. Olivier dug out a fire pit and gathered the driest firewood he could find, while Mitchell tended to the horses. He brought them water from a stream he found in the woods and fed them each a portion of oats and barley. A bag of horse food was among the supplies they carried from the farm. It was stored in a drawer built beneath the back of the wagon.

Only a little light was left of the day when they had finished setting up the tent and sat on the ground beside the fire. Though hungry and impatient to eat, Mitchell, a Deist, politely waited until Olivier had prayed aloud before he took his first forkful of food. Prayers were never said in his nephew's kitchen, but he had learned to listen to them out of respect for Olivier and LeClerc. Once the prayers were said, they quickly devoured the scraps of pork still left on the leg, the two soup-spoon sized pieces of venison remaining from their morning meal and the hardened end of the last piece of bread. Everything else Elizabeth had packed for their journey was gone.

"Well, that's all of it." Mitchell made a face. "There's nothing for the morning. Course, I could shoot us a rabbit or squirrel pretty quick, but I don't suppose …" He saw Olivier shake his head from side to side. "No, I didn't think you would want to spend the time needed to cook one of them over a fire. Well, if the road's improved from here on as we were told and we leave here at first light, we should be fine. I can wait until tomorrow afternoon when we reach Galvez and eat at Mama Mellete's house. How about you, Father?"

Olivier smiled. "I'll be fine until then, William. Once we're in Galvez, how many more days do you think we'll be on the road?"

"Let me think. Tomorrow is the first of April, isn't it? I think two more days after Galvez should do it. We should arrive in New Orleans on the third – probably near dusk. Of course, that depends on the horses and the condition of the road. I'm also counting on three to four hours on the road tomorrow afternoon after leaving Galvez."

The two men sat beside the fire until a cold wind blew out of the west, chilling the night air. They stood to close down their campsite for the night. Olivier covered the fire pit with dirt and put their remaining kindling in the wagon, while Mitchell picketed the horses between two water oaks, where there was abundant grass for grazing. A moment before entering their tent for the night, they looked up to see the full moon. It stood out like a yellow melon in the cloudless sky covered with stars.

Arriving well after midnight, the murderer stared at the front of the tent. He stood hidden between two water oaks that had grown only a foot apart. He could see the army tent clearly in the moonlight and knew there had been no movement inside for almost an hour. An earlier walk around the tent had confirmed that the two men were sound asleep. At the time, he had paused briefly and carefully placed his left ear against the canvas side for several seconds, listening to their heavy breathing. Now, with his plan in mind, he decided to take one more trip around the tent. He wanted to make certain no one else was in the vicinity. The murderer knew the value of caution; it had served him well time and time again in the past. The walk, he told himself, would be his last. He intended to take two concentric circles around the campsite, one close to the tent and the other eight to ten or so feet away in the surrounding woods.

Thirty minutes later, certain there was no one lurking among the trees, the murderer stood in the front of the tent with his knife in hand. He quickly cut the three ties that closed the tent's opening. With his sharp knife, it was done without the slightest sound. He cut through the top tie first, then the one in the center and finally the tie at the bottom. He had to kneel to cut the lowest one near the ground. On the left side he saw Olivier's white bandage in the moonlight. Standing up, he slid his knife into the sheath on his belt and took the iron bar from its scabbard.

The murderer listened again and, hearing nothing, he leaped through the opening into the tent. He held the bar up to hit the man who lay asleep on the right side of the interior. Too dark to see his head, he brought the bar down on the spot where he thought it lay on the bed roll. The murderer heard the bar break his skull and knew he had killed him. He then turned and struck the other man, whom he knew was Oliver, on the chest. Olivier gasped in pain, though the murderer had not hit him as hard as his first victim. It was over in seconds as had been planned.

The murderer dragged Olivier to a water oak only a few feet from the tent. He sat him up against the trunk and, with the roll of rope that hung over his shoulder, he tied him tightly to the tree. The murderer ran the rope a number of times around his body and right arm. He knew the priest's left arm, which was still in a sling, was too weak to be of any use. After tying Olivier, to the tree, Charles Laroux stepped back and looked down at him. He could see the priest clearly in the moonlight.

"Well, Olivier, what say you now?"

"What do you expect me to say? I suppose you killed Mitchell?" Olivier grimaced as he spoke. His ribs ached where he had been struck and he assumed at least one was broken. Once Laroux had hit him with the bar, he had been in too much pain to resist anything that followed.

"Oh, yes, he's dead." Laroux showed him the iron bar with blood on the end. "I'm told he's Timothy Mitchell's uncle. Or should I say *was* his uncle? A veteran of the Revolutionary War my agent tells me. He's one of a long list who are yet to die. But we'll talk about them a little later. For now, I want to know when you suspected I was the one so many fools tried to find. I've a notion you knew before you met Suzanne."

Olivier nodded. There was no reason not to talk to Laroux. He knew the murderer would kill him when they finished talking. Olivier looked up at the star-filled sky and prayed silently.

"I suspected you after you set fire to the Villièrs house."

"Oh, is that so?" Annoyed, Laroux made a face.

"You knew too much about the treehouse and path from the river road to the field south of the Villièrs house. The most telling knowledge was revealed in your question to me about the sentry in the treehouse. You asked, 'How could the sentry miss seeing him moving on the path far below him?' At the time, I wondered how you knew the treehouse was so high up in the live oak and that the path was '*far below.*' It was two days after the fire that Lieutenant Palacios Leguia discovered the treehouse was twenty feet up from the ground."

Laroux smiled, but there was no humor or warmth in the smile. "Good for you, Olivier, I knew you were clever. Anything else?"

"Yes, there was also your … sessions with the girls in darkness. It was obvious that you didn't want the girls to see your face and, of course, the mark on it." Olivier saw a muscle twitch in the murderer's jaw and knew he had angered him.

"If you knew so much about me, why did you sail to Natchez in search of Suzanne? Why didn't you accuse me in New Orleans?" Laroux smiled again, thinking Olivier had exaggerated his knowledge of him.

"No one would have believed me. I had too little information to accuse you and, more important, you are too well regarded in town. Everyone prefers to talk to you rather than Jean Bertin. As you probably know, it's often said, 'Avoid Jean Bertin and speak to Charles Laroux. He's the reasonable and thoughtful one." Olivier tried to shift his sore back against the tree, but immediately stopped moving when he felt a searing pain in his chest.

Laroux ignored the grimace of pain he saw on his captive's face. "Are you flattering me to save yourself, Olivier? If so, it's futile."

"No, Charles, I know you intend to kill me. I've known it since you attacked me in New Orleans. But there's no need to kill anyone else. I'm the only one who knows about you. I've told no one else."

Laroux stared at Olivier. "Is that so? Why should I believe you?"

"It's the truth. I call upon God as witness to my soul that I tell the truth."

Laroux continued to study Olivier, crossing his arms over his chest.

Olivier tried to look sincere. Laroux stared into his eyes. He hoped the man believed him. It was the truth, he had not revealed his name to anyone, not even to Father Antonio.

Laroux abruptly turned and looked into the trees behind them. He cocked his head to the side as if listening to a sound or sounds he heard in the woods. He remained unmoving in that position for several seconds before returning his eyes to the man bound to the tree.

Olivier did not speak. He knew pleading would not persuade the murderer.

"It matters not whether you have told anyone, Olivier. You must die as well as everyone you met on your trip to Natchez. It would be foolish of me to spare any of them." He shook his head. "No, they all must die."

"There's no need to kill anyone else No one else knows."

Laroux sneered. "I told you it doesn't matter. I must take every precaution. It's what I have done in the past and what I will do now. They all must die. The list of them is long and your trip has made it longer." Laroux saw the priest's face contort and he knew his words had wounded him.

"Suzanne is the first on my list."

"Suzanne has no knowledge of you. She doesn't know your name and has no notion of your appearance. The curtains were closed, the candles were unlit and the room was in darkness when she was with you in the Villièrs house. It was your demand for darkness, not anything she said that identified you. She is an innocent!"

"I told you it's of no matter to me. She's first on the list along with her husband. I know they left Natchez, but I'll find them. You can be sure of it!"

Laroux smiled, seeing the anguish on Olivier's face. "Then, of course, there's the little whore, Rochelle, the Mosqueras – everyone of them, the Mitchells, the physician, yes, even Doctor Standish, And don't think I've forgotten your young sycophant, Francis, and Madame Boudreaux. They're on the list as well as all the Dumonts." Laroux nodded as if confirming the names on the list.

Olivier said nothing. He refused to give the man the satisfaction of a reply or plea for the lives of those he intended to kill. Instead, he prayed silently for their survival, hoping with every word that God would save them. He stared into Laroux' eyes, unafraid of the death to come.

Laroux frowned and again turned to look into the dark woods. He saw nothing moving, but listened for almost a minute before returning his eyes to the Dominican.

"You know, Olivier, there's no help for any of them. No, none! Prayers won't help, no one can help them. Least of all Castañedo, who is blundering around not knowing what to do. He will never know I'm the one, no matter how many die in New Orleans. I'll begin with them upon my return to New Orleans and, in due time, they'll all be dead and gone." Laroux smiled.

"Yes, I know there is a lot of work yet to be done, but I'll manage it."

Olivier continued to stare into his eyes, saying nothing.

"Nothing to say, Olivier? Cat got your tongue?" He snickered. "Well, then I suppose it's time to close this conversation." Laroux looked down at Olivier and reached for his knife.

His fingers never touched the knife's handle as the boom of a flintlock rifle startled him. The sound of the shot was instantly followed by a burst of spraying bark in the water oak above Olivier. Laroux turned to look for the plume of smoke from the rifle. He saw it rise up behind the wagon and knew in the moonlight he was easy to see from that distance. He immediately ran into the woods as another shot sounded from a spot nearer the road. Laroux heard the ball strike a second oak as he fled into the darkness. He knew at least two men were attacking him and his only recourse was to find his horse and escape.

The wagon rolled into Galvez on the first day of April. Fearful of surprise attacks from the woods, they moved cautiously and it was after dusk when they finally arrived. Except for candles and oil lamps that could be seen through windows, the houses were in darkness and they looked like assorted boxes, one building blending into another.

LeClerc was driving the wagon and Olivier and Mitchell sat on the second bench behind him. Durant rode his horse alongside on the right and his oldest son, Félix, rode on the left. His two younger sons, Bastian and Lazare, rode behind. All of the Acadians were armed with pistols and two of the boys had flintlock rifles.

Mitchell also held a rifle in readiness. His head was bandaged and, though he would not admit it, he felt dizzy and nauseous. His head also ached where he had been hit by the iron bar. Unable to see clearly in the darkness, Laroux had hit Mitchell a glancing blow on the head. The sleeping man lay facing Olivier when the murderer struck him and the bar scraped the back of his head rather than striking it solidly. The blow opened his scalp, produced a flow of blood and left him unconscious.

Laroux thought he had cracked Mitchell's skull and killed him. The bar actually broke the sleeping man's pipe, which was in a pocket of his winter coat. Before lying down to sleep, he put the pipe and pouch of tobacco in his coat pocket, rolled up the coat and placed it beside his pillow; he wanted them near for a smoke if he awoke at night. In his attack, Laroux heard the pipe break when he struck the sleeping man and believed the bar had cracked open his head. The blood he saw on the end of the bar confirmed his belief.

Arriving in Galvez, Mitchell was taken to a physician. Durant, who had relatives in town, knew the physician, an elderly white-haired man named Édouard Renault. The doctor, bandaged Mitchell's head and gave him potions for his dizziness and headache. By that time, the nausea was gone. The physician told Mitchell the dizziness would disappear after a night's sleep, but the headache might linger for as long as a fortnight.

Doctor Renault also examined Olivier, whose ribs still pained him after Laroux' attack. Mitchell helped the priest heave himself up on the examination table. Even with the help, Olivier grunted as the movement exerted pressure on his ribs. The physician gently moved the palm of his hand over his chest and then used his forefinger to probe the red and swollen area apparent on his left side. He also looked at Olivier's upper arm where Laroux had stabbed him. Finished, he smiled at Olivier. His smile was wide and showed a mouth full of white teeth.

"Well, Father, fortunately only one of the ribs is cracked, the others are bruised. They'll all heal in time. I'll bandage them to keep them secure and cause you less pain. But you will be uncomfortable for four to five weeks. There's nothing to be done about it. However, the knife wound looks clean and there's no sign of infection. I expect the arm will be fully useful in ten or so days, though a scar will remain on the site to remind you of the murderer – Laroux." His wide smile appeared again. "You know, Father, it seems Laroux was fond of your left side."

They stayed overnight in the home of Durant's cousin, Aristide Gallard. Gallard, a stout bearded man, owned the only general store in Galvez as well as a spacious house in the center of town. He and his wife, Adelaide, welcomed the tired men into their home. The visitors were instantly given glasses of hard apple cider followed by large bowls of deer stew. Despite the necessity of moving their children to the floor, the guests were given beds for the night.

When they awoke in the morning, they were greeted with plates of eggs, sausages, grits, rice cakes, beignets and hot coffee. The entire Gallard family, including five children all under fourteen years of age, crowded around the kitchen table along with the visitors. The three oldest children were girls and they helped their mother serve food, fill cups of coffee and retrieve used plates and tableware. With all the movement around the table, loud talking and laughter, it was a noisy but joyous occasion.

When breakfast was over, the adults sat about the table talking and drinking coffee. The children had gone about their chores and Durant's sons left to walk about town. After some talk about the higher prices of imported goods and the lower prices of farm products. Gallard politely asked Olivier what had brought him so far from New Orleans.

"I understand you have even been to Natchez, Father."

"That's correct, Monsieur." He smiled. "Well, it's quite a story and it will require help from your cousin, Monsieur Durant, as well as Monsieur LeClerc." Olivier looked at the men and saw their nods of agreement.

"I see. Adelaide and I will look forward to hearing your story. As you have heard in the last few minutes there's not much to talk about in Galvez."

"I, too, would like to hear your story, Father," said LeClerc. "I was told to follow and guard you and know nothing else." He looked at Durant, who shook his head showing he also wanted to hear the priest's story.

Olivier spoke for more than an hour telling them about the murderous rampage of Charles Laroux. The others listened intently, though his account was often interrupted by exclamations of horror and words of disbelief. When he finished, there was a moment of silence.

"We must alert the town. Immediately!" Gallard's commanding voice broke the silence. "Since the monster still lives, he may lurk nearby."

Olivier held up his hand. "Please wait, Monsieur Gallard. I'm certain Laroux poses no threat to anyone in

Galvez. I've thought about him all the way here in the wagon and if you will permit me a moment or two more, I'll tell why you have nothing to fear from him." He smiled and looked at everyone sitting at the table.

Seeing their nods of agreement, Olivier sighed and then began to speak.

"Laroux poses no threat to Galvez because he's gone. He's on his way to New Orleans at this moment! His only concern now is to find a place of refuge. It must be a place he knows and therefore not in the vicinity of Galvez. He's a stranger here and doesn't know the surroundings."

"But he can hide here in the woods even if he doesn't know the surroundings." Gallard spread his hands out wide to his sides indicating the immensity of the woods. "In New Orleans there's no place to hide."

"True, but only for a while. Without food or shelter, he couldn't survive here for long. No, Laroux is riding as fast as he can to New Orleans where he has lived his life. He knows he must reach the city before anyone there hears about him – hears that he's the murderer. He has little time, no more than a day or two before everyone knows what he has done. For now, he can ride the roads without fear of arrest. But once we reach New Orleans, he will have to go into hiding or flee the city. Whatever he does, the mark on his face will force him to remain out of sight in the woods or swamps around New Orleans. This is his last chance to escape …"

Olivier did not finish his sentence. One of Gallard's sons opened the door and ran into the kitchen. Panting, the excited boy saw his father and shouted, "There are two soldiers from New Orleans looking for Father Olivier." He pointed to the priest.

Four hours later, Olivier once again sat on the second bench of the covered wagon. One of the magistrate's men drove the wagon and three others rode beside and behind guarding the man they had been sent to find. The uniformed men who met Olivier in Galvez were joined by two others when the wagon left Galvez and reached the main highway running between Baton Rouge and New Orleans. It was a coincidental meeting since the two others were returning from their futile search for the priest on the river road north. Guarded by four armed men, Olivier sighed, knowing he was safe and soon would be in New Orleans.

Olivier felt better than he had in days. Some of his strength seemed to be returning and he felt more like himself. Although the bandages around his ribs restricted his breathing, his left arm now moved freely without any pain. There was an occasional pinch, but nothing more. His only complaint was a sore bottom from sitting so long on the hard bench.

"What a journey it had been!" he thought, sighing loudly. "Well, it's almost over now." Three armed men from Galvez had been sent ahead to New Orleans. They were told to inform Castañedo about Laroux and then notify Father Antonio of Olivier's return. The murderer's fate would be sealed once the magistrate was notified. Laroux would be immediately arrested if he remained in the city or relentlessly pursued if he avoided capture. "Remerciez Dieu, c'est finalement fini (Thank God, it's finally over)" he said to himself.

Olivier left Mitchell behind in Galvez. Since the wounded man still felt light-headed the doctor recommended he remain another few days with the Gallards. It was agreed that when his health improved, he would be given a new wagon and horses for his journey home to Natchez. Olivier promised to reimburse the Acadian once he reached New Orleans. He was certain Father Antonio would support his promise, probably from a donation made by a wealthy parishioner of the cathedral. It occurred to Olivier that Jean Bertin would undoubtedly be the one to make such a donation. Given the identity of the murderer, he was sure the parish pastor would see to it that Jean Bertin made that donation as well as many more in the future. The priest smiled, picturing a scowling Jean Bertin shaking the pastor's hand after promising the donations.

Olivier was now finished with the long investigation and he looked forward to returning to Santa María and his people in the lowlands. He sighed again and reached in the pocket of his cassock for the flask of rum Gallard had given him. The considerate Acadian had handed it to him a moment before he had climbed up into the wagon.

Olivier thought about all the Acadians who had helped him. He knew they had saved his life at least twice on his journey. LeClerc had saved him from death aboard the *Concordia* and then stopped Laroux from killing him at their last campsite. It was LeClerc who fired the first shot at the murderer as he reached for his knife. The young blacksmith had watched over him from the time of his arrival in Natchez to their last wagon trip to Galvez.

Durant was another Acadian who had followed and guarded him. Durant had fired the second shot that sent Laroux fleeing into the woods. Like LeClerc, the big man had been his hidden protector following him with his three sons and, after the murderer was gone, guarding him until they reached Galvez. Then, there was Doctor Renault who had bandaged his ribs and, finally, the amiable Aristide Gallard and his family who had welcomed him into the warmth of their home. They all had treated him as if he were an Acadian himself. Olivier recalled the last words Gallard had said to him as he thanked him for the flask of rum.

"We Acadians have many failings, Father, but we have a

few virtues that make us a great people. Perhaps, our commitment to each other is our most important virtue. "Allez avec Dieu. (Go with God) You are one of us."

CHAPTER FIFTEEN

NEW ORLEANS APRIL 2, 1800 – OCTOBER 24, 1810

At eleven o'clock, on the night of April 2, Laroux left his house for the last time. Before leaving, he fed his tired horse and left him with water. It was as if he intended to return the next morning to ride him to his office. Laroux walked into the darkness carrying only a cloth satchel. The satchel held all the pesetas he would need for the foreseeable future. Laroux needed nothing else. Everything of possible use to him was already stored in the cabin a carpenter had built for him many years ago. The cabin was located fifteen miles northeast of New Orleans and hidden in an almost inaccessible swamp. Trying to anticipate all possibilities, Laroux had prepared a place of refuge for himself in the event his scheme to take over the Dumont enterprises failed. His uncle owned the tract of land where the cabin stood, but, since Jean Bertin never visited his properties outside of New Orleans he was unaware of its existence.

The streets were empty as Laroux walked toward the

southeastern entrance into the city. Still to be cautious, he stayed in the shadows and close to buildings along the way. Busy telling bawdy jokes, the two guards did not even look at him as he walked out through the gates. Once outside the city, he picked up his pace, hoping to reach the cabin by three in the morning.

It was a bright moonlit night and Laroux had no trouble seeing the path he had carefully marked before pursuing Olivier. In the swamp, he had painted white spots on forty trees, all at eye-level, so he would not lose his way in the dark. When he awoke in the morning, he would come back to cut out the white spots, making certain no one else would find the path. His only worry now was the possibility of stepping on or too close to a snake as he walked to the cabin. The woods were full of rattlesnakes and the lethal water snakes seemingly lurked everywhere in the swamps. Laroux held his sword in readiness as he walked, but to his relief, no snake or any other animal crossed his path. He walked very slowly especially in dark places overhung with vines, but, except for one misstep off the path into swamp water, he arrived safely at the cabin earlier than anticipated. It was two-thirty when he looked at his pocket watch in the light of an oil lamp. He went to bed soon after drinking a cup of tea.

Laroux spent most of the next day planning his future. His first concern was where he would go to begin the next phase of his life. He knew a city with a population of at least 10,000 people would be needed for him to move about unnoticed or be of little interest to people passing him in the streets. The city also had to be far away from New Orleans. That meant he could not think of moving to Spanish Florida. St. Augustine and Pensacola were too close and too small to be considered. In any similar city, he would live in constant dread of being seen and recognized by someone who knew of him in New Orleans. For that reason, he dismissed Charleston, though it was a city that appealed to him. St. Louis was far enough away, but its population was under 5,000 and he had met a number of its merchants, who sailed down the river to conduct business in New Orleans. Some had negotiated contracts with him and would surely remember his face.

Laroux also ruled out living in the northeast. Montreal and Quebec were the best places for his use of French, but the bitterly cold winters convinced him to reject Canada. Boston, New York, Philadelphia and Baltimore were large enough for him to be lost among their populations, but his accented English along with the mark on his face would sooner or later bring attention to him and perhaps recognition. The northern cities also had much colder winters than New Orleans which he found intolerable. Cold winter was also the reason why he had not considered far away Chicago as a place to live in the future. Sitting outside in the warm sun the first morning after his arrival, Laroux nodded knowing where he would go.

"I'll go west," he said to himself. "I'll go to the Spanish lands in the west. It's said that California has become a destination for homesteaders and San Francisco is a city on the rise. The population is still small, not yet 1,000, but growing fast." He nodded, thinking his command of Spanish would make a move to California easier than any other place, with the exception of the small Spanish presidios in Florida. In addition to a multitude of Indians, he had heard there were Franciscan missionaries, Spanish soldiers, and a wide variety of foreigners in California. In such a mixture of people, he hoped to be unseen and unknown among them. A new name might even assure himself of anonymity for the rest of his life. He smiled. "Yes, I'll wait until the summer when the search for me loses momentum and then I'll go west to California."

In the meantime, he would be comfortable enough in the cabin. Food was plentiful in the surrounding area. There were any number of animals in the woods as well as fish in the nearby streams. He had fishing gear and a flintlock rifle in the cabin, though he intended to use a bow and arrows to hunt land animals. Laroux realized the sound of him shooting a rifle might attract unwanted visitors to the cabin. He also had other food stored at the cabin. Before pursuing the priest, as a precaution, he took two trips into the swamp with staples for a prolonged stay. Laroux brought a bag of rice, a bag each of carrots, onions, potatoes and turnips, two breads, a chunk of cheddar cheese and a container of hard cider. There was also a full barrel of rain water available outside the cabin.

With what hunting and fishing produced, Laroux assumed he had a sufficient supply of food for the sixty days he planned to remain in the swamp. Even if it was necessary to limit his intake at the end of May, he did not intend to risk any midnight visits to nearby farms for food. Laroux would not jeopardize his hidden existence by angering the Acadian farmers. He knew they would search endlessly for anyone who took their products, no matter how few were taken.

Laroux dreamed that night of his new life in California. He saw himself as the owner of a grand hacienda with hundreds of Indian peons. His last view of his property was from a high promontory on the Pacific coast, where he stood looking down at his Spanish styled stone house and the many similar buildings that stood in the center of his 500 acre hacienda. His beautiful thirteen-year-old wife stood beside him smiling with happiness.

The next morning, Laroux awoke with less enthusiasm for his move to California. He lay under the blankets, thinking about everything he would lose when he left New Orleans. Despite the stench of the city, he liked its Spanish architecture, the picturesque view of the flowing river, and the surrounding lowlands, swamps and pine forests. He would especially miss the autumn colors on the river when he usually sailed to the gulf in late October and early November.

Then there were the lovely young girls prancing about the plaza as well as all those who were available to him whenever he wanted. He had become accustomed to them eagerly coming to him to be his compliant mistresses, willingly accepting any bodily act he required. He pictured the last one with the pitch-black hair and almost boyish body. Once her clothing fell to the floor, she had pounced on top of him, probed his mouth with her tongue and then licked every surface of his body. Laroux closed his eyes and exhaled a long breath; he knew all those joys were gone, perhaps, forever.

He gritted his teeth, thinking of all he was losing. Not only was he losing the place of his birth, childhood and growth to be a man, it was where he had eventually become well respected and regarded as a gentleman. In New Orleans, he had been a man of meaning, despite his facial disfigurement. He was viewed as an up and coming community figure by both Spanish officials and French residents. Only a month ago, a wealthy landowner told him that in a conference with the governor he had been mentioned as a future member of the Cabildo, the governing council of the city. Prominent people had come to him for advice and, in commercial dealings, many of the businessmen in town requested meetings with him rather than Jean Bertin. He was the man who best represented the Dumont enterprises – not Jean Bertin.

Laroux sat up in bed and leaned his head against the backboard, thinking of how much he had done for the Dumonts and how little he had been appreciated. He had been the one who did most of the daily work, not Jean Bertin. On the contrary, his uncle did less and less in the office. Jean Bertin had become little involved in commerce, leaving many, if not most, of the business decisions and organizational work to him. He was the one who supervised the daily operation of the office, scheduled appointments and meetings, hired and fired employees and tried to mollify discontented customers. He was the one who met with clients at all hours and often far outside of New Orleans. He was the one who carried out every irritating task that bedeviled Jean Bertin. In fact, everything his indolent uncle disliked doing, he turned over to him. Of course, the obese owner of the Dumont enterprises continued to attend city conferences and luncheons, where he ate endlessly and got fatter by the day. It seemed each week he did less and less in their office and left more and more of the work to his *indispensable nephew.*

Laroux grimaced, recalling how he had hated Jean Bertin's smile when he praised him to others. Those who heard his words thought they were spoken by a proud uncle, but Laroux saw them as condescending, the words of a superior to an inferior. Though Jean Bertin was unaware of it, his mouth curled into a sneer whenever he complimented him.

Laroux frowned and then nodded knowingly. That was why he had decided to take over the Dumont enterprises. It was a reasonable decision and only required the deaths of Jean Bertin and his three sons. He had made a murder sequence and planned their killings one day in July as he sailed his sloop south on the river. Jean Bertin, of course, was his choice to be the first to die, but his murder unfortunately had to wait for a while. According to the sequence he created, his young cousins, Jacques and Matthieu, would be killed first followed by their father a few months later. Laroux initially planned to spare Alain, the oldest son, temporarily if he stayed in France, but his scheme changed when Alain arrived in New Orleans following his brothers' funerals. He was uncertain of how and where Alain would be killed, but it was only a matter of time.

It was then that he decided to poison the entire family. Laroux knew he risked the deaths of everyone when he mixed the spotted water hemlock into the family's rice. But he was weary of Jean Bertin's endless demands and anxious to take charge of the Dumont enterprises. He also assumed at least one of the family members would survive the poisoning and ask him to manage the business. Anyone who survived, even Jean Bertin, would want him to continue his work for the family. It was well known he was aware of all the intricacies of the business. He, of course, was a family member himself, though not from the immediate family. Unfortunately, not one of the Dumonts died and, by that time, Jean Bertin had contracted with the damned Dominican to discover what had happened to *La Bonne Chance.*

The only good result of the poisoning was Jean Bertin's decision to draw up a will. The deaths of his two sons made him think about his own mortality and the need to provide financial protection for his remaining family. A week later following the funeral of Lucille, Jean Bertin approached him to be the executor of his will. His uncle also asked him to serve as manager of the Dumont family's enterprises upon his death. He, of course, had reluctantly accepted Jean Bertin's request and a will was prepared soon afterward.

As expected, his son, Alain, was made the principal heir of his father's estate. His wife, Paulette, daughters and mother were also mentioned as beneficiaries and provided with lifetime legacies. Laroux was included next in the will and, in addition to his designation as manager of the family's holdings, he was given two dilapidated rental houses and ten acres of an unsightly and uncultivated tract of land southwest of the city. A variety of trivial monetary distributions were also extended to older and favored employees and family servants.

Determined to contain his fury, Laroux closed his eyes and exhaled a long breath. Despite his many years of devoted service for Jean Bertin and his family, his penurious uncle had willed him a mere pittance – an insulting pittance.

It was as if he were one of his uncle's servants who were also left trivial gifts.

Laroux shook his head, thinking of how little he had been appreciated by Jean Bertin. He had given more than half his life to his uncle's enterprises – all in vain. The ungrateful bastard had no appreciation for all the money he had made for him, never mind the effort he had put forth to make the wealthy man even wealthier.

Laroux sighed, thinking there was no point in being angry. Jean Bertin was now living the final weeks of his life. The fat fool had actually forfeited his life the day he signed his will. His uncle had no idea that the will allowed him to be killed whenever it was convenient. At the time, Laroux knew it would be necessary to wait at least a year to kill him to avoid suspicion of his involvement. For that reason as well, the murder of Jean Bertin had to look as if he had died naturally or in an accident. Alain's eventual death would have required a similar appearance.

He nodded, curling his lip. "Now, of course, such concerns do not matter. Jean Bertin will be struck down like a scorpion on the floor."

The thought of killing his uncle brought to mind the plans he had made to take control of the Dumont enterprises. The faked murder attempt was one of his favorite schemes and allayed any suspicion of him that might have emerged when other killings followed afterward. Laroux smiled, recalling how he had staged it in the late afternoon darkness before the street lamps were lit. To make the assault look authentic, he hit himself hard on the head and had fallen stunned to the ground. He touched his head where the bump from the blow had remained for more than a week. It was long gone now, but not the memory of his performance which still pleased him.

"It was as good a performance as a thespian could give," he said aloud, picturing himself as the protagonist in

Molière's play, *L'école des Femmes* (The School for Wives). He chuckled, remembering how the clever scene he set up on the street had convinced Jean Bertin he had been attacked and almost killed. If his skeptical uncle had ever distrusted him before, he did not doubt him thereafter. His performance as a deathly sick man, who almost died from the poisoned rice, was also fine piece of acting. It fooled the doctor as well the others who sat by his bedside when he appeared to be near death's door.

At the time, everything had been proceeding exactly as he had planned. Laroux closed his eyes as he recalled his life less than nine months earlier. He had all the money he needed, a fine home with furniture imported from France, a sleek sloop made of Jamaican mahogany and costly clothing only a man of means could wear. He appeared, behaved and was regarded as a wealthy gentleman everywhere he went. And, in addition to the judiciously selected virgin he enjoyed every month in Madame Villièrs' house, he maintained at least two young mistresses in town at any given time.

He sighed. Everything he owned came from years of hard work for Jean Bertin. He was not paid generously because he was Jean Bertin's nephew. He earned every peseta given him for all his toil year after year. The so-called *cheapest man in town* paid him what he was worth and nothing more. There were never any annual bonuses or seasonal gifts that other men gave their best employees. Not only was he denied the status and salary of a family member, Jean Bertin also denied him the deserved benefits bestowed upon others like him.

"God, how I hate that man," he shouted, his hands thrust upward with fingers extended. He pictured his hands around the fat man's neck, choking the life out of him.

All his careful plans, everything he had worked so hard and long to put into place began to deteriorate when that bâtard gros (fat bastard) hired the Dominican. The deal he made with Olivier was not only stupid, it was excessively expensive. He had wasted 10,000 pesetas! Jean Bertin gave the priest's pitiful little church more money in one foolish transaction than he paid him for three years of hard work. In return for the extravagant contribution, Olivier was of little help in the futile investigation. His explanations for the sinking of *La Bonne Chance* and the deaths of Jacques and Matthieu were dubious at best. Of course, Jean Bertin believed them, but not the magistrate or the governor. They regarded his suspicions as the befuddled beliefs of a grief-stricken father His uncle had foolishly squandered 10,000 pesetas of the family's money, but more important, his hiring of the damned Dominican resulted in the discovery of the drowned girl.

Laroux inhaled deeply and then let out a long breath. "It was ironic," he thought, "the girl was a gift to the boys for their last evening on earth." He snickered. "It was a thoughtful gift for the two lustful lads so they would not die virgins. Of course, she was an ordinary girl in life and nothing more; I cannot even recall her name. But, in death, she became the bane of my existence. Once she was found all my accomplishments began to slip away." He shook his head astonished at the unfortunate turn of events.

The discovery of the girl distracted him from his scheme to take over the Dumont family enterprises. Instead, it forced him to focus all his attention on the Villièrs house. The murders of Madame Villièrs and her niece naturally followed as well as his pursuit of the girls he had known in the past year. They were routinely removed like the protruding rocks on the surface of a busy road. But, unfortunately, his search for them required time and effort, delaying the completion of his plans. The lengthy hunt for the girls also added other risks when the magistrate became involved seeking his arrest.

It was all because of Jean Bertin and Olivier. They had spoiled his plans and ruined his life in New Orleans. He was now a pariah in the city of his birth and where he had lived all his life. He had risen from near poverty to become a man of prominence and a gentleman in New Orleans and now was compelled to leave his home forever. His house, office, sloop and even the streets of the city were forbidden to him. He could never walk or ride his stallion through New Orleans again. The city was lost to him with the exception of the pictures of it that remained in his mind's eye.

"I am now am exiled from the city I love," he muttered as tears filled his eyes.

Laroux dried his eyes on the sheet that covered him. He realized it was useless to lament the past. There was nothing to be done about it. He had to leave his home and begin a new life elsewhere, perhaps, in California. He nodded, confidant of his success in the west. It was only a matter of time and he had plenty of time in the future. The thought of how long it would take to reach the privileged position he had enjoyed for years in New Orleans changed his mood and his face flushed in anger.

Laroux spoke through gritted teeth. "Well, since I must leave because of Jean Bertin and Olivier, so must they. I will go to the west and they to death."

Laroux pictured himself, hot and sweaty, digging graves in the soft soil of the swamp. Jean Bertin and Olivier lay bound and gagged on the ground, their eyes open wide with terror. He did not yet know how it would be done, but, before his departure, they too would disappear forever. Like the others, they would be dead and gone.

Olivier arrived in New Orleans in the early evening of April 3. His guards took him to the magistrate's home and then to the cathedral. His meeting with Castañedo was brief, lasting fifteen minutes, and his reunion with Antonio lasted only a few minutes longer. The exhausted priest then rode in the pastor's carriage to Madame Lefevre's house. Hearing Olivier had arrived in town, Madame Lefevre had a hot meal ready for him. Famished, he quickly devoured the food on his plate, thanked her and then went to his room. He was asleep seconds later. Olivier did not undress or drink his usual three drams of rum before dropping down on his bed.

The following morning, Olivier found more than a hundred people awaiting him at Santa María. Many met him outside the city gates and walked beside and behind him to the church. He was surrounded there by the lowlands residents who hugged, kissed him on the cheeks and smiled simply to see him. Francis was among the crowd of Acadians and, like them, he had tears in his eyes. Olivier tried to speak, but, with tears trickling down his cheeks, he could do little more than thank them for welcoming him home. Outside the church, he kneeled on the ground and, when the large crowd joined him, the priest prayed aloud, thanking God for his survival and reunion with his people.

On the first Friday after Easter, Ana Luisa and Honorè were married in Santa María at eleven o'clock in the morning. Olivier presided at the celebration and blessing of their marriage with Antonio by his side. The wedding was not only well attended, it filled the lowlands church to capacity with a crowd of people standing in the doorway. A large group of latecomers stood outside straining to hear Olivier's service and the exchange of vows. To Olivier's surprise and Ana Luisa's delight, Sylvie Dubois and the remaining girls from the Villièrs house were among those who sat inside Santa María. Mother Marguerite and Sister Helene from the convent also attended the wedding and the prioress smiled at Olivier as he left the church after the ceremony.

Ana Luisa was initially disappointed not to be married in the cathedral, but brightened happily when she saw the fête de marriage (wedding celebration) the Acadian women had set up outside the church. While the wedding was in progress, they had decorated the grounds around Santa María with baskets of colorful leaves, wreaths of pine cones and the first flowers of spring. The older parishioners said the church grounds had never looked so beautiful.

The women also brought pots of food and laid them out on tables made from the left over wood from the church's renovation. Wine and other home-made alcoholic drinks accompanied the Acadian food, which included redfish and rice, rabbit and rice and squirrel stew. Three men took turns playing fiddles while everyone ate and they continued afterwards when many of the Acadians danced away the afternoon. The wedding celebration ended abruptly with the arrival of mosquitoes and gnats after dark.

On the following Monday, Antonio walked to Santa María to talk to Olivier. He arrived at the church at midmorning and found the Dominican on his knees repairing one of the benches. A nail at the center of the bench had risen from the wood and Olivier was hammering it back into place. He stood when the pastor entered the church and, after their exchange of greetings, they went to the benches that stood beside the bayou. It was a chilly morning, but they sat beneath a cloudless sky and a warm sun.

Antonio inhaled deeply. "It's so good to breathe the fresh air here outside the city. It's so foul-smelling these days and undoubtedly will smell worse in the future. I must say, Olivier, there are times that I envy you here at Santa María."

Olivier nodded, a smile on his lips. "I certainly understand such envy, but, as you well know, Father, no priest from this little church will ever be summoned to Rome."

Antonio shook his head and smiled. "I suppose I deserve your teasing. Needless to say, Olivier, you know I have no such aspiration. I would rather be sent to some obscure parish than the Vatican … which brings me to the reason for my visit today."

Olivier frowned. "Don't tell me you have been sent to a diocese in South America!"

"No, no, not me." Antonio sighed. "But that's where Meléndez is going at the end of the month. Bishop Peñalver y Cárdenas will be returning from Cuba at that time."

"My God! Where in South America has he been assigned?"

"Asunción." Antonio exhaled a long breath. "Malheureux (Unfortunate wretch)!"

"Malheureux indeed! What an awful appointment."

"What do you know about Asunción, Olivier?"

"I heard about the town from a Jesuit I met before coming to Louisiana. He spent four years in Asunción." Olivier stroked his chin, remembering what the Jesuit had told him. "He said the town has about 10,000 inhabitants and most of them are poor Mestizos. The Asunción diocese is the only one in that vast territory. The weather is insufferably hot and humid most of the year with storms and downpours day and night from October to April. There are clouds of mosquitoes during the rainy months and the people sleep on six-foot high platforms with layers of netting to keep them from being bitten all night long. In the morning, the netting is dark with hundreds of mosquitoes clinging to them. Apparently, everyone there drinks a strange tasting tea called *Yerba Mate* and the Mestizos, including the women, smoke dark-leaf cigars. The Jesuit said Asunción was the worst place he had lived in his life."

"Mon Dieu! That's no place to send a man of his age. Meléndez won't last six months in Asunción. What in God's name is the archbishop thinking?" Antonio struck the stump between them with the palm of his hand.

"I doubt the archbishop made the appointment by himself. The Church in Havana is now full of young priests who handle most of the petty administrative duties. They are, of course, in the archbishop's office as well and serve him in a variety of clerical capacities. And one of their tasks is to provide him with the needed information to make his decisions. It's therefore likely that one of those priests read a request for a bishop in Asunción, found Meléndez' name on a list of bishops awaiting new appointments and passed his name to the archbishop's aide … who then recommended Meléndez to the archbishop for the appointment in Asunción."

Antonio frowned. "I'm certain you are right, Olivier, unfortunately for Bishop Meléndez. It's the way of the world these days. Church and crown appointments are all too often made as a consequence of aristocratic status, financial gifts and convenience. Capability and commitment often seem to be ignored as criteria for appointments."

Olivier nodded.

Antonio sighed. "Well, I must tell the mahheureux I wish him well. He has a hard road to travel in the future and I will pray for him as well."

"Yes, indeed, so will I."

The priests looked at each other and together kneeled on the ground to pray for the future welfare of Bishop Meléndez.

Olivier and Francis went to María Adela's house on the evening of May fourteenth. The day had been dark and dreary, but the sun finally appeared in the late afternoon sky and colored the remaining clouds pink and purple. The two priests stopped several times to enjoy the sunset as they walked from the lowlands into the city. There was also a sweet fragrance in the air and, though they looked about for a few minutes, they never found its source.

Upon arrival, Olivier and Francis sat with María Adela on her upper porch and watched the last of the sun fall below the horizon. All of the color in the sky instantly disappeared with the exception of a thin orange line above the trees in the west. As soon as the line was gone, they descended the stairs to the dining room for their evening meal. After eating, an Acadian seafood stew, they moved into her living room and talked until ten o'clock.

María Adela asked Olivier about Laroux as she lit the candles in the room. Awaiting his reply she handed him a glass of brandy and poured herself half a glass. Francis, who still held his wine from dinner, sat in a chair beside Olivier.

"The magistrate thinks he has left Louisiana. There still are sightings of him, but most of them are reported at night and probably related to excess drinking or imagination. With what is now known about him, Laroux would be foolish to lurk in town and he's certainly not a fool."

"What do the townspeople know about him? I doubt the Spanish officials would ever tell them everything he has done." María Adela made a face. "They would never admit the number of his murders or the manner in which his victims were killed."

Olivier nodded. "True. The townspeople only know he killed Jacques and Matthieu and poisoned the entire Dumont family. Of course, there are a number of others who also know he murdered Madame Villièrs, her niece Gisella and Raphael Portillo at Mosquito Creek. A few likewise know of his killing of Valarie Poulin. The magistrate told me they feared there would be panic in the community if the exact number of murders were known."

"That's the excuse the Spaniards always use to keep the truth from the people. What the Spaniards really fear is a community uprising that might threaten their rule of the colony."

"Perhaps. But that's certainly understandable considering what has happened in France after the revolution. The unfortunate country has suffered the fall of the monarchy, mob rule, the ruthless persecution of the Church and the Reign of Terror. It's said hundreds were guillotined in Paris in those years."

"And thousands more have been killed in the endless wars of Napoleon," added Francis, looking at Olivier for his agreement."

María Adela nodded. "Well, Father, what do you know about Laroux' killings?" She wanted to mention what she considered to be the more important consequences of the French Revolution, but knew her comments would fall on deaf ears. The priests would not think the end of aristocratic privilege, the loss of monarchial and Church authority, the abolition of feudalism or the *Declaration of the Rights* of Man were worthwhile results of the revolution. She therefore changed the subject.

Olivier studied María Adela and paused before speaking.

"Father, I do not repeat anything you tell me."

Olivier smiled. "I know that, María Adela. I only paused, thinking of the number of the fiend's murders." Olivier frowned, knowing he had lied again. He actually had wondered why María Adela had changed the subject so abruptly, but did not want to ask her.

"I assume there were at least ten murders. Were there many more?"

"Yes, unfortunately. Laroux kept a list of them in his diary, which he left behind when he fled from the city. The magistrate found it when he went to his house to arrest him. It appears he killed more than twenty people – most of them young girls."

"Mon Dieu!" María Adela's face paled and her mouth dropped open.

"Are you feeling ill?" Olivier and Francis both stood, intending to go to her aid.

"Sit, sit. I'm fine." María Adela waved them back to their chairs. "I assume Jacques and Matthieu's names were on the list."

Olivier nodded. "Yes, the list included everyone's first names. Their family names were ignored except for Madame Villièrs, whose first name was omitted for some unknown reason."

"What else do you know about Laroux? Did he leave his diary behind on purpose?"

"The magistrate doesn't know whether he forgot the diary or left it on purpose. I asked him the same question."

"I assume he mentioned Jean Bertin in his diary."

Olivier nodded. "Laroux hated him. It seems he loathed the whole family, although his intense hatred of Jean Bertin stands out above all else in the diary. He conceived of a number of plans to kill him, but kept putting them off for fear of being suspected. Laroux realized he could not murder Jean Bertin and take over the family's holdings at the same time – which was why he continually made and cancelled plans to kill him. His last plan was written in early March and he vowed to take his uncle's life by the end of the year. He hoped to make Jean Bertin's murder look accidental."

"I'm not surprised he hated Jean Bertin. The man is a selfish beast and I'm sure anyone serving him for so many years would have hated him. It's ironic, isn't it, that the man Laroux detested is still alive and more than twenty innocent people he probably didn't detest are dead instead." María Adela frowned. "I understand Jean Bertin is quite contrite these days."

"I've not seen him since my return to Santa María."

"I expect he will avoid you. Seeing you would remind him of all the foolish complaints he made about you to Father Antonio. Jean Bertin is not a man who admits his mistakes. He has not even admitted hiring Charles Laroux was *his* mistake. No, instead, he has intimated his father suggested hiring the boy before he died." María Adela sighed in exasperation. "He's now hired Tristan Surette to serve in Laroux' position, and I've heard the Acadian also hates him."

"Jean Bertin is not easy to like." Olivier recalled his last meeting with him. "However, Father Antonio met with him a few days ago and, to the pastor's surprise, he offered to support the enlargement of Santa María." He saw María Adela raise her eyebrows. "That's not all. Jean Bertin also offered to pay the costs of constructing a school beside Santa María for the Acadian children. Antonio, of course, instantly accepted his offer."

Olivier smiled and both Francis and María Adela laughed.

"Well. Father, that's his payment to you for finding the murderer of his sons. He would never admit it, but it's also an apology for criticizing your investigation."

Olivier continued to smile. "He also offered, without the parish pastor's encouragement, to pay for the costs of my journey to and from Natchez. And that includes the cost of the new carriage and horses Gallard gave Mitchell for his journey home to Natchez. Needless to say, the pastor quickly accepted that offer as well." They all laughed again.

"I wanted to take the money myself to Gallard, but the magistrate warned me against it. Since Laroux has not been found, he wants me to avoid traveling for the time being. He urged me to be accompanied by an armed man wherever I go." Olivier chuckled. "So, Francis here has been by my side every day from morning to night. Malheurusement (Sadly), Francis does not tuck me into bed before he leaves at night nor does he help me dress in the morning."

María Adela smiled. "It seems for once Castañedo has made a sensible suggestion." She looked at Francis. "His advice for you to carry a pistol also makes sense."

Francis shook his head. "Capuchins are never armed, Madame."

"I'm aware of that, but it's a sensible precaution with

Laroux alive and perhaps about."

Olivier nodded. "It is sensible, María Adela, but we will trust in God's protection rather than walk about armed. However, I've something else I must tell you about Francis."

The young priest's face turned crimson. "You are making too much of it, Father."

"No, I'm not, Francis, and I am certain María Adela will appreciate it."

"What is it, for goodness sake?" María Adela clucked her tongue. "Has Francis become pastor of Santa María and you are returning to the cathedral?"

"No, but the former may indeed take place in the future. What I want to tell you concerns the search for the murderer's identity before my journey to Natchez. Do you recall the talk we had here before I left?" He saw María Adela nod her head. "We discussed Francis' suggestion that the magistrate's men should interview the boot makers in town to see if one of them made a pair of cordovan boots for a customer in town."

María Adela nodded. "Yes, the murderer was seen wearing cordovan boots at the brothel. I recall you said Ana Luisa, the girl who was recently married, saw him wearing *new and shiny* cordovan boots. Ah, so, one of the bootmakers in town has now remembered making a pair for Charles Laroux."

"Exactly! Francis, tell María Adela about it."

"I met the bootmaker at Honorè and Ana's wedding. He's Italian and his name is Luigi Canolo. He made shoes for the couple to wear at the wedding and he and his wife were invited to the celebration. Canolo speaks only enough French to be understood with hand gestures. We talked briefly when we met and he identified himself as the oldest bootmaker in town. Of course, I then inquired if he had made cordovan boots for Charles Laroux and he nodded and touched the left side of his face."

"Ah, to indicate the purple spot on Laroux' face." María

Adela stared at Francis, shaking her head. "So, only a brief interview with each of the bootmakers in town would have identified Laroux as the murderer."

Francis nodded. María Adela shook her head. "I was too quick to the give that pompous Spaniard credit for giving you advice. Now, we know Laroux could have been stopped in March – *two months ago*, if the incompetent fool had ordered the interviews of the bootmakers in town. Who knows how many on his list would still be alive if Castañedo had listened to you."

Olivier sighed, exasperated at María Adela's continuing criticism of the magistrate. "He didn't have any men available at the time to do the interviews. Half his men were stationed at the governor's house for the French envoy's reception. The others were ill with the plague and unavailable for duty."

María Adela frowned. "I recall what Castañedo told you. That's why he said there was no one to accompany you to Natchez."

Olivier nodded. "That's right. He urged me to wait to leave until at least two of them were fit enough for the trip."

"What about after you left? Why were the bootmakers not interviewed when the envoy returned to France and the sick men returned to duty? Laroux would then have been arrested as the murderer and you could have been recalled from wherever you were at the time."

"I don't know why the bootmakers were not interviewed. There may well be a perfectly good reason for it." He saw the doubt in María Adela's down-turned mouth. "But I do know the magistrate did everything possible to protect me on my return from Natchez. As soon as he knew I was on the way here he sent four men to find me. Father Antonio even praised him, saying no one could have acted any faster to protect me. And you know how critical the pastor has been of the magistrate in the past. Incidentally, he now thinks highly of him."

María Adela did not reply.

"I owe my life to both the Acadians and the magistrate."

"From what I've heard, it was the Acadians who actually saved your life." María Adela stared at Francis, shaking her head ever so slightly. She was signaling him to say nothing.

Only Francis knew she had contacted one of the Acadian elders and informed him of the perilous trip Olivier was taking to Natchez. María Adela met with him the morning after Olivier told her about his planned departure. Her housekeeper, Renée Latour, arranged the meeting with the elder at Santa María. Since it was Francis' turn to perform first Mass, María Adela met the man, Lucien Maillet, at the church. Maillet immediately agreed to do whatever was necessary to help Olivier. He said the Acadians would never forget how the bon père (good father) had helped them after the hurricane and would gladly guard him throughout his trip. His only concern was the cost of food, lodging and travel if a ship's passage or carriage fare was required. Asked how much money the Acadians might need for the journey, Maillet paused briefly and then said 100 pesetas should cover all their expenses. María Adela handed him 200 pesetas, hoping twice his request would assure his pledge to protect Olivier.

Eight men including Emile LeClerc, eventually took turns following the priest. Olivier was watched every day from the early morning he boarded the *Santa Teresa* in New Orleans to the night he arrived at the home of Aristide Gallard. Unaware anyone was following him, the preoccupied priest did not know the Acadians and the Parsall brothers both were watching him. The Acadians also watched Louis and Jean Jacques Parsall without them knowing it.

André Durant and his sons were not among the Acadians sent to guard Olivier, but they accompanied Emile LeClerc when he told them the dangers the priest faced on the bypass road to Galvez. Durant's sons joined their father and LeClerc at their farm and, riding horses, they set out after Mitchell's carriage. Durant and LeClerc rode off first with the farmer's two horses and his three sons followed an hour later on horses borrowed from neighbors. The Acadians, almost four hours behind Olivier and Mitchell, found themselves in darkness as they proceeded slowly along the road. Reaching the stone littered portion of the road, they dismounted and walked their horses forward. They had two lanterns, but hesitated to light them fearing the murderer might see them approaching. Moving carefully and quietly, Durant and LeClerc finally spied the campsite in the moonlight. The snort of one of the picketed horses made them look from the road to where the wagon stood. Their eyes accustomed to the dark, they entered the woods behind the wagon, tying their horses to saplings by the side of the road.

They walked bent over at first and then crawled to spots where Mitchell's tent could be clearly seen. Durant lay close to the bypass road and LeClerc was hidden deeper in the woods on the other side of the wagon. They had no sooner settled into their observation positions when they saw Laroux drag Olivier from the tent and tie him to the oak. Since the bottom of the tree was obstructed by thick underbrush, they had to change positions to aim their rifles at Laroux. Durant's sons arrived moments after the two shots missed the murderer. Though they wanted to pursue him, the young men realized the futility of a search in the darkness. Instead, they joined their father and LeClerc, guarding Olivier and Mitchell as the wagon was driven to Galvez.

The Gallard family and the Acadians of Galvez knew of Maillet's pledge to protect the priest. They were awaiting his arrival. Neither Olivier nor Mitchell saw them in the dark – fifteen of the townsmen, armed and posted all along the road from the wooded outskirts of Galvez all the way to Gallards' house. The Acadians had been in position for the whole of three days and nights.

Olivier nodded. "Yes, they saved my life and I will be forever grateful for their care and kindness. I knew none of them before my journey and yet they loved me as if I were one of their family. They helped me out of the goodness of their hearts – no one asked them to help and they asked for nothing in return – not one peseta! They expressed the love our Lord came to this earth to give us and share with all others. The Acadian people are closer to God than any other people I've known in my life and I am fortunate to serve some of them as their pastor at Santa María." Olivier looked away as tears filled his eyes.

"The Acadians, not the magistrate, saved your life and watched over you." María Adela did not tell Olivier they had guarded him the entire time of his trip nor did she tell him her part in his protection. She was pleased he believed the Acadians alone had saved his life and would not tell him what actually had happened. There was no reason to alter Olivier's appreciation of the Acadians, who were rarely, if ever, praised as a people. They usually were regarded as a difficult people who too often ignored the laws of the colony. Looking at Francis, María Adela doubted the young priest would tell him either. He nodded to her as if he knew what she was thinking.

Olivier smiled. "They didn't let me out of their sight until the magistrate's men arrived in Galvez. What a wonderful people!"

On Tuesday, the third of June. Olivier learned he would be leaving Louisiana. Antonio heard about it on Monday afternoon, but, suffering a sick stomach, he waited until the next day to tell him the news. Antonio left the cathedral at midmorning and, walking briskly, he arrived at Santa María twenty-five minutes later. The pastor had seen Francis earlier at the cathedral and knew Olivier would be at the church supervising the renovation. From 100 some feet away, he saw him talking to a man and woman in the doorway of Santa María. Antonio could see that the couple was about to leave and, to his surprise, he saw the woman lean up against Olivier and kiss him on the cheek before she turned toward their carriage. The priest was waving to the couple as Antonio arrived beside him. They waved back as each of them climbed into the carriage.

"That's Aristride Gallard and his wife, Adelaide," Olivier said to Antonio as the carriage driver urged the horses to a trot toward New Orleans. Olivier waved again when he saw the slim hand of a woman extend out of a carriage window.

Antonio smiled. "I assume they are shopping in town."

"They are. They come to New Orleans every two months or so to purchase a variety of items unavailable in Baton Rouge. They arrived in town last night and came here for a brief visit this morning. Let's talk outside; the carpenters are working on the roof and it's much too noisy inside." Olivier gestured to the benches by the bayou.

Once seated, Antonio told Olivier the news. "Olivier, I'm truly sorry to t-tell you …" He sighed., "You have a new assignment in Havana. A Dominican priest on his way to Mexico told me about it late yesterday afternoon. He said his name was Father Modesto. His ship stopped in New Orleans for provisions and he came to the cathedral while they were being put aboard. He said an official letter from the master general of your order would soon be forthcoming with the details of your new assignment. I know you are disappointed, Olivier, but … "

"I am disappointed, but not surprised. Although I've come to love my life as pastor of Santa María, I'm sure the master general regards my service at a parish church as inappropriate for a Dominican priest. He would say such service should be the responsibility of the Secular Church. And, of course, he's right." Olivier sighed and made a face. "Did Father Modesto say anything about the nature of my new assignment?"

"He thought it had something to do with teaching Church history and theology. I assume the assignment will be in Havana"

Olivier nodded, his mouth turned down. "That makes sense. It's what I've done most of the time since my ordination in 1777." He turned his eyes away from Antonio and looked at the church, it's new cross bright white in the morning sun. Olivier stood abruptly and strode toward Santa María, his eyes brimming with tears.

Olivier left New Orleans on June 24, 1800, three weeks to the day when Antonio told him of his new posting in Havana. The magistrate came to see him the afternoon before his departure. Castañedo visited him at Madame Lefevre's house and the two men talked for an hour outside on the patio. Olivier had always liked the magistrate and he was pleased the Spaniard had come to say goodbye. Castañedo squeezed his hand warmly when he met him in the living room.

"Well, Father, I am sincerely sorry to see you leave New Orleans. You are truly a man of God and I am only one of many in this colony who knows the truth of that statement." Olivier held up his hand to protest. "No, Father, what I say is true and you know it! It is also important for me, as magistrate of New Orleans, to praise and thank you for what you accomplished in the murder investigation. I don't know who else here could have exposed the identity of the clever fiend. Only God knows how many lives you saved by pursuing him."

"Speaking of the murder investigation, is there anything

new in the search for Laroux." Embarrassed by the magistrate's praise, Olivier hoped his question would change the subject of their conversation.

"No, except for the reduction of the endless sightings. Finalmente gracias a Dios (Finally, thank God)! I was beginning to think Laroux would continue to be seen the rest of the decade."

"I think he's gone. He's too clever to stay here and risk arrest."

Castañedo nodded. "I'm sure you're right, but I wish I could see his execution and know with certainty he was dead. "You know, Father, the fiend killed twenty-seven people! The list tells us twenty-two were women – probably young girls with the exception of Madame Villièrs and her niece. He killed the last girls as well as Villièrs and her niece because they could identify him. It was the purple spot on his face, of course." The magistrate shook his head. "In his diary, he complained that the killings in Mosquito Creek *distracted* him from his more important task of taking over the Dumont enterprises. Can you imagine it? The murders were a *distraction* to him. What kind of man born of a Christian woman thinks in such a manner?"

Olivier nodded. "Laroux is evil incarnate, perhaps a demon from hell."

Castañedo shook his head. "He is evil incarnate. He killed twenty seven people! And, proud of his murders, he recorded them in his diary. Laroux used the last several pages of his diary to list them in the order they were murdered. He wrote their names neatly in large letters, without a mistake or blot of ink anywhere. The dates of their deaths and the methods of disposal were written beside the names with the same care."

"Mon Dieu! How did he dispose of his victims?"

"Those he murdered in town were weighted down and dropped into a tidal inlet south of the city. He followed a five-step process in New Orleans, where he murdered most of the girls. His would kill a girl, take her body to his boathouse late at night, where he left it tied and ready for disposal until the next day. Then, boldly in the light of day, he would sail leisurely down the river to drop the body in a deep-water inlet. Afterwards, that night at home, he added the name of the victim to his list along with the date and the phrase '*Dead and Gone'* in parentheses. On a page of his diary he wrote in late February, I forget the date, he described the entire process."

Olivier gasped. "Quel monstre! Nous espérons que nous ne verra jamais son pareil." ("What a monster! Hopefully, we will never see his like again.")!

Castañedo held up a finger. "Never mind a similar monster in the future. Let's hope we never see this one again."

After sunset that evening, Olivier, Antonio and Francis ate dinner together at Madame Lefevre's house. She prepared Bouillabaisse for them which they enjoyed with a freshly baked bread and two bottles of white Bordeaux wine. Antonio brought the wine and they opened one of the bottles before dinner to toast Olivier. Madame Lefevre and Gervaise were there to join the toast and then left the house to visit a neighbor while the priests ate their meal. The clergymen sat in the kitchen after dinner, talking and drinking almost half the bottle of cognac María Adela had given Francis to contribute to the occasion. They ended the evening at ten-thirty and Antonio and Francis walked back to the cathedral together.

Olivier stayed up a half-hour more to play one last game of checkers with Gervaise. The boy yawned throughout the game since he was awake much later than his usual bedtime. There were tears in his eyes as Gervaise put the checkers away and, before leaving the room, he threw himself in Olivier's arms and sobbed until it was time for the priest to pack his belongings.

María Adela, Madame Lefevre, Gervaise and Francis accompanied Olivier to the docks the next day. They rode in María Adela's carriage, the four adults inside and Gervaise outside sitting up beside the driver. The drive took less than ten minutes and they had little time to talk about anything except the early arrival of the heat and humidity.

"It seems the summer is already here," said Madame Lefevre as the carriage stopped and the doors were opened.

Olivier sailed on the schooner, *La Nuestra Señora de Dolores*, which was bound first for St. Augustine and then Havana. The last passenger to board the schooner, he stood amidship, waving to the crowd of people standing on the dock. There were more than two hundred of them there. They had come at first light, most of them walking in from the lowlands, to wish him bon voyage. Immediately surrounding him as he stepped down from the carriage, they had reached out to touch his hands as he walked toward the gangplank. Men and women alike, everyone had tears in their eyes. Once aboard the schooner, Olivier waved to them as the mooring lines were untied. He continued to wave until he could no longer see the dock and the ship was in full sail, heading south toward the Gulf of Mexico.

Laroux died four days after he arrived at the cabin. He was bitten by a rattlesnake on his second morning in the swamp. The snake struck him above his left ankle. Though neither deep nor full of venom, the bite left two open wounds on his leg where the fangs had penetrated the skin. The wounds became infected and the infection, not the snake's venom, killed him.

It happened as Laroux turned over a pirogue that was covered with leaves. The pirogue lay beside the cabin on two logs with its bottom up. He heard the snake's rattle, but moved away too slowly to escape the strike. The rattlesnake had been curled up beneath the center section of the pirogue where he stood turning it over. After striking him, it instantly slithered away into the pine woods behind the cabin.

Laroux hurried inside the cabin and treated the snakebite as he had been taught. Since he could not reach the bites with his mouth to suck out the venom, he widened them with his knife and, using all the strength in his forefingers, squeezed out a quantity of blood from the wounds. It was his hope the bleeding would include most if not all of the venom. Laroux then covered the wounds with a mixture of gunpowder and salt. The treatment at the time called for a potent that included those two substances mixed with the yolk of an egg. But without any eggs in the cabin, Laroux hoped the yellow liquid of the yolk was only added to make the potent into a sticky paste for application purposes.

Despite a little soreness around the wounds, Laroux felt better after applying the mixture. He had lunch at midday and ate a full bowl of rice and vegetables, while drinking two glasses of cider. Later in the day, Laroux felt increased pain in his leg and saw pus in the wounds. Seeing pus pleased him since he had heard its appearance suggested healing was taking place. Feeling nauseous, Laroux did not eat anything for supper, but did drink two more glasses of cider. He recalled someone saying that alcohol was also helpful in the treatment of snakebite. He sighed, hoping what had been said were not the words of a tippler at a tavern and remembered by other drunken men.

Intense pain awakened him in the middle of the night. He was hot and sweating when he awoke and, in addition to the pain, he noticed his leg was swollen with red streaks stretching out from the wounds. He now knew his leg was infected.

Laroux immediately put another mixture of gunpowder and salt on the wounds, this time with extra salt which burned as he applied it.

His condition worsened the next day and he had trouble walking. By late afternoon, his whole leg was red and swollen and the pain was excruciating. He could no longer walk without intolerable pan and even sitting up brought tears to his eyes. Unable to rise up from his bed, he eventually peed and dirtied his drawers. As evening approached, Laroux thought about applying another mixture on his infected leg, but he was too weak to leave his bed. That evening, his arms seemed too heavy to move and he struggled to breathe. Laroux now knew his end was near and, frightened of what would follow, he wept.

He slept little his third night in the cabin. The pain and endless effort to breathe kept him awake. Laroux tried with all his might to ignore his suffering, but, with the exception of a few brief moments of relief, he could not escape it. The one time the dying man managed to sleep for any length of time, he saw a procession of the young girls he had killed pass before him pointing their fingers at him. A rainstorm began before sunrise and his last awareness was a flash of lightning that briefly lit up the cabin and an explosion of thunder that followed seconds later. Laroux did not hear the hailstones that then clattered on the cypress roof.

A hurricane struck New Orleans later that summer and destroyed the cabin. The storm's hundred-mile winds blew the building apart and the flooded waters carried the logs into bayous deeper in the swamp. Everything inside the cabin, including the skeletal remains of Charles Laroux, likewise were washed away. Several days later when the storm had lost its strength inland, the receding flood left a layer of mud over the area. Heavy rains in the autumn added more mud to the site and by the following spring there were saplings shooting up where the hidden cabin had once stood.

What was left of the broken building and the murderer had disappeared into the soft sand of the swamp.

Since Laroux's death was never discovered, he lived on in New Orleans. Though unseen or hidden during daylight, he lurked in the late afternoon shadows and the dark of night. He was recognized by his wide-brimmed hat which he continued to wear slanted over the purple spot on his face. There were thirty-three sightings of Laroux the first week following Olivier's return to town, twenty-seven the second week and more than a hundred by the end of the month. Reports of seeing him in the streets of the city continued in number throughout the summer and fall. In the winter, there were still as many as four sightings each month. The number increased to seven during the Christmas season and twelve people swore they saw Laroux on New Year's Eve.

Worried that the mass murderer still lingered in the vicinity, the magistrate and his men spent an exhausting year investigating every sighting told to them. It was therefore with relief that the number of reports of Laroux they received dwindled in January and February of the New Year. One sighting was claimed in March, but there was none in April or May. The magistrate's office received only a handful of reports of him the rest of the year and all but one of those were made by drunken men.

By the end 1802, the sightings had ceased as well as any mention of him in town. By that time, Charles Laroux was almost forgotten. Assuming he had gone elsewhere or died, few of the residents ever thought of his name. Whatever had happened to him, he no longer frightened the townspeople as he had three years earlier when his murders were revealed. But, while the city's residents had lost their fear of Laroux, he had become a nighttime goblin to their children. The children had heard countless number of conversations in which he was mentioned as a *mercilesss fiend,* a *monster* or the *devil's disciple.* And, eventually with so many of his sightings at night, he became known to them as the goblin *Laroux*. He was imagined as a bent over old man wearing a wide-brimmed hat. The hat was slanted on his left side to hide his grotesque purple face.

Aware of their children's fear of the goblin, parents soon began to use his name to control their behavior. "Look out for the Laroux!" therefore became a warning most of them used at one time or other. It also was typical for an impatient parent to hurry a child home with the shouted words, "It's getting dark and you better be home before the Laroux comes out!" But the warning they expressed most often was, "The Laroux will get you if you don't watch out."

On the early evening of October 24, 1810, Father Francis left Santa María at five-thirty to attend the weekly meeting of the Capuchins at the cathedral. It had been a dark day with clouds overhead all afternoon and dusk came early that evening. He noticed the street lamps were being lit as he entered the city. Moments later, Francis reached Conde Street and proceeded hurriedly toward the cathedral.

There were a number of people ahead of him. Anxious to arrive on time, Francis took long strides, passing people with a polite nod or smile. Within sight of the cathedral, he came up behind a man and his son. From the boy's height, he assumed him to be six or seven years old. Only fifty paces from the cathedral, Francis was about to pass the man and boy, when the little lad gasped, stopped short and pointed to an old man leaning against the wall of the cathedral. The man was bent over from age or infirmity and he wore a wide-brimmed hat slanted over the left side of his face.

"Look, Papa!" the boy exclaimed, "There's a Laroux!"

ABOUT THE AUTHOR

ROBERT L. GOLD

Robert L. Gold is a Professor Emeritus of History, an entertaining speaker and a prolific writer. He has contributed articles and reviews to many magazines and newspapers in the southeast and especially in Florida, where he has lived for more than thirty years. In St. Augustine, he has written the popular newspaper column, *Essays from El Dorado*, a script for sightseeing train guides, and *The Story of St. Augustine*, a brief history of the city given to millions of visiting tourists.

Extensive research in English, French and Spanish history and his book, *Borderland Empires in Transition*, have provided the historical basis for his current project, a trilogy of colonial murder mysteries. *Dead to Rights*, set in Savannah, *Cut of the Cross*, set in St. Augustine, and now *Dead and Gone*, set in New Orleans – all published by Marcinson Press. In addition to the suspenseful mysteries, the trilogy offers readers a penetrating look into the cultural and political life of colonial America in the eighteenth century. Each of the novels reveals the colonists' everyday struggle for survival, their search for meaning in the world and the simplicity and shortness of their lives. The series also offers a graphic view of the lush and virtually undisturbed landscape that once existed in what is now the southeastern United States.

The author has enjoyed a long professional career in Florida. He has served as state historian in St. Augustine, professor of Latin American history at the University of South Florida and executive director of the Historic St. Augustine Preservation Board. Dr. Gold also has been a speaker for the Florida Humanities Council, giving presentations entitled, "Characters and Crooks in Florida History." A bit of a character himself, he continues to offer those talks throughout North Florida.

He's also published a beautiful new book on the history of St. Augustine with photographer William LaMons, *St. Augustine: A Brief History of America's Oldest City*.

Robert Gold lives in Jacksonville, Florida, with his wife, LaDonna Morris, and two beloved Airedale Terriers – Baxter and Spencer. A devoted dog servant, he confesses to being led by the nose of the furry-faced beasts, walking them at least six miles a week and spoiling them rotten. With Baxter at his feet and Spencer snoring somewhere nearby, he's begun another historical mystery series, set in the south during the Civil War.

AUTHOR'S COMMENTS

DR. ROBERT L. GOLD

Although most Americans think of New Orleans as uniquely Cajun, the colonial city's history is actually more French and Spanish. France initially colonized Louisiana at the end of the seventeenth century and founded New Orleans in 1718. The colony remained in French control until 1763 when it was ceded to Spain following the Seven Years War (known in America as the French and Indian War). Spain ruled Louisiana, obviously including New Orleans, for the next forty years. And the city retained its French character during that time. In 1800, the huge territory was secretly returned to France, but Spanish officials administered the colony until 1803, when it was purchased by the United States.

Fires destroyed much of New Orleans in the last two decades of the eighteenth century and all the major buildings remaining from that time were built while Spain still controlled the city. With the exception of the *old* Ursuline Convent erected in 1745, the Cabildo, St. Louis Cathedral and most of the French Quarter buildings were constructed during the Spanish Period. Though perhaps a useless suggestion, the oldest section of New Orleans might more accurately be called the Franco-Spanish Quarter. It doesn't look or sound right, does it?

The Acadians, ancestors of the Cajuns, came to Louisiana in the middle of the eighteenth century. Most of them actually arrived after 1763 in what is called the *Great Expulsion*. They refused to swear allegiance to the British monarchy during the French and Indian War and were subsequently deported. Most of the Acadians came from Nova Scotia, New Brunswick and parts of Quebec in Canada as well as northern Maine in the United States. Today's Louisiana Cajuns are descendants of the Acadians who initially settled in the Spanish colony and later people who married or mixed with the original Acadian settlers.

Father Olivier is a fictional character. He shares a name, however, with a Jesuit priest I knew years ago while in graduate school. Father Olivier was a great friend and, in addition to the meals and conversations we enjoyed together, he gave me, a non-Catholic, an understanding of Catholicism that I still appreciate. Like the fictional Olivier, he was a well-versed scholar of Church history and philosophy, particularly the writings of Thomas Aquinas. Unlike the novel's Olivier, he did not have a drinking problem. Although he was a lifelong Jesuit, I made Olivier a Dominican in *Dead and Gone*. It was historically necessary because the Jesuits were expelled from Spanish America in the eighteenth century when the story takes place. Pope Clement XIV banished the Jesuits in 1767, apparently as a consequence of their determined independence and refusal to accept the Spanish monarchy's authority in America.

Father Antonio, the cathedral pastor in the murder mystery is based on Père Antoine the Spanish Capuchin who served as the pastor of St. Louis Cathedral from 1785 to 1790 and then again from 1795 to 1829. He died at the age of eighty-one. Père Antoine's first service in New Orleans ended with his deportation. The governor of Louisiana, accusing the priest of rebellion and insubordination had him seized at night and put aboard a ship bound for Spain.

At the time, Père Antoine had been named Vicar and Ecclesiastical Judge of the Inquisition in the colony. He apparently conducted heresy investigations in the eighties and, fearing a local rebellion in New Orleans, in 1790, the governor exiled him to Spain. Confronting the disobedience and defiance of Father Antoine, the bishop of Louisiana supported the priest's removal.

Five years later, Père Antoine returned to Louisiana, reinstated by King Charles IV to his former position as rector of the cathedral. Unchanged by his lengthy exile in Spain, the Capuchin priest continued to defy his Church superiors following his reinstatement. However, in the years that followed, Père Antoine was revered in New Orleans as an abstemious, pious and charitable priest, known for his devotion to the poor and children. At his death in 1829, thousands of people filed for three successive days past his grave.

Despite the many scientific discoveries of the eighteenth-century Enlightenment, blood-letting (venesection) was still a common treatment for many illnesses. And pneumonia was one of those illnesses believed to be cured by blood-letting. It is therefore not surprising that Doctor Standish used leeches to treat Olivier's pneumonia and it is also not surprising he survived the treatment. Recent pneumonia research, in fact, suggests that venesection might actually help some patients suffering the disease. The bacterium that causes pneumonia apparently needs a form of iron in red blood cells to thrive. So, blood loss would be helpful for those patients who have that form of iron. I guess we should keep that in mind since anti-biotics these days are not always reliable as an effective treatment for bacterial infections such as pneumonia. That might mean that after almost a century, a jar of leeches would once again be seen in pharmacies. In my mind's eye, I can see the leeches now, several hundred of them, stuck to the sides of a large glass jar standing on the pharmacy counter at Walgreens.

A final note. There were no Airedales in America or anywhere else in the world in 1800. They were bred in Yorkshire, England in the middle of the nineteenth century from a mixture of terriers and otterhounds. I put, Vandal, the Airedale in the Laurent home simply as a whim. My own Airedales, Baxter and Spencer, made me think the Laurent family needed an Airedale to love when Valarie was lost.

Also from author Robert L. Gold:

Dead and Gone (first in the Colonial City Series)

Cut of the Cross (second in the Colonial City Series)

St. Augustine: A Brief History of America's Oldest City

Other titles from Marcinson Press:

Wisdom from Adoptive Families: Joys and Challenges in Older Child Adoption

Awakening East: Moving our Adopted Children Back to China

Geezer Dad: How I Survived Infertility Clinics, Fatherhood Jitters, Adoption Wait Limbo and Things that Go "Waa" in the Night

Little Birds Big Adventures

Sam's Sister

Zero Gravity

Pink Baby Alligator

Dear Creator: An Anthology of Hope & Prayer in Word, Image, and Song

Jazzy's Quest (Young Readers adoption series)

Available from online, major, and independent booksellers throughout the U.S.

For bulk purchases or
to carry this book in your
library or bookstore,
please contact the publisher
through marcinsonpress.com.

Made in the USA
Columbia, SC
13 August 2018